I0725391

RIP TIDE

RIP TIDE

ELENA GRAF

PURPLE HAND PRESS

Purple Hand Press
www.elenagraf.com
© 2025 by Elena Graf

This is a work of fiction. Names, characters, places, and incidents are the product of the author's imagination or used fictitiously, and any resemblance to actual persons, living or dead, businesses, institutions, companies, events, or locales is entirely coincidental.

Trade Paperback Edition
ISBN-13 978-1-953195-24-1
ePub Edition
ISBN-13 978-1-953195-23-4

Cover photo © EyeEm - Freepik.com, used by license.

03.25.2025

To Sheila, as always

Note

For a character guide to the inhabitants of Hobbs, Maine, please visit: https://elenagraf.com/hobbs-characters/

Chapter 1

From the window of the church library, Lucy Bartlett gazed at the ocean across the salt marsh. The rising September sun cut a brilliant path of light on the waves. The view of the row of colorful beachfront houses on the barrier island looked like a postcard. Lucy murmured a little prayer of gratitude for being blessed to live in such a beautiful place.

The morning air had been brisk, whipping up Hobbs' famous beryl waves. Lucy and her wife, Liz, had walked at the edge of the damp sand to keep the water out of their shoes. As usual on chilly mornings, Liz had held Lucy's hand in the pocket of her sweatshirt. She respectfully gave Lucy the silence she needed for her prayers, a condition of being allowed to accompany her on her morning walks. But as much as Lucy loved her wife, she occasionally missed the solitude of walking alone. When she did, the sea gulls followed her. She considered them her most faithful congregation. If the beach was empty, Lucy might sing to them, always surprised and pleased when they sang back.

Singing had unexpectedly taken a more prominent role in Lucy's life. The Met had engaged her as the soprano soloist in its pre-season *Verdi Requiem*. The first performance was only a few weeks away, which meant she and Liz would be in New York for rehearsals. As much as Lucy looked forward to returning to the vibrant city that had once been her home, she still wondered how to balance her original career as an opera singer with her vocation as a priest and rector of St. Margaret's Episcopal Church.

She could be justifiably proud of what she had done for this church. The old building had been neglected for decades. The congregation had been in decline. With the support of a group of influential women, especially the town's richest woman, Olivia Enright, Lucy had saved the historic building, with its inspiring stained-glass windows and famous organ, from ruin. She'd assembled a competent vestry that brought home the parish diaspora and welcomed new families.

She couldn't have done it without the help of Tom Simmons, who had stepped back from leading a prominent New Haven church, to live in Maine as an openly gay man. His guidance of St. Margaret's inexperienced new rector had made all the difference. He'd justifiably earned his retirement to Florida with his new husband, but he'd returned without question after the horrific shooting at Hobbs Elementary.

Although the reason for Tom's return to the parish was sad, Lucy was glad to have him back. His sturdy presence had steadied St. Margaret's during the pandemic. In the aftermath of the shooting, his long experience as a rector and his counseling skills were invaluable. The vestry was wise to reverse his retirement and take him back without question. Now, they just needed to find him an office in the rectory. Until they did, he was sharing Lucy's.

On her way to the break room, she passed the closed door. Behind it, Tom was meeting with Liz, who hadn't been the same since she'd been forced to shoot Peter Langdon. She'd formed a special bond with the young man, who'd been her patient since he was young. Although he'd shot nine little boys and their teacher, killing him, even in self-defense, was devastating. For months, Liz couldn't return to work as senior doctor at Hobbs Family Practice or her many leadership roles in the town's civic organizations. Eventually, time and talking to Tom had brought her back to at least the appearance of normality.

Whenever Lucy wondered what Liz and Tom might be talking about behind closed doors, she stifled her curiosity. It was none of her business what Liz said in her sessions. Lucy was simply grateful that Liz was talking to someone. Although Tom wasn't a licensed therapist, he was a gifted counselor. Their intelligence was well matched. Liz liked to play with people, but Tom was smart enough to see through her little games.

***

Liz Stolz scrutinized the man sitting across from her. Tom Simmons' rapidly thinning hair was now more salt than pepper. To disguise the loss, he'd been wearing it shorter. His ruddy complexion, merry blue eyes, and warm smile were unchanged, despite the pandemic and Erika Bultmann's sudden death at only sixty-two. They'd once been lovers as well as graduate school rivals, so Tom took her loss especially hard. But the ultimate shock had been the mass shooting at Hobbs Elementary. After that, Tom had grayed rapidly. And he wasn't the only one. Liz's hair had gone from iron gray to snowy white almost overnight.

She was relieved that Tom wasn't wearing his clerical shirt today. The informality helped preserve the illusion that what they were doing was having a friendly chat, not, God forbid, psychotherapy. The stiff linen collar of Tom's rugby shirt was unbuttoned, showing a pink streak of raw skin where his razor had scraped too hard. His bare throat looked so vulnerable when his Adam's apple rose and fell. He swallowed frequently. The waiting had made him anxious.

Liz knew it was standard therapy practice to allow the client to open the conversation, but she always stalled until he looked at the clock.

"Why do I think you're getting ready to say something important?" he finally said, breaking the stalemate.

"Whatever gave you that idea?" Liz grinned slyly. Tom was exceptionally observant. Was noticing every detail a part of seminary training like it was in medical school? "Usually, I'm better at hiding my intentions," she said, stretching out her long legs in front of her.

"Yes, but I've known you too long."

"Forty-two years," said Liz, subtracting the dates in her head. "Has it really been that long? I can't believe it." She gazed out the window toward the churchyard, where her friend lay buried. "And you've been nothing but trouble since Erika introduced us."

At the mention of Erika, Tom sighed. "Liz, tell the truth. You're glad I'm here. Otherwise, your wife would make you see a real therapist."

"Since you're not billing my insurance, your credentials are irrelevant." But he was right. Liz would prefer to talk to an old friend than an official "shrink." She'd had few options after Lucy had blackmailed her into "getting help." Liz could choose Tom or someone else, but Lucy had insisted that she needed counseling.

As if Liz could share her burden with anyone. She'd asked both Lucy and Tom, in their role as priests, to give her absolution, hoping the magic from her Catholic childhood would make the guilt go away, but it hadn't...not even for a moment.

"You bastard! The suicide fantasy was between us. Why couldn't you keep your big mouth shut?"

"As a doctor, you know why. I couldn't keep something so important from your wife."

"But you told me our talks were confidential. I thought I could trust you!"

"You *can* trust me...to do the right thing."

Liz shot him a skeptical look.

Tom looked sad. "You'll never forgive me for that, will you?"

"Probably not," said Liz. "But I know you mean well...so does Lucy."

Tom pursed his lips. "All right, Liz, stop prevaricating and cut to the chase. What do you want to tell me?" Tom never wasted her time, which she appreciated.

"I want my guns back. Please tell my wife I'm no longer a suicide risk."

Tom adjusted his posture and studied her with a little frown. "The shooting was almost eight months ago. In all that time, you have shown no interest in your guns. Why do you suddenly need them *now*?"

Liz gazed into his blue eyes, now steely with resolve. No matter how much she complained, she loved Tom and valued their long friendship. She wouldn't insult him with more bullshit. "My gun club asked me to teach my 'firearms for women' class. There's a long waiting list, so they're pressuring me."

Tom lowered his shoulders to their normal position, but he wasn't done with her. "Liz, we've talked about your overdeveloped sense of responsibility. You don't always have to save the day."

"I need to do this," she said, meeting his penetrating gaze. "Things have been a little tense at my gun club. My interview on *Sixty Minutes* didn't sit right with some people. Besides, I'm on the board and the only NRA certified instructor."

"You're still a licensed surgeon, but you retired from the operating room because of your arthritis. Consider the PTSD from the shooting another impairment and step back from teaching gun classes. At least, for a while..."

"I'm fine, Tom. I swear to you I've gotten over it."

The flinty look returned to his eyes. "You're not fine, Liz. You have PTSD. You know as well as I do that you will never get over it. Neither will anyone who was in the school that day. That trauma will be with you as long as you live."

"Well, dammit. That's exactly why I want my guns back. I want to be able to fire my pistol without cringing."

Looking surprised, Tom sat back in his chair. "You mean, practice tough love on yourself? That's so typical of you."

"Why not? It always works," said Liz under her breath. She gazed out the window at Erika's grave. "I learned that trick early. When my high school classmate died, I joined the volunteer ambulance service to overcome my fear of death. It worked. I believe in facing my fears head on."

"Like volunteering to negotiate with a man who'd decimated a third-grade class?" The memory of that day made Liz queasy, but she forced herself to hold Tom's gaze while the scene vividly replayed in her mind—Peter's glassy-eyed stare across the room, the overwhelming stench of cannabis smoke. "I thought I could convince him to release the hostages. I wasn't trying to prove anything."

"Hah! You're always trying to prove something. As long as I've known you, you've been trying to prove something. You never turn down a dare or an impossible challenge. The harder, the better."

Liz hated that Tom knew her so well. "Really, Tom, it was about the hostages."

"Even Susan, whom you've never liked?"

"I don't dislike her per se," Liz protested. She was lying. Susan, with her insipid worship of Lucy, annoyed the hell out of her. "I didn't like her interference in my relationship with Lucy, and all the subterfuge around why she'd come to Maine. But when Peter had a gun to her head, none of that mattered."

"And you protected her. I think you still believe if you had said or done something else, there might have been a different outcome."

He's leading me like a witness, thought Liz. "Yes, I thought I could reason with Peter. He trusted me."

"Legally and morally, you did the right thing."

Intellectually, she knew that he was correct. "So why do I still feel so fucking awful?"

"Because you cared for Peter and wanted to save him. Except he didn't want to be saved. He wanted you to end his life because he couldn't do it himself. You keep thinking you could have prevented his death. He wanted to die."

"Susan often reminds me that I saved three lives that day including my own. Not bad odds, considering how many others died."

"Nine kids and their teacher. One permanently brain damaged."

Liz continued the countdown. "One who will have gut issues for the rest of his life. One who will never walk again. Others with lifelong health challenges from their wounds. We always talk about the dead, not the injured survivors."

Tom sighed. "Unfortunately, that's true."

"As a surgeon, I used to patch up people like that. They're never right again. Their bowels leak or their breathing is compromised. Never mind the muscle damage. An assault rifle turns the tissue into mincemeat." Tom looked slightly nauseated by her descriptions, so Liz stopped.

"Liz, if you swear to me that you will not harm yourself, you can have your guns back."

"Thank you."

"Now for your end of the bargain."

"Oh, really, Tom. I'm a doctor. If I wanted to kill myself, I could think of less messy ways to do it. You're not serious."

He glared at her from under his brows to show that he most certainly was. Liz rolled her eyes, but she raised her right hand like a court witness. "All right, Tom, I swear. I will not use my guns to harm myself."

Tom sat back in the club chair and rested his ankle on the opposite knee. Unconsciously, Liz mirrored his pose. "Liz, I've always known you to keep your word. After you leave, I'll call Brenda and Lucy and tell them I signed off on access to your guns."

"That was too easy."

Tom shrugged. "Honestly, I never thought you were serious about killing yourself. I think you were right. It was just a thought experiment. You were trying the idea on for size."

"So why did you tell on me to Lucy in the first place!"

"I couldn't take a chance, and I was professionally obligated. I know you do things your own way up here in Maine. But sometimes, I need to play by the rules."

"Fuck you, Tom."

He laughed heartily. "Oh, come on, Liz. I'm not that bad."

"No, you're not. And I have a soft spot for you, you old bastard. But I do have something else to tell you." Liz paused to allow him a moment to prepare. "I want to end our sessions."

"Just when things were getting interesting," he said with exaggerated disappointment. "I'd hoped I'd find out why you need to save everyone."

"I don't save people, Tom. I treat them for medical conditions. Saving people is your job."

"You tried to turn Peter Langdon around. You talked him into taking your gun safety class. You got him a job working in Sam's renovation business. You kept checking on him to see how things were going..."

Liz crossed her arms on her chest. "I was only doing Lucy a favor. His mother was her client. She was worried about all those guns in her basement. Lucy didn't know what to do, so she called me. I told Brenda what was going on. You know, the unconventional way we do things up here in Maine," she said, mocking him. "Peter had been my patient since he was a boy, so when he came in for an exam, I casually mentioned my safety class. And Sam needed help with her tiling business. Too bad I didn't know the whole story." Liz stared at her fingernails the way men did, her fingers rolled into her palm. "I thought I had a rapport with the kid."

"You did. That's why he chose you to hear his terrible secret."

"Why do abused children always seem to grow up into abusive adults?"

"Those who get the right care don't. Unfortunately, if we don't know about the abuse, we can't help," Tom said in a sad voice.

"Churchmen do such a good job of covering it up," said Liz with an accusing look. "How could we?" She drew a long breath of frustration. "Why don't they just kill themselves before they go on a rampage and shoot so many innocent people?"

"Because mass shooters are screaming to be heard. The shooting is their way of making a statement." Tom studied her. "Liz, please don't quit counseling. I'm not playing now. I'm here for you." The kind pleading in his eyes forced Liz to look away.

"I know you are, and I appreciate it."

"I've already told Jeff I'm staying this winter."

"I bet he's not too happy about that."

Tom shrugged. "No, but we can go down to Florida for long visits. He loves this town, and he can see there's so much to do. Everyone is still a wreck. Besides, with all her singing engagements,

Lucy can use the help." Liz realized that Tom liked being associate rector. He'd only quit to please Jeff.

"Tom, please understand. I need a break. I need to get back to normal life. Our sessions keep reminding me of that awful day."

"Quitting counseling won't help you forget or make your life go back to the way it was."

Liz knew that Tom was right, but she was determined to end these ridiculous sessions.

✾✾✾

Lucy always found preaching on this Gospel frustrating. After browsing the commentaries in the library, she knew she was not alone. She decided that a caffeine jolt might stimulate her thinking. As she headed toward the break room, the sound of Tom's voice, booming from behind, startled her. "Good morning, Mother Lucy. You can have your office back now."

"Good morning, Father Tom. I was just about to go back to the library to work on my sermon."

"That's right. Wednesday is homily day, isn't it? I always write them on Fridays."

"I like to give myself lots of time to prepare because something always comes up."

"A smart practice. I admit to cheating occasionally and recycling some of my old sermons from Trinity. This congregation hasn't heard them, so they don't care."

"Bad boy."

Tom grinned. "And damn proud of it!"

"Coming from your session with Liz?" Lucy asked ingenuously. "Still going okay?"

"Well, it was, but sadly, now it's over."

"She didn't," said Lucy, gripping his arm.

"Oh, yes, she did. Come on, Lucy. We both knew that project was on borrowed time. Liz hates the very idea of psychotherapy. I'm surprised she can stand being married to a 'shrink.'"

Lucy rolled her eyes. "She still uses that word no matter how many times I tell her I hate it."

"It's Liz. Like a kid, the more you discourage something, the more she'll do it. Maybe she'll change eventually, but at her age, I doubt it."

"Oh, I don't know about that. I've seen positive changes. I just wish she hadn't quit therapy. She still wakes up with nightmares about the shooting."

"I'm sure she does, but we can't force her to do counseling." Tom sighed. "Oh, and I'm supposed to tell you, I okayed getting her guns back."

"Tom, please say you didn't."

"Lucy, I had no choice. She gave up the guns voluntarily. She's as sane as we are."

"Which isn't saying much."

"No, but if asked by a judge, I can't honestly say she's a suicide risk. She seems like the old Liz to me. You know—contrary, skeptical, sometimes snide. All the things we know and love about her. She says she wants things to go back to normal."

"Don't we all wish for that?" said Lucy with a long exhale. Since the pandemic, everything was different. Her congregation was growing again, but many families had never come back. Most of the Sunday school classrooms went unused. Merchants were still trying to rebuild their businesses. Kids were struggling to catch up to where they were before Covid shut down the schools, and then the shooting...

"Yes, but she's right," said Tom, watching Lucy's face. "At some point, we need to let go of the grief and try to get back to some semblance of normality. Obsessing about what happened just keeps reinforcing it in people's minds. That doesn't mean we forget about the victims or their families, we just ease into a more positive approach."

"Easier said than done. The news media won't let go of it. The local paper just did a big story on the boy who'll be in a wheelchair for the rest of his life." Lucy patted Tom's arm. "But you're right... as always. Dwelling on the sadness can become oppressive. People need a sense of security and a return to normal. We'll continue to counsel the survivors and raise money for the families. It's the best we can do."

"How is the foundation doing?"

"We've exceeded our target by over a million, and we're forging ahead. We may soon need to hire a part-time director."

"That's certainly a good problem to have."

"Liz and I will be doing some fundraising while we're in New York. That pro we hired is doing a great job. Olivia recommended her from past charity work. They worked together on many fundraising campaigns, and Olivia is leveraging her ties to the New York financial community. They seem to be getting past the insider trading scandal. After all, it was her son who committed the crime, not Olivia."

"Eventually, people forget," Tom said. "The newest and nastiest takes precedence in people's minds. Olivia just had the misfortune of being Jason's mother. Like Renee was Peter's mother. Yes, they raised those men, but they're not responsible for what they did. I'm all for redemption. After all, it's what we preach."

"How did you know that's the theme for my sermon?" asked Lucy.

"Because I'm riffing on the same Gospel." Tom winked. "And we both live the truth that, even late in life, we can strive for authenticity and forgiveness." Tom gave Lucy a quick half hug. "Let me not keep you from your creativity, and I have some home visits to make."

"Are you coming to the *Verdi Requiem*?"

"Wouldn't miss it! Jeff made hotel reservations and got tickets as soon as they went on sale."

"I'm always glad to have a sympathetic listener in the audience," said Lucy.

"Oh, I wouldn't worry. They love you in New York."

Tom whistled as he headed down the hall. With a prayer of gratitude for his ministry, Lucy gratefully reclaimed her office. On impulse, she sat in the chair where Liz usually sat during her sessions and found it still warm. Smiling, Lucy decided to work there instead of at her desk.

She'd barely written two sentences when there was a knock at her open door. "Come in," she called and looked up to see a smiling dark face. "Good morning, Reshma."

"Good morning, Mother Lucy," said the young curate. "Are you working on your sermon? If so, forgive me for disturbing you."

"That's why I work here every other Wednesday. I expect to be disturbed. What can I do for you?"

"Ah," said Reshma, grinning. "It's what I can do for *you*. I'm on my way to the pâtisserie for a chocolatine. Would you like one?"

Lucy closed her laptop to show that Reshma had her complete attention. "You've developed a real taste for chocolate croissants," she said. "What happened to your usual granola with yogurt breakfast?"

She guessed that Reshma's face was flaming even though her dark skin hid the blush. "I know yogurt with granola is healthier, but I *really* like chocolatine. Don't you ever binge on something you like?"

Lucy smiled, knowing that Reshma's addiction to the French treat was only part of the story. The real reason Reshma wanted to go to the new pâtisserie was the proprietor. They'd met when Tiffany had created the pastries for Lucy's wedding. Later, the young pastry chef had volunteered to make them for Reshma's ordination.

"Thank you, Reshma, but I've eaten breakfast, and I need to fit into my dress for the Met concert."

Reshma looked skeptical. "Like you need to worry."

"You're young. You don't know how easily the weight can come on after a certain age, and how it sticks around."

Again, the skeptical look. "I won't be long," Reshma promised.

Yeah, right, thought Lucy and smiled to herself as she opened her laptop.

***

Reshma John patiently waited her turn to order. During the tourist season, every coffee shop and café in Hobbs was jammed. Reshma had always favored Awakened Brews, which featured organic, free-trade coffee. That was before Tiffany had sent a special birthday pastry, as gorgeous on the outside as it was delicious on the inside. The delicate napoleon with its crispy layers and the luscious custard filling had been dusted with confectioners' gold. The glittering box was tied with a golden bow. Attached was a sweet note with a mildly suggestive original poem that intrigued Reshma. Now, she was a devoted regular at Wicked Pleasures Pâtisserie. She wasn't too sure about the name, which could equally apply to an adult toy shop as a bakery. But that didn't matter. The main attraction was Tiffany Taylor, the owner and chief pastry chef.

In Reshma's eyes, Tiffany was the living embodiment of an angel. She sparkled like the confectioners' gold she used to brighten her petit fours and chocolate tartlets. She was as blond as the angels in the children's Bible Reshma had been given when she'd arrived in an Episcopal boarding school as a charity student.

Some of Reshma's seminary friends accused her of internalizing colonialism by admiring European religious art. The historical Jesus hadn't been a blond, blue-eyed Scandinavian. He was a dark-skinned Semite from the Middle East, who'd probably looked more like Reshma than the white teachers in her upscale religious school. Yet Reshma still found art depicting a black Mary cradling a dark baby Jesus unsettling. Her friends tried to explain that was the result of brainwashing by the dominant culture, subtler than how religious schools tried to force assimilation on Native Americans or the colonial missionaries on Africans, but no less harmful. They told her she must replace the European images with something more culturally correct. But why? Reshma found European art beautiful and inspiring.

The wait in line gave Reshma the opportunity to observe Tiffany. The people who came for her fancy pastries were as smitten by the proprietor's radiant smile as by her beautiful creations. Reshma watched anxiously as a young man in fluorescent green biking clothes bent to speak confidentially. Whatever he'd said made Tiffany giggle.

It hadn't occurred to Reshma that her beautiful angel might like men. Maybe the special birthday gift had been nothing but good marketing. As St. Margaret's curate, Reshma knew many people in town. A recommendation from her could go far. Reshma glanced at the line behind her. Tiffany was still busy with the bicyclist. Maybe Reshma could slip away unnoticed. The moment Reshma thought of escaping, Tiffany turned and smiled in her direction. Reshma froze where she stood.

Tiffany went back to her customer. Reshma felt the attention of a woman eyeing her collar. She was wearing it today because she'd taken over online morning prayers now that Susan had returned to teaching. The glaring woman's haircut, shaved on the sides, with a long purple tuft at the top shaped into a point, suggested she was some version of queer. Reshma only used that word with people of her own generation. Her colleagues at St. Margaret's remembered a time when "queer" was a slur and cringed whenever she said it, even Mother Lucy, who was younger than the others.

Reshma smiled at the staring woman, who responded with a dirty look and faced forward. Reshma wondered what she had done to deserve such contempt. Did the queer woman have a problem with Reshma being black? That was unlikely from a person her age. Maybe she was one of the many victims of religious abuse who now hated religion. Reshma sighed. As a newly ordained priest, she was proud to wear her collar, just like the woman in front of her was proud to wear a queer hairstyle. Why couldn't people be proud of who they were without the need to make someone else *wrong*?

Reshma's day, which had started out being greeted by the

rising sun pouring through her window, had been so full of hope. She'd read some beautiful scripture to her faithful Facebook prayer group, and now she was in line to order coffee and chocolatine from the beautiful Tiffany. But the idea that everyone was being forced to take sides made Reshma grumpy. Her perfect smile drooped. When it was her turn to step up to give her order, Tiffany anxiously asked, "Reshma, is everything all right?"

Reshma smiled, revealing her perfect teeth. "It is now."

Tiffany's blue eyes smiled back. "The usual?"

"Please."

"Do you have a few minutes?" Tiffany asked shyly.

Reshma glanced at the long line behind her. "Do you?"

"I'll get Kristen to watch the register for a few minutes. I can use a break. I've been on my feet since five." Tiffany went into the kitchen, which prompted some grumbling from the line behind Reshma. Kristen, a slightly darker version of her boss, but just as perky and bright, came out from the back and took Tiffany's place at the register.

"Come on," said Tiffany and put two super-size coffees with a shot of mocha and plates of chocolate croissants on a tray. She opened the gate by the register and nodded to Reshma. "I know a quieter place to sit." She led the way past the pile of enormous bags of flour and sugar to a door. It opened onto a bright office, fully equipped with the latest technology, and a bistro table with two chairs. "This is my office. I don't get to spend a lot of time in here because I'm always baking. Forgive the mess." Tiffany brushed some papers off a table and invited her to sit down.

Reshma glanced around. Apart from the stack of unopened envelopes on the desk and an empty coffee cup, the small room looked tidy. "Thanks for inviting me into your private space."

"You're welcome. I've been wanting to talk to you."

Reshma's heart rate sped up a few beats. "You have?"

"Yes. One of my other customers said you've been experimenting with African cuisine, and you cook it well."

Reshma tried to figure out the origin of this opinion. She thought of Susan, who'd often been her dinner guest and had sampled some of Reshma's Sudanese favorites. It seemed unlikely that Susan, who saved every penny, would fritter away her money on fancy pastries.

"Who told you about my African cooking?" Reshma finally asked.

"Your friend Teresa Gai. She comes in to get scones. She says mine are the closest to those from the British bakery in Khartoum," Tiffany said proudly. "Her daughter really likes them."

"Oh, Teresa! I've learned so much from her about cooking dishes from my homeland. I was away at boarding school, so I never had the opportunity to learn traditional recipes from my mother. She passed when I was in college."

"I'm so sorry," said Tiffany, her blue eyes clouding with sympathy.

"Thank you. She suffered so much from the cancer, so her death was a mercy. It left me alone in this country, but I was lucky to have the support of friends at school and my teachers."

"That's good. Friends can be like family too."

"Yes, they can," said Reshma in a hopeful voice. "But tell me. Why are you interested in African cooking?"

"Well, I have some friends from the CIA coming up this weekend, and African cuisine is our theme."

"The CIA?" That sounded like a government agency.

Tiffany laughed. "No, not the place with the spies. The Culinary Institute of America. People who went there, like me, always call it by its initials. When I get together with my friends, we cook because that's what chefs do. So much fun! I wondered if you might like to join us."

Reshma wanted to jump out of her chair with excitement. Tiffany was inviting her to dinner at her place. Then her enthusiasm sank like a lead fishing weight. She would be cooking with trained chefs. Not long ago, she couldn't even make a hard-boiled egg that wasn't runny or green around the yoke. "Are you sure? I'm just an amateur. I don't want to embarrass you or myself in front of your culinary school friends."

"You're ahead of us. We're looking up recipes we've never cooked before. Maybe you can look over mine to see which is worth the effort." Tiffany leaned forward and there was a little twinkle in her eye.

"Sure," said Reshma. "When?"

"How about tonight? I eat early though. A baker has to get up early to make the pastries and open the store for the coffee crowd."

"How early?" asked Reshma cautiously.

"Five o'clock. Does that work? You can come over any time after four."

Reshma mentally scanned her calendar. She had a pastoral team meeting at three, but they seldom ran more than an hour.

"Great! I'll be there. Just give me the address."

"Oh, it's here. I live upstairs."

"Well, that's easy."

Tiffany nudged Reshma's plate closer. "Go on. Eat up. I need to get back to work, and I'm sure you do too."

❊❊❊

"Liz! Where are you?" called a familiar voice upstairs. Liz stood up from dragging boxes across the floor. She turned around and saw stylish pumps and well-toned legs heading down the basement stairs. Maggie's face appeared above the stair rail. "Down here already? Couldn't you wait?"

"I'm moving some stuff away so I can get to the safe. It's been months since it's been opened, and all this crap has piled up in front of it."

Maggie clucked her tongue. "So unlike you, Liz, to accumulate boxes. You hate clutter."

Liz lifted a box onto the relocated stack. "It's not my clutter. This shit belongs to Lucy."

Maggie pursed her lips. "That's right. Blame it on your wife. You're good at that."

"Oh, for fuck's sake, Maggie, don't start with me. It is Lucy's shit. These are her theology books from the beach house. She dumped them in an empty office in the rectory when she moved. She's cleaning out an office for Tom, now that he's back full time, so they've landed here."

"He's back full time? That's a lot of clergy at St. Margaret's," said Maggie with a frown of disapproval.

The implied criticism of Lucy annoyed Liz. "Reshma's brand new. Susan's only part time, so is Tom. Besides, what's it to you?"

Maggie gave Liz a hard look. "Why are you such a crab ass? Here I am doing you a favor."

"You asked me a question, and I answered it," Liz replied irritably. "And you didn't have to come over. You could have just called me with the combination, or I could have waited until Brenda got home and got it out of her gun safe."

"I know, but I didn't mind bringing it over. I don't see you very often." Liz listened carefully to the subtext. Maggie missed her. Maybe she was lonely with Sam off building skyscrapers again. Either way, it wasn't surprising that she'd come to Liz, now that the dust from the divorce had finally settled. Maggie was the kind of woman who had many superficial friendships with other women, but few close friends. That's why her deep friendship with Lucy was so surprising and its end such a loss to both women. Maggie eyed her cautiously. "How about a hug? Or doesn't Lucy allow it?"

"Of course, she does. She hugs everyone." Liz clamped Maggie close.

"Careful. The implants."

"Oh, that's ridiculous," Liz said, letting her go. "A big squeeze is not going to hurt them."

Maggie opened her bag and took out a piece of paper. "Here you go. I had it in my jewelry box."

Liz took the paper and tapped the numbered keys until there was an audible click. "And there we are. It worked!" Liz opened the door. It gave her a strange sense of relief to see all the fitted plastic cases containing her handguns and the long guns neatly stowed in their slots. The colorful boxes of ammunition were piled up on the shelf just as she'd left them. Nobody, not even Lucy, had had access to the safe in the eight months since Brenda had locked it and changed the combination. It looked like everything was there, but Liz took a quick inventory, touching each item. She could trust herself now to handle these things, and others did too. She was a normal person again, no longer a suicide risk who needed surveillance.

"Happy now?" Maggie asked.

"Yes, I'm glad to have my guns back."

Maggie shook her head. "I don't get it, but it's your thing, not mine."

From a nearby shelf, Liz took a roll of blue masking tape and taped the paper that Maggie had brought to the safe door.

"What's the point of the safe if you have the combination taped to the front?"

"Well, I'm not going to leave it there. I'll memorize it after you leave. Then I'll put it in a safe place." She locked the safe again. "Have you had breakfast?"

"No, I didn't have class today, so I slept in. I'd barely had my first cup of coffee when Brenda messaged me, but knowing you, I figured I'd better get over here ASAP! I know how impatient you can be when you want something." After fifty years, Maggie probably knew her better than anyone.

"Come on upstairs and I'll make you some breakfast," said Liz. She moved a box that wasn't too heavy away with her foot so they could pass.

"I can make you breakfast," said Maggie when they were in the kitchen. "I bet you don't get that often." Everyone knew Lucy wasn't much of a cook.

"When you're in my house, *I* make the breakfast." At first, Maggie grinned at Liz's tough guy imitation, but then her eyes misted.

"It used to be my house too."

Liz scooped her up, more gently this time. "Oh, Maggie. Things change. Come on. I'll make you some blueberry pancakes."

Liz filled two pods with coffee. "Don't be a stranger, Maggie. Sit down and make yourself comfortable," said Liz, getting cream for the coffee out of the refrigerator while the coffee brewed.

"I still feel like I should be making you breakfast."

"Why? You did me a favor. Just relax. I don't get to make blueberry pancakes very often. Lucy loves them but says they make her fat. The kids don't come up much, now that they're growing up and in every sport and after-school activity."

"I know, it's the same with the girls," said Maggie wistfully. "Like you say, things change."

Liz gazed into the refrigerator. "Luckily, I do have fresh blueberries. If I'd known you were coming, I would have picked up some buttermilk."

"You can make some with milk and white vinegar."

"I know, but it's not the same."

"Your pancake recipe is the best," said Maggie as Liz brought her coffee to the table. "Katrina and Nicki love them."

Liz smiled at the thought that Maggie still made her blueberry pancakes for her grandchildren. "I know Sam likes them too," said Liz.

Maggie's expression changed and she looked away.

"What's the matter?" asked Liz.

"Oh, nothing." Maggie waved dismissively.

"Don't bullshit me, Maggie. We've known each other too long for that."

"I don't really want to talk about it."

"Okay," said Liz with a shrug and went to get her coffee. "If you change your mind, I'm here to listen."

"Why would I want to talk about my current partner with my ex?"

"Because I've known both of you for decades, so my perspective might be helpful."

Maggie made a face. "You were jealous when I got together with Sam."

"Yes, but not for the reason you think. I never thought Sam would side with you against me. I mean she knew how you fucked that kid actor to get back at me." Liz was instantly sorry she'd said that and busied herself with preparing her coffee. "I shouldn't have brought that up."

"You're still angry, and so am I. It was on the tip of my tongue to say you kissed Lucy on the boat. And now I brought it up anyway." She sighed deeply. "Why can't we just put this behind us?"

"Because it happened, and nothing we can do can change it."

"You know I really loved you."

"And I really loved you too," murmured Liz, mostly to herself.

"I still love you, but I can't be married to you. Can we just be friends? I mean, real friends. No pretense?"

"We can try, but we've both said and done plenty of stupid things, mean things too," said Liz. "Let me get breakfast started."

"You know what? Skip the pancakes. Just make something simple."

"Fried eggs okay? I can make you an omelet."

"Never mind. Fried would be fine," Maggie said quickly. "You like them that way." Liz got up and put a skillet on the stove and cut a knob of butter into it. "What would Lucy say if she knew you were making me breakfast?"

"She'd probably be happy that we're getting along better." Liz put bread into the toaster. "You could join the truce. She misses you."

"I know. It's just hard. So much has happened."

Liz could feel Maggie's eyes on her back while she tended

the eggs. When they were done to her satisfaction, she efficiently scooped them out of the pan and buttered the toast. She brought their plates to the table. "So, tell me what's going on with Sam."

"Liz, I'm afraid to tell you because you'll interfere."

"If she's not treating you right, you're damn right I'll interfere."

Maggie looked up from her plate. "See? That's what I mean. You always think it's your job to fix things."

"Well, it is my job. That's what I do. I *fix* things."

"Why can't you just listen?...without judgment if that's even possible with you?"

Liz pursed her lips. "Of course, it is. As a doctor, I listen to a lot of stuff without judgment. You'd be surprised."

"Not at all. I know you're very good at pretending you don't have emotional reactions, but I know better."

"Okay, you're right," said Liz to stop the conversation about her. She wanted to know about Sam. "When is Sam coming home?"

Maggie put down her fork. "Maybe she's not."

"What?"

"She loves Chicago and wants to move there."

"Did she ask you to come along?" asked Liz, as casually as she could.

"She did, more out of loyalty, I think, than she really wants me there. She's with her architecture friends. They're mostly a younger crowd."

"You're assuming that."

"Yes, but you know my instincts are usually good. Like I knew your proposal was mostly a need to prove you'd stand by me despite the cancer diagnosis."

Liz wanted to argue that it was more, then decided it was more important to find out about Sam and the move. "Trust your instincts, but you should also have a heart-to-heart with Sam. Maybe she really does want you to move with her."

"I don't need to tell you how complicated it is. I'm seventy.

I don't want to make another big move, and most of the reason Sam wants to leave is she wants to get away from Hobbs. The stigma of being responsible for giving the shooter access to the school haunts her. I think people have mostly stopped blaming her, but she feels guilty. She thinks going to Chicago will give her a fresh start."

"The geographical cure never works, but I can see why she might think so."

"It worked for you," Maggie pointed out. "When you were fed up with your job as chief of surgery at Yale, you moved up here."

Liz didn't want Maggie to read her feelings, which as a theater director, she excelled at doing, so she focused her attention on her plate. "I'm glad that Sam is making friends with other architects. She always felt on the outs with that community because she was a woman in a man's profession. I get that. I felt the same. There weren't a lot of female surgeons when I started. Younger women have a different perspective."

"Yes, they do. They're reaping the benefits of the battles we fought."

"Will Sam sell the house?" asked Liz, focusing on the practical aspects.

"I don't know. If she does, I'd have to buy it or I'm homeless again. I knew I shouldn't sell the Scarborough house to Alina."

"You hold the mortgage, so technically you still own it."

"Technically."

Liz had finished eating, so she crossed her cutlery on her plate. "Alina said you can always move back into the apartment in the basement."

"Now that she's engaged, she doesn't really want me there. The kids are getting older and don't need grandma to babysit them. That basement apartment was always dark and damp and cold in the winter. I put up with it because I needed to get away from you and Hobbs, and the kids needed me."

"Oh, Maggie, I'm sorry. Don't take it personally. Sam's relationships never last."

"I know, and I didn't really have any expectations."

"Honestly, I was surprised you got involved with her so fast."

Maggie's hazel eyes scanned Liz's face. Liz guessed she was deciding whether to trust her. "I needed her then," Maggie finally said. "She was kind to me after the cancer came back. She told me I was attractive despite my mastectomies and the difference in age. She told me what I needed to hear."

Liz looked at her ex-wife. She was attractive, not a natural beauty like Lucy, but Maggie knew how to make the most of her assets. She kept her white hair long and wore it in elaborate braids or updos. Her makeup was always just so. Liz reached for her hand. "You're beautiful, Maggie. Don't ever think you're not."

Maggie squeezed her hand. "Oh, Liz, you're prejudiced. Look at me. I have fake breasts. I'm old."

"I'm old too," said Liz, "but I'm not done yet." She got up to brew another cup of coffee. "You could buy the house from Sam. It's worth a lot because it's waterfront property, and it was renovated by a prize-winning architect. I'm sure she'd give you a good price."

"Liz, it's awful being out there without Sam. I'm used to having close neighbors. There are only a few houses on Jimson Pond, and they're summer homes. It's so dark out there at night."

"Sam's house is isolated, but so is this place. Were you afraid when I went off to a conference or down to New York to visit my mother?"

"No, I knew you had all those security cameras, and when the place is locked up, it's like a fortress. But even more, I knew you'd be home soon, and I'd be safe." Maggie's voice broke on the last word.

Liz was torn. Should she brush off the emotion to spare herself and Maggie the indignity of showing how moved she was? There was also the possibility that Maggie was just acting. She had the uncanny ability to accurately portray a feeling summoned from nowhere. Liz's intuition told her this was genuine. Then, Maggie's

colorful scarf slipped. The sudden view of her neck, pale and as delicate as crepe, made her look so vulnerable. Liz swallowed the lump
in her throat, and tried to pretend she hadn't seen Maggie's tears.
Then a hand reached across the table and covered hers.

"Thanks for listening," said Maggie. "I'm sorry to burden you
with my troubles."

"I'm your friend, Maggie, and I care about you. How long have
you been frightened to be alone on Jimson Pond?"

"In the beginning, Sam was always there, so I never noticed how
isolated we were. Then she went out to California to make her pitch
for the museum project, and I realized there was no one around.
Winter's long nights are the worst. And there are so many noises in
the woods—the loons calling each other on the pond, unidentified
growls and howls. When it freezes, you can hear the ice groaning as
it expands. The acorns sound like artillery when they hit the metal
roof. In a storm, you can hear the water slapping against the dock."

"But the acorns won't hurt you, and that house was built on high
ground to avoid flooding. Burglars are more likely to hit the empty
summer homes than Sam's place. And the police patrol regularly."

Maggie's hazel eyes held Liz's gaze. "Brenda gave me your gun
for protection, the one you used to kill Peter Langdon."

Liz's breath caught. Brenda had offered to buy the CZ-10 to take
it off her hands, but Liz wouldn't take the money. That was the last
they'd spoken about the gun, Liz's favorite carry pistol, manufac-
tured in the Czech Republic to old world standards. It was rare and
valuable, and it had nearly broken Liz's heart to give it away.

"Maggie, you're terrified of guns. Why did you let Brenda give
it to you?"

"She was in a bind. Cherie wanted it out of the house."

"Why? Brenda's the police chief. She has her service weapons
and personal pistol in the hall closet. What's the difference?"

"You know why. She's hated guns since that trooper shot
her sister. She felt creepy about this gun because you killed Peter

Langdon with it. That and Brenda's fascination with it. So I offered to keep it at Sam's until you were ready to have it back."

"Where is it now?"

"On the sideboard in the hall."

Liz wanted to jump up and run into the hall and get it, but that would send the wrong message. Instead, she picked up the toast crust she'd left and chewed thoughtfully. "Thanks for bringing it home."

"You're welcome." Maggie picked up her fork. "And thanks for listening to my tale of woe."

Liz nodded and finished her coffee in silence.

Chapter 2

"**O**uch! Your nails are sharp!" Liz flinched dramatically.

Lucy laid her hand on her cheek to soothe her. "I'm sorry, sweetie. I let them grow for the concert."

"You claw your lover so you can be glamorous? Why couldn't you use press-on nails for the performance?"

Lucy was intrigued that her wife, who always disparaged anything 'girly,' even knew nail extensions existed. "How do you know about them?"

"I was married to Maggie Fitzgerald, glamor girl *par excellence*, no one can hold a candle to her...except maybe you."

"I only do glamor because it comes with being an opera star. Fans expect it."

"Don't bullshit me, Lucy. You never leave the house without makeup. You won't even host online morning prayer without putting on mascara and lipstick."

"That's because the ring light washes out my features. My congregation expects their rector to look professional, not like some old hag," protested Lucy. "You're a doctor. It's the same."

"Done with all that dress for success nonsense. What you see is what you get."

Liz's attitude was trying Lucy's patience, not because she was expressing opinions she'd vocalized for years, but because she was wasting time. Lucy had to be at rehearsal soon.

"I didn't really hurt you, did I?" asked Lucy, feeling her fingernails. They were only slightly longer than usual and carefully filed.

"No, but try to be more careful."

"I'll make it up to you," said Lucy, diving under the covers, where the musky scent of their morning lovemaking filled her nostrils. That alone was an aphrodisiac. "Now, just relax, my love, and let me take care of you." The touch of Lucy's tongue made Liz jump and instantly stopped the silly conversation. As usual, it didn't take long before her body shuddered with pleasure.

"You're so easy," said Lucy, nestling in the crook of Liz's arm.

"Some women fake orgasms. I've never heard of any pretending the opposite."

"I still haven't learned your pace. One touch, and you come."

"Don't complain. When we have morning sex, coming fast keeps you on schedule."

Lucy gently pinched Liz's thigh. "You and your Teutonic efficiency. Erika never watched the clock." Lucy sighed and nuzzled against Liz's breast. "Sometimes, I miss her so much."

"Me too." Liz sighed. "She was my wingman. I still feel lost without her."

A few tears came to Lucy's eyes, wetting the space between her cheek and Liz's skin. Shouldn't she be getting past the grief by now? Erika had been gone for almost two years. Yet Lucy frequently found herself bursting into tears. God knows there was plenty to cry over—wars, homelessness, the brutal murder of innocent children right in their own town. Now that the wound of Erika's death wasn't so fresh and searing, Lucy could finally probe its depth. The rehearsals for Verdi's gorgeous, operatic Requiem were churning up deep emotions.

Even though she was a professional, she sometimes struggled to express such powerful feelings without losing control. Her mother had trained her to focus on technique rather than the meaning of the text. That was easier when she was young. Then, it was all about the singing. She hadn't yet experienced the terrible hurts of adult life—the loss of her parents, her promising career, and her spouse. The deaths were awful, but so was the rape and having to give up her baby daughter for adoption. It took great discipline not to show how much the words that she sang meant to her, especially when she remembered the teachers and fellow singers who'd taught her so much. It was just the natural cycle of life, but as she edged toward sixty, it suddenly had much more significance.

Liz seemed to sense that she was weeping. She rolled over and pulled her against her breast. "I'm selfish to whine about losing my friend. Erika was your lover, your wife." Of course, that only made Lucy cry harder. Liz kissed her forehead, her eyelids, her cheeks and moved down her face to her mouth. The deep kiss rekindled Lucy's desire, but unlike Liz, she liked a long, slow plot to an orgasm. She'd already had one this morning. Wanting another was just being greedy. Besides, she had a rehearsal at nine-thirty, and she couldn't be late.

"Sweetheart, I love you dearly, but I need to get up and shower," said Lucy, slipping out of her arms.

"Leave some hot water for me," said Liz, taking the gentle rebuff in stride. "I'm coming with you."

"You don't always have to come to my rehearsals," said Lucy. "I mean, I appreciate it, but don't feel obligated."

"I don't. I enjoy hearing you sing. Plus, I always learn something from hearing the conductor's instructions to the orchestra." That was one of the many things Lucy loved about Liz. She was so curious, always wanting to learn more. "This new kid is full of surprises."

"I love Yannick!" Lucy declared.

Liz looked thoughtful. "But I've never seen a conductor, male or female, paint his fingernails black."

"I like that he doesn't care what anyone thinks. He's so confident, so full of joy!"

"Reminds me of Leonard Bernstein in the days he was broadcasting his young people's concerts. He was flamboyant too. Obviously, people knew back then that he was gay, but no one talked about it. And I was just a kid. I'd sit in front of our black and white TV and conduct along with him." Lucy imagined young Liz, waving her arms in time to the music. She'd seen enough photos of the wiry, tall girl to create an accurate movie in her head. If she'd met the young tomboy, they might have bonded over music, but they were nearly a decade apart in age. Lucy was just an infant when Liz was playing conductor.

"Is that how you learned to love classical music?" asked Lucy, sitting up.

"No, I got that from my father...and Saturday morning cartoons. By the time I got a 'phonograph' as they called LP players in those days, I was familiar with the most famous tunes."

"I never know if familiarity is a benefit or a curse. Some popular compositions become such clichés I can't stand hearing them anymore."

"Hey, don't knock popular classics. They have their place. It's why you still have a job."

Lucy chuckled and got out of bed. She felt Liz's eyes following her to the bathroom. At the door, she stopped to wiggle her rear suggestively and heard Liz laugh.

"Yes, dear, you have a nice ass. Don't forget to pee."

Lucy turned and bowed. She dreaded UTIs since she had come home from her honeymoon with Erika with a nasty one. That's when she learned Liz made house calls for special patients. Unsolicited medical advice after sex was one of the downsides of being married to a doctor, but there were also benefits.

Lucy undressed and got into the oversized shower. Despite its reputation for luxury, the bathroom in the Plaza was not nearly as big or as well-appointed as their bathroom at home. Of course, Liz had planned it that way. She loved a long, very hot shower in the morning.

Before pinning up her hair, Lucy brushed it out. More and more strands were fading to blond in the peculiar way that redheads "gray." When she'd shown up for the costume fitting for *Der fliegende Holländer*, the wig master had been so intrigued by the variety of tones that he decided Lucy didn't need one. Lucy couldn't be happier. Wearing a heavy wig while singing for hours under the hot stage lights could be torture. It occurred to Lucy that the man had made the decision out of kindness. At her age, most sopranos were thinking of retirement, and here she was, restarting her career.

Roger Weinstein, her agent, was taking maximum advantage of the Met's refusal to investigate Lucy's sexual assault when it happened, using the leverage to get more roles close to home, mostly because Lucy was reluctant to do the overseas travel expected of an international opera star.

Roger often threatened her with the obvious fact that her future as a singer was limited, but Lucy mostly ignored his ominous warnings. The way she saw it, she was enjoying the gift of a revived singing career, a reason for gratitude, not fortitude. She'd made a life for herself as a priest and a home in Hobbs, where she had a loving wife and supportive friends. As much as she enjoyed performing again, she was not about to abandon everything that made life worth living.

That's what she told herself, but sometimes the allure of the stage was irresistible. She loved being with other musicians again. Working with an energetic and creative conductor like Yannick Nézet-Séguin was inspirational. She loved his flamboyance and enthusiasm for all kinds of music. Working with him reminded her of why she'd come to love her singing career, despite being pushed into it by her mother, who'd never achieved her own operatic aspirations.

As Lucy was rinsing off, she felt warm hands on her waist and a pubic bone pressing gently against her buttocks.

"Liz! What are you doing in here?"

"You were taking so long I figured I'd better jump in with you, or we'll be late for your rehearsal."

"Likely story. You just wanted a little water play." Lucy pressed Liz's hand to stop the motion. "You know how much I enjoy making love in the shower, but not on a day when I have to be somewhere."

Liz grinned. "Okay, but let me under the shower, so I can wash my hair."

"You can have it all to yourself. I'm getting out."

Liz sighed contentedly as she doused her face with hot water. Lucy realized that displacing her had been the plan all along.

***

Although they were sitting at the back in the auditorium and couldn't be heard, Roger whispered into Liz's ear. "Lucy is singing better than ever. Whatever you're doing, keep doing it." He grinned suggestively as if sex were the only reason Lucy was in good voice.

Liz deadpanned because Roger annoyed her. He was always making assumptions, and he pushed Lucy too hard. Lucy found it hard to say no because he'd stuck with her when her career was on the wane. She left Liz to set boundaries. She didn't really mind because she could be tough when she needed to be.

While Roger might insinuate that sex was improving Lucy's voice, it was Liz's attentive care. She made sure Lucy was fed and watered like an exotic plant. Although she was no longer Lucy's doctor, Liz scrupulously monitored the condition of her throat. Every morning, she sat in their media room with the perfect acoustics she'd designed for it while Lucy practiced. She patiently listened to Lucy sing her exercises before rehearsing for upcoming engagements. She offered gentle but honest critiques, which Lucy seemed to appreciate.

Roger didn't need to know any of that. It was their business. Liz deliberately turned the subject away from the personal to the professional. "Lucy's right. Her voice has darkened."

"Well, that's natural. But her voice is more powerful than ever, and she brings so much to her interpretations. It's crazy but being away for a decade has probably extended her career. Too bad she lost so much momentum."

"I don't think she really cares."

"Yes, I know," said Roger, making a face as he parroted Lucy's words. "She's grateful for the opportunity to sing again. I just wish we could put some fire in her belly. Liz, this is her time! People are begging for her to sing. Even Bayreuth."

"The Wagner festival?" asked Liz incredulously. "Really?" The

Bayreuth festival had been on Liz's bucket list for decades. "She didn't tell me."

"I know she doesn't want to be typecast as a Wagnerian. But she has the voice and they noticed. Hard to believe someone so small can make such a big sound." Again, Liz hid her smile. She could attest that her tiny wife had an enormous impact in many ways. "Could you talk to her, Liz?" Roger asked, patting her arm. "Please?"

"You know I never interfere in Lucy's career."

"Bullshit, Liz. You're her shadow manager."

"I'm her wife. Not the same. I support her to do what makes her happy."

Roger's lips compressed into a line. "She's lucky, and so are you. I was married once. Didn't last. She complained that I worked too much."

"See? That's the moral of the story," said Liz. "Pace yourself and let Lucy do the same."

"Yeah, I get it, but I work for myself. If I don't hustle, the money doesn't come in. And you should talk, I bet you worked your ass off to become a surgeon."

"I did, which is why I didn't have a serious relationship until I finished my training." She smiled. "Lucy works hard in her day job. She doesn't need this."

"Hard to have a career in classical singing as a sideline. Right now, her stock is high. The sympathy over being driven out after reporting that prick, Alex Dupuis, made her a sensation, but it won't last. Most people have a short attention span."

"She hates being known for the Met apology."

"I know, but it jump started her career, and she needs to capitalize on the momentum. You always say you don't interfere in her decisions, but I know she listens to you."

"Roger, why are we having this conversation again? Lucy has a mind of her own. Don't you know that by now?"

"I do, but I need to convince her to perform more often. Bayreuth is a big deal."

It was a "big deal." The Bayreuth festival was the pinnacle of a Wagnerian singer's career. And if Lucy performed at Bayreuth, Liz would certainly get free tickets instead of languishing on the waiting list for years. "Maybe if you got her some non-Wagnerian gigs, she would consider it. There are a lot of operas in her *Fach*."

"Covent Garden is reviving *Otello*."

"One of her favorite roles."

"And Paris has a *Faust* in the works. I've already put her name in the running for both."

"Good. Get her off the Wagnerian circuit, and I'm sure you'll find her much more receptive."

They were distracted by the conductor clapping his hands to announce that they were ending rehearsal for the day. Lucy lingered to speak to the mezzo soloist before coming down the stage stairs into the auditorium.

Roger got up and stretched. "Will you ladies join me for lunch?"

"Can't, Roger," said Lucy. "We have a date with my old professor at Union."

"Dinner?"

Lucy shook her head. "Sorry. We're having dinner with a friend, who's in town for the performance."

Roger looked glum. "Maybe we can do lunch tomorrow," Liz suggested. "That way, Roger can get all the business talk out of his system before the opening night gala."

Roger brightened at the suggestion. "You'll come too, Liz, won't you?"

"Of course, she'll come," said Lucy. "I drag the poor woman everywhere, so she's not jealous I'm getting all the attention!"

Liz made a face. Lucy rubbed the small of her back to assure her she was only teasing. "My wife is very patient," she explained, smiling adoringly. For some reason, that made Liz blush.

They parted on the street when a cab pulled up. "See you tomorrow," he said, kissing each of them on the cheek. He caught Liz's eye before she got into the cab. "Remember what I said."

Lucy gave the taxi driver instructions, and they headed up Broadway. "How did I do today?" she asked, patting Liz's thigh.

"Great. Roger says you've never been in such good voice." Liz gazed innocently out the window. "He thinks it's because you're getting regular sex."

Lucy feigned shock. "Did you agree? I know you like to brag about what a stud you are."

"I value my life, so I wouldn't dare."

"Good. Our sex life is no one's business." Lucy gently stroked Liz's thigh. "You sure I did okay?"

"Where's this insecurity coming from?"

Lucy moved closer and leaned into her. "Working with Yannick reminds me how much I love performing. I'm afraid I'll want to go back full time."

Liz nodded slowly. "It's okay if you do. I'll support you."

"No, it's not okay. I have an obligation to St. Margaret's. You have your practice. We'd need to live closer to an airport."

As Liz listened to Lucy enumerate the many reasons why she couldn't go back to singing full time, she wondered if her practicality had rubbed off on her. "So far, you're managing," Liz said after Lucy finished. "And now that Tom's back, you could take on more engagements. Why didn't you tell me about Bayreuth?"

"Because I knew you'd insist I do it."

"Well, of course I would. Other singers would die for that opportunity. What's the role?"

"Elisabeth in *Tannhäuser*."

"What would your mother say if she knew you'd turned down Bayreuth?"

"She'd probably kill me." Lucy grinned. "No, that's an exaggeration, but she'd probably never speak to me again."

"I might not either. I've always wanted to go to Bayreuth."

"Well, dear, I hope you'll understand that I'm not going to sing at Bayreuth just because you want tickets. If I accept, it will be because I only have so much time to give to my singing. I never aspired to be a Wagnerian soprano, and I'm annoyed Roger can't find other roles for me to sing."

"He told me he's working on it."

"Liz, you promised to stay out of my decisions about my singing career unless I ask for your advice."

"I did, didn't I?" said Liz sheepishly.

"Yes, you did. And part of the reason I didn't tell you about the Bayreuth booking is I knew exactly what you'd say. I am thinking about it. I promised I'd let Roger know this week. When I decide, you'll be the first to know." Lucy sat up straight and stared out the taxi window at the congested traffic around them. Clearly, she was conflicted, and the topic of Bayreuth was sensitive. Liz suspected it went beyond her worry about being typecast.

"I'm sorry, Lucy. Only you know what you can take on and what will benefit your career most. I know you'll make the right decision."

Lucy's answer was to reach over and take Liz's hand and squeeze it.

The traffic finally broke up as they left Midtown and headed through the Upper West Side. They passed the building where Lucy had once lived. "Sometimes, I really miss New York," she said wistfully. "Don't you?"

"I enjoyed living here while I was in college and medical school, but now I can't think of living anywhere but Hobbs."

Lucy nodded but said nothing.

❋❋❋

When they arrived at the La Salle Dumpling Room, Lucy's dissertation advisor, Jerry Spangler, wearing a Hawaiian shirt and jeans, was waiting outside. "Don't look at me like that Lucy," he said, grinning as he bent to kiss her cheek. "It's my day off."

"How am I looking at you? I'm happy to see you looking so casual and relaxed." Lucy gave him a warm hug.

"Hello, Liz." As he extended his hand, his blue eyes gave her a careful inspection. "You look great," he said, sounding almost surprised. He held the door open and gestured for them to go inside.

"If I'd known it was your day off, I would have picked another day," said Lucy apologetically.

"Why? This is a social occasion, not work. And I'm only teaching one class this semester. Part of my plan to wind down before I retire completely."

Lucy frowned. "I'm sorry to hear you're going to retire. Their loss."

"Oh, it's the right thing to do. I don't feel like I fit in. Union has always been a progressive place, but now, I have to watch every word I say. You know me, Lucy. I'm the kind of teacher who thinks out loud in the classroom. You can't do that anymore without someone playing 'gotcha.'"

"But it makes me sad that you'd give up teaching," said Lucy, looking more than sad. "You have so much more to say. Your theology is an inspiration to me and many others."

Spangler shook his head. "It's not like it used to be. You should know. Remember how that trans woman attacked you in your lecture last fall? You always have to say the right thing, no matter what you think. I'm not the only one thinking of quitting. Many of the others are worried about their jobs and being intimidated into silence."

Liz studied Spangler's lined face. She shared his worries. Censoring free speech on campus was a bad sign.

After they ordered, Lucy excused herself to use the ladies' room, but it was lunchtime and there was a line to get in. Spangler smiled pleasantly.

"I'm glad to see you looking so well, Liz. Lucy told me you were having a hard time after the shooting."

Liz wondered what Lucy had told him. And she didn't like the idea that he might be trying to counsel her as a pastor. "We were all having a hard time," Liz said evenly, "but yes, I had a harder time than most."

"I can't imagine how you must feel about being forced to take a life."

"I don't think you can. I don't think anyone can."

"Of course not, but it must be especially hard because you're a doctor and took an oath to do no harm."

"That's nonsense," Liz replied bluntly. "Doctors do lots of deliberate harm. Causing pain through surgery is harm."

"Hadn't thought of it that way."

"Peter Langdon wasn't some random nutty kid waving an AR-15. He was my patient. I cared about him. I tried to turn him around. Turns out he had a deep, dark secret he'd been hiding."

"The sexual abuse?"

"If I'd only known…"

"But you didn't. You did the best you could under the circumstances."

"I know. Some people think Peter deserved to die because he killed all those children. They say I shouldn't even think twice about shooting him. Easy for them to say." Although Liz usually didn't drink during the day, she signaled the waiter and ordered a beer and a glass of white wine for Lucy. "Something for you, Jerry?"

Spangler shook his head. When the waiter departed, he said, "Give yourself a break, Liz. You're a good person, who was caught in a bad situation."

"That's what everybody says. But I keep thinking I should have said or done something differently…"

"You did the only thing you could."

When Lucy finally returned to the table, Liz smiled brightly, but the conversation had put her in a dark mood.

❋❋❋

"Liz didn't want to come?" Rebecca asked, when Lucy appeared at the table alone.

Gazing into Rebecca's dark eyes, Lucy knew that anything less than the truth wouldn't satisfy her. Although she was younger, Rebecca had more experience in pastoral counseling, and she knew Lucy better than anyone. "She wanted to give us some private time, so I left her back at the hotel. Don't worry. She'll get room service and read medical journals and be perfectly happy. Liz can be sociable when she feels like it, but she prefers her own company."

Rebecca nodded. "She's one of those introverts who play a good game. I guessed that about her. Actually, I'm glad to have you all to myself."

"Why didn't Judith come down with you?"

"Judith is getting ready to leave for Israel to visit her parents. Looking after the twins on my own for a month won't be easy, but honestly, I'm glad for a break. Even in a marriage, there's such a thing as too much togetherness, if you know what I mean."

Lucy shrugged. "I guess I don't. Liz leads a busy life, and I do too. I love spending time with her."

Rebecca listened as if she'd heard this story before and knew it had a different ending. "The glow hasn't worn off yet. I bet you still have sex every day."

Usually, they were completely open about their intimate lives. Lucy quickly realized that telling Rebecca the truth could make her feel bad about her own sex life, so she responded with a canny smile and a shrug.

Rebecca waved dismissively. "Don't give me that. I bet Liz can't keep her hands off you. Enjoy it while you can. Who has time for sex when the girls need to be driven here, there, and everywhere? Thank God, they'll be driving soon. I can't wait!"

Lucy sat back and listened to Rebecca tick off her concerns about the twins driving. Lucy knew they weren't really twins, even though they looked alike, not surprising because Rebecca and her

Israeli wife resembled one another, and they shared a sperm donor. The girls also shared a birthday because their mothers had chosen to be pregnant at the same time, implanted with each other's fertilized ovum, and delivered on the same day by Caesarian.

Rebecca had described their debates surrounding the choice of a donor. Judith wanted the father to be a scientific genius, like her geneticist friend, who ran a biotech startup. Rebecca worried about the potential for autism, so that suggestion was nixed. They'd finally agreed on a history professor who moonlighted as a jazz musician.

"I understand Judith needs to visit her parents," said Rebecca after the waitress took their drinks order. "But she has this deep connection to Israel that I don't share. She lost family in the holocaust. Her parents grew up in a Kibbutz. She served in the Israeli army. I find Israel beautiful and historic, but as an American Jew, it doesn't mean as much to me."

"It's where she grew up," Lucy said. "It's part of her identity."

"I have issues with Zionism. I support Israel, but I don't think there should be settlements in the West Bank. There needs to be a two-state solution."

"Nationalism can be dangerous, especially when it's wrapped up with religion. Look at the white nationalists who are giving Christians a bad name. No wonder people are fleeing churches."

"They're leaving because they found other things to do on the Sabbath, like chauffeuring their kids to activities. Good thing I have gentile friends who can take my daughters to their Saturday practices and games. Mom says it looks bad for the rabbi's kids to be absent from temple, but what can I do?" The waitress delivered their drinks and appetizers. Rebecca shoveled fried calamari from the pile onto her plate. "I have to eat this where no one knows me. Squid isn't kosher." Lucy had never thought of that. She watched Rebecca enjoy her guilty pleasure.

"You're right. People fell out of the habit of going to services during Covid. Getting them to come back isn't easy."

Rebecca peered deeply into Lucy's eyes. "Doesn't it worry you?"

"You mean, do I worry that I'll be out of a job? A little. But since we've gone back to in-person worship, we've experienced a revival. People realized they were missing something. Mostly, they're older, but if they still have a pulse, we take them. Lots of ex-Catholics."

"What are they looking for?" said Rebecca, twirling a piece of calamari in the savory marinara sauce.

"Part of it's nostalgia. They're looking for a community they remember from childhood. The familiarity of the rituals gives them comfort."

"Not just insurance for when they die?"

Lucy considered the question. "The Catholics always want to make their peace with God before they die. Older people tell me, and it makes sense, when you're no longer running around like a crazy person for your job and your kids, you finally have time to think about the meaning of life."

"You're older, Lucy, so I'll have to take your word for it."

"I'm not there yet. I'm still running around like a crazy person."

"Rushing down here for rehearsals. Catching up with all your New York friends. Opening night gala, then three performances of the Requiem. I can understand why Liz decided to take the night off."

"Liz wants me to do more performances. She's pushing me to sing at Bayreuth."

Rebecca looked surprised. "Why wouldn't you want to sing at the Bayreuth Festival? That's a big deal in your world, isn't it?"

"For Wagnerians, it's the biggest thing, the pinnacle of success. That's also why I'm leery about it."

"Oh, come on, Lucy. You can't be having imposter syndrome at this stage in your career."

"It's not that. I never set out to be a Wagnerian soprano. If I sing at Bayreuth, I'm committed. It's not like the old days, when people crossed *Fachs* easily. Nowadays, only superstars like Renée Fleming can do it."

"Well?" Rebecca crossed her arms and gave Lucy a penetrating look.

Lucy laughed. "No, Becca, I'm not in her league. Maybe if I'd stuck with singing, I could have been, but I've been gone too long. A great diva is the sum of her performances. There's a big hole in the middle of my career that can never be filled."

"So Fleming can rest on her laurels, while you still need to hustle. Of course, you need to sing at Bayreuth. Break the rules, Lucy. You're good at that."

Lucy blushed a little because she knew Rebecca was right. "Gee, thanks."

"Well, you are. Who else could write about the theology of sex, question every church doctrine ever written, and get away with it? It's that smile, Lucy. People will forgive you anything."

On cue, Lucy smiled broadly.

"Besides," Rebecca continued, "life is short. What's that they say? 'Buy the shoes. Eat the cake.' Let's add, sing at the Wagner festival. You might never get another chance."

Lucy fell silent because she knew that Rebecca was right.

✻✻✻

Liz snatched a glass of champagne from the passing tray and retreated to what appeared to be a quiet corner. From there she could admire Lucy, who was dazzling everyone with her opening night splendor. Now that she was in demand again, fashion designers were lining up to dress her. Despite Lucy's diminutive height, she carried clothes beautifully. Tonight, she was wearing a retro dark red satin dress with a form-fitting bodice and black lace accents. Usually, Lucy preferred classic elegance, but this gown had a steampunk look that would have suited Helena Bonham Carter in her Tim Burton era.

The general manager, the same one who'd nearly choked when Lucy demanded an apology for covering up the sexual abuse, had laid claim to Lucy and was making the rounds, showing her off to the Met's wealthiest patrons. Lucy looked entirely at home in this glittering crowd. Older, obviously gay men were fawning over her. Some of them probably remembered her from her first career at the Met.

"Hiding?" asked a voice. Liz turned to see Lucy's agent at her elbow.

"Schmoozing with big donors was never my favorite thing."

"I bet you had to do lots of it when you were chief of surgery at Yale."

"Which is why I hate it now. Besides, that's ancient history, and I'm out of practice."

"Nah, you're doing great. I noticed your suit coordinates with Lucy's dress. You make the perfect couple."

Liz managed a polite thanks and took a gulp of champagne. Roger's obvious patronizing annoyed her. She wished he would save it for the music critics, but it appeared he had already done his rounds.

"Thanks for talking Lucy into Bayreuth," said Roger. Liz assumed her impassive doctor look to hide her surprise. She didn't know that Lucy had decided. "I understand that it means missing the Aix festival," Roger continued, "but it's a small price to pay for the boost it will give her career."

"Despite the collar, she's not a saint and can't be in two places at once. Although I never know what she'll do."

Roger chuckled and raised his glass to Liz. "I completely understand. But thanks for helping her come to her senses. She might never get another shot at Bayreuth."

"I think you're giving me more credit than I deserve." Liz pointed across the room. "That's Rebecca Morgenstern, Lucy's rabbi. They had dinner last night. I'd bet money she's the one who convinced Lucy to sing at Bayreuth."

"Glad she listens to someone."

Having backup like Rebecca certainly helped. When it came to performing, the more Liz pushed her point of view, the more stubborn Lucy became. Now that Liz was wise to her game, she often pretended she didn't care. She'd make her case and drop the subject. Nine times out of ten, Lucy would come around. "Would you like to meet Rebecca?" Liz asked. "She's a New Yorker like us, but now she leads a synagogue in Portland."

"She's a real rabbi?" said Roger, looking surprised. "I thought you meant she's the person Lucy goes to for advice."

"She's that too. Come on." Liz nudged Roger with her elbow and led him across the room.

"You're not introducing me because I'm Jewish?" he asked anxiously. "I mean, I'm not practicing. Haven't for years."

"No, and it wouldn't matter to Rebecca. She's cool. And it's good to cultivate allies since you're not getting anywhere with me."

"If she's a rabbi, she won't encourage Lucy to quit the church and focus on her singing," said Roger, stopping in the middle of the crowd, which forced Liz to stop too. "Liz, being a classical singer is not a hobby."

"Neither is being a priest. Come on." Liz tried to encourage Roger with a gentle pull on his elbow, but he dug in and held his ground.

"Liz, you know that Lucy needs to choose," he said, searching her face.

"Maybe she does, but I don't suggest you put it that way because you may not like her answer."

"You don't get it, do you?" Shaking his head, Roger headed to the exit.

Chapter 3

Reshma decided to use the battered Dutch oven that came with the studio when she'd moved in. Besides being exactly the right size for the recipe, it would be an efficient means to transport the ingredients. While she assembled them on the counter, she tamped down her anxiety, reminding herself that she'd made this dish many times. Denise and Susan had always raved about it.

Luckily, chicken legs had been on sale. As much as she wanted to impress Tiffany and her friends, she had to be practical. Her first thought was to make Kofta, but the price of ground lamb was excessive. The shortages might be over, but everything in the supermarket was so expensive.

Her salary used to go much further. Even with the big raise she'd gotten after her ordination, she struggled to pay the grocery bills. For a curate, she was already being paid on the high end of the pay scale, so she didn't feel right asking for a raise. She'd been sharing the cost of groceries with Susan. She was now spending more time with Bobbie, so Reshma was cooking solo, and it had put a sizable dent in her food budget.

Fortunately, onions were cheap. This recipe called for two pounds, and Reshma never skimped. A good Yassa was all about the onions. To save time, she'd peeled and sliced them beforehand. Gathering the pungent rings into a plastic bag, Reshma realized the smell had permeated her skin and clothes. Prepping food in the outfit she'd intended to wear had been a poor choice. What would Tiffany's friends think if she arrived reeking of raw onion? Probably nothing, of course. Professional chefs would be accustomed to the smell, but Reshma desperately wanted to make a good impression on Tiffany's friends.

She stripped off her blouse and vigorously scrubbed her hands and forearms with dish soap in the kitchen sink. A faint onion smell remained, but it was better. Flipping through the tops in her closet, she flung the hangers back and forth, seeking an alternative. The African-inspired patterns she usually wore were an obvious choice for an ethnic dinner, but Reshma worried that Tiffany and her friends would find the colors too loud. Instead, she chose a classic boatneck T-shirt from the L.L. Bean outlet.

Reshma changed her top, grabbed her pot of ingredients, and raced down the stairs. Susan, returning from her teaching job, crossed her on the way up. "You shouldn't run on the stairs, dear," she admonished, "especially not with that big pot."

"Unfortunately, I'm late, as usual. I was invited to cook with Tiffany's friends from the CIA. We're making an African meal together."

"You've gotten so good at cooking recipes from your homeland, I'm sure your contribution will impress them," said Susan, her blue eyes full of fondness. Since she'd helped her young colleague get over her doubts about ordination, she'd assumed a protective, grandmotherly role and always had something positive and encouraging to say. "You've become very fond of Tiffany, haven't you?"

Reshma drew breath to answer, but the clock in the hall chimed, reminding her how late she was. "I like her very much, but I can't talk now. I'll tell you tomorrow." She hurried down the remaining steps.

"Have a great time," Susan called after her.

"Don't forget to record Lucy's concert!" Reshma called back.

Reshma regretted missing the live broadcast of The *Verdi Requiem* from the Met. She knew that Susan would do her best to record it, but she was a self-confessed technophobe. Determined to bring her into the twenty-first century, Reshma had been coaching her. As a result, Susan could operate her smartphone and use Facebook Live to do morning prayer.

Reshma stowed the Dutch oven behind the driver's seat of her vintage Prius and headed into town. The pâtisserie was on the border between Hobbs and trendy, gay-friendly Webhanet. Tourists came from both towns and as far away as Portsmouth and Portland to buy Tiffany's artistic pastries. The location ensured there was always enough business to keep her afloat, even in the off-season. Evidently, Tiffany was a savvy businesswoman in addition to making the best chocolate croissant Reshma had ever tasted.

A tall woman with very short curly hair opened the door of Tiffany's apartment and looked Reshma up and down. Happy female voices emanated from inside. "Am I the last one?" Reshma asked anxiously.

"Looks like it. Good thing you made it. Tiff was starting to worry."

Tiffany pushed past the woman at the door and scooped Reshma into a hug. She sniffed audibly. "Onions! Yum!" Reshma cringed. Despite all the scrubbing, the pungent aroma persisted. Reshma reminded herself that chefs were known to have sensitive noses. "Are you making a Yassa? Oh, Goodie." She clapped her hands vigorously. "I hoped you would."

"This is Brianna, by the way," said Tiffany, pointing to the tall woman who'd opened the door.

"You must be Reshma," said the woman, eyeing her. "Tiffany told us she was inviting a real African, who would put us all to shame."

"How could you say that?" Reshma asked, turning to Tiffany. "You've never eaten my cooking."

"I wanted them to up their game. We might be pros, but nothing beats authenticity."

Wondering if she'd been set up, Reshma followed the women into the apartment. It reminded her of the lofts she'd seen in big cities. The open floor plan was dominated by the enormous kitchen. The surface of the island was almost completely covered with bowls and pans. Gathered around it, young women were enjoying wine and cocktails. Only one woman looked like she really enjoyed food.

The others were slender as twigs. All eyes turned to her, subtly taking her in, when they weren't staring outright. Reshma was the only woman of color in the room, but she wondered if Tiffany had also told them she was a priest. That information was guaranteed to draw strange looks.

"What can I get you to drink?" asked Tiffany. "I made Rooibos tea, but everyone is going for the Ngolos." When Reshma looked puzzled, Tiffany explained: "Kind of like a Moscow Mule, but spicier."

"With alcohol?" asked Reshma.

"Bourbon and ginger beer."

"Sounds intriguing."

"You've never had one?"

"Africa is a big continent with many cultures," Reshma reminded her with a smile.

"Of course," said Tiffany, blushing charmingly. "What am I thinking?"

While Tiffany mixed Reshma's cocktail, the others introduced themselves. Brianna, who'd met Reshma at the door, was a chef in a high-end Boston restaurant. Jess was head chef in a trendy New York bistro, where her girlfriend, Jamie, was the sous chef. Amber was a pastry chef in a big Manhattan hotel. Kirsten was the test kitchen manager for a well-known food magazine. As Reshma had feared, she was the only amateur cook.

Tiffany handed her a glass. "Wow! That's good!" exclaimed Reshma, after tasting the Ngolos. "Sweet, but not too sweet."

"Maple syrup," revealed Tiffany as if she would burst if she didn't tell.

Reshma frowned at what seemed like an obvious cultural contradiction. "I never thought of Africa as a maple syrup producer."

"Me neither. I learn something new every day, and since you've done a deep dive on Sudanese cuisine, I'm hoping you can teach us about it."

"Then you should have invited Teresa. She's the real expert. I'm completely self-taught."

Tiffany took Reshma's arm and pulled her gently away. "I invited you because I wanted you to meet my friends." She smiled. "Any excuse to get you over here. Please be okay with it." Slender fingers entwined with hers and Reshma found herself lost in Tiffany's blue eyes. "You look nice. I kinda expected you to wear bright colors like you usually do." She glanced at Reshma's L.L. Bean top.

She wanted me to look authentic, like a real African, instead of an imitation New Englander. "I could go home and change. I can even put on my collar," she teased with a grin.

The smile disappeared from Tiffany's face. "I didn't tell them about your job," she whispered.

"Well, in that case, I won't either. If someone asks, I'll say I'm a counselor. It's true, after all." Tiffany looked a little too relieved. "Don't you need to get your Yassa going soon?"

"I should, although it doesn't need to cook long."

Tiffany watched her remove the ingredients from the battered pot. "You can use my Le Creuset, if you like," she whispered, glancing furtively at the others, who were busy sampling skewered Kenyan barbecue and mixing more cocktails. She was obviously embarrassed by the state of Reshma's cookware. Reshma wasn't. If it had served generations of St. Margaret's clergy, it was good enough for her.

"It's pretty beat-up," said Reshma, "but it works fine." Tiffany looked doubtful. Reshma ignored her and turned on the flame under the pot.

The sizzle of the chicken legs as they hit the hot oil got the attention of the other guests, and they gathered around the stove. "The recipe calls for a habanero, but I never remember to buy one, so I just use canned chilis. Don't tell." There was some laughter. Reshma looked up to see Tiffany's smile of approval. The self-effacing attitude seemed to be working. Jess and Jamie were craning to get a look into the pot, so she tilted it for all to see. "Golden brown is what you're looking for." She asked Tiffany for a plate and removed the chicken so she could brown the onions. Soon the pot was ready to go into the oven to braise. The next cook stepped up to prepare a sweet potato stew.

"How often do you get together?" Reshma asked, intrigued by the combination of cooperative cooking with girls' night out.

"We try to meet every other month for dinner," the short one called Amber explained. "Sometimes, we eat at a new restaurant we all want to try. Other times, we cook together, like tonight."

"Fortunately, we've stopped having debates about whether it's cultural appropriation to do these ethnic dinners," said Brianna dryly. "I'm glad because I really enjoy them."

"What do you think, Reshma?" asked Jess, whose long, blond hair was nearly the same color as Tiffany's. "It's your culture we're celebrating tonight."

Reshma thought for a moment. This could be a fraught topic. "I think celebrating is the right word for what we're doing. I spent much of my childhood in an Episcopal boarding school, which couldn't be farther from my village in Sudan. In the refugee camp, we were on UN rations, so traditional cooking was impossible. I taught myself to cook as an adult." Reshma looked up. They were staring at her, probably some of them were shocked by her sad story. "But I didn't answer your question. I think sharing our ethnic heritage helps us appreciate our diversity." The others nodded in agreement. She'd given the right answer.

"I think people are inserting politics into places where they don't belong," Brianna said. "I have a curious palate and love to eat all kinds of foods."

"Me too," some of the others murmured.

Red-haired Amber declared, "I'm sick of being told what to think. I'm as liberal as they come, but some of this stuff is over the top for me." She glared at Reshma. "I hate group think," she added vehemently.

"You're not the only one," Brianna chimed in. "It's gotten out of control."

"Reshma, what do you think?" asked Jess' diminutive girlfriend, Jamie. She wore her short hair shaved on the sides, yet she looked softer than her partner.

As the only, brown-skinned person in the room, Reshma wondered how she'd been chosen to represent all marginalized minorities. She glanced around at the curious faces. "I'm not the best one to ask. I've only recently rediscovered my African identity. My education was designed to turn me into a WASP and a faithful Episcopalian. I do think assuming the worst about people shuts down conversation."

"They don't want conversation," said Brianna, crossing her arms. "They think they're right and everyone else should either put up or shut up."

Tiffany looked alarmed that the conversation had gotten hot so quickly. Reshma glanced at her for cues, but she stared back with wide eyes. Finally, she said, "Reshma, please. Help me out here."

All eyes were on Reshma. She smiled. "I love a good discussion, but I think Tiffany invited us to cook, not debate. For the sake of our appetites, why don't we hold the political conversation until after dinner?"

Brianna engaged her eyes in a clear challenge, but Reshma continued to smile, and soon she saw it mirrored in the faces around her. Finally, Brianna's expression softened.

"Why don't we relax and enjoy some snacks while our dinner cooks?" suggested Tiffany, heading to the sitting area on the other side of the apartment. She waited while people found seats. Under her breath, she asked Reshma, "How did you do that?"

"I don't know, but Mother Lucy can calm everyone with a smile."

"Well, now you know you can too." Tiffany moved closer to Reshma until their thighs touched. "Thank you!"

✳✳✳

That smile! Tiffany wondered if they taught smiling in priest school. No, that wasn't right. What did Reshma call that place? *Seminary.* Reshma's boss, Lucy Bartlett, smiled the same way, like no one in the world mattered more than you. When you basked in such a smile, all the fear, anger, or whatever negative feeling you'd been feeling just melted away. It was pure magic.

Tiffany had no idea what to make of it or the fact that Reshma was a priest. Tiffany's parents had no use for religion. They were proud atheists. Her mother was a psychiatrist. Her father was the president of a national foundation that provided grants for the performing arts. They'd imbued in their only child an appreciation of humanistic values and a deep respect for critical thinking. She wondered what they'd think of her attraction to a to-die-for Episcopal priest.

They'd like the idea that Reshma John was a refugee from Africa, who'd made the most of her education. Brad and Mary Taylor were big on education. They were disappointed when Tiffany chose culinary school over a prestigious college. She'd gotten into Vassar, Barnard, and Sarah Lawrence, but chose the CIA. Mary had objected more than Brad, whose failed career in music helped him understand his daughter's impulse toward creating fanciful pastry. All her life, they told their daughter they'd support her in whatever career she chose. When the time came, they weren't so sure.

Loading the dinner dishes into the dishwasher so she wouldn't wake up to a mess, Tiffany listened to the relaxed and civil conversation her guests were having in the sitting area. Reshma sat in the center, effortlessly facilitating the discussion. Maybe moderating debates was another subject they taught in priest school.

The party would be breaking up soon. Some of the guests had a long drive ahead. Brianna was staying overnight, otherwise Tiffany would have made an overture to Reshma. The impossibility of it hadn't stopped her fantasies of Reshma's reaction. Although they all ended the same way, with Reshma's generous lips kissing her deeply. Her imagination had Reshma primly proposing a wait-and-see approach then capitulating once Tiffany puckered up. In the movie in her mind, she enjoyed watching Reshma's sunny self-confidence unravel. Then there was the scenario in which Reshma took the lead, and Tiffany swooned in her arms.

Reshma suddenly glanced at her from across the room, making Tiffany wonder if she could hear her wicked thoughts. Her guilty look made Reshma excuse herself from the group and head to the sink where Tiffany stood.

"Dutifully playing Martha to my Mary, I see," whispered Reshma. Tiffany had no idea what she was talking about. She stared at Reshma until she explained. "It's from scripture. One sister does the cooking and cleaning while the other sits at Jesus' feet to hear his teachings." She stared contritely at the dish drainer "I'd offer to help, but it looks like you're done."

"Don't worry. I'm grateful you're keeping my guests entertained and happy."

"My pleasure," said Reshma with a little bow. "I always enjoy talking to intelligent women."

Tiffany glanced at her friends in the sitting room. "For a bunch of cooks, they're pretty smart."

Brianna raised her head and looked in their direction. Her eyes narrowed.

"Brianna says she's staying over," whispered Reshma.

"She is," replied Tiffany casually. "Otherwise, I would have asked you to stay."

Reshma's dark eyes widened, leaving Tiffany to wonder if her fantasies had made her too bold. Maybe she'd jumped to conclusions. "I don't have far to go," Reshma added rapidly. "I live right here in town...and it's not like it's late."

For God's sake! Reshma couldn't be *that* dense, could she? Or maybe she was giving Tiffany an out by ignoring the all-too-obvious invitation. Tiffany couldn't resist testing her hunch.

"If you drank too much, you'd consider staying, wouldn't you? I'd hate for something to happen to you."

"My limit is two drinks when I have to drive," Reshma assured her virtuously.

Tiffany tried not to show her frustration. "Just know that you are always welcome."

Reshma smiled one of her winning smiles, and Tiffany just melted. "Thank you. I appreciate the invitation should I ever over-imbibe."

Well, that was hopeful, but Tiffany wanted to make sure Reshma understood. She leaned closer until their hips touched. Reshma pressed back against her. Message understood. But now Brianna was glaring at them. Maybe it was time to wind the party down. Jess, Jamie, and Amber were driving all the way to New York, fortunately together.

"Okay, gang. I'm throwing you out," Tiffany called to the women in the sitting room. "Four o'clock comes awfully early."

"Really? That's when you get up?" asked Reshma, concerned.

With an exaggerated nod, Tiffany confirmed her statement. "When do you think we bake your chocolatine?"

The guests came into the kitchen to collect their cookware and dishes. "In New York next time," said Jess. "Anyone who wants to stay at our place, bring a sleeping bag. We have air mattresses."

Tiffany packed Reshma's spice bottles into the battered pot from the rectory kitchen. "I have an extra Dutch oven if you want one. I almost never use it."

"Thanks, but this one has fed many hungry priests. I'll use it until it wears out."

"Looks like the end is near. See those pit marks?" Tiffany pointed to the inside of the pot. "They're caused by salt. Try waiting until the water is boiling to add salt." She grinned. "That is, if you want to preserve this relic for posterity."

Tiffany felt Brianna nearby, listening intently to every word that passed between Tiffany and Reshma. She really needed to stop this possessive hovering.

With their canvas bags filled with pots and folded thermal bags, Tiffany's guests departed. Their voices echoed in the hall and stairwell as they said their goodbyes. That was one bad thing about living in the same building with a storefront below. Sound carried. Taking a nap during the day was impossible.

"Thanks for including me," said Reshma, bending to kiss her on the cheek.

"Your Poulet Yassa was delicious. You can cook for me anytime."

"I'll have to make you Kofta." Reshma leaned closer to speak privately. "I couldn't afford the ground lamb for a group this size, but I can make it for the two of us."

"I'd like that." Tiffany gave Reshma's slender body a quick squeeze, delighted to feel that she was soft in the right places. She still smelled faintly of onions beneath a bright scent redolent of rosemary and lemon. "Thanks for coming." She pushed her out the door to block the temptation to keep touching her.

When she turned around, Brianna was staring at her. "Hungry priests? What the hell is she talking about?"

"Nothing." What she really wanted to say was 'none of your business.' When they were in a relationship, Brianna could stare her into answering a question. Tiffany finished loading the dishwasher to avoid her gaze.

"You're not really interested in that black woman."

Tiffany bristled but tried not to show it. "Why not?"

"Not your type. Too femme."

"How do you know what my type is? Maybe I don't have a type." Tiffany hoped they weren't going to have a fight. She needed to be in bed and asleep within the hour and didn't want to get worked up.

"I thought you said you weren't interested in another relationship."

"Well, maybe I changed my mind. And it's not a relationship yet. We're just getting to know one another."

"It's too soon. I know. It's too soon for me."

"I don't have to do everything you do."

Brianna took a step closer, which made Tiffany tense. "You know you're only dating a woman of color to show how 'woke' you are." Tiffany fought to control her temper. This was the kind of provocative statement Brianna liked to make to lure her into an argument.

"Bri, don't make me regret inviting you tonight. The others weren't sure they wanted to come when they heard you'd be here."

"Thanks. I like you too."

"No one wants to listen to exes bicker. Talk about a way to wreck a nice social evening."

"I wasn't sure I wanted to come tonight."

"I only invited you because you keep saying you want to stay friends. Everyone was getting along great until you started the political argument. Good thing Reshma shut it down."

"I wanted to hear her point of view."

"Tonight wasn't the time or place. This is why we don't work, Brianna. You're always angry, always looking for a fight. Your anger is always percolating below the surface. Why can't you be happy for a change?"

Brianna's face darkened. "I was stupid to come tonight. Maybe I should go home."

"Maybe you should."

"You're throwing me out."

"No. It was your idea to leave."

"Fine. Fuck yourself."

Tiffany watched Brianna collect her things and go into the bedroom for her overnight bag. She kept her hand on her phone while she waited for her to leave. In past arguments, Brianna had shoved her or knocked her around, but then they still had a connection. Now, Tiffany wasn't sure what she would do.

It seemed like it took a long time for Brianna to get herself together. "Thanks for reneging on the invitation."

"Get home safe," said Tiffany and meant it.

"Like you really care," Brianna replied before slamming the door.

Tiffany locked it right away. Why did she think it was a good idea to invite Brianna? Yes, she was feeling generous after a few glasses of wine the night they'd discussed arrangements. Then, she was hopeful that after a year they were both in a better place.

Her phone vibrated in her pocket. A text from Reshma. *Thanks for a great time.*

I loved having you here.

I loved being there.

See you soon?

Bright and early. Rest up so you can bake the croissants. Three purple hearts.

Tiffany sent five pink ones in return.

***

Reshma tiptoed past Susan's door, but she got caught anyway. She guessed Susan had seen her shadow moving past the gap under the front door. Ordinarily, Susan would be so absorbed in reading, but this was opening night for the *Verdi Requiem* at the Met, and it was being broadcast live. Susan would never miss the opportunity to hear Lucy sing.

"Reshma!" Susan called in a loud whisper, even though they were the only ones in the building. "It's still on. Come in and listen." Reshma quickly put the bag with her pot and supplies inside the door of her studio. "Make sure you lock the door!" Susan chided. "Lucy will be after you if you don't."

Reshma hurried back and Susan closed the door. "I don't want to miss anything, but I want to make sure I'd set up the recording correctly. I'm glad you're home early."

"How far along is it?" asked Reshma, sitting down at Susan's open laptop.

Susan glanced at her watch. "About a half hour in. They're singing the "Rex Tremendae" right now."

"I can hear," Reshma said, adjusting the volume slightly. She checked the other settings and found them all correct. "Good job," she said.

"Would you like a cup of tea?" Susan whispered into her ear.

"Actually, I'd love one! But I don't want you to miss the concert."

"I can listen to the recording later. And I just made a pot. Let me get you a cup."

Since Reshma had shared that the boarding school where she'd been a charity student used high tea to teach the girls proper etiquette, Susan always used the "good" China. Reshma knew Susan preferred traditional ways. She often said she found the formality of using a tea service reassuring in a world that had become excessively casual. Reshma had never seen her drink from a mug.

"I'm surprised you're home so early," said Susan, refilling her teacup.

"Tiffany has to get up early to bake for the shop."

"Of course. Hadn't thought of that."

"She said she would have asked me to stay, but she has a friend spending the night." Reshma had shared the information in a casual tone, but now she worried she'd revealed too much. Surely, after sharing her deepest secrets while she was debating whether to be ordained, Reshma shouldn't be worried about Susan judging her, but she was.

"Would you have stayed?" Susan's tone sounded interested, but not invasive.

Reshma stirred her tea as she considered what to say. "It's probably too soon for that. We don't really know each other."

Susan made no attempt to hide how much Reshma's answer had pleased her. "You haven't spent much time together. Admiring her from afar doesn't count."

"No, it doesn't," agreed Reshma. "Plus, it would have been messy and inconvenient." Reshma focused on her cup, wondering if that had been too much information. Susan looked like the kind of person who never discussed private things like menstruation.

Then Susan surprised her by saying, "Ah, that time of the month. Always a good excuse."

Reshma checked the recording settings again to avoid showing her surprise at Susan's answer. "We should pay attention," Reshma said, "or we'll miss the whole concert."

"Good idea."

Together they drank their tea and listened to the wonderful Met orchestra and Lucy's superb soprano slay Verdi's amazing requiem. Eventually, the performance wound to a close. Lucy began to sing the "*Libera me.*"

"Sublime," said Reshma. "Her pianissimos are perfect."

"No one sings the *Verdi Requiem* like Lucille Bartlett," Susan agreed, her eyes shining with emotion. "She has such control of her voice, but that is the sound of a woman who's experienced great loss." Susan smiled. "I only wish we could see her face."

"Maybe you will. I wouldn't be surprised if Liz comes home with a video recording like last time."

"Now, let's listen. The ending is my favorite part." Susan sat back and closed her eyes. Her face took on an almost Beatific expression. The second part of the "*Libera Me*" wound down to an exquisitely executed conclusion, followed by the expansive last chords, and then, spoken words, always a surprise after such an operatic piece. The orchestra played the final notes. Reshma imagined the conductor holding back the applause with his arms still raised. Finally, the hall erupted into clapping and cheers. The opening night performance had truly been memorable. Reshma hoped that someday she could witness it in person.

"May I?" asked Reshma, approaching Susan's laptop to stop the recording.

"Please just play a little so I can see if I did it right."

Reshma set up the recording for playback. The instrumental opening began with evocative cello notes followed by the violin's higher voices. Next, the chorus entered, singing softly at first, then progressively louder. Reshma allowed the passage to finish before cutting off the sound. "Perfect," she declared. "You did a great job, Susan. Couldn't have done it better myself. I look forward to listening to it later. Mind if I send myself the link by email?"

"Go ahead. That's why I recorded it." Susan was obviously still back in the performance, smiling an otherworldly smile.

"You're a real Lucy Bartlett fan," Reshma observed lightly.

Susan turned her eyes on her, and said, "You have no idea."

Chapter 4

"**I** was expecting your voicemail," said Sam, sounding confused. "No, I'm done for the day. Just writing up the notes from my last exam." Liz was surprised, but pleased to hear from Sam, who wasn't the best communicator and never called without a reason.

"What's up?" prodded Liz. She was anxious to leave the office and get some outside work done. This time of year, dark came so early.

"Maggie called a few minutes ago," Sam explained, sounding frustrated and slightly annoyed. "The water conditioner is out of sync. It's going on at the wrong time, right in the middle of her morning shower."

"Storm must have knocked out the power. Not surprising. The rain in New York was torrential. The streets flooded, even the subway tunnels. We were stranded in our hotel. Sam, I lived in New York for years and never saw the subways flood like that. This isn't normal."

"But climate change isn't real," Sam said sarcastically. The environment was one of her hobby horses. If she got started on that topic they could be on the phone for hours. Liz glanced at her watch. She should have left the office by now. She was only hanging around because Amy Hsu had left early for an appointment, and the other physicians were off that afternoon.

Liz looked out the window and saw the light was fading fast. So much for her plan to harvest the rest of the tomatoes before the frost that had been predicted. "I'm surprised the generator didn't kick in," she said, closing her laptop. "Could you be out of propane?"

"That's a good question. With all the back and forth from Hobbs to Chicago, I might have forgotten to order it."

"What do you need me to do, Sam?" Liz asked, trying not to sound impatient. "Want me to drive over to your place and reset the timer?"

"If you don't mind."

Liz hoped her sigh wasn't audible. Of course, she minded. "Can it wait until tomorrow? I wanted to get some fall cleanup done this afternoon."

"I suppose she can work around the water cycle being off. You did say you'd look after the place while I was away." Sam knew that reminding Liz of a promise was a guarantee she'd keep it.

"No, if I said I would do it, I will," Liz said reluctantly. "And I'll check on the propane and the generator while I'm there."

"Thanks, Liz. That's a load off my mind. If Maggie weren't there, I would have winterized the place and shut it down."

Liz debated whether to bring up what Maggie had said about Sam's plans. Maggie hadn't asked her to keep it confidential. "What's this I hear about you moving to Chicago?"

"Oh, she told you," said Sam, sounding annoyed.

"Old habit, I guess. While we were married, she told me everything."

"Well, you're not married anymore," Sam briskly reminded her. "And it's not a done deed. I'm just thinking about it. Dammit. I wish she'd keep her mouth shut."

"Don't be angry. You can understand that she'd be worried about where she's going to live. She just sold her house to her daughter, thinking she had a home with you."

"Liz, it's not about Maggie!" The vehemence of Sam's tone made her frustration obvious. "I just don't feel welcome in Hobbs anymore. It makes me so sad. I love the place. I never felt more at home anywhere. My friends are there. My business was finally starting to make money. Now I can't even go into the supermarket without people staring and pointing at me. I know exactly what they're thinking: 'there's the idiot who let the shooter into the school.'"

"You don't know what they're thinking," Liz said in a completely rational but soothing voice. She heard Sam's pain and ached for her friend.

"Are you kidding? They don't need to say a word. Their faces say it all."

Through the telephone, Liz heard a hard swallow and imagined Sam trying to hold back tears. She'd known Sam for decades and had only seen her cry once—when her favorite aunt died. Sam was as stoic as they came.

"Remember when we were living in Connecticut," Sam asked, "and I was renovating that old Arts and Crafts bungalow. I'd bought into the idea that 'if you build it they will come.' While I was carving the fireplace surround, I was dreaming of sitting on my Morris couch with a beautiful woman who would love me for who I am, not mind my hard edges or rough hands. I wanted a feminine woman who would accept me, butchness and all. I wanted to be cared for, cooked for, comforted when I was hurting. Maggie gives me all that and more. I want to be with her for the rest of my life."

"Well, maybe you need to tell her that," Liz suggested. But she saw the disconnect between Maggie's feelings about the relationship and Sam's. Sam really cared for Maggie. Maggie was ready to end the relationship at the mere suggestion that Sam might want to move.

Liz tried to remember when she'd figured out that Maggie chose relationships based on the security they offered. That's why she married her football star husband the week after she graduated from college. She'd been dating Barry since high school, but when Maggie and Liz were college lovers, she'd confessed that she'd only dated him because her mother thought the engineering student was a good catch. It never occurred to Maggie or her mother that Liz, who was bound for medical school, had even better prospects. It troubled Liz to think that Maggie had married her for protection and stability. But after all, wasn't that what she'd offered? Even if Liz hadn't explicitly said, "Come live with me. I'll take care of you," it was implied.

"I shouldn't be giving you relationship advice, Sam. My own track record isn't great."

"Yeah, but your relationships last more than a couple of years."

"Just let Maggie know how you feel. She doesn't want to move again, and you're putting her in a difficult position."

"I know, but I find it so hard to face all those incriminating looks."

"You could try shopping in Webhanet, where people don't know you. Just keep a low profile until the anger dies down."

"Get real, Liz. You know it will never die down."

Sam had a point. The shooting had changed the town forever. People still came up to Liz in the store to thank her for her bravery. She never knew what to say to them because she hadn't felt brave, just scared shitless. She asked Lucy what she should say.

"Don't offer explanations or deny the compliments," Lucy advised. "They mean them. They're grateful. You are a hero to them, no matter what you think. Like beauty, being a hero is in the eyes of the beholder. When they thank you, just nod and smile."

"So will you help Maggie with the water conditioner?" asked Sam, bringing Liz back to the present.

"I'll head over as soon as I finish up here. You can tell your girlfriend I'll be there within the hour."

Liz tapped off the call and tossed the phone on her desk. She hated to be in the middle between Maggie and Sam. Thinking of them as a couple had required serious rearrangement of her mental landscape. Swapping partners was common in small lesbian communities, but at this stage of life, Liz preferred a more predictable social order.

Liz unlocked the safe to take out her gun purse and headed out to her truck. Although resetting the water heater didn't require tools, she'd stop at home first to pick up her tool bag. While she was out there, she'd ask Maggie if there were other things that needed attention, which could save her a future trip to the pond.

Before Maggie had moved in, Liz would just honk the horn when she arrived, in case Sam was outside. With Maggie there, Liz was more civilized. She got out of her truck and tapped on the window glass, but there was no answer. It was a warm day for early October. Maggie could be outside enjoying the nice weather. Her genetic predisposition to skin cancer meant she couldn't spend much time in the sun, but like all Mainers she hoarded every moment of warmth before winter trapped them inside.

There was no sign of Maggie on the dock. Liz climbed the steps of the rear deck and saw that it was covered with colorful leaves and pine needles. She made a mental note to ask one of the kids at Awakened Brews to come by and blow off the debris. Sam usually did those chores, including plowing the snow for herself and her friends, but since she'd been traveling for her architectural jobs, everyone had to fend for themselves. Apparently, she hadn't arranged for someone to do fall cleanup. Liz wondered if that meant she'd planned to come back and do it herself, despite her reluctance to face the disapproving townspeople.

Liz peered inside the sliding glass door. The light was on in the kitchen. Liz tapped gently on the glass. Maggie looked up from her laptop. Her entire face smiled.

"Why don't you come to the front door like a normal person?" Maggie asked, after she opened the door.

Liz laughed. "Why should I change? I did knock. I guess you didn't hear."

"I wish Sam would install a doorbell instead of that ridiculous ship's bell." Maggie glanced at Liz's tool bag and looked worried. "Is resetting the water conditioner a big deal?"

"No, but I figured while I'm here, I'd fix anything else that needs attention."

"That is so sweet." Maggie stood on her toes to give Liz a kiss on the cheek. "Off hand, I can't think of anything but give me a minute."

Liz set down her bag near the kitchen door. "Everything in this house is so new, there shouldn't be many repairs. Remember this place when she first bought it? What a dump! She could get big bucks for it now." Maggie's distraught face made Liz sorry she'd mentioned selling the house, even though it was an idle remark. "If it makes you feel better, it doesn't sound like Sam's in any hurry to put it on the market."

"You know Sam. She mulls things over for a long time before talking about them. She's like you that way. Used to drive me crazy."

"I'm sorry, but I don't like to inflict my half-baked ideas on people."

"No, shocking them instead is much better." Maggie grinned to soften the sarcasm and gave her a playful pinch on the arm. "Thanks for coming to rescue me."

"Come on. I'll show you how to reset the conditioner, so you can do it next time."

"You know I won't remember."

"Use your phone to take a video while I do it. Then you won't need to remember."

"Why, when I can get you out here to do it?" Maggie asked with a dazzling smile. Liz made a face, which earned her another playful pinch. "I'll take a video, but that doesn't mean I'll be able to do it." Liz rolled her eyes. "Oh, don't huff, Liz Stolz. You know I'm an idiot when it comes to mechanical things." Maggie said such things, then wondered why people doubted her competence.

"Maggie, I know you're a femme, but you don't have to be a cliché. Isn't it easier to do it yourself than putting up with chemicals when you shower?"

"Probably, but the damsel in distress act makes you feel big and strong, and it always works, doesn't it?"

"Except I know you're smart and capable, so don't play that card too often. Come on. Let's do this so I can get home and harvest the last of the tomatoes."

Maggie glanced outside. "Looks like you don't have much time."

"Damn right. Now, come on!"

They went to the storage area that housed the furnace and water conditioner and other important mechanical systems. Being adjacent to the pond, which occasionally overflowed, the house didn't have a basement, only a crawlspace. All the mechanicals, including the service panel, were scrunched into a closet off the kitchen. Liz switched on the unshaded bulb. Of course, energy-conscious Sam had replaced the incandescent bulb with an LED. It blasted the tiny room with light.

"Ready?" asked Liz. Maggie took out her phone and set up the camera for video. "First, you press this button to reset the time, hour first, then minutes." She tapped the buttons.

"Whoa! Slow down."

Liz repeated the process. "Now, we're going to double check the time settings for the iron filter and the water conditioner. It's usually set up to go off in the middle of the night while you're supposed to be asleep." While she had the instrument panel open, Liz changed the backup battery. "Got that?"

Maggie was distracted by storing the video file, but she nodded.

"Now, let me get home so I can harvest my tomatoes. We might have frost tonight."

"You and your vegetables. I bet you have bushels of tomatoes and peppers and eggplants already picked."

"I do, but I hate to waste food, and I enjoy fried green tomatoes."

"I have a better proposition for you. I couldn't eat the whole bag of apples from the farm stand fast enough, so I made a tarte Tatin."

"It's not easy cooking for one, is it?" Liz commiserated.

Maggie smiled sadly to acknowledge the sympathy. "Come on. I'll make you some coffee. I know tarte Tatin is one of your favorites."

While Maggie prepared the coffee, Liz sat at the kitchen table, admiring the woman, who used to be her wife. Her white braid had gotten so long that it went down to her attractive backside, trimmer than usual. She'd lost some weight, which caused Liz's physician's antennae to twitch. "Mag, are you on a diet?"

Maggie obviously stopped what she was doing and stood

straight. Finally, she turned around and scrutinized Liz's face. "No, but with Sam gone, I don't need to cook as often."

Hearing the weight loss had an innocent cause made Liz relax a little. "Let me know right away if it's more than you planned."

"But my tumor markers have been good," said Maggie, looking up sharply. "You check them every time." She raised crossed fingers.

"Yes, your numbers are fine." Liz's eyes were already tasting the picture-perfect tarte Tatin. She leaned forward in anticipation as Maggie sliced the confection into perfectly even sections.

"Now that we're not married any more, you could be my doctor," Maggie suggested casually.

"No, it's better this way. Cathy can be more objective."

"Yes, but she's not an expert in breast cancer, like you are."

"If she has any concerns, she always asks me. We're a team."

The piece of tarte Tatin that Maggie set in front of Liz could be a feature photo in *Food and Wine*. Liz would freely admit how much she missed Maggie's elegant cooking and baking. Preparing meals all the time was tiring, but cooking wasn't Lucy's thing. Olivia, who was also a trained chef, had taught her to make a few classic dishes. After that, Lucy had lost interest, and her repertoire remained limited.

Maggie poured them each a cup of coffee. She sat down and gazed directly into Liz's eyes.

"It was the sex, wasn't it?"

"What?" asked Liz, almost choking on a mouthful of tart.

"I didn't give you enough sex, so you started looking at Lucy. You couldn't resist her smile and perfect boobs."

"No," Liz protested, trying to swallow so she could speak clearly. "Maggie, you know that's not how it was. We discussed how the Tamoxifen would suppress your libido. When I asked you to marry me, I knew what I was signing up for."

"But I didn't give you enough sex."

"Why are you bringing this up?" asked Liz, annoyed at being

distracted from her enjoyment of the delectable tart. When they were married, Maggie would often cook one of Liz's favorite dishes to soften her up for a difficult discussion. But that wasn't the case here. She hadn't been expecting Liz, and the story about the excess apples was plausible.

"I worry that I don't give Sam enough sex," said Maggie, picking up her fork. "She's always horny like you."

Liz felt her face warm, not from anger or jealousy, but because she was embarrassed by the intimate confession. "Mag, if you don't mind, I'd rather not discuss your sex life."

"Who can I talk to? Not Lucy. She's married to you, or Cherie. She works for you. Everyone in this town is connected to *you*." The last word was full of accusation and a little disgust.

It was true. Being the town doctor and involved in so many civic organizations, Liz had a connection to almost everyone in Hobbs. "What about your old therapist, Gloria Parrish? She's been coming up twice a week to counsel the families of the shooting victims. I'm sure she could squeeze in some time for you."

Maggie raised a forkful of pastry to her mouth. "That's not a bad idea. I'll think about it."

Feeling good about making a positive contribution, Liz happily demolished what remained on her plate. No one made tarte Tatin like Maggie. "Well, I guess I'll have to leave those last tomatoes for the critters."

"Knowing you, you'll be out there with a flashlight."

"Not a bad idea," said Liz, pressing her fork into the crumbs to get up the last delicious bit.

❋❋❋

Lucy heaved her bags onto a stool at the kitchen island. Liz had been harping about how dragging around so much stuff could hurt her back. Lucy was so tired of listening to everyone's complaints and advice that she often tuned out her wife, even when she was right. She just didn't have the energy or patience to explain why her bags were heavy. She simply had no time to clean them out. They accumulated all kinds of odd things—little gifts from the Sunday school children, pens she forgot to return after borrowing them, pretty stones from her beach walks. Switching to digital editions of her favorite books would lighten the load, but the dog-eared pages of her favorite devotionals with their yellow and pink highlights were like old friends. In many cases, she could remember where and when she'd first read the words. The tactile experience of touching the highlighted paper reinforced the connection.

"Hi Mom," said a voice that made Lucy instantly smile. She turned around and hugged the exceptionally tall redhead. Her daughter looked like her in every way except for her height and blue eyes. Having a child who so closely resembled her was a special gift. Lucy could see both her past and the future every time she gazed into Emily's pale, freckled face.

"Hello, sweetie." Lucy reached up to kiss her daughter. "Glad you could come for dinner."

"Thanks for having us," added Denise, Emily's girlfriend. The trans woman was even taller than Emily and towered above petite Lucy. Despite her height, Denise "passed" very well. An observant person might notice the size of her wrist bones and hands and wonder, but most people would take her gender at face value.

Lucy glanced at the clock. "Where's Liz?"

"We don't know," said Emily. "I used my key to come in through the bridge, and we helped ourselves to wine. Hope that's okay."

"Of course, it's okay," said Lucy, frustrated that her daughter, who'd made such an effort to find her birth mother years after her adoption, still doubted her place in the family. "Emily, you're always welcome here."

"We've been watching the sunset from the enclosed porch," explained Denise. "We turned on the propane stove because it's getting a little chilly." Emily's girlfriend apparently had no trouble making herself at home.

"Let me get some wine," said Lucy, "and I'll join you."

"Don't you want to take your collar off?" Denise asked.

Lucy touched her throat and felt the stiff linen. Usually, she took off her collar as soon as she left work, but she'd been distracted by a difficult conversation. Joyce, Bobbie's former partner, was in the end stage of dementia and rapidly failing. Bobbie had asked Susan to perform the last rites, but she felt uncomfortable, given their relationship, so she'd asked Lucy to do it.

Lucy would never withhold the prayers of the Church from anyone who sincerely asked for them, but Joyce wasn't an Episcopalian or even aware of the request. Susan had confided that Bobbie only came to church because of their relationship. Lucy knew the most compassionate way to deal with this ethical morass was to take a pastoral view and agree to help, but she resented being put in this position.

"Can I pour you a glass of wine while you change?" asked Denise. "We found another bottle of pinot in the fridge. I can open it."

"Perfect," said Lucy. She glanced at her smart watch to see if there were any messages from Liz. The last text was from yesterday.

Where are you? Lucy quickly typed.

At Sam's. Water conditioner problems. Be home soon. Five red hearts.

Emily and Denise are here. What about dinner?

No reply. After Lucy changed, she checked her watch again, but still nothing from Liz, which made her wonder. Liz was often late at the office, but she usually explained if guests were expected.

When Lucy came downstairs, Denise and Emily were sitting at the kitchen island. They'd found the salsa Liz had made and were scooping it up hungrily with corn chips.

"I hope you don't mind that we helped ourselves, Mother Lucy," said Denise apologetically.

"Of course, I don't mind, Denise, but don't you think it's time you stopped calling me 'Mother Lucy'? You're dating my daughter and practically living in my house. Just call me Lucy, all right?" It was meant to be a good-natured invitation, but it came off as impatience. She was aware that Denise was studying her curiously. "I'm sorry, Denise. But first, Liz invites you to dinner, and then she's late."

"No worries. We can help get dinner together. Right?" Denise glanced at Emily for support, but she shrugged. "Do you know what Liz had planned?" asked Denise.

Lucy was tempted to answer, 'beats me,' but it was her own fault she didn't know. She never paid attention. Cooking was Liz's thing. She enjoyed it and so Lucy left it to her. Maybe she should have learned her lesson after Erika's death. For weeks afterward, maybe months, she had no interest in food. She became nearly skeletal from lack of nourishment. But the lack of appetite was an aberration due to grief. Once Lucy's friends forced nutritious food on her, she became like a hungry wolf gobbling it down. Before Erika's death, Lucy had always managed to feed herself. When she was on the opera circuit, she ate in restaurants. As a new priest, she couldn't afford to eat out, so she threw together rudimentary meals like salads topped with hard-boiled eggs or tuna. They weren't always satisfying, but at least they were healthy. As a side benefit, she'd kept her figure.

"Honestly, Denise," Lucy said as patiently as she could. "I have no idea what's for dinner. Liz does all the shopping and meal planning."

"Do you mind if I poke around in the refrigerator and see what's there?" asked Denise, slouching a little to see Lucy's face.

"Be my guest," Lucy waved dismissively. "I hope you can find something."

Emily's high-end autism sometimes cramped her emotional perceptions, but she picked up that Lucy was out of sorts. "I'm sorry you had a bad day, Mom."

Lucy gave Emily a half hug. "I'm sorry, honey. I didn't mean to take it out on you and Denise."

"What's going on, Mom?" Emily asked so tenderly that Lucy was nearly moved to tears.

"Oh, just the usual, flying in all directions at a hundred miles an hour and bumping into things."

"I don't know how you do it, Lucy," said Denise, dumping more corn chips into the bowl. "Now that my singing career is taking off, I hardly have time for anything else. How can you sing professionally and run a church?"

"I've begun to wonder that myself," Lucy murmured.

Denise's blue eyes grew large. "You're not thinking of resigning?"

"Not yet, but I need to figure out how to do right by my congregation, sing, and still have time for the people I care about."

They stared at her sympathetically.

"You know what Mr. Rogers said: 'look for the helpers,'" Denise said. "And here we are! I can report that my search of the refrigerator turned up a large piece of salmon and a steak. My guess is that Liz intended to cook the salmon first because it's more perishable."

Lucy wanted to hug Denise both for her practicality, and even more for her willingness to make decisions about areas where she felt incompetent. "That sounds like a good guess, and even I know how to roast salmon."

"Never mind, Lucy," said Denise, gently leaning on Lucy's shoulder to keep her in her chair. "You sit and relax. Emily and I will make dinner. I see Liz has all these baskets of beautiful veggies from her garden. We'll roast some peppers and summer squash, and I'll put together a tomato salad.

"I can make the rice," offered Emily.

"We'll have a feast!" said Denise. "See, Lucy? We've got all the major food groups covered."

Lucy watched with gratitude as her young daughter and her girlfriend worked together in the kitchen. Denise's hands were square and sturdy. Emily's were slender with long, tapered fingers that recalled her father, Alex Dupuis, the Met producer who'd forced himself on Lucy after befriending her over a professional dispute. When she'd reported him to management, he'd denied it and had her blacklisted. Emily was the product of that rape.

At first, Lucy hated to see signs of her father in Emily. During her discernment for the priesthood, Lucy had forced herself to forgive the man who'd assaulted her and ruined her singing career. Forgiveness was one thing, but Lucy had resolved that he would never be part of her life or know that he'd fathered a child. By the time her daughter had petitioned the courts to unseal her adoption and reconnected with her birth mother, Lucy knew Alex was dying, but still she kept his identity from their daughter. She came to regret keeping them from meeting one another.

"What are you thinking about, Mom?" asked Emily. Counterintuitively, her autism allowed her to observe people without their knowing. The ability always surprised Lucy. She smiled to dispel Emily's worry. Despite her neurodiversity, Emily was shrewd and wasn't taken in. Her skeptical look said it all.

"How we resemble our parents."

Emily's face twisted in pain. Sometimes her efforts to respond emotionally went overboard. "Please don't hate him, Mom." Lucy knew that Emily was really saying: "Please don't hate me, because he raped you." Fearing exactly that reaction, Lucy had held off telling Emily how she'd been conceived. When she wrote about it in her book on sex, she'd been forced to tell her.

"I don't hate him, sweetie," Lucy said, affectionately rubbing her daughter's arm. "And I love the parts of him that make you you— your tall, beautiful body, your brilliant mind, your musical ability..."

"You're sure?" Doubt clouded Emily's blue eyes.

"I'm sure."

"I get music from you too."

"Yes, you do, dear."

Denise, preparing an eggplant dish that looked like something she might have learned from Reshma when they were cooking together, had been pretending not to be paying attention. Lucy knew that Denise had sharp ears and wondered what she thought about the intimate exchange between mother and daughter. Then she heard the garage door open and close.

Liz came into the kitchen and carefully placed a large, covered plate on the island. "Maggie sent us some tarte Tatin for dessert. I sampled it, and it's delicious." She gave Lucy a quick peck on the cheek. "Sorry to be late," she said, briskly moving on to inspect the dinner preparations. "Since you seem to have everything under control, I'll just run out and pick my tomatoes."

Grabbing her by the elbow, Lucy held her back. "Don't be crazy. It's already dark outside. It can wait until tomorrow."

"We're supposed to have frost," Liz protested.

Lucy nodded toward the baskets of tomatoes, peppers, and squash cluttering up the kitchen. "Like we need more?" Liz looked stony and crossed her arms on her chest. Of course, she wasn't happy that Lucy had scuttled her plan. "What's this about a water tank?" Lucy rarely asked her wife to account for her time, but when she did, Liz never liked it. Her face hardened.

"The water conditioner is set to go off at a certain time, usually one in the morning when no one is using the water," Liz explained with exaggerated patience. "The power went off so many times last summer, it wore out the battery backup, so I had to reset the timer."

"I thought Sam had a generator," Lucy said, frowning.

"She does, but with all the travel she's been doing, she forgot to order propane. I called the fuel company and ordered a delivery."

Lucy glanced at the two young people. As before, Denise pretended to be deliberately deaf. Emily wasn't a good enough actress to disguise her curiosity. Lucy's concerns about Maggie's manipulative hold over Liz were none of their business. She'd address it later when she and Liz were alone. Then she realized Maggie must have felt the same twinge of jealousy on the many occasions when Liz had rescued Lucy from some electrical or plumbing disaster.

"Since I've been *forbidden* to harvest more tomatoes," Liz said, scowling at Lucy, "I'll grill the salmon."

"No, I've got it," Denise assured her, gesturing to a pan where the fish was decoratively covered with lemon slices and fresh dill. "I was going to roast it in the oven. Just relax and have a glass of wine with your wife." She glanced in the direction of the screen porch. "I think we left the propane stove on. You should probably check it." She wasn't even trying to be subtle about wanting them out of the kitchen.

"What a good idea," said Lucy, getting up to pour herself another glass of wine. She felt generous so she poured one for Liz too. "Come on, Liz. They're doing fine. Let them take care of dinner." When Liz hesitated, Lucy gave her a firm look and a side wag of her head to indicate she wasn't taking no for an answer.

When Liz opened the door to the porch, they were greeted by an oppressive blast of super-heated air. "Guess we'll be ordering propane too," Liz grumbled.

While she was adjusting the thermostat, Lucy sat down and slipped off her shoes. She'd been on her feet more than usual today, and they hurt. She wished she weren't at odds with Liz because she would love a foot rub. Given the situation, asking for one was out of the question.

"That was kind of you to help Maggie with the water conditioner." Lucy said, hiding her irritation under the most neutral tone she could manage. "I hope you didn't pay for the propane."

Liz turned and gave her a filthy look. "No, she gave me her credit card."

"You really should teach her how to adjust the timer herself." Lucy was on shaky ground with this one. She wouldn't know how to adjust the timer either. She didn't even know where it was.

"I tried," said Liz, shaking her head. "You know how Maggie is."

"I sure do." Lucy realized her nonjudgmental act wasn't convincing when Liz turned and eyed her.

"Gee, Lucy. I can remember a certain party begging for my help to start Erika's portable generator during an ice storm."

"Yes, I did. I'm grateful you came. It was getting cold in the house without heat."

"I promised Erika before she died that I'd always look after you." Lucy stared at Liz. She'd heard that before, but she didn't remember it until now. "I promised Sam I'd look after the house while she was gone. I keep my word."

"Your integrity and generosity are some of the things I love most about you, but..."

"But what?"

"Just be careful, Liz."

Liz got up from her place next to Lucy. Their proximity had obviously become uncomfortable for her. "You have nothing to worry about," Liz declared resolutely and plopped down on the adjacent settee. "It's fucking hot in here. I don't know how the kids could stand it." She was obviously trying to change the subject, but Lucy wasn't having it.

"Maggie's put you in a tough position before. When you were staying at Jenny's before her surgery, she crawled into bed with you."

The firelight reflecting Liz's eyes emphasized her fury. "It's shitty of you to bring that up, and you know it."

"I didn't say it to make you feel bad, only to remind you that Maggie knows exactly how to manipulate you. You're susceptible because you're hardwired to take care of people...and you still love her."

Instead of denying it, Liz took a long drink of wine. It was obvious she wasn't a white wine drinker because she tended to guzzle it like a soft drink. "Don't worry. I have her number now."

"Maybe you do, Liz, but she has yours too, and you two go back a lo-o-ong way. I hate to say this, Liz, but Maggie has the advantage. She's an expert at reading people's emotions."

Liz stared into the fire. "Why are things always so complicated?" she asked glumly.

"Because people are complicated. They use different means to get what they want." Lucy moved next to Liz and gently stroked her thigh. Like a cranky puppy, Liz always responded to petting. "I trust you, sweetie," Lucy said gently, "but Maggie knows how to maneuver you into doing exactly what she wants. Sam's gone and she's lonely."

"She's also scared to be out at the pond all alone."

"I wouldn't want to be alone there, either. In the winter, the place is completely deserted, and there's no one for miles."

"Brenda gave her my gun for protection. She knows how to use it, not that she ever would. She gave it back to me."

"She did?" Lucy asked, surprised. She sat up and scanned Liz's face, tinted orange by the stove light. "I thought you gave that gun to Brenda."

"I did, but Cherie wanted it out of their house, so Brenda gave it to Maggie for safekeeping."

Lucy frowned at the reminder of how much in Hobbs went on behind the scenes.

"You killed Peter with that pistol. How do you feel about having it back?"

"Don't shrink me, Lucy," Liz warned, moving away from her hand.

"I'm not. I'm just curious."

Liz finished her wine and put the glass on the table. "I don't know yet. When I do, I'll let you know." She sat back again. "And don't worry about Maggie. I'll handle her," she said confidently.

Lucy recognized this ploy, a clear message that Liz no longer wanted to talk about this subject. Lucy was tempted to calm her again with a touch, but Liz crossed her legs and rested her ankle on the opposite knee. Her foot barred Lucy's path. She got the message. "I trust you, Liz. Just be careful. Okay?"

"Okay!" Liz agreed defensively. The silence that followed meant Liz was thinking about what Lucy had said. "Maggie pulls the same shit with Sam."

"That's Sam's problem. They're in a relationship and need to work it out, just like we need to work out our issues."

"I appreciate that you don't manipulate me."

"Oh, I do. But I don't try to hide it, and you're good at calling me on it when I do."

"Why is it different with Maggie?"

Lucy thought for a moment. "I don't know. Maybe it's because you were both very young when you got together and unconsciously playing the gender roles you learned from your parents. Was Maggie's mother manipulative?"

Liz picked up her glass, looking disappointed that it was empty. "Maggie's mother was a total bitch!"

"That doesn't tell me much."

"If you're asking if she called the shots, she did, with her husband and her children. It was never obvious, but she always got her way."

"Sounds like Maggie learned from an expert."

"You'd never know her mother meant any harm. She was always smiling," said Liz with a distant look in her eyes, apparently remembering a scene from the past. "People like that worry me."

"All smiles are not equal," Lucy said. "But somewhere along the line, Maggie learned that playing helpless worked for her. You fall for it, and that's why you need to pay more attention."

Liz slid closer, indicating she'd realized Lucy wasn't the enemy. She tolerated Lucy's hand when she rested it on her thigh. Lucy ventured higher, lightly touching Liz's cheek. "Kiss me so I know you're not still angry." Liz welded her mouth to hers and kissed her so deeply that Lucy felt faint.

Behind them, the sliding door opened. "Hey, Mom. Dinner's ready."

****

Reshma stared at the little breaded cakes on her plate. She'd seen similar patties at the fish counter in the supermarket. The sign beside them read: "Just brown and serve."

"Fish cakes," Susan explained in response to Reshma's inspection. "Maybe I should have asked whether you like them. Some people don't."

"I don't know if I do. I've never had them before."

"Oh, then you're in for a treat! When I was a girl, this was my favorite meal on Friday nights. In those days, Catholics weren't allowed to eat meat on Fridays. Please forgive the indulgence." Susan's words were apologetic, but her eyes shone with anticipation as she heaped pillows of homemade mashed potatoes on Reshma's plate. She passed a steaming bowl of peas, glistening with melted butter. It was a simple meal, but Reshma's eyes grew hungry just looking at it. "After we left my grandparents' house," Susan continued to explain, "my mother often made this dinner because it was cheap. In those days, you could buy six fish cakes for two dollars. They're made of cod and potatoes. Irish Americans used potatoes in everything. When I finally got to Ireland, I saw 'potatoes, three ways' on the menu in a pub and realized it wasn't just an ethnic joke."

"No wonder the potato famine was so devastating," Reshma observed. "Another casualty of British colonialism."

"That's a sad subject for another time," said Susan with a long sigh. "Thank you for coming tonight." Reshma basked in Susan's affectionate smile. "I can use the company," Susan admitted quietly. "Bobbie's been so busy with Joyce. I hardly ever see her."

"Have they called in hospice yet?"

Susan looked up sharply, which meant Reshma now had to reveal her source. It was so difficult to keep confidentiality in a small town where everyone was connected. Even among clerical colleagues the boundaries could get confusing. "Teresa told me that Joyce isn't doing well," Reshma confessed.

"Yes, it won't be long now. Bobbie didn't like giving up control to their nurses. They're overworked and stretched thin, but it's a necessary step and wise to do it now."

"So sad that she's spent so many years in cognitive decline. The 'long goodbye' is an apt description."

"It's heartbreaking to watch, especially for Bobbie, who knew Joyce as a brilliant woman. She told me Joyce was once the center of a social network, like our Dr. Stolz, always getting people together. Bobbie's love for Joyce and her loyalty are touching." Furtively, Susan glanced at Reshma.

Reshma felt Susan's eyes on her. "I hope you don't still feel guilty about getting involved with Bobbie."

Susan chased the peas around her plate with her fork. "Lucy seems to think I should have waited to get involved."

"She's not in your relationship. It's not her place to judge." Reshma didn't add what she was thinking, namely that Lucy hadn't wasted any time getting involved with Liz Stolz after her divorce. Reshma had heard the rumors whispered in the parish. No one dared to say them aloud.

Now that Reshma was ordained and privy to the inner workings of the church, she was getting a different point of view.

"I'm sorry these fish cakes are so salty," Susan apologized, reaching for her glass of lemonade. Because she was a recovering alcoholic, she never served wine at dinner. Reshma guessed that anxiety had made Susan's mouth dry, not the salt in the food. "Bobbie asked me to give Joyce the last rites, but I don't feel comfortable doing it. After all, I replaced her in the relationship."

This time, Reshma couldn't avoid rolling her eyes. "You did nothing wrong, and neither did Bobbie. She was kind and loyal to look after Joyce during her decline. You shouldn't let other people's opinions make you feel bad."

"It's not other people. It's my own conscience."

Reshma was about to blurt out her thought—that Susan's

conscience was excessively sensitive. Then she remembered Lucy's first rule of pastoral counseling: "Never judge someone else's feelings." Finally Reshma said, "It must be hard to feel so conflicted about helping a friend. What did Bobbie say when you told her you couldn't do it?"

Susan compressed her lips. "She reminded me that it's my job as a priest to do it. She said that when Lucy comes into the office with a sore throat, she doesn't send someone else to treat her because of our past."

Reshma was confused. The past with Bobbie or Lucy? "What past?" she asked innocently.

The frank look of terror in Susan's blue eyes told Reshma she'd revealed something she'd meant to keep hidden. Reshma thought back to the night when Susan had urged Reshma to get past her doubts and embrace her vocation. She'd alluded to an affair with a woman when she was in seminary. Guilt over the same-sex relationship had nearly derailed her ordination. Could that woman have been Lucy Bartlett? Whenever Lucy spoke, Susan simply glowed. Her eyes followed Lucy everywhere. When Lucy sang, Susan looked like she'd heard an angel.

Susan, pushing her food around her plate, had obviously sensed that Reshma was connecting the dots. "Now, I've shocked you," she murmured.

Reshma didn't know what to say. She was surprised that it had taken her so long to figure out what had been so obvious. Now, she had so many questions, she didn't know which to ask first. "I guess I don't understand why you would want to be here, working for her. It must be..." Reshma searched for a word. "...uncomfortable."

"It is, but I didn't have a choice. I wanted a priest's license in this diocese. The bishop knew about my relationship with Lucy. He has a high opinion of her abilities as a therapist. He thought she could oversee my recovery and keep me from embarrassing the church."

"Was your drinking that bad?"

"It was more than the drinking. I abandoned Lucy after ordination because I felt guilty about being involved with a woman. I didn't even let her know where I was going. I wanted to get as far away as I could, so I took a curacy in a remote part of South Dakota. The rector there was known for being conservative, and didn't support the idea of female priests, but I was the only one who applied."

"So, you were in a church without much support from your rector."

"He wasn't that bad when I got to know him, strict, but basically kind. But you can't imagine how isolated it was in the Black Hills and how desolate in the winter. I missed Lucy and felt terrible about how I'd left things. I began drinking...a lot. My rector counseled me several times. I got written up for DUI twice. My driver's license was under suspension when I got involved in an accident, so I ran. The only place I could think to go was Hobbs because I knew Lucy was here. When I arrived, I had only a few hundred dollars. I was living in my car. But Lucy wasn't here. She was in New York preparing for her dissertation defense. I told Tom Simmons that I'd been in seminary with Lucy."

"But that part was true," said Reshma. "You were in seminary with Lucy."

"Yes, I was, except we hadn't exchanged a single word in years. Tom was taken in by my story that I couldn't find a motel room because it was high season. He let me use the same apartment where you're living."

What Reshma was hearing was a tale of subterfuge and misrepresentation. She focused on her plate to avoid Susan's curious eyes.

"When Lucy returned from New York, she was so kind, despite how I'd treated her, but eventually she figured it out. She gave me an ultimatum—join AA or vacate the apartment in the rectory. I was desperate, so I agreed to abide by Lucy's rules. Then the police chief discovered I was wanted in South Dakota. Lucy convinced me to return and face justice."

Reshma reminded herself to close her mouth. She found it hard to believe that kind, motherly Susan could have been involved in a hit and run accident, never mind a fugitive.

"How did you end up back in Hobbs?"

"I made restitution for the accident. Thankfully, no one was seriously injured. My bishop convinced the court to expunge my police record and reinstated my priest's license. I lost my teaching job, but my rector took me back after I completed my rehab and community service. The accident got wide news coverage, and my standing in the community was wrecked. Who can minister to people who shun you? I came back to Hobbs, where I knew at least one person cared about me. Two, if you count Liz, who pulled strings to get me into a rehab facility."

Reshma needed a moment to absorb so many surprising revelations. These older women, whom she looked up to, had been embroiled in a sordid and scandalous mess. When Reshma could finally form words, she said, "Many people care about you, Susan, and I'm one of them."

Susan's eyes glistened with tears. "I know, but when you're an addict, you can't see how much people care. Lucy, Liz, Sally, my AA sponsor, even Brenda Harrison, who reported me...they saved me. And then Liz faced a crazed gunman, and literally saved my life. She could have been killed! I know she must be a mess after shooting that boy." She raised her eyes. "God help me. I wish I could do more for her."

"Dr. Liz looks like she's doing fine. She's back at work. She's even smiling again."

"Don't be fooled, Reshma. As a doctor, she's trained to put up a good front, just like we must when we're having a bad day. But you don't get over that kind of trauma in a couple of months, not even years. Maybe never." Susan's face was suddenly pale. Reshma realized she was also speaking about herself.

While they'd been talking, their food had been getting cold.

Reshma forced herself to eat it because she knew how tight Susan's budget was and how much effort she'd put into recreating this favorite meal from her childhood. She also ate it because she'd known hunger as a child in the African refugee camp and never wasted food.

"I should have told you about this long ago," murmured Susan. "You probably think less of me now."

"No, I don't. In fact, I admire you more because you've reclaimed your life after such struggle and humiliation. But I hope you don't mind me saying you need to get past all that guilt. It's only making you miserable."

"That's pretty hard when you grew up Irish Catholic."

"Obviously, you're in a much better place. Allow yourself to enjoy it."

"Easier said than done."

"What can I do to help?"

Susan stared at the table. "I don't know if anyone can," she murmured in a barely audible voice.

"Susan, guilt has been stealing your happiness your entire life. You need to let it go."

"I know. I've tried." Susan covered her face with her hands and began rubbing her forehead with her fingertips. "You don't know how I've tried."

Clearly, the poor woman was suffering, and Bobbie's request had made it worse. How could Lucy turn away a friend like that? There was one thing Reshma could do to help. "I can give Joyce the last rites. Bobbie knows me, and I think it would be okay with her."

"You'd do that for me?" asked Susan hopefully. "Oh, Reshma, Bobbie would be so grateful, and so would I."

"This would be my first time, but you'll be there to help me, won't you?" Reshma felt confident that she could manage the ritual, but she knew Susan couldn't resist a request to mentor her.

"Of course, I will." Susan reached across the table and patted Reshma's hand. "And you'll also be taking the pressure off Lucy."

That was obvious, but Reshma couldn't decide whether Lucy deserved it after being so judgmental. Then she realized a woman was dying. Her friends were grieving, and her rector needed to learn how to forgive. They could all use some grace.

Chapter 5

Lucy shuffled into the kitchen in her favorite fuzzy slippers and headed directly to the coffee maker. There was too much noise and activity around her. Alexa was blaring the friendship duet from *Don Carlos*. Liz, slicing peppers with her favorite chef's knife, was singing along with gusto. Vats of red liquid bubbled on the stove. It was all too much for someone who had just crawled out of bed.

"Liz, you'll wake the neighbors," chided Lucy, waiting for her coffee to brew.

"Won't be a problem. Sam soundproofed the whole house." Liz went back to singing. Lucy was glad Liz had gotten over her shyness over singing in the presence of a professional, but why did she have to prove it first thing in the morning?

Lucy saw she needed to take charge of the situation. "Alexa! Lower volume three levels."

"You're no fun," said Liz with an exaggerated pout.

"Liz, I just woke up." Lucy glanced at the wall clock. "Why did you let me sleep so long?"

"Well, I was tempted to wake you for a little activity." Liz suggestively wiggled her brows. "But you were sleeping so peacefully I just couldn't." She kissed the top of Lucy's head on her way to stir the pots on the stove, "... and you had such a bad day yesterday."

"Bad day is an understatement." Lucy took a few sips of coffee. "What are you doing?" she asked in a small, worried voice.

"Processing the last of the vegetables. We lucked out. No frost last night, so I harvested everything this morning." She pointed to the huge pots on the stove. "Tomato soup and marinara sauce."

"Looks like enough for an army. Isn't the freezer full?"

"Not yet, and I always end up giving some away. I hope you don't mind that I asked Maggie to come over and help me make eggplant rollatini."

"When?" Lucy's eyes flew open. The idea of having Maggie there on a day Lucy hoped to relax was unnerving. Since the rupture in their friendship, Lucy always felt she had to be on alert in Maggie's presence, watching every word she said, often needing to bite her tongue.

"I don't expect her till ten-thirty or eleven. She likes to sleep in on Saturdays. You have plenty of time to get decent."

"Good," said Lucy, mostly to herself. Like a turtle finding refuge in her shell, she pulled her head deeper into her polar fleece. Despite the simmering pots on the stove, the kitchen was cold. Being a red-head, Lucy was more sensitive to temperature changes. She looked at Liz, who was in shorts and a hoodie. "No fire this morning?" She hoped Liz would get the hint.

"I'm trying to save our firewood until it gets really cold, but I can't have you shivering." Humming the melody Alexa was playing, Liz headed into the living room to start a fire. While she was gone, Lucy asked Alexa to lower the volume again. "It should warm up in here in a few minutes," said Liz, returning. She handed one of her Yale hoodies to Lucy. "Put this over your fleece. I'll turn on the furnace." She fiddled with the thermostat. The furnace fired in the basement, causing the floor to vibrate. "Real Mainers don't turn on the heat until Halloween."

"I'm from Massachusetts. I never claimed to be a real Mainer."

"Well, I'm from New York, but Maine women are tough and resilient. I aspire to be one. You know, some people up here don't turn on their heat until Thanksgiving!"

"Not if you want to find a frozen body in your bed," warned Lucy, flipping up the hood of Liz's sweatshirt. Snuggling into its warmth, she sipped her coffee and tried to heat her freezing hands around the cup.

"It will warm up soon." Liz returned to chopping vegetables, but mercifully, she asked Alexa to turn off the music.

Lucy crawled into the breakfast nook to drink her coffee in

peace. "You know I could have helped you with the rollatini," she said, watching the mountain of pepper slices grow. She felt slightly hurt that Liz hadn't asked her before calling Maggie, but she understood. Maggie was a trained chef, and Lucy... Well, she often cut herself on Liz's unbelievably sharp knives. When she looked up, she saw that Liz was studying her. She often forgot that as a doctor, Liz could read faces as well as she could. She'd sensed her insecurity.

"Okay, what's going on?" asked Liz.

"I could have helped you cut up vegetables."

Liz instantly got the picture. "We'll have plenty of work for you. We have all those eggplant slices to roll." She covered the bowl of sliced peppers with plastic wrap and washed her hands. "How about some breakfast? I feel like having eggs and bacon this morning. What do you think?"

"I'm in," said Lucy.

Liz rearranged the stove to make room for a skillet and took a slab of bacon out of the refrigerator. She could cut slices as thin as paper, but for a country breakfast she liked it cut thick. The delicious smell of it frying reminded Lucy of the weekend mornings when her father would make breakfast. He was a better cook than Lucy's mother, who was always busy with her voice students or preparing for a recital.

"Does it bother you that I can't cook?" Lucy asked.

Liz looked up. "Well, you can cook when you want to. And I like to cook, so it's fine."

"When you were married to Maggie, she cooked for you."

"We shared the cooking, but before Maggie moved in, I cooked for myself."

"But you invited her over because I'm a zero in the kitchen."

"Hey, I don't like that negative self-talk. I invited Maggie over because we have a system for processing the end-of-season harvest. We make a good team."

They were a team now? It wasn't long ago that Lucy had to keep them from killing each other. It was hard to keep up with them.

Liz turned around to hand Lucy a plate of eggs. She stopped short. "Uh-oh. You look pensive. Luce, what's going on?"

"I'm just glad you and Maggie are getting along better."

"I wish you'd join the ceasefire. I know you miss her."

Lucy inhaled a deep sigh. "Liz, I've done everything I can to patch up our friendship. It looks for a while that things are better, then they fall apart again. She still blames me for 'stealing' you."

"She knows that's not true. I was an asshole. I kept teasing you."

"But I went along with it," said Lucy.

"Giving as good as you get is one way to avoid unwanted sexual advances."

"Who said they were unwanted?"

Liz's fork stopped on its way to her mouth. "What?"

"I enjoyed the attention. Don't get me wrong. I loved Erika, and I would never have cheated on her. When she suggested I should sleep with you to get it out of my system, I was shocked."

Liz frowned and looked thoughtful. "Erika looked at sex differently. For twenty years, she had an odd relationship with that artist at Colby. Jeannine Sanders would have fucked every woman on campus, if she could."

"Liz!" Lucy didn't usually call out Liz for expletives, but the tone of this one was especially nasty.

Liz reacted to the scolding with a shrug. "I liked Jeannine, but not her awful so-called feminist art. Wall-sized paintings of obese women with excessive pubic hair aren't exactly my taste. You should have heard what Stefan had to say about them."

"I have heard. I asked his advice about what to do with the paintings Erika had inherited. He said, 'burn them all!'" Lucy had perfectly mimicked Stefan's German accent.

Liz laughed. "Erika's father and I think alike on many subjects."

"I did find Erika's ideas about commitment more casual than I'd like," Lucy admitted, getting up to make another cup of coffee. "But didn't you have an open relationship with Jenny?"

"Not exactly. We didn't break up when one of us strayed. At

least, we pretended to be monogamous. With Jeannine and Erika, it was never even on the menu." Liz, who always ate quickly, scooped up the remaining egg with her toast. "Gotta get back to work. I want to have the eggplant sliced by the time Maggie gets here."

"And I should get showered and dressed."

Liz, who was rinsing her plate at the sink, turned off the water. "By the way, you might think about giving your friend, Rebecca, a call. There was a Hamas attack on Israel overnight. Isn't her wife over there?" Although Liz's face didn't register any particular emotion, her tone was grave. Lucy felt prickles of worry on her skin.

"Yes, Judith is visiting her parents. Is it bad?"

"Sounds bad to me. Hamas fired over two thousand rockets into Israel."

"Gracious God have mercy," Lucy murmured.

"The Christian God, the Jewish God, or the Muslim God?" asked Liz, but the set of her mouth told Lucy she wasn't trying to be funny.

"They're all the same God, if only people would remember that!"

"Should I turn on the news?" Liz asked.

The last thing Lucy wanted to see on a Saturday morning that had already started off with too much noise and activity was scenes of violence on the other side of the world. Concern for her friend Rebecca and her family trumped her wish for quiet. "Yes, please."

Liz located the remote and switched on the small TV hanging in the breakfast nook. It was always set to CNN because Liz liked to catch up on the news while she was making dinner. In the Middle East, it was already nighttime. The newscast showed intercepted rockets exploding in the night sky like firework duds.

"I'm not surprised this is happening," Liz said with a sigh. "The Saudis have been cozying up to Israel. The Palestinians feel like they're being left out. The right-wing Israeli government is encouraging new settlements in the West Bank. Unfortunately, violence was inevitable." Lucy always listened carefully to Liz's assessments of news events. During the day, she followed political and international events through her news feeds. Her analyses were always precise and accurate. "This could escalate into a proxy war with Iran or even Russia. Just what the world needs, with Putin pummeling Ukraine."

"Considering we could be on the verge of World War Three, you seem pretty calm."

Liz raised her shoulders. "There's nothing I can do. But you should give Rebecca a call. With Judith over there, she's probably losing her mind."

Lucy noted the time on the TV screen. "She might not even know about it. She'll be officiating at her Sabbath service now. I have to think about what to say." She glanced at Liz.

"Don't look at me. You're the shrink."

Lucy rolled her eyes. She'd given up correcting Liz for using that word, but it still annoyed her.

***

After Lucy left the kitchen, Liz finally allowed herself to experience her concern about the events in Israel. After decades of practicing medicine, she was adept at controlling her expressions. In surgery, she'd had to set an example of calm even when there was blood in all the wrong places and monitors were screeching. She could deliver the worst news without upsetting already anxious family members. Maintaining a professional demeanor was such second nature now, she often had to remind herself to emote. Maybe that was why she got along so well with Emily. For her, as for Liz, the expression of feelings required deliberation.

Only one event had totally defeated Liz's self-control. When she saw Peter Langdon's still body lying in a growing pool of dark, sticky blood, she fell to her knees and screamed like a raving banshee. The piercing sound had shocked Susan out of her own horror. She'd been staring at the perfectly round hole in the boy's throat. Susan's fingers reached out and clutched Liz's shoulder, trying to keep her in this world, but only Lucy's voice could make words understandable again.

The memory was still as vivid as the moment. It played in Liz's mind like a movie. Sometimes, the smell of marijuana smoke could trigger it or the sound of gunfire on TV. When Tom asked how often Liz had flashbacks, she lied with a straight face. She had to get out of therapy. She'd always handled her shit on her own, and she'd deal with this too. She hadn't told anyone how often she lay awake at night, twitching so hard she wondered if she were developing a degenerative neurological disease. Her father's mother had Parkinson's, and Liz's aunt. Maybe someday, the disease would come for her too.

Liz went out on the deck to take some deep breaths. When she felt better, she lined up the sterilized jars for her sauce on the countertop. She estimated that the pot would yield at least a dozen pint jars of sauce, plus enough for the rollatini. She ladled the sauce into the jars with an ancient aluminum funnel. The battered metal had been scrubbed with steel wool to a bright sheen. The wide end was dented in places, but Liz had smoothed out the worst of them with a peen hammer and opened the spout with a dowel. The old funnel had belonged to her grandmother, so Liz would never replace it. As she filled the jars with sauce, she imagined her grandmother's rough, rope-veined hands filling glass jars with foaming strawberry jam or pickled beets.

Nowadays, most people bought their preserves from the supermarket. The wealthy felt virtuous buying them from a farm store. With Liz's many obligations, growing and preserving her own food made little sense. It didn't save money. In fact, she'd once calculated that each tomato she grew was many times more expensive than it would cost in the store. She always planted too much but couldn't resist the new pepper or eggplant varieties or rediscovered heirloom tomatoes in the seed catalog. Every January, she started flats of seedlings under grow lights in the basement and always ended up with too many. She donated the extras to the church's Mother's Day plant sale.

"Okay, I'm *decent* now," said Lucy, arriving at Liz's side in skinny jeans and a hoodie. "Put me to work."

Liz selected onions from a bushel. "Peel these while I slice the eggplants."

Lucy wrinkled her nose, which made Liz smile. No one liked to peel onions. "When you enjoy those sausage and pepper heroes this winter, it will be worth it."

"Grinder. That's what we call those sandwiches at home."

"Whatever," said Liz dismissively, knowing her New York chauvinism could drive Lucy crazy. But this time, Lucy ignored her.

Liz finished filling the jars with sauce and put them into the canner to sterilize. Next up was the tomato soup destined for the freezer. She carefully ladled it into quart containers and brought them down to the basement on a tray. As she ascended the basement stairs, she heard Maggie's voice. Liz glanced at her watch. Maggie was early for a Saturday, almost as if she'd been eager to come.

Liz found them in the kitchen, watching the coverage of the Hamas attack. The reflection of the screen flickered on Maggie's dramatic rimmed glasses.

"I couldn't believe it when Lucy first told me," said Maggie, turning to Liz. "How can they be so stupid?"

"Desperate times call for desperate measures," Liz said with a shrug.

Maggie turned to Lucy and said, "Professor Stolz will now explain the geopolitical situation."

Liz shot her an impatient look. "I don't know why anyone is surprised. Israel turned Gaza into a ghetto. They shut off access to jobs in Israel, turned off the electricity and water at will to assert their control. The world looked the other way because criticizing Israel is 'anti-Semitic.'"

"I wouldn't say that too loud, Liz," Maggie cautioned. "Your friends won't speak to you again."

"I don't know about that. I've had long talks with Sid Birnbaum about the situation over there. His father was a holocaust survivor. Sid taught modern history at Yale before he retired. He says that expanding settlements in the West Bank is a shameless land grab. Netanyahu's right-wing government has been spoiling for a fight. Now, they've got one." Liz picked up a wooden spoon and dipped it into the sauce. She cupped her hand under it as she offered it to Maggie. "Here. Tell me what you think."

Maggie closed her eyes as she focused on the sauce. "Like that little kick at the end."

"I threw a couple of hot peppers in."

"So daring of you, Liz."

Liz felt Lucy's eyes on her as she and Maggie bantered. She'd had the sense that feeding her ex had made Lucy tense and smiled in her direction. "Let me get these eggplants sliced so we can rock and roll." She chuckled at her own joke.

Maggie looked to Lucy for sympathy. "How can you stand it?" she asked Lucy.

Lucy responded with one of her high-wattage smiles. "I've never found it a problem."

Maggie exhaled a dramatic sigh. "You knew what you were getting when you married her."

"So did you," Lucy replied without missing a beat.

"Actually, I didn't. She looked at me with that earnest, intense look and I thought I was getting the same, sweet kid I knew in college, but I wasn't. Not even close."

Liz wanted to say she didn't know that when she married Maggie, she'd be getting the same cheating woman who slept with men. She didn't want to get into it this morning. She'd slept badly and didn't have the energy for a fight. Besides, it would put Lucy into the role of referee. She led therapy groups in her day job and wouldn't appreciate moderating an argument on her day off. Liz distracted herself by sharpening her favorite chef's knife.

With her newly honed, dangerously sharp knife, Liz began

cutting thin slices of eggplant. Maggie mixed the ingredients for the filling in a steel bowl. Liz and Maggie fell into their old roles in the kitchen, forming an assembly line to produce neat rows of rollatini ready for sauce. Except for the sound of the CNN pundits and rocket fire in the background, there was silence as they worked together.

Lucy finished peeling the onions. "I think I'll give Rebecca a call," she said, looking like she couldn't wait to get out of there.

"Don't they have coffee hour after the service like we do?" Maggie asked.

"No, most people go home afterward for the Sabbath dinner," Lucy explained, "but with this mess over in Israel, some may have stayed behind to comfort one another, and they'll be looking to their rabbi to be a role model. I'd find that hard if my wife were in a war zone. Liz, I'm going to use your office, okay?"

"Help yourself. You don't need to ask."

After Lucy left, Maggie said, "You let Lucy use your office? It was always off limits."

"I never said that. You just assumed."

Maggie grunted. "Thanks for telling me now."

Liz took a deep breath in the hope of staying calm. Maybe inviting Maggie to help this morning wasn't a good idea after all.

Lucy must have connected with Rebecca because she didn't return. Liz and Maggie continued their tasks. Suddenly, Maggie gave her a sharp look. "You had to insert yourself, didn't you?"

"What?" asked Liz, mentally scanning the morning's events to figure out what she'd done wrong.

"Sam called last night all lovey-dovey to assure me she wasn't going to sell the house. You put her up to it."

"I did not!" Liz protested indignantly. "It came up when she called about the water conditioner. We were just chatting."

"Yeah, right," said Maggie cynically.

"I can understand why Sam doesn't want to come home. She feels unwelcome here."

"Me too. I'm living with her, so I must be guilty too."

"Everything's not about you, Maggie. Try to see it from Sam's point of view."

"I know she's your friend Liz, but what she did was stupid. I can see why people blame her. She should have locked the door behind her or gone the other way. Maybe the shooter still would have gotten in, but it would have taken longer."

"Haven't you ever cut corners or done something stupid? Give Sam a break. There were a lot of what-ifs. The lock was old and flimsy. The school board only hardened the front entrance for show but diverted the money to secure the back. It's on them."

"If Sam hadn't run out of patience with Peter and fired him…"

"Maggie, stop! We can't undo it. It's done. Sam didn't kill those kids. Peter did. And if any one of those what-ifs hadn't happened, I wouldn't have had to kill Peter. But he's dead, and the kids are dead, and there's nothing we can do about it." Maggie was staring at her because she'd been ranting. Liz lowered her voice. "Melissa thinks Sam's actions meet the standard of negligence. The families could still bring a lawsuit. The school would be involved because they deliberately diverted the funds for fixing the lock."

"Shit!" Maggie said under her breath.

"Yes, shit." Liz glanced at the door, watching for Lucy's return. "So far the work of the foundation has prevented legal action. But it just takes one greedy family and one ambitious lawyer."

Maggie's face, usually pale, blanched. "God, I hope not. It would rip this town apart."

"It would. And it would destroy Sam. She really needs you to stand by her, Maggie. You would have stood by me if I were in her situation." Maggie glanced away, raising flutters of doubt from the pit of Liz's stomach. "You would have, right?"

Maggie focused on spreading filling on the eggplant slices. "Of course," she muttered. Liz perceived that it wasn't Sam's ability to commit to the relationship that was threatening it.

Liz was about to defend Sam when Lucy returned to the room.

"How did it go?" Liz asked.

"She's upset. She's trying to hold herself together for the kids and her congregation. She's heading down to Hobbs to be with her mom and Jack. Melissa and Courtney are coming over. She needs to be with family right now."

"That's good."

"She said there are reports that Hamas attacked a music festival and a Kibbutz near the border. Everyone's asking why the government wasn't prepared."

"I'm curious myself," Liz said. "Unless Netanyahu let it happen to divert attention from his legal issues. Most secular Israelis can't stand him or his right-wing government. I'll be curious to see if the reservists show up. They threatened not to after he pushed that law limiting the Supreme Court."

"Judith is in the reserves," said Lucy. "Rebecca's worried she might be called up."

"But she has a family and a teaching job here," Liz said. "She can't just run off to war."

"Why not?" said Lucy with a shrug, "When Russia invaded Ukraine, you wanted to volunteer."

Maggie stared at Liz. "No! Liz, you're too old. You can't really be that crazy." She shook her head. "Of course, you are. You always have to be a hero. Lucy, how did you talk her out of it?"

"I didn't. Fortunately, she talked herself out of it, after I reminded her of her responsibilities *at home.*"

"At least, she listens to you," said Maggie. "When I talked to her, it was like she was deaf."

The sound of the CNN announcer and explosions in the background, combined with the conversation, began to annoy Liz. She switched off the TV. "Mind if I put on some music? Too much to think about this morning."

"Fine with me," said Lucy. "Just no opera, please. I love it, but not today."

❊❊❊

"Well, that's interesting," said a familiar voice. Reshma had been engrossed in watching the town manager, Olivia Enright, and the new doctor at Hobbs Family Practice, Amy Hsu, engaged in an intimate tête-à-tête. She hadn't even noticed Tiffany standing right beside her.

Reshma leaned down to whisper, "Do you think they're together?"

"You mean, are they a couple?" Tiffany whispered back. She studied them carefully. "They're sure acting like one, but they're so old. Do they have sex?"

Reshma gave her the side-eye. "That's an ageist comment, you know."

"Yeah, I know," Tiffany said, staring at the floor. "But it's hard to imagine."

"I'm sure you could if you tried," Reshma dared wickedly.

"But that would be like imagining my grandmother having sex!"

"Well, how do you think you got here?" asked Reshma, raising a brow.

"That was a long time ago. My grandparents have been dead for years."

"Come on, Tiffany. You're creative. Olivia and Dr. Hsu were young once, just like you and me."

Tiffany shook her head. "Not going there. None of my business. Besides, Dr. Hsu is my PC. My mind would explode thinking about her in bed."

Reshma laughed, but she'd forbidden her mind from imagining Lucy and Susan together. The ban was unnecessary. Her imagination simply couldn't conceive of vibrant, sexy Lucy in bed with prim, sexually repressed Susan. At least, Lucy's attraction to Dr. Liz made more sense. With her deliberately messy spiked hair and studied casual style, Liz had some sex appeal. Reshma had shut down that thought too. There were some lines her mind just couldn't and probably shouldn't cross.

The town manager had noticed them talking and waved pleasantly. "Oh God," said Reshma under her breath. "Olivia saw me and knows we're talking about them."

"Just smile at me and pretend you didn't notice."

"I can't do that. She's the junior warden and a big donor to the church."

"Well, then go over and say hello, and I'll grab some ham and cheese croissants out of the counter. That's why you're here, isn't it?"

"Do you have time to eat with me?"

"Yes, if you don't spend a lot of time with Ms. Enright. Remember the way to my office?"

"Through the kitchen to the right?"

Tiffany cocked an eyebrow. "I thought you might remember." Her hand brushed against Reshma's, and she caught her pinky with her own. "Don't be long." She released Reshma's finger. "Go," she urged, nudging her with her hip. "I'll meet you upstairs in my office." She grinned. "It will give me time to do a little cleanup before you get there."

Reshma's eyes followed Tiffany's blond head as it wound through the crowd. It vanished when she bent to take some sandwiches out of the counter display. The pâtisserie always had piles of premade sandwiches, reminiscent of displays in European department stores. Just the sight of the stacks of turkey clubs, lox sandwiches, and ham and cheese croissants made Reshma salivate. It was late for lunch, and she hadn't eaten anything except a yogurt for breakfast.

Reluctantly, Reshma headed to the table where Olivia and Dr. Hsu sat. "Hi, ladies," she said brightly. "Nice to see you here."

"Mother Reshma, those colors are just gorgeous on you!" Olivia gushed. Reshma looked down at her favorite blouse, a bright, patterned button-down that relieved the dreariness of the black stock and collar beneath.

"Thanks," she murmured. "Two dollars at the thrift shop."

"Oh, I find some of my favorite clothes in there," said Olivia, shocking Reshma with the thought that the richest woman in town shopped in thrift stores too. Olivia seemed to enjoy watching Reshma try to square the circle. "I know what you're thinking, Reshma. Don't you know that rich people stay rich because they don't spend money?"

Reshma had heard that expression from the ridiculously wealthy mother of one of her boarding school friends. Reshma, who'd arrived as a penniless refugee didn't understand it at the time. The churches who'd sponsored her provided Reshma with an allowance, but otherwise, she never had any money. Every bit of her earnings from part-time work when she went to college and then seminary went toward paying her expenses. Her only extravagances on her meager earnings as a priest were her purchases from Wicked Pleasures. Lately, Tiffany had been slipping her freebies, which eased the burden on her budget.

Reshma turned to Olivia's companion. "How are you, Dr. Hsu?"

"Enjoying my day off. Thanks for the inspiration. I'll encourage Olivia to visit the thrift shops this afternoon. I could use a few things now that the weather's getting colder."

Reshma stared at Dr. Hsu, finding it hard to believe the elegantly dressed woman bought secondhand too. "I'm from a warm place," said Reshma, recovering her poise. "I'm never ready for winter."

"None of us are," said Olivia with a sigh. "Hobbs is so empty, and the wind! To make it worse, we have this horror in Israel."

"Terrible," Dr. Hsu agreed, shaking her head in disapproval. "Those poor people in the Kibbutz, attacked in their homes. Young people hacked up at a music festival. It's terrorism."

Reshma understood the terror of living under constant threat of attack in a way these women never could. She remembered her mother showing her where to hide if the soldiers came. She was to run into the undeveloped land behind their house. One day the soldiers arrived, sitting on top of Jeeps, their black rifles ready to shoot anything that moved. Crouched behind an oil drum, Reshma watched the soldiers slash her father with a machete. They bludgeoned her grandmother with a rifle butt. The word, "terrorism," meant something different to her than to these smartly dressed American women, but she continued to smile pleasantly. She was in her role as curate of St. Margaret's, not Reshma, the terrified child, who'd prayed every night that the soldiers would not come for her family, until they did.

"I hear that Mother Lucy is planning a vigil for Israel," said Olivia, bringing Reshma back to the present.

"She is," Reshma confirmed. "She'll be sending out an email soon with the details."

"You can tell her we'll be there," said Olivia, glancing at Dr. Hsu, who nodded her assent.

"Excellent," said Reshma. "We need a good show of support. Well, ladies. I must excuse myself. My sandwich and Tiffany are waiting for me."

"I'm sure both will be delicious." Olivia smiled like a cat.

What a provocative thing to say to a priest! thought Reshma as she gingerly walked away, moderating her step and maintaining perfect posture to hide the fact that she wanted to run. *Is it that obvious?* Reshma wondered as she walked through the kitchen. She reminded herself that Olivia had been a force on Wall Street, where success or failure in business depended on seeing opportunities others didn't. Amy Hsu seemed unfazed by Olivia's insinuation, but doctors were good at hiding their feelings.

"I was beginning to wonder if you were going to stay and eat with them," said Tiffany, batting her long lashes, which could make Reshma feel weak. She slid into the chair closest to her. "What's the matter?" asked Tiffany.

"Everyone's onto us."

"So? We're not doing anything wrong."

"I'm a new priest. I need to protect my reputation."

Tiffany laughed merrily. "You're so funny." Then she stopped smiling. "But you look sad." Her blond brows dipped into a frown.

"We were talking about the Hamas attack on Israel. Made me think of Sudan. There's trouble there again."

Tiffany's blue eyes were instantly sympathetic. "There's trouble everywhere. What did they say?"

Reshma shook her head. "Not now. Let's eat our lunch. I'm hungry." Biting into the delicious sandwich, Reshma reflected that words like "terrorism" and "hungry" were relative terms. She remembered standing in line with her mother for hours for a sack of meagre supplies. When you are literally starving, even packaged rations and hard tack can taste delicious. This ham and cheese sandwich would be considered an extravagant feast.

Reshma wiped some mustard from the corner of her mouth with her thumb.

"I should have asked if you wanted mustard. I always put it on my ham and cheese sandwiches. How do you like this Artisan cheddar? It's new."

"Tasty. How do you find these things?"

"I get emails from the state promoting local growers."

"That's cool."

Tiffany's eyes were fixed on Reshma's mouth as she took another bite. "I love watching you eat, but I hope you're not just hanging around for the food."

Reshma struggled to finish chewing so that she could protest, but Tiffany reached over and gently stroked her hand.

"Relax. I'm just teasing." The gentle stroking didn't end. Tiffany's eyes looked deeply into hers. "Your skin is so silky and smooth, like velvet." Reshma tried to swallow the mouthful, but it refused to go down.

Tiffany's merry laughter surprised her. She was such a tease, but the smoldering gaze that followed confirmed that it had been more than flirtation.

Reshma finally swallowed and cleared her throat. She pointedly changed the subject. "I meant to ask. Mother Lucy is holding a vigil for the victims and hostages in Israel. Will you come?"

Tiffany took another bite of sandwich before she answered. "You know I'm not religious. I hope that's not a requirement."

"There will be prayers, but the vigil is to show support for the people of Israel."

"I didn't mean going to the vigil. I want to make sure you'll still like me, even though I'm an atheist."

"Whether you believe or not is between you and God." Reshma felt hurt that Tiffany feared rejection because she wasn't a believer. "I only invited you, so we could spend time together, not to evangelize."

"Yeah, that isn't a good word to use with me. I hate evangelicals."

"Sorry, but it's what we call talking about our faith to others. Please believe me. I'm not trying to convert you." Reshma kept her next thought to herself—*I have something else in mind for our relationship.*

"That's good because I'm definitely not interested in religion," Tiffany stated bluntly.

Reshma was disappointed that Tiffany even felt the need to warn her. She'd gone out of her way to avoid talking about anything overtly religious. "The vigil is a public event. It wouldn't hurt to be seen there. It could be good for business."

"I don't know about that," said Tiffany, her blond brows dipping. "A lot of my friends think the Palestinians are right to push back."

"Push back maybe, but not with violence. Attacking a music festival and a Kibbutz, where many of the people were sympathetic to the cause of peace, is terrorism."

"I agree, but we don't have time to get into it now. Eat. I need to get back to work."

Reshma was surprised that she'd been shut down for a simple

invitation. Her phone began vibrating in her pocket. "I'm sorry, but it's the church. I need to take this."

"What's the matter?"

"A parishioner is dying, and the family has requested a priest."

"Oh! I'm sorry. Is it anyone I know?"

"An elderly woman with dementia. Her death has been expected."

Tiffany jumped up and whipped away Reshma's plate. She took an industrialized size box of plastic wrap from a cabinet and expertly wrapped the half-eaten sandwich. "Eat it on the way."

Reshma leaned down and lightly kissed her cheek. "Thank you."

***

Liz sloughed off her jacket and hung it on the hook by the door. She stepped out of her shoes and headed down the hall in stocking feet. She found Maggie spooning sauce over a tray that appeared to be eggplant parmigiana.

"I'm sorry. I ask you to come over to help and then abandon you."

Maggie raised her face for a kiss. Liz pasted a quick peck on her cheek. "I'm used to it. I was once married to a doctor."

"Well, I'm getting paid back for it being married to a priest." Liz patted Maggie's shoulder. "Thanks for being here. I wasn't sure you'd come back after the tension last time."

Maggie shrugged. "There was a lot going on that day between the Hamas attack on Israel and Lucy's rabbi friend. Stuff like that makes our squabbling seem trivial."

"But you stuck around until the job was done."

"I know you value doing what you say you're going to do. Besides, I find processing the end-of-season harvest comforting. Reminds me of better times." Maggie emptied the pot and ran water into it. She was all business.

"I know what you mean. That's why I wanted my guns back. And thanks for bringing back my CZ. I really love that gun."

"I know you do. I was here when you brought it home from Cabela's. You and Brenda sat out on the porch oohing and aahing over that thing, taking it apart, and putting it back together. I couldn't believe two grown women could be so crazy about an inanimate object, but don't make me regret giving it back, Liz. I'd never forgive myself if you used it on yourself."

"Don't worry."

"I don't. I never believed you were a suicide risk. I thought Lucy was overreacting. You're too full of yourself to take your life."

Liz stood behind her ex-wife, staring at her back, as she listened to Maggie reveal knowledge of her personality accumulated over fifty years. Their long history enabled Maggie to know her better than Lucy, despite her therapy skills.

"How did it go at Bobbie's?" Maggie asked, laying a gentle hand on Liz's arm.

"Joyce will be gone by tomorrow."

Maggie's sympathy was genuine. Liz could tell by the catch in her voice when she said, "It's hard, even when it's expected."

"Reshma did a good job with the prayers."

"You stuck around?"

"She was my patient. I remember her before the dementia." Liz put a cookie sheet under two trays of eggplant to support them. "Lucy's not home?"

"No. Haven't seen her."

Liz whipped out her phone to send Lucy a message but saw her wife had already left one: *Quick meeting with Tom about tomorrow's services. Be home in twenty minutes.*

Liz held up the phone so Maggie could read it. "See what I mean about being married to a priest?"

"What can I say?" asked Maggie with a shrug. "Payback's a bitch." She covered the trays with foil. "I made this one for your dinner," she said, obviously switching to a less controversial topic. "Do you want to bake it now, or should I put it in the fridge?"

"Why don't you stay and eat with us? It will be like old times."

"Not really," said Maggie. "And if I'd known how things would turn out, I probably would have done things differently."

"Like what?" asked Liz, pulling out a stool from the island. She crossed her arms, then remembered Lucy's oft-repeated advice to avoid striking a defensive posture. Instead, she leaned her elbows on the counter and leaned forward to look interested.

"For one thing," Maggie continued, "I wouldn't have let Lucy insinuate herself so deeply in our life."

"You were the one who kept inviting her. I thought she was silly. But you did girly things together, which took the heat off me." Liz screwed up her face into a look of disgust.

"I know. You hate shopping. And I enjoyed her company. She's very chatty. Unlike you."

"Sounds like you two are more compatible. Maybe you should have gone after Lucy after you divorced me."

"Not my type," Maggie replied bluntly as she dried the pot. "And she wasn't 'into me,' as the kids say. But I could tell she thought you were hot. You might have been ignoring her, but she was very aware of you."

"See? I missed all that."

"That's because you don't pay attention, Liz. When you're doing something, the ceiling could collapse on your head, and you wouldn't notice. Oh, you're very observant when you play doctor, but otherwise, you miss the most obvious things. I've said it before, Liz. When it comes to women, you're stupid."

"Gee, thanks."

"What can I say? It's the truth." Maggie opened the refrigerator and took out a bottle of pinot grigio. "At least, Lucy has good taste in wine. Want a glass?"

"No, thanks, but I will take a beer."

"Which one?" asked Maggie, surveying the supply on the door, "There are five different kinds."

"I don't care. Pick one." Fortunately, Maggie picked a double IPA that Liz really liked. She got up to get a glass because she didn't want to listen to Maggie complain about her drinking from the can. "When can we stop talking about why our marriage failed?"

"When I'm done processing it."

"And when will that be?"

Maggie shrugged. "I don't know. Whenever it happens. By the way, I took your advice. I've gone back to therapy."

"Glad Gloria found time for you. She's been so busy counseling the families of the victims."

"She made time for me because I'm an old client."

"That's nice," said Liz, carefully pouring the beer down the side of the glass.

"Whenever therapy comes up you always sound so dismissive."

"It's no secret I'm not a fan."

Maggie pulled the cork out of the wine bottle. Unlike Lucy, she carefully unthreaded it from the opener and threw it out. "Lucy's a therapist. How does she stand your contempt for her profession?"

"Lucy's a lot of different things. She's a priest too. Not a fan of that either."

Maggie gave Liz a hard look. "I don't know about that, Liz. I think that's one of her attractions. You just won't admit it."

Liz took a sip of the sudsy, perfectly bitter IPA and tried to ignore Maggie's needling. The garage door opened, which meant Lucy was home. When she came into the kitchen, she looked at each of them in turn to take the emotional temperature of the room.

Maggie's attitude instantly changed. Liz could tell she'd slipped into her actress mode because she was all smiles and her voice was warm when she said, "Sorry to have taken over your kitchen, but I'm done now."

"Luce, I asked Maggie to come out to dinner with us," Liz explained quickly. "She made a tray of eggplant parmigiana for us, but she's sick of looking at it, so I suggested we go out." In fact, the idea had just occurred to her, but a restaurant would be neutral territory. Liz was emotionally exhausted from attending Joyce and wrangling with Maggie. Lucy looked like she could use a break.

Lucy scrutinized Maggie, evidently sizing up her interest in joining them. Maggie smiled coyly. "If you don't mind, Lucy. With Sam in Chicago, eating alone every night gets boring."

"I don't mind," Lucy said with a sincere smile. "It will save me and Liz from talking about grim stuff, like how long she thinks Joyce has and why." She turned to Liz. "How was Bobbie when you left?"

"You know how she is, trying to hold it together to prove how professional she is."

"But it's different when it's your own. Look how I fell apart when Erika died."

Maggie put her arm around Lucy's shoulder and gave her a little hug. "You did your best. What a shock, going upstairs to get ready for bed and finding your wife unconscious. I would have completely fallen apart. At least, you had the presence of mind to call Liz."

Liz remembered that awful night. Erika was unresponsive when she'd arrived. The CT scan revealed an aneurysm that had left her friend's brain so damaged she could never recover. Because of the pandemic, they weren't letting any visitors into the hospital. Fortunately, Liz had surgical privileges. She'd pulled strings so that Lucy could say goodbye to her wife.

"It's never easy," said Lucy. "Erika's death was a shock. She was only sixty-two and looked so healthy. Joyce is close to eighty. She's been battling dementia for years. But it doesn't matter, when the end comes, it's always a shock." She reached up to unpin her clerical collar. "Let me get out of my work clothes. Fancy place or casual?"

"I don't know about you," Liz said, "but I just want to relax."

"Me too," Lucy agreed.

"I'm dressed for cooking, not stepping out," said Maggie, but she always looked terrific. She was wearing classic gold jewelry. She'd throw on a simple scarf and look "dressed up."

After Lucy left to change, Maggie asked Liz, "Are you sure you want me along?"

"Yes, Lucy's right. It will keep us from talking about grim stuff. God knows there's enough of it to go around. Lucy has been up in Portland and on the phone with Rebecca. She's freaking out because Judith is still with her parents. She won't be drafted, but she's still talking about reactivating her status in the IDF."

"Is she crazy?" asked Maggie incredulously. "She has two teenagers."

"I know, but Israelis are passionate about defending their country, especially after that brutal attack. I'm worried too. It sounds like there will be a full-scale war."

"God, I hope not," Maggie murmured.

"If there is, we'll all have something to worry about." Liz shook her head and took refuge in her beer.

Chapter 6

Reshma wondered if she was ready for her first solo funeral. Other than the usual jitters of a first-timer, she had no reason to be nervous. Susan, considered St. Margaret's best homilist, had reviewed her sermon and pronounced it pitch perfect. Tom, who would be concelebrating, had done a dry run of the ceremony with Reshma, and it had gone smoothly. So why was she trembling?

Joyce wouldn't have relatives to judge Reshma's performance, or even friends. Many people outlived the people who'd been important in their lives. Some died in places far from the community where they'd lived. Elderly and weak, they'd moved to be near their children. Often, the attendance at such funerals was sparse, but this one wouldn't be.

Bobbie had many patients at Hobbs Family Practice who appreciated her practical, no-nonsense approach to their care. She taught training classes to the first responders. The immigrant community thought she was a saint for taking in Teresa and her daughter when they were homeless. It was entirely possible that most of Hobbs might show up.

Susan would be sitting in the first row with Bobbie and couldn't come to Reshma's rescue if something went wrong, but she'd have reinforcements. Lucy and Tom had agreed to concelebrate. Reshma wondered if Lucy was trying to make amends for being so judgmental. In the last few weeks, Reshma had learned many things about Lucy she'd never wanted to know. It was painful to see her idol fall from her pedestal, but now Reshma could appreciate Lucy for who she was, a flawed woman who did her best to love everyone, but often made mistakes, sometimes big ones.

Reshma adjusted the chasuble on her shoulders. The vestment still showed some hard creases from the shipping box. The altar guild had tried to steam them out, and it had been hanging on the mannequin for over a week. The wrinkles persisted because the sizing and tight stitching made the brocade inflexible. It bulged when Reshma gathered it closer to move her arms. Fortunately, it wasn't right next to her skin, which would be intolerable.

Bobbie had donated the new vestments and altar cloths to St. Margaret's in Joyce's memory. She'd made this expensive gift along with a substantial bequest from her deceased partner's sizable investments to thank the staff for their attentive ministry. Reshma wondered if wearing the new vestments was payback for the sin of kindness. She shifted the ritual garment on her shoulders, trying to get it to drape properly.

"Sorry you got stuck with the new vestments" said a sympathetic female voice, "They're always stiff in the beginning." Reshma turned and saw Lucy, smiling with maternal pride. Despite seeing the cracks in Lucy's perfect image, Reshma still thought of her as a second mother. She basked in her warm smile.

Reshma inspected herself in the full-length mirror. The brilliant white of the new vestments was a shocking contrast. Only High-Church Anglicans still wore black for funerals. White was the modern color, reflecting the hope for the final resurrection. Most of the liturgical colors—blue for Advent, purple for Lent, red for Pentecost—complemented rather than highlighted Reshma's dark complexion. Even green, worn for the long stretch between Pentecost and Advent, looked good on her. Fortunately, a rich church like St. Margaret's had green vestments in many shades, from the brilliant green of spring to late summer's rich olive. The dazzling white brocade of the new chasuble made Reshma's face and hands appear almost preternaturally dark.

"I'm so black!" she exclaimed, staring at her image.

Lucy's spontaneous laughter sounded odd before a funeral, but it forced Reshma to smile too. "Yes, you are," said Lucy. "Vestments are meant to call attention to the wearer's role, not the person wearing them, but they always seem to accentuate personal traits. I never realize how red my hair is until I wear green. And God knows, during ordinary time, we wear it a lot."

Lucy patted Reshma's shoulder affectionately. "Don't worry, Sister Priest. You look absolutely beautiful." Reshma's cheeks flamed. Her dark complexion hid blushing, an advantage she had over white people. No one could ever tell from her face that she was embarrassed.

Reshma allowed the warmth in her cheeks to subside before asking, "Any final words of advice?"

Lucy thought for a moment. "You can keep the eulogies from going on too long by getting up from your seat as if you're approaching the pulpit. It nearly always forces the speaker to wind down. If not, wait for an appropriate pause and interrupt."

"But don't we want people to express their grief?"

"Yes, we do, but we also want to give everyone a chance to speak."

"I have the list of eulogists right here." Reshma patted her *Book of Common Prayer*. She raised her eyes. "Oh, Lucy! There are so many things to think about!"

"When you're the celebrant, you're not just the star of the show. You're the producer, stage manager, and director all rolled up into one. Don't worry. Between me and Tom, your supporting cast has decades of experience." Lucy gave Reshma a half hug. "I need to get the procession organized. See you in the back after your greeting."

Lucy's departure left Reshma alone with her worries. She made one last adjustment of the stiff chasuble, then willed her hands to stop fussing with it. In the mirror, she saw Susan come into the room.

"Reshma, you look fantastic!"

"Thanks, but these new vestments are like wearing cardboard!"

Susan felt the offending fabric and nodded. "Yes, but it is an honor that you are the first to wear them."

"I hope Lucy didn't feel slighted that Bobbie requested me as the officiant."

"Nonsense. Lucy's always in the spotlight. I'm sure she's glad to share it with you. You know how proud she is of you." Reshma puffed up with pride at hearing Lucy's opinion reported second-hand. "I am too," added Susan. "You are a gifted priest."

All the compliments somehow added to the pressure Reshma felt. "Are there a lot of people out there?"

"It's a big crowd. I can't imagine where they're all coming from. I guess most of these people are Bobbie's friends or patients of hers."

"And also people from the parish, supporting you."

Susan lowered her eyes. In times of stress, she still reverted to the odd convent custom. "I hope it's for Joyce and Bobbie, not me."

Reshma bent a little so she could look directly into Susan's gray eyes. "People love you, Susan. They want to be here for you today."

"How do they even know I'm connected to Bobbie? We've been so discreet!"

Reshma stifled a smile to avoid seeming disrespectful. Everyone knew Susan and Bobbie were a couple. In a small town, it was impossible to hide secrets for very long. But Susan was already anxious enough about her reputation. Reshma didn't need to add to her worry.

"It's okay," she said soothingly. "No one's judging you."

"I don't know about that," said Susan, now staring at the door as if she expected an invasion of witch hunters.

"Susan, you worry too much. Let people support you. You're among friends here."

"I guess so," she said, but she didn't look sure. "I should get back to Bobbie." Susan moved toward the door but stopped to inspect the vestments for Sunday on the manikin. "Did you need something?" asked Reshma. It seemed unlikely. Susan had explicitly declined any role in the service.

"No, I only came in to wish you luck. It's your first funeral, and it can be hard." Reshma wished Susan hadn't reminded her. Until now, she'd mostly had her unexpected stage fright under control.

"How's Bobbie holding up?" she asked to change the subject.

"Okay. She keeps telling me she feels guilty because she's relieved it's finally over."

"But that's natural. It's been an ordeal. She's been Joyce's caregiver for decades."

"Not quite decades, but a long time. Now that Joyce is gone, she feels lost. The role she's had for so long, the person she'd organized her entire life around is...gone. That has left a big hole in her life. She suddenly doesn't know what to do with herself."

"I'll tell you what I'd do in that situation," said Reshma. "I'd take some of that money Joyce left her and book a long vacation. I'd go to Europe, or Alaska, cruise the Greek Isles, or fly to Iceland to see the Northern Lights..." Reshma had signed up for emails offering vacation packages that allowed her to vicariously travel the world, so she knew all the most sought-after destinations.

"She could travel. She doesn't need to work, but her job as an NP gives her structure, especially now that she doesn't have to care for Joyce. But a vacation isn't a bad idea." Susan's eyes shone with possibility.

"Where would you go, if you could?" asked Reshma tenderly.

"Ireland. My sister took me there years ago, after I came out of the convent. I'd always wanted to visit the Emerald Isle and see where my ancestors came from. It's beautiful."

"How long has it been since you had a vacation? I mean a real one, where you went away for a while?"

Susan shook her head as if dismissing a daydream. "I never had that kind of money, not when I was putting myself through seminary and certainly not since I've been a priest." Reshma understood. The last time she had a vacation was a week at Lake Winnipesaukee when a college friend invited her to her family's sprawling summer "camp" on the water. That was years ago.

"I'm sure Dr. Liz would give Bobbie some time off," said Reshma confidently. "Maybe you could go too."

"The only school break coming up is Christmas. As you know, it's our busiest time of year. So many events and services."

"But Father Tom is here, and I can help. Why don't you ask Lucy for some time off?"

The person under discussion poked her head into the sacristy. "Reshma, we should get started soon," Lucy urged with a firm look. Her eyes turned to Susan.

"And I need to see how Bobbie is doing," said Susan, hearing Lucy's silent order loud and clear. "Lucy, give me a moment to get back to my seat."

Lucy watched Susan leave. When she was out of earshot, Lucy added, "Don't worry, Reshma. I'll be right there with you. Just follow the rubric and you'll do fine." Then she was gone.

Alone again, Reshma felt prickles of anxiety on the back of her neck. She bowed her head and murmured a little prayer. Before she went into the sanctuary, she made one last adjustment to the rigid chasuble and hoped for the best.

Every pew in the old church was full, and there was a crowd standing in the back. Reshma recognized most of the parishioners, but there were many others—Bobbie's coworkers from Hobbs Family Practice, a contingent of faculty from Susan's school, including the principal, Courtney Barnes, and her partner, Melissa Morgenstern.

"Thank you all for coming to honor Joyce's memory and to support her family." Reshma gazed directly at Bobbie and Teresa and the others who lived in the house. Reshma had considered not using the word "family" because Bobbie and Joyce had never married, and it seemed cruel to emphasize the lack of blood relations attending the service. There was no one left except some distant cousins who were too frail to come to the funeral. Ultimately, Reshma decided to use the word to emphasize the idea of chosen family versus blood kin.

Hobbs was known to welcome LGBT people, and had many examples of the connections that often ran much deeper than blood. Reshma's eyes fell on Cherie and Brenda with their two adopted children. Looking dapper in a designer suit, Liz sat with Emily and Denise. Melissa seemed to have adjusted to the role of co-parent to Courtney's tween, Kaylee. Reshma could count many more unconventional families sitting in the church, but now she needed to clear her mind and focus on the service.

"For those who aren't part of our church, welcome to St. Margaret's. If you would like to receive communion, please know that everyone is welcome at God's table. If you'd like to have a blessing instead, simply cross your hands in front of you like this." Reshma demonstrated. "And now, to ground us, I would like to read this poem by Mary Oliver, which was one of Joyce's favorites. It's called 'In Blackwater Woods.'" She reverently read the poem, lingering on the last stanza.

> "…to live in this world, you must be able to do three things: to love what is mortal; to hold it against your bones knowing your own life depends on it; and, when the time comes to let it go, to let it go."

When Reshma looked up, she could see how much those words had moved her listeners. It had brought her to tears the first time she'd heard it at the funeral of her favorite seminary professor. Amanda Cotton had been one of the first black women to be ordained in the Episcopal Church. Like too many of those women, she'd discovered that ordination didn't mean acceptance. She couldn't find a congregation to hire her, so she'd gotten a theology degree and taught in a seminary. After hearing her backstory from the source itself, Reshma had admired her even more. Professor Cotton had never become bitter, only more philosophical. She'd continued to fight for the rights of female clergy until the day she died.

Reshma awoke from the memory when she saw Lucy beckoning her to the back to join the procession. The order of participants was determined by their role in the service. As the celebrant, Reshma was last in line. Lucy, wearing a simple Alb and white priest's stole, was ahead of her. In front of Lucy, Tom's sturdy figure blocked the view.

The organist launched into the entrance hymn and the procession stepped off. The members found their seats in the chancel. Once everyone was settled, Reshma recited the collect for funerals. Looking up between phrases, she saw Tiffany sitting near the back of the church. Her golden hair shone in the overhead light as if lit from within. She looked exactly like the angel from Reshma's childhood Bible. Reshma quickly dropped her gaze to her prayer book.

She began to relax after she'd gotten through the first part of the ritual and could sit down for the readings. Mother Lucy's green eyes met hers. She looked relaxed, which meant things were going well. Susan was smiling at her proudly. Then she seemed to remember it was a funeral and assumed a more solemn expression. Cherie Harrison was the first reader, followed by Liz. Reshma imagined her reading at medical conferences in the same practiced, measured tone. Lucy read the passage from John's Gospel about the many rooms in the Father's house.

Natalie, the student who'd helped care for Joyce, approached to eulogize Joyce, followed by Teresa. The only other person who stepped up to talk about Joyce was Liz, who had known her from when she first came to vacation in Maine. She spoke about Joyce's sharp intelligence and her interest in current affairs, her love of the rugged Maine shore, and her philanthropy. For a moment, it seemed that Bobbie might get up to speak, but then she faltered and sat down. It was always better when someone sensed their limits and avoided sobbing at the lectern. Reshma waited another minute for any spontaneous eulogizers, but no one else stood.

Reshma liked to preach her sermons from the aisle in the nave instead of the pulpit. She launched into her prepared text, but the words she'd once thought were so brilliant, now sounded vague and hollow. She did something she had never done before—she abandoned her prepared sermon and preached from the heart.

"You heard Dr. Stolz remember a different Joyce, not as a woman whose mind had faded, but as a brilliant business leader and philanthropist. Joyce was born to wealth and privilege. For many years, she ran the family business and successfully led it through challenging times.

"Joyce could have used her wealth solely for her own enjoyment, but she didn't. She invested in scholarships for young women to attend business school, in programs that trained women in the building trades. She gave millions to arts institutions, including our own Webhanet Playhouse. She supported shelters for abused women and homeless teens. Some of you might dismiss her generosity as smart tax deductions but think of all the people who benefitted. And Joyce didn't only give away money. She was committed to every charity she supported, served on the boards of these organizations, using her business acumen to help them thrive. Her contributions benefit them to this day.

"Joyce wasn't just the fading Alzheimer's patient of her old age. She was once someone important, not only because of business success or wealth, but because she dedicated herself to the service of others. She made things better for many by mentoring other women, supporting ways to inspire minds and hearts, and building community.

"The idea of heaven, portrayed in the Gospel, with its many rooms, or 'mansions' in some old translations, might be comforting to people as they grieve, but Jesus' real message was creating God's kingdom here on earth. He was teaching us how to live with one another. He knew it would be hard. There is so much broken in the world and so much work to do, but we need to keep trying. Joyce did, and so must we." Reshma looked around the congregation. They were really listening. Encouraged, she went on.

"Some people think death should be welcomed when an elderly, sick person dies. They've lived their lives. It's their time, they say. Their death is a mercy because it ends their suffering. As Christians, we believe that death is the beginning of eternal life. Jesus' resurrection gives us hope that we too will rise again.

"But no life should pass unacknowledged, especially not the life of a generous woman who contributed so much to the lives of others. We should honor her by emulating her generosity and kindness to others, and her desire to make the world a better place. I never knew Joyce before her disease stole her memories and finally, even her ability to speak. But even in her silence, God heard her voice and loved her." Reshma tapped the place over her heart for emphasis. "And God loves each of us too, more than we can ever imagine."

Reshma decided to end it there. She sat down to let everyone absorb her message. The sermon had been quite a ramble, not very elegant or profound, but she'd made her key points. Lucy, sitting across from her, nodded in approval. Tom leaned forward and smiled. From her seat in the front pew, Susan smiled too.

From here on, Reshma only needed to follow the rubric and she'd be home free. She basked in the warmth in Susan's eyes when she took communion. Then Tiffany stepped up to the communion rail. Gazing directly into those celestial blue eyes, Reshma said the ritual words, "The body of Christ, the bread of heaven." To avoid dropping the host, Reshma forcefully pressed it into her hand. She could hear the delicate wafer loudly crack.

"Amen," Tiffany declared emphatically. Out of the corner of her eye, Reshma watched the blond head bend to drink from the chalice Lucy offered. She tried to stay focused on the next communicant instead of wondering why Tiffany had come. *Stop thinking about her!* Reshma ordered herself and held up the host to the next communicant.

As Reshma recited the post-communion prayer, she noticed Tiffany getting up to leave. She'd hoped to find out what Tiffany had thought of the service, so she was very disappointed. Then she noticed others getting up to leave and realized that they were all members of the hospitality committee. They were leaving early to ready the post-service reception. Reshma's heart rate speeded up. Tiffany was probably helping them.

Tom, Lucy, and Reshma gathered around the stand where the urn containing Joyce's cremains stood next to a vase of Japanese irises, her favorite flower. Together, the three priests recited the words of the commendation. Then they joined the procession out of the church to the choir, led by Maggie Fitzgerald, singing "I am the Bread of Life."

It was over. Reshma breathed a profound sigh of relief. She joined Lucy and Tom to shake people's hands as they left the church. The line seemed interminable. Finally, she headed to the vestry to change. Tom was quick. He could get out of his vestments in minutes. Whistling, he headed off to the reception. Lucy was silent as she took off her Alb and hung it up in the closet. Reshma noticed how carefully she handled the white stole.

"That's so beautiful," Reshma said, noticing the delicate red and gold embroidery.

"It is, isn't it?" said Lucy, gazing at it fondly, "Susan gave it to me for my ordination." Afraid her eyes might reveal that she knew their secret, Reshma focused them on the stole. When she'd finished admiring it, Lucy carefully rolled it up and put it in her bag. Now Reshma knew why she never left it with the common vestments.

She was anxious to hear her mentor's opinion of her extemporaneous sermon. She asked before she burst. "Was my sermon okay?"

Lucy nodded. "Yes, I'm still thinking about it."

Reshma hung up the stiff white chasuble, hoping Lucy would say more. When she didn't, Reshma prodded her. "Is that good or bad?"

Lucy took a moment to reflect. "It's always good to make people think. That's the point of a homily, isn't it?" Reshma was disappointed she didn't say more. Before she left, Lucy stopped at the door and turned around. She looked directly into Reshma's eyes. "You spoke from the heart, Reshma. A few times, I worried that you were losing the plot, but you found your way back and tied up everything perfectly." She smiled. "Stop worrying. Now, get changed. People will be looking for you at the reception."

That was the closest thing to an order Lucy had ever given her, so Reshma hurried to change. She slipped a dark suit jacket over her clerical shirt. She'd passed on her usual brightly colored, patterned top in favor of something more subdued because it was a funeral.

By the time she entered the parish hall, there was a long line of people waiting to fill their plates. The elderly church ladies who prepared meals for everything from fundraising dinners to post-service coffee hour were stationed at the tables to serve the food. Reshma spotted Tiffany brandishing tongs at the dessert table and made a beeline to where she stood.

"Hello, Reshma. Looking for sweets?" Tiffany asked coyly. Her cherubic mouth smiled primly, but the look in her eyes was positively devilish.

"Well, of course. But you're the best sweet of all," replied Reshma, not to be outdone. She looked over her shoulder to see if anyone had heard, but most people were in line for more substantial fare.

"There are ham and cheese croissants on the lunch table. You should grab one before they're gone," said Tiffany, levering an éclair onto a plate eagerly held up by an elderly gentleman. "But come back later."

Reshma headed to the back of the food line but was ambushed by Susan before she got there. "Oh, Reshma. Your sermon was absolutely inspired!" Because Susan had reviewed the draft, she'd known exactly when Reshma had deviated from her prepared text.

"I'm glad you think so. Lucy said she's still thinking about it. I'm not sure she was as impressed as you were."

Susan batted away her concern with a wave. "Take it from me, it was brilliant. Maybe Lucy's jealous. She's always struggled with sermon prep. That's why she starts so early in the week. But if she says she's still thinking about it, I'd take that as a high compliment, not a criticism." Reshma had been stealing glances at the dessert table. "I won't keep you," Susan said. "I see you looking at your girlfriend."

Reshma was surprised by the spark of annoyance she felt. "She's not my girlfriend yet," she corrected briskly. Susan shrank away at Reshma's sharp tone. "I'm sorry," Reshma added, "I meant we're not that far."

"I understand. And you're wise to wait. Go, get some food," Susan said kindly. "I need to get back to Bobbie. Come sit with us if you can."

As the line wound its way by the food table, people kept ambushing Reshma to compliment her on the service and her sermon. In the rare moments of peace, she watched the women on the hospitality committee serving the food they'd prepared for the reception. They were doing what women had done since time immemorial—comforting and sustaining mourners with nourishing food.

When she looked for a place to sit, Susan jumped up and waved. Reluctantly, Reshma joined them. She only hesitated because it looked like Bobbie was already overwhelmed by people offering sympathy and Reshma's presence would only draw more attention.

Reshma wolfed down the delicious ham and cheese croissant. She ate three deviled eggs, a standard feature at Episcopal coffee hours. Every priest knew to grab some after a service because they were high in protein and easy to eat while talking to congregants. She finished her coffee and cast her eye at the dessert table.

"Will you excuse me?" she whispered to Susan, who gave her a knowing look and gently nudged her arm.

Now that the funeral crowd had scoured the food table, they were looking for sweets. The line for Tiffany's pastries had grown longer. Reshma stood a few feet away to admire Tiffany's angelic face and golden waves, today neatly worn in an updo. Eventually, Tiffany, who'd been chatting with the mostly elderly people seeking her offerings, became aware of Reshma's presence and looked up. Reshma used her collar as a ticket to break through the line and stand behind the table.

"I was so surprised to see you at the service," Reshma whispered near Tiffany's ear.

Tiffany grinned. "I'm sure you were, but I got here early to drop off the pastries and sandwiches. And one of the kitchen ladies asked if I would like to see the church, so I stuck around."

"I'm glad you came in for the service."

Tiffany fixed her blue eyes on Reshma's. "I was curious to see what you do in your job." Her expression changed to one of concern. "I hope that was okay, and I wasn't a distraction."

Of course, she was a distraction! "It didn't matter. I was so happy to see you, especially after all your warnings not to talk about religion."

"I'm sorry. I don't really care if you talk about it or how much you like your job," said Tiffany, smiling at the boy practically drooling over one of the eclairs. "Just don't try to convert me."

"I can understand your curiosity, but you came to communion."

"You invited me. Remember? You said, 'everyone is welcome at God's table' and looked right at me. That meant a lot to me."

Reshma studied her face and realized she had taken the formula as a personal invitation. "I believe that everyone is invited, but there's a lot of debate in theological circles about whether the unbaptized can be given communion. Have you been baptized?"

Tiffany giggled, then quickly assumed a serious expression. "No disrespect, but my parents are total atheists. You'll meet them soon."

Reshma gulped. Meeting Tiffany's parents meant taking the relationship to a new level. Reshma wasn't sure she was ready, but she managed to say, "Of course, I'd love to meet them."

"They're coming for Thanksgiving, so you'll have your chance."

Reshma noticed Teresa beckoning to her from the door of the institutional kitchen at the end of the hall. "Excuse me a minute," Reshma said.

"Sure. I'll put aside a napoleon for you."

As Reshma approached, she saw that Teresa, who was perennially cheerful, was twisting her fingers.

"Was that you calling to me before?" Reshma asked.

"Yes, but I had duties today in the kitchen, so I couldn't wait for you," said Teresa. "Can you spare a moment?"

"Yes, of course. Let's find a quiet place to sit down."

"Not here," said Teresa. "Some place more private."

Reshma thought for a moment. The place was swarming with mourners and church personnel. She glanced at her watch. "We can go into the sanctuary. The altar guild should have finished their work by now." Reshma led Teresa into the church. Only the lights in the chancel were lit, so they sat down in a pew near the altar.

"What's wrong, Teresa? You look so distressed."

"Well, I am. I'm happy for Joyce that her long agony is finally over, but obviously, this changes things."

Teresa didn't have to say more. She'd been a certified nurse in Sudan, but her credentials had been lost in the country's unrelenting wars. She needed training to be licensed in Maine. While she got it, Reshma had arranged for Teresa and her daughter, Grace, to live in an old office annex to Bobbie's house in exchange for their help in caring for Joyce. With her passing, the quid pro quo was moot.

"I understand," said Reshma. "Joyce's death will change so much."

"Has Bobbie mentioned what she intends to do about her tenants?" Besides Teresa and Grace, there were two students living in the big oceanfront house.

"No, it's way too soon for that," said Reshma.

"I know, and it's not appropriate to ask, but, Mother Reshma, I can't afford an apartment while I'm going to school. I love my job at Hobbs Family Practice. My Grace is so happy in her new school. I don't want to uproot her again. You cannot imagine how hard it was for her in that refugee camp. Her schooling was spotty, and she's so smart."

Reshma could hear the poor woman's anguish at the thought that their stable home, even though it was only a couple of small rooms in a former office, would be suddenly taken away.

"Teresa, you and I both know that Bobbie is a kind and generous woman. She won't just throw you out on the street. You always did more than take care of Joyce. You cook for everyone, and Grace helps take care of the garden."

"But she doesn't need us or the student boarders anymore. Joyce left her all that money. She's rich! She doesn't even need to work as a nurse anymore."

"She never did," Reshma said. "She went back to work to keep her skills active and to stay engaged in the community. She needed a break from taking care of Joyce and working at Hobbs Family Practice was the perfect escape."

"But now she doesn't need an escape."

"Oh, I disagree. She needs it even more. Most people work to make a living, but some people really have a passion for their profession. They look forward to going to work and love doing their job. Bobbie is one of those people, and so are you, I think."

"Bobbie inspired me to become a nurse practitioner too. I intend to ask Dr. Stolz to recommend me."

"I'm sure she will. Bobbie tells me that everyone thinks highly of your work at the practice."

"People think we would rather be doctors but just couldn't make it into medical school. That's not true. We nurses are on the front lines, healing people in a way doctors can't or won't." Teresa clutched Reshma's hand. "You will tell me if Bobbie says she wants me and Grace to leave?" she asked in a pleading tone. "I need to know, so I can make plans."

"Of course, I will, but maybe you should talk to Bobbie directly. Yes, this is a difficult time, but I'm sure she'll understand your need to know. You might also mention it to Mother Susan. As you know, she has a special relationship with her. She may be able to influence the situation."

Teresa sighed and nodded. "Wise advice. I'll look for a time to talk to her."

"You bring so much to our community. I think keeping you here would be a good thing, but let's see what happens."

"Thank you. You are very kind. But now, I must go. They will be looking for me in the kitchen."

After she left, Reshma decided to remain and pray. It amazed her that the end of one woman's life could impact the fate of so many.

Chapter 7

Lucy hated doing dishes. By the time she was a teenager, she'd figured out a surefire way to avoid it. If she promised to sing extra vocal exercises, her mother would clean up the kitchen. It was an easy bribe. Peggy Bartlett desperately wanted her daughter to have the opera career she'd never had. To afford the travel to Lucy's competitions, she'd sung for weddings and given private voice lessons. After all her mother had sacrificed for her, Lucy felt guilty for tricking her, but the extra exercises hadn't hurt.

Liz was harder to manipulate. For one thing, she hated housework, which was why they had a house cleaner. And Lucy never liked to take advantage of Liz's protective instincts because she cooked every night. After a busy day of listening to her patients' complaints, she managed to pull things out of the pantry and refrigerator and put a delicious, healthy meal on the table.

Fortunately, Liz was a neat cook, who used a minimum of pots and pans and cleaned up along the way. By her own admission, Lucy was a slob. She'd had to clean up her act or risk eviction from the shared walk-in closet in their bedroom. Liz bought her see-through plastic boxes to organize the bags of shoes she'd brought over from the beach house. She'd hung another rod so Lucy could keep her clerical wear separate from her other clothes. Seasonal items had been banished to the downstairs bedroom that doubled as Lucy's office. At first being forced to maintain order put Lucy off balance, although she agreed it was better than spending an hour looking for a pair of shoes. Erika, despite similar Teutonic influences, had indulgently let Lucy get away with everything.

Lucy's eyes misted at the thought of her first wife, gone too soon and too abruptly. She counseled others that grief showed up in unexpected ways, but she was always surprised by it when it happened to her. The pain was less intense now, but it hadn't gone away.

Lucy turned on the small light under the cabinet and shut off the bright overhead fixture. It was their signal that the kitchen was closed. Liz might slip down later for a salty snack, especially if they made love. Liz was always ravenous after sex. Lately, she'd been addicted to a spicy trail mix she made for herself.

Lucy climbed the stairs to the second-floor bedroom that Liz had converted to a TV room. Lucy used the enormous media room on the first floor for practice, so she associated it with work, and it was just too big. Liz had obligingly turned one of the second-floor guest rooms into their TV room. Liz half-listened to CNN while she cooked, but Lucy, who didn't have time to look at her phone during the day, liked to watch the evening news.

Sprawled on one of the sofas, Liz was reading on her iPad. Before Lucy lived with Liz, she'd had no idea how much doctors needed to read. Liz moved down a little, creating a space big enough for Lucy to sit, and rested her head on Lucy's thigh. Eventually, her head would become too heavy. Until then, Lucy enjoyed winding her fingers in Liz's hair while she watched the news. Her wife never complained about the petting, and it seemed to calm her after a difficult day.

"Thanks for cleaning up," Liz said as Lucy settled in beside her. The unexpected courtesy from someone who could often be dismissive and gruff pleased Lucy. Liz stretched out her long arm to grab the remote. She switched on the news channel and went right back to her tablet.

"I bet you already know everything that's going on in the world," said Lucy. "Maybe I don't need to watch the news, and you can just tell me what's going on."

Liz closed her iPad and sat up. "Well, let's see... The Israelis are bombing the shit out of Gaza. I was hoping the president could talk Netanyahu into restraint, but he's got those right-wing nuts breathing down his neck."

"The Hamas attack was horrific," said Lucy, "but retaliation isn't the best solution."

"Tell that to the people who invented 'an eye for an eye.'"

"Liz, that sounds anti-Semitic."

Liz shrugged. "My Jewish friends agree with me. Are they anti-Semites?"

"They could be. Self-loathing is common among marginalized people."

"You've met Sid and Bev Birnbaum. They are devout Jews. I doubt their criticism of Israel is 'self-loathing," said Liz in an acid tone. "And my colleague, Jack Dreyfus, is an observant Jew, and he feels the same. But this war isn't about religion. A nation is violating international law with complete disregard for civilian lives. The holocaust doesn't justify the slaughter of women and children. Saying that people without political power chose to shelter terrorists is pure bullshit."

Lucy smiled. Liz's succinct and accurate summaries of the news always came with a side of expletive-laced opinion.

"You're right," said Lucy, because it was easier. She could see that Liz was just warming up and like Erika, she was a formidable adversary in a debate.

But Liz wasn't deterred by the quick capitulation. "I tend to side with Jews because of my history. Of course, my father didn't have much choice when he was drafted into the Wehrmacht in World War II."

"And his guilt isn't yours."

"Some people think there should be reparations, whether it's for church abuse of Native Americans or slave owners. Germany did pay some reparations for the Holocaust. But where does it end? Genocide and territorial expanse are as old as humankind."

Lucy stroked Liz's thigh. "Sweetie, calm down. Don't get so agitated before you go to bed, or you won't sleep."

Liz huffed in indignation. She turned the TV on again and picked up her tablet.

Lucy snuggled closer. She hated Liz's sleepless nights, when she crept down to her first-floor office and answered emails or listened to music until dawn lit the windows. Since the shooting at Hobbs Elementary, Liz had been more restless. Lucy tried singing her to sleep. Liz would fall off within a few minutes, but a few hours later, she'd be roaming the house. If she hadn't gotten out of bed yet, Lucy might use sex to settle her, but their memory-foam mattress didn't transmit motion, so catching Liz before she got away wasn't easy. She'd offered to sleep in another room, but Lucy would rather have the comfort and security of Liz's body than uninterrupted sleep.

In the pocket of Lucy's fleece jacket, her cell phone vibrated. She stuck her hand in to silence it. The call was unlikely to be a pastoral care request because Reshma was on duty. Reluctantly, Lucy looked at the screen. The image was a smiling blonde with her hair pulled back. The name below read "Brenda Harrison." Lucy lowered the TV volume before she opened the call.

"Hi, Brenda," Lucy said calmly, although she didn't feel calm. Usually, communications with Brenda went through Liz because they were old friends. "How are you?"

Brenda got right to the point. "Lucy, I'm calling you instead of your wife because I'm afraid the news might set her off." Below the forced steadiness in Brenda's voice, Lucy could hear the splintery tension. "There's an active shooter in Lewiston."

"What the fuck!" Liz exclaimed and sat up so suddenly she almost dumped Lucy on the floor.

"Too late, Brenda. I think she knows." said Lucy, trying to read the headlines running on the bottom of the TV. "It just hit national news."

"Tell Liz to stay home," Brenda ordered. "She has no business getting involved, and if I catch her heading up there, I'll... Well, I don't know what I'll do, but she won't like it. If you need help with her, let me know and I'll come over."

"Aren't you going to the scene?" asked Lucy.

"No, they've got a slew of local departments searching for the guy. I need to stick close to home in case he shows up here."

"Put her on speaker," Liz demanded. Her fierce look made Lucy instantly comply. "What do you know, Brenda?"

"Not much. We have some fuzzy photos of a guy with an assault rifle entering a bowling alley. Then he went to a nearby bar. Some deaf people didn't hear the shots and couldn't take cover."

"My God!" exclaimed Lucy under her breath. Out of the corner of her eye, she watched Liz becoming more agitated. "Liz, take it easy. It's not your problem."

"No? It's my problem because it's everyone's problem!"

"Brenda, thanks for calling," said Lucy to get her off the phone. "Get back to us when you know more."

Lucy closed the call and dropped her phone on the couch. "Liz, calm down. I know this triggers you, but there's nothing you can do. Take some deep breaths."

Liz tuned her out and stared at the TV. The national news cut away to local coverage. The gunman had shot multiple people at a local bar and grill and the police were rushing to the scene. The Maine state police had issued a "shelter in place" warning. Lucy hoped it might deter Liz from getting involved, but then she headed to the door.

"Where are you going?" Lucy demanded.

"To get a drink," muttered Liz on her way out.

"You know that will only make things worse," Lucy called after her.

"How can it get any worse?" Liz called back.

Lucy heard Liz's feet pounding down the stairs. Liz was probably heading for the bottle of whiskey she kept in the kitchen. Lucy hoped she'd think to bring her a glass of wine. She could use a drink too.

***

When the announcement broke into the broadcast, Reshma was listening to the classical station on Maine Public Radio. The NPR announcer's usual monotone voice couldn't hide his alarm when he explained that an armed, active shooter was on the loose in Lewiston.

"Dear God, not again!" whispered Reshma aloud as she plucked out her EarPods. She so seldom watched the tiny TV mounted over the passthrough to the kitchen that she had to search for the remote. Then she needed to refamiliarize herself with the controls to navigate to a local news station. The broadcast opened on a reporter speaking outside a bowling alley. The young man was probably a recent journalism school graduate, who'd come to Maine to get his start in news broadcasting. He desperately tried to focus on the camera, but his eyes kept darting in every direction. Flashing red and blue lights reflecting on his face indicated he was being distracted by passing emergency vehicles.

A chill went through Reshma when he reported that the gunman's location was still unknown, and he could be anywhere. Reshma thought of Susan down the hall. She'd been a hostage in the school shooting. After having a gun pointed at her head and watching Liz Stolz shoot her assailant in the throat, Susan could be triggered by the news.

Reshma turned off the TV, dug her hoodie out of the bedding, and hurried down the hall. She knocked softly at first, knowing that since the episode at the school, Susan was startled by loud noises. When no one came to the door, she knocked again, louder this time. She didn't want to disturb Susan if Bobbie was visiting, but she almost never spent the night in the rectory. While she waited, Reshma looked out the window facing the parking lot. There was no sign of Bobbie's SUV.

Susan's door finally opened. "Reshma? Are you all right?"

"Yes, I'm fine. I came to see how *you* are."

"I'm fine. Why wouldn't I be?" Blinking in the bright light of the hallway, Susan's gray eyes searched hers. Reshma realized that she'd likely been settled into the comfy club chair in the rector's sitting room, reading the latest historical novel. She had no idea what had happened. "You look like you just saw a ghost," Susan said. "What's the matter?"

"Can I come in?" Reshma asked, resorting to formality to cover her confusion and fear.

"Of course, you may." Susan stepped aside, but she stared at Reshma, looking equally curious and apprehensive. "Has something happened?" she asked, closing the door.

"Maybe you should sit down," suggested Reshma.

"Would you like a cup of tea?"

"No, thanks. That's not why I came."

"You can still have a cup of tea."

"Please sit down," said Reshma firmly, trying not to sound impatient.

Susan's eyes were fixed on Reshma's face as she found her way to her chair. On the side table, a large volume lay open, the place marked with a colorful bookmark.

"Now, will you please tell me what's going on?" said Susan, her eyes wide with worry.

Reshma sat down on the hassock in front of the chair and took Susan's hands in hers. She looked into Susan's eyes and spoke to her in the calming voice she used to deliver bad news. "There's been a mass shooting in Lewiston. Several people have been killed and many others injured. The shooter is still at large. The police are searching for him."

Susan's eyes had registered no emotion during Reshma's report. She was eerily calm. Finally, she said, "Lewiston is over an hour away. You don't think he'll come here, do you?"

Reshma allowed her mouth to part in surprise. That was certainly not the response she'd expected.

"Well, we have no way of knowing where the man will go. He

shot people at a bowling alley before moving on to a local pub. The police don't even know who he is yet. They're trying to identify him from some fuzzy security footage."

The sound of a loud ring startled them. "That's probably Bobbie. She'll be worried," said Susan, reaching for her phone. "I'm fine," she said after she swiped open the call. "Don't worry."

Of course, Bobbie would be beside herself. She'd witnessed Susan's sorry state after the Hobbs shooting. Reshma had tried to imagine how Susan felt with the cold steel of a gun barrel against her temple, or when she'd seen her eight-year-old students in caskets. Susan had dutifully taken her turn at the wakes with St. Margaret's clergy, even though Lucy had offered to excuse her.

"Bobbie's coming over to pick me up," Susan explained to Reshma after she ended the call.

"Good. You shouldn't be alone now."

"It's that caregiver instinct, but I am perfectly fine. I don't know why everyone is so worried!" She sounded slightly annoyed, which puzzled Reshma until she realized Susan was in shock.

After a deep breath to consider her words, Reshma said, "We're worried because you experienced a terrible trauma, and not that long ago."

"Yes, but that doesn't mean I'll fall apart every time someone gets shot. We should be focused on the new victims and their families, not me. Everyone's worry is excessive. It's beginning to aggravate me."

"We're worried because we love you."

"I mean no disrespect, Reshma, but please let me handle my own issues in my own way. Helping others is the best way to heal."

Reshma realized that Susan wasn't prattling some pious maxim. Arguing with her could only make things worse. She was glad Bobbie would be there soon. As a nurse, she was experienced in managing difficult situations. Plus, she knew Susan in a way Reshma never could.

"Maybe I'll take you up on that cup of tea. Do you mind if I make a pot while we're waiting?"

"You don't have to ask, Reshma. Please help yourself! I can use one myself but let it steep. In an emergency, my grandmother swore by strong, sweet tea. You might need to refill the sugar bowl, dear."

Reshma went into the kitchen and filled the battered tea kettle with water. She'd seen whistlers for sale in the church thrift shop. Maybe they should splurge and replace the rectory pots and pans with newer models. Although Susan, who saw the old kitchenware as a link to the past, would likely resist the idea. She treasured the old China teapot. The inside was permanently blackened. Reshma had tried to scour out the stains from the teapot she'd found when she moved into her studio. Finally, she realized that she would damage the porcelain if she didn't stop.

Reshma brought the tray out to the sitting room. Susan had turned on the TV to watch the coverage of the shooting.

"Have they caught him yet?" asked Reshma, setting the tea service on the butler's table.

Susan shook her head. "They're taking the dead and wounded out of the bar now. They're still looking for him." Susan switched off the TV. Reshma felt her eyes on her while she poured the tea into the delicate floral cups. She was confident in her technique—at her boarding school, high tea was an excuse to teach the girls social etiquette. A glance at Susan's face told her that the older woman's mind was far away.

"Susan, are you okay?" Reshma asked in a steady voice. In her required first aid class, she'd learned about the potentially devastating effects of shock. Now, she tried to remember what to do about them. Fortunately, Susan returned to the present and smiled.

"Before we have our tea, I would like to pray for the victims and their families."

"That sounds like a perfect idea." Reshma knew a traditionalist like Susan would be comforted by the familiar words more than anything she could say.

They bowed their heads, and Susan recited by heart the prayer in times of tragedy: "O Lord our God, source of all goodness and love, accept the fervent prayers of your people; in the multitude of your mercies look with compassion upon all who turn to you for help; for you are gracious, O lover of souls, and to you we give glory, Father, Son, and Holy Spirit, now and forever."

Susan watched Reshma spoon sugar into a cup. She gathered air with her hand to indicate she should add more. Reshma dumped more sugar into the cup and handed it to Susan, who nodded in satisfaction once she'd taken a sip. "How can we be here again?" she asked with a sigh.

Reshma realized she meant another mass shooting. "According to statistics, there is a mass shooting every day. We just don't hear about them."

Susan shook her head. Reshma couldn't figure out if Susan didn't believe the statistic or was denying it. They drank their tea in silence until there was a knock on the door.

"That will be Bobbie," said Reshma, quickly swallowing what remained in her cup. "I'll clean the pot."

"Don't waste the tea! There's a mason jar in the cabinet over the sink. Put the left over in the fridge." Reshma remembered Susan's tales of her impoverished childhood. Obediently, she poured the remaining tea into the old-fashioned jar. She'd never seen Susan drink iced tea. Maybe she would heat it in the microwave for a quick jolt of caffeine.

She returned to the sitting room to find Bobbie and Susan in a tender embrace. Bobbie was stroking Susan's face and hair. Reshma tried to tiptoe back to the kitchen.

"It's all right, Reshma," Bobbie assured her without letting Susan go.

"Now that you're here, I'll just let myself out," said Reshma, pointing to the door.

"Thanks for looking after Susan," Bobbie called after her.

Although Reshma thought Lucy's order to keep all rectory doors locked was excessive, she checked the hall before leaving Susan's apartment. Hurrying to her studio, she kept looking over her shoulder. Her hands shook as she tried to get the key into the lock. For the first time since she'd moved into the rectory, she felt scared.

Bobbie would take Susan back to her big house with security cameras everywhere. Reshma would then be alone in an old building with its antique and unreliable keyed locks. Lucy had deadbolts installed on all the downstairs doors after someone had broken into Cherie Harrison's office. The police said the proximity to the main road invited break-ins. When the officer began complaining about the undocumented immigrants boarded in local motels, Reshma was incensed. When he noticed Reshma standing there, he instantly dropped the subject.

Reshma put on the worn yoga suit that doubled as pajamas and opened her *Book of Common Prayer*. She quickly navigated to the prayer in time of tragedy that Susan had recited. She remembered the victims who'd been taken to the hospital and recited the prayers for the dying, reading them slowly to linger on the significance of the words. The familiarity of the prayers lulled her into a peaceful state. Then the wail of her cell phone pierced the silence, and her hand flew to her chest.

She smiled at the image of the golden-haired woman looking back at her. "Tiffany? Are you okay?"

"Yes, I'm okay." There was a brief silence. "No, of course I'm not okay. I'm terrified. Aren't you?"

"They still haven't caught him?"

"No, and Lewiston is only an hour away. By now, he could be in Hobbs!"

Reshma weighed the likelihood of such a thing. "Yes, I guess he could be. But why would he come here?"

"Why not? The train station's here and roads to everywhere." Tiffany's perverse logic made a kind of sense. "Can you come over? *Please?*"

Tiffany saw her as a protector, which made her grin. The expectation wasn't unjustified. Reshma was taller and more substantial than Tiffany, who looked like a waif when she wasn't disguised as an angel. Reshma had taken a self-defense class when she was attending classes at Yale's seminary because parts of New Haven were so dangerous. But how could her basic martial arts defend them against a crazy person with a gun?

"I can, I guess, but how will that help?"

"You can keep me talking. Then I don't have to think about how scared I am. Please come. I don't want to be alone."

"All right," said Reshma with a long sigh, trying to sound reluctant. In fact, she was secretly delighted by the invitation. "I'll be there in a few minutes."

***

Liz knew Lucy meant well. Anticipating the shooting could trigger her PTSD was perfectly logical, but her wife was trying to use therapy skills on her, which annoyed Liz to no end. Usually, Liz played along, knowing it was how Lucy showed love, but this was not a game. In Lewiston, innocent people had been shot to death and others had been seriously wounded. Liz knew from covering in the ED in New Haven that more would likely die, despite the ED's best effort. The reporter had noted that Maine Med was dealing with more trauma victims in one night than it usually saw in a year. Shots of the emergency entrance showed every light ablaze. Liz itched to go up there to offer her help, but she knew Lucy wouldn't let her out of her sight, and if Brenda caught her, there would be hell to pay.

Although Liz hated the television news, especially the cable networks, for their repetitive and obsessive coverage of the latest headlines, her eyes were riveted to the TV screen. She wondered if this was what viewers were doing while she was trapped in the principal's office with Susan and Peter Langdon. Had they watched with their mouths slightly ajar while an unthinkable tragedy was unfolding right before their eyes? Like the Lewiston shooting, this was too close to home. Mass shootings were tragedies that happened in other places, not in friendly, quiet Hobbs. Until now, the massacre at Hobbs Elementary had been Maine's largest mass shooting with ten dead. The carnage in Lewiston had already eclipsed that sad statistic, and the fate of the wounded was still unknown.

The state police had enhanced the security footage of the shooter and had identified him as ex-military. Maine was full of retired military personnel, so that was no surprise. Vets owned a disproportionate number of Maine's guns. Liz saw them at the range testing the latest models of assault weapons. Most hunted deer and turkey, like many Mainers, but the ex-military and police seemed obsessed with tactical weapons. When she'd brought that up in the fish and game club board meetings, they'd dismissed her concerns. The thinking was, better the nuts get their dose of gun porn on a shooting range. With a presidential election coming up, more members were showing their political stripes and were clearly taking sides.

Lucy was holding Liz's hand so tightly it was getting numb. "Really, Lucy. I'm okay," Liz said, disengaging from her grip. She flexed her fingers a few times to encourage the circulation.

"Well, I'm not okay," said Lucy with a little pout. "I'm terrified."

Liz put her arm around her and pulled her closer. "Sweetheart, there's nothing to be afraid of. The perimeter of the property has sensors. The house is alarmed. We have security cameras everywhere. I hate to say it, but this house is better protected than Hobbs Elementary was the day Peter Langdon showed up."

Lucy's face showed she was processing the information. Then she looked sad. "If Sam had only locked that door..."

"The lock could be opened with a credit card. I can't believe the school board didn't fix it when they could." Liz knew why. By focusing on reinforcing the front entrance, they could point to a visible improvement. Meanwhile, the town had been lulled into a false sense of security. How easy it was to look back at mistakes and realize what should have been done differently. She wondered which warning signs people in Lewiston had ignored—obvious things that could have prevented the deaths of innocent people.

The news was now reporting that police had surrounded a private home under the assumption that the suspect could be inside. The reporter's position down the road gave a view of the flashing lights of the police cars but no more. The police had pushed back the reporters to protect them in case the shooter opened fire.

"At least, they think he's still up there and not here," said Lucy, snuggling deeper into Liz's body. Liz kissed the top of her head.

"Don't worry, Lucy."

"I'm not worried for us. Look at all those people. They're terrified. You remember how it was for Hobbs."

Liz felt a vibration in her pocket. "That's probably Brenda with an update," said Liz, digging into her pants for her phone. But it wasn't Brenda. It was Maggie. Liz gently nudged Lucy to move so she could sit up.

"Hey, Maggie," said Liz. "Are you okay?"

"No," replied the distraught voice. "Who can be okay with this happening...AGAIN!"

"Are you home?"

"I'm driving down from Biddeford. I had class tonight. One of the students interrupted to tell us the news. We ended early because of the shooting."

"That's probably a good idea."

"Liz, I'm scared to go home. Sam's house is in the middle of nowhere. It's a perfect place for the shooter to hide."

"Sam has a state-of-the-art security system over there."

"But I still have to get from my car into the house when I get there." Liz glanced at Lucy because she knew what was coming next. "Can I stay with you until they catch him?"

"Hold on a minute," Liz said and muted the phone. "Maggie

wants to come over," she explained. "She's afraid to go back to Sam's house."

To Liz's surprise, Lucy didn't roll her eyes. She nodded thoughtfully. "Well, it's so isolated out there on Jimson Pond. I can understand why she doesn't want to be alone."

"Sam has that whole place alarmed. There are security cameras everywhere."

"Liz, when someone's breaking into your house and you're all alone, what good are security cameras?"

She could call the police, Liz thought, before calculating that it would take at least twenty minutes for a squad car to get to Sam's house. A lot could happen in that time. She unmuted the phone. "Sure, Maggie, you can come here. You can stay in the downstairs guest room. Call me when you're five minutes out, and I'll open the door for you."

"Thank you! Thank you!" Maggie said dramatically. "You have no idea how scared I am."

Lucy patted Liz's arm and nodded her approval. "Drive carefully," said Liz. "How long before you get here?"

"Twenty minutes, if not sooner."

"Don't rush," Liz cautioned. "The police will be watching for speeders, thinking any one of them could be their guy. And don't hurry on our account. We'll be awake. No one's going to sleep with this drama going on."

Maggie promised to drive carefully, and Liz hung up. She turned up the TV volume and slouched into the sofa.

"I hope she calls Sam to let her know what's going on," Lucy said.

"If she doesn't, I'll call her. Maggie's got enough going on just to get here in one piece." Liz noticed Lucy was frowning. "What's the matter? You think Sam will be upset to know Maggie's coming over?"

"It is somewhat unusual to run to your ex-wife when you're

frightened." Lucy sat up to scrutinize Liz's face. "And here I was worried about how you would react to the shooting. You're so busy protecting other people you don't have time."

Liz grinned ironically. "Don't tell, but that's my secret. I take care of other people, so I don't worry about myself."

"I knew that, but you better watch out," said Lucy philosophically. "One day it will catch up with you."

"Oh, I think it has. Isn't that why you had my guns taken away?" said Liz, getting up. "I'm going downstairs to make sure there are enough towels in the guest bathroom. I don't want to be hanging around down there when Maggie comes. You know her. Any excuse for a long conversation."

"She's lonely with Sam away," said Lucy. Liz was surprised to hear her defend Maggie, but Lucy was compassionate by nature. "And Sam doesn't talk much."

"Then she should have chosen a partner who does."

"Careful, Liz. The same could be said about you." Lucy smiled to lessen the sting and blew her a kiss. "I love you just the way you are."

"Thanks. Glad someone does." Liz scooped up their glasses. "More wine?" she asked. Liz groaned a little as she got to her feet. Kneeling to do fall garden cleanup hadn't helped her knees.

"If you're buying, sure." Lucy's attempt at a smile fell short. Liz certainly understood.

In the first-floor guestroom, Liz turned down the bed and checked the bathroom cabinet for towels. She rooted through the box of guest supplies, mostly collected from hotels while Lucy traveled. She found a new toothbrush and travel size toothpaste and set them next to the sink. Maggie had used the guest suite before and knew where to find a T-shirt to wear to bed. Satisfied that everything was ready for their unexpected guest, Liz went into the kitchen to replenish their glasses.

"Thanks," Lucy said idly when Liz handed her the wine. Her eyes were trained on the TV.

"What did I miss?" asked Liz, collapsing into the spot beside her.

"The police have no idea where the shooter is. It doesn't look like they found the guy in the house they surrounded."

Liz's phone began to vibrate in her pocket. She pulled it out and saw it was Sam calling. "Hey, Sam. You heard." She got up and went into the hall to avoid distracting Lucy.

"What the fuck is going on over there?" Sam asked.

"Which part?" Liz said, grinning, although this was no time to be a smart ass. "Did Maggie tell you she's on her way over here?"

"Yes, and thanks for looking out for her," said Sam, which came as a relief to Liz. Being an ex could be a minefield, especially when friends were involved. "She's always been afraid to be out there alone," Sam added. "I keep telling her the entire place is alarmed. If anyone tries to break in, the system calls the police."

"Well, I can understand. Your house is in the middle of nowhere. It would be spooky for anyone to be out there alone. She can stay here until they catch the guy."

"I can't believe they haven't caught him yet. On TV, it looks like they have every cop in Maine looking for him."

"Not Brenda. She's staying here and has me under house arrest."

On the other end, Sam chuckled. She understood what passed as Liz's humor. "She knows you, Liz. You hear a siren and can't stay away."

"Bad habit from the old days."

"How are you doing?" Sam asked, her tone turning serious.

Liz looked through the door toward the sofa, where her wife pretended she wasn't listening. Liz lowered her voice slightly. "Lucy's stuck to me like glue because she thinks this shooting will trigger me."

"Did it?"

"It's fucking upsetting," Liz admitted. "Can't even get through the year without another mass shooting."

"I know what you mean. Brings back the wrong kind of memories." There was a long pause on the other end. "What the fuck is wrong with people?" asked Sam in disgust.

"I don't know. Just when I think things couldn't get crazier, I remember all those assassinations when I was a kid—JFK, Martin Luther King, Bobby Kennedy. There were riots. Cities being burned. Bombings and kidnappings. It's always been crazy, not just now."

"But now people have more guns," said Sam gloomily. "But I'm glad you got your guns back. Just in case…"

"Me too. I just hope I don't need to use them."

"Amen," Lucy chimed in. So, she had been listening…to every word.

***

Tiffany was so relieved to see Reshma she grabbed her bag and yanked her into the loft. Once she was safely inside, Tiffany locked all three deadbolts.

"Well, that should keep him out," said Reshma with exaggerated gravity.

"You don't really think the killer would come here?"

"I don't know," Reshma teased with a perfectly straight face. "All those pretty pastries in the window might make him hungry enough to break in."

"Reshma, that's not funny. It wouldn't be the first time a pâtisserie was robbed because the offerings looked too inviting."

"Maybe in Boston or Manhattan, but here in Hobbs with a population of what, eleven thousand max? I don't think so. Besides, the killer has other things on his mind than your chocolate eclairs."

Reshma dropped her duffle bag and opened her arms. Tiffany fell into them and clung to her with all her might. "Thank you s-o-o much for coming."

"Honestly, I'm glad you invited me. That old rectory is spooky enough without a killer on the loose." She heaved out an enormous sigh and attempted a smile. *God, she's beautiful,* thought Tiffany.

She wondered if Reshma was even aware of how stunning she was. She wasn't the least bit conceited. "I'm counting on you to protect me!" Reshma declared.

"You can't be serious," said Tiffany.

"No, of course not." Reshma straightened to her full height and flexed her shoulders. "I'm bigger than you, so I guess it will be my job."

"Are you into role play, Reshma?" asked Tiffany, stroking her arm. The muscles were toned and felt powerful. The prospect of strong, aggressive sex made Tiffany tingle. She liked when women took the lead and handled her assertively. Brianna always gave Tiffany what she liked, but to her ex being butch also meant being bossy and directive. Tiffany thought it was part of the package. She tolerated it until things got too rough.

"Role play?" asked Reshma, tapping her chin with her fingertip, as if she didn't know what Tiffany was suggesting. "You mean like butch and femme?"

"Exactly!" Tiffany replied enthusiastically.

Reshma eyed her, weighing her response. "Maybe. What about you?"

"Depends. If it means being protective, I could really go for that right now. I'm terrified."

"I hear you," Reshma said. "I guess we'll have to protect one another."

"Guess so," Tiffany agreed, tugging on the arm of Reshma's coat. "If you're staying, you need to take this off."

Reshma pushed her bag further into the room with her foot and slipped off her coat. Tiffany gasped. She hadn't been prepared for the sight of Reshma in a snug fleece top that emphasized her high, firm breasts, bigger than Tiffany had suspected. When Reshma was in uniform, they were usually hidden under a loose clerical shirt, layered under another top. Of course, when you call at ten-thirty at night to ask someone to come over because you're scared, you can't expect her to arrive dressed for work.

But Reshma's snug top wasn't the only surprise. Her clingy, hot-pink yoga pants revealed the outlines of the gentle folds where her lithe body met long, shapely legs that seemed to go on forever. Tiffany caught a quick glance at the spot but dared not allow her eyes to linger. The glimpse was enough to turn the spark she'd felt earlier into an inferno of desire. She focused on Reshma's anxious face so her eyes wouldn't reveal everything she was thinking. Then she ruined it by blurting out: "I love your outfit," she said, unable to avoid glancing at Reshma's breasts. "It's so you!"

"I hung some clothes in the car for tomorrow. Just in case." Reshma's generous lips twitched into an anxious smile. "That's okay, I hope."

"Yes, I want you to stay."

"But If they catch the shooter, I can go home," said Reshma, apparently trying to leave herself an out.

"Do you want to go home?" asking Tiffany, appreciatively running her hand up Reshma's arm. Oh, those muscles in her arms were delicious. When did she have time to work out?

Reshma shook her head. "No, Susan left to be with her friend. I swear that old rectory is haunted. All those dead priests hanging around to make sure the living behave."

"Ooh, I love haunted houses!" declared Tiffany. "Come in and tell me about it." She led Reshma into the sitting room, where she'd made up the sofa bed and piled it high with fluffy pillows and comforters. She watched carefully while Reshma evaluated the arrangement.

"Thank you for not assuming we'd sleep together," Reshma finally said.

"I wanted to give you options."

"I appreciate it," said Reshma, "but don't think I'm not interested." The quiet admission made Tiffany's heart flutter with anticipation, but Reshma quickly added, "Call me old fashioned, but I think we need to spend more time together before we make love."

The flutters instantly stopped. At least, Reshma had admitted they were heading to bed, maybe even sometime soon.

"Does cuddling on a scary night count as getting to know one another?"

"Probably counts more than fancy dinners with your chef friends, rushed lunches, or flirting over the pastry counter."

Tiffany gestured to the loveseat across from the sofa bed. "Sorry. There aren't many places to sit. That's the problem with a loft."

"I love your place," said Reshma, looking around. Tiffany wondered what she thought of the wall art, mostly minimalist ocean scenes. In the kitchen were classic food posters, including one that rated chili peppers by heat. "I'd love to have this much space."

"Maybe some time you'll show me your studio."

"Maybe," Reshma said without enthusiasm.

"Should we put on the TV and see what's going on?" said Tiffany, reaching for the remote. "What news do you usually watch?" she asked, trying to be polite.

"None. I usually get my news online," said Reshma. "I almost never watch TV."

"Neither do I," Tiffany said, although she often had it on for background noise while she cooked or baked. Avoiding TV was a sign of intelligence in certain circles. Tiffany didn't want Reshma to think she was one of the dummies.

Tiffany clicked through the local channels. Every station was covering the shooting nonstop, so she stopped at the third channel and settled next to Reshma. The programming switched from the Portland studio to a boat launch on the Androscoggin River where the shooter's car had been found. It cut away to a reporter announcing that hundreds of law enforcement officers from all over New England had converged on Maine to search for the perpetrator.

"I wonder where he's hiding," said Reshma, moving her trim rear closer to the other side of the loveseat. Tiffany instantly missed the radiant warmth of Reshma's thigh pressed against hers, but she stared ahead and pretended she hadn't noticed a change.

The reporter began explaining that the area surrounding Lewiston was densely forested. The gunman, now identified as an Army reservist, was well-trained in survival skills and knew the woods from hiking and hunting. Police feared the search could go on for days and advised everyone to stay at home until he was caught.

"We're just recovering from the pandemic, and now we need to keep our businesses shuttered? When I close my shop, even for one day, I lose money. Right now, people are up here sightseeing and getting ready for hunting season. I need to make money while I can. Winter is rough for small businesses."

"I bet." Reshma gave her hand an encouraging squeeze. "They'll find him," she said confidently.

"I could use a glass of wine to calm me down," said Tiffany, mentally tasting the expensive Cabernet she'd opened earlier. "How about you?"

"Thanks, but I want to stay alert...in case I'm needed."

"What do you mean?"

"I have pastoral care duty this week."

"Even when there's a shelter-in-place order?"

"The sick and dying need prayers no matter what else is going on."

"I really hope you don't have to go out," said Tiffany, reaching for her hand.

"Me too."

Tiffany knew it was part of Reshma's job. She admired her sense of duty, but she really wanted a drink to calm her nerves. She managed to keep her thirst at bay until the thought of the open Cabernet bottle on the counter became so tantalizing that she could no longer resist. She got up to pour herself a glass. "Sure you don't want any? This Cab is excellent."

"Thanks, I'm good," Reshma murmured, her eyes riveted to the screen. She suddenly sat forward.

"What's happening?" Tiffany asked.

"They discovered his boat was missing from the launch. They're going to dredge the river."

"That could take days!" Tiffany returned to her seat. She savored a sip of the wine, noting hints of pepper over a rich cherry base. "You're missing something special, Reshma. Here, have a sip." She offered her the glass and watched Reshma's face as she tasted it. Her eyes closed in pleasure.

"Ooh, that's good."

"Pricey, of course. Dad liked it, so he sent me a case."

"Good. Then I can have a glass next time I'm here."

Tiffany liked the idea that there would be a next time. "I just can't believe we're sitting here watching a manhunt for a killer."

"Well, we don't have to spend the whole time waiting for nothing to happen. We could turn off the TV and talk. I can set my phone to ping me with news alerts."

"Sounds like a plan," said Tiffany, switching off the TV. "You're so smart." Reshma smiled modestly. "You want some sparkling water? How about some cookies?"

"You don't have to feed me. I ate dinner. But I would never turn down your cookies."

Tiffany jumped up to fill a plate with almond cookies she'd baked that afternoon. She poured a glass of milk to go with it.

"I'm surprised you and your chef friends stay so slim with all the delicious food you make," said Reshma, biting into one of the soft, fragrant confections. "How do you do it?"

"Oh, that's easy. If you eat truly good food, a small portion is satisfying, so you don't need much."

"I think if I regularly ate with you and your friends, I'd want to gorge. Everything you cook is amazing." Tiffany felt her face warm and guessed it was bright red. "You don't have to be modest when it's true," said Reshma, helping herself to another cookie. "Take the compliment. I meant it."

"What I find amazing is your kindness. You always tell the truth, but it's never mean or hurtful."

"I try, but sometimes, I'm so angry I can't help myself. The senseless killing of all those innocent people infuriates me. If there weren't so many guns out there..." Reshma took a deep breath and exhaled it slowly. "We need to stay calm. How about some music? I was listening to a classical music broadcast before the bad news. Do you mind if I stream it to your speaker?"

Tiffany controlled her face. Even though her father was a classical music impresario, she wasn't a fan, but unlike most of her friends, she didn't hate it. And if Reshma liked classical music, she'd listen to it. "Sure," said Tiffany, trying to sound enthusiastic. "But now that you're finished eating your cookies and won't leave crumbs, we could sit on the sofa under the covers." Reshma stared at the mountain of quilts and pillows on the sofa with a mixture of skepticism and dread. "To keep us warm," Tiffany added as a selling point. "You said cuddling is okay."

"I did." Reshma slipped off her shoes. They relocated to the sofa and covered themselves with the comforter.

"Cozy. Don't you think?" asked Tiffany. "When I was a kid, I used to pile up all the pillows and comforters and pretend I was in a castle."

"And you were the little princess," Reshma guessed.

"Of course! Didn't you want to be a princess when you were growing up?" Tiffany realized she'd said something wrong when Reshma began scrolling through her phone for an app. "I'll turn on some music." She connected to the remote speaker, but the public radio station, like all the TV channels, was reporting on the shooting. Reshma looked frustrated. "Can't get away from it. Never mind. I can play the album of religious music that Lucy recorded. It's soothing. Okay?"

Tiffany shrugged. She didn't know what to expect, but Reshma fiddled with her phone for a few seconds and a beautiful soprano voice began singing a familiar tune. "That's "Jesu, Joy of Man's Desiring," Tiffany said, delighted to have recognized it.

Reshma nodded in approval. "Bach is always good in times of stress. His music is so structured and orderly. It measurably lowers stress."

Tiffany closed her eyes and listened. Reshma was right. The music was calming. "Is that really *our* Lucy Bartlett?"

Reshma grinned proudly. "Yes, *our* Lucy Bartlett!"

"Wow! She's fantastic!"

"You don't get to sing at the Met unless you're the best." Reshma moved a little closer. "Is this okay?"

"You bet! And it would be even more okay if you put your arm around me."

Reshma draped her long arm around Tiffany's shoulder. "This feels good. We should do it more often."

Tiffany moved closer. Her palm rested on Reshma's thigh. Beneath the silky fabric of her yoga pants, the warm flesh felt so alive. Reshma's quick look warned her away from roaming too far. Under the quilt, a long fingered, delicate hand took hers. Tiffany was afraid to meet Reshma's eyes, but when she did she met the gentlest, most loving look she could imagine.

"I'm not ready yet," Reshma whispered.

"I'm sorry."

"Don't be. I love being here, so close to you. Let's listen to the music."

"Okay," said Tiffany.

Although a terrible event had brought them together, sitting there, snuggling with Reshma felt just right.

Chapter 8

Since Emily had moved into the garage apartment, Lucy had gotten used to complete privacy. Liz's family came to Maine less often now that her niece's kids were older, so except for a few weeks in the summer, they were completely alone. Most mornings, Lucy came down to the kitchen for her first cup of coffee in nothing but her sheer nightgown. In the summertime, often nothing at all. Lucy doubted Maggie would appreciate a glimpse of her red pubic hair or her barely concealed naked body, so she headed to the bathroom to shower.

It felt so strange to have Liz's ex-wife sleeping under the same roof with them. Lucy had only slept in the first-floor bedroom once. Feeling sorry for herself because Erika hadn't been answering her emails, she had drunk too much wine at dinner. Liz forbade her to drive and had offered to drive her home. Maggie nixed the idea because if anyone caught them, it would reflect badly on the new rector. Ironically, it had been Maggie who'd invited her to spend the night.

Lucy had awakened in the cozy guest room. In an orgy of self-recrimination over finding herself there, she imagined Liz and Maggie in bed upstairs. She usually avoided thinking about other people's sex lives, but her response to Erika's interest had reminded her that she was still a sexual being. But here she was in another state, a first-time rector with a falling down church, and a declining congregation. After Liz had appeared at the carols and lessons service with her entourage, Maggie had become Lucy's best friend. During those winter months, Erika had only replied to one of Lucy's chatty emails. Meanwhile, Maggie offered her companionship, and Liz always set another plate at the table. Now the situation was reversed.

Lucy felt a pang of sympathy for Maggie, who openly admitted her loneliness since Sam had begun traveling so much for her architectural projects. All the warning signs had been there before they'd gotten involved. Sam was painfully shy and inarticulate about her feelings, whereas Maggie talked nonstop. In the beginning of a relationship, a taciturn partner can be drawn out by a loquacious one, but eventually the chatty one runs out of stories to tell. Lucy knew how to pry things out of Liz, something Maggie had never learned how to do. Maggie always needed an audience. Lucy had also spent much of her life on the stage, but as a therapist and a priest, she'd been forced to learn how to listen.

Why, Lucy had once asked Liz, had she succeeded in getting her to talk about her feelings where others usually failed? "Because I trust you," Liz replied bluntly. Realizing the implications for Liz's broken relationship with Maggie, Lucy felt genuinely sad on her behalf.

When Lucy turned off the shower, she could hear hangers slinging across the rod in the closet on the other side of the wall—Liz choosing clothes for the day.

"I guess you don't want to face Maggie undressed either," she observed as Liz came into the bathroom.

"No. It's strange how the rules change when you're not in a relationship anymore. When Maggie and I were married, I never thought twice about being naked in front of her." Liz turned on the hot water and stepped in. "Do you feel uncomfortable having her here?" Liz called through the cloud of steam.

Lucy moved closer to the door. The shower was huge, and it was sometimes hard to hear over the sound of the water. "I'm trying to figure out how I'm feeling. I'm not angry that you invited her."

"She invited herself," Liz reminded her. "With a killer on the loose, I didn't think I had any choice."

"We always have a choice, Liz, but you made the right one."

"According to the news, they haven't caught the guy yet. There's still a shelter in place advisory."

"Are you going to close the practice?"

"No, but we'll only have essential staff. I called around to see who's willing to come in. We have enough people to manage. What about the church?"

"I closed the office today, but I have clients and lots of calls for appointments. Some I can do online. Others insist on coming in."

"What a fucking mess," said Liz, shutting off the water. "Are you going to sing this morning?"

"I'll sing my exercises. Otherwise, I'll feel my mother's ghost breathing down my neck."

"Dead ancestors are very effective at keeping us in line," said Liz, kissing Lucy before she grabbed her towel from the hook. "We should try to get downstairs before Maggie wakes up. Once she gets your ear, you won't have time to practice."

"Okay, but first, I need a cup of coffee."

Delicious aromas greeted them as they descended the stairs. The kitchen was brightly lit. Huddled over a coffee cup, Maggie sat at the island.

"Good morning," she announced brightly. "I hope you don't mind, but I thought I'd make myself useful by making a breakfast casserole."

Liz glanced at the mixing bowl by the sink. "I see you found everything, despite your complaints about my kitchen organization."

"I think I've finally figured it out," replied Maggie mildly.

"I don't know why it was such a big deal. My method is simple. Like in surgery, things you use most should be closer to where you work than those used less often." Liz took two cups down from the cabinet and handed one to Lucy. "My mother used to say two women can't live in the same house, which made no sense to me because she'd had her mother living with her for a decade before she died. But my grandmother quickly learned to be the sous chef."

"I think that's a generational thing," Maggie said. "I always thought we cooked together well."

"We did," Liz reluctantly agreed. "But I didn't find your kitchen organization efficient. That's why I changed it."

"Efficiency is in the mind of the beholder," Maggie parried.

Lucy knew this bickering would go on unless she said something. "Okay, ladies, we're in a tough situation. Let's try to make the best of it." Maggie's cold stare was a practiced theater gesture, but Lucy smiled in return. Maggie's gaze warmed considerably. "Thank you for making breakfast, Maggie," Lucy added. "I'm sure it will be delicious."

Liz thrust her cup under the single-serve coffee maker. "Lucy doesn't usually eat before her singing exercises. Will your breakfast keep for a while?"

Maggie glanced at the clock. "It's in the oven for another forty-five minutes. Will that be enough time?"

"That's fine," Lucy said quickly.

Maggie gestured with a wag of her head toward the door. "Go on with your practice. I'll keep Liz company."

Lucy looked at Liz, wondering if it was safe to leave them alone. She understood their resentment after the divorce. They each accused the other of cheating. The impulsive kiss on the boat had been a mistake, but Maggie had slept with a young actor out of spite. If they were still so angry, why did they seek out each other's company? And why was Liz so gruff with Maggie, when she still obviously cared about her. It seemed she kept Maggie at arm's length to protect herself, but from what? Her anger or her affection?

"I won't be long," Lucy said. "Just the basics this morning." She gave Liz a penetrating look. "Try to behave. Remember. Maggie is our guest."

Liz rolled her eyes. Maggie smiled triumphantly. *Oh, God,* thought Lucy, *now she thinks I'm on her side.* This was their problem, she decided, and headed to the media room.

***

Tiffany watched Reshma pick at the chocolate croissant on her plate. She'd never known Reshma to be fussy where her baking was concerned. The croissant was two days old because items didn't move as quickly in the off-season. Tiffany had removed it from the display case in the shop, but it was still perfectly fine to eat. "Don't you like it?" asked Tiffany, her fingers walking across the tabletop before taking Reshma's hand. "I can get you a fresher one downstairs."

"No, this one's fine." Reshma ripped off a corner and popped it into her mouth to prove it, but she made no move to take more.

"Reshma, what's wrong?"

"You're disappointed," she murmured, staring at the half-eaten croissant.

"Kind of, but we agreed the night of a mass shooting wasn't the time to make love."

"But I think you expected me to change my mind." Reshma's dark eyes finally focused on hers.

"Well, yeah. I kind of hoped you would."

"Our generation is so big on consent," said Reshma. "Sometimes, I wonder if we're killing all the spontaneity and passion."

"You think?" Tiffany's smart-ass remark didn't land as she'd hoped. She wanted Reshma to laugh, or at least, smile. Now she looked even more miserable. But she hadn't done anything wrong. She'd merely set a boundary, and Tiffany could respect that.

"It's okay, Reshma. Yes, part of me was hoping you'd ravish me like in those steamy romances."

"You did not!" Reshma's large eyes grew even bigger. "Not really?"

"Sure I did." A smile now would seem coy, so Tiffany struggled to keep a straight face.

Reshma leaned forward and peered at her. "What if I said I expected you to seduce me?"

"I tried, but the minute I put my hand on you, you chased it away." The memory of Reshma's warm thigh under her palm caused a definite tingling between Tiffany's legs.

"I'm sorry, Tiff. When we make love the first time, I want it to be special, without excuses or distractions."

"That's very romantic."

"Better than ripping your clothes off?"

"I don't know," said Tiffany, mocking intense consideration. "I'd probably like that."

Reshma huffed out a sigh and made another run at defending herself. "A lot of people our age seem to think sex doesn't matter. That it's just something you do for fun."

"Sex shouldn't be fun?"

"Yes, of course, it should be fun," said Reshma, looking frustrated. "But it should be more, don't you agree?"

"Actually, I do. The reason I hang around with you is you take me seriously."

"I do. Because I...I...like you a lot!"

Tiffany studied Reshma's face. "Reshma, you're blushing."

"You can't see me blush!"

"No, but I can tell you're blushing now." She leaned closer until their faces were almost touching. "I can feel the heat, even if I can't see it." Reshma blinked, then closed her eyes. Tiffany gently pressed her lips against Reshma's. They tasted of coffee and chocolate. "You're delicious. I think I'll eat you all up!" She drew back slightly, and Reshma finally opened her eyes. Tiffany sat back in her chair. "You're not afraid, are you? You've been with a woman before, right?"

Reshma stared at the tabletop, then gazed at her from under her eyebrows. "Depends on your definition of woman."

"What do you mean?" Tiffany chewed on her lip, while she puzzled over her own question. When the answer popped into her mind, she felt stupid for not thinking of it right away. "Reshma, you don't mean a trans woman, do you?"

Reshma ripped another piece off the croissant and stuffed it into her mouth. Tiffany doubted she'd suddenly found an appetite.

More likely she'd rather chew a slightly stale croissant than answer the question.

"When did that happen?" Tiffany asked, trying not to sound accusatory. Here she thought Reshma was so sweet and innocent. She'd slept with a trans woman!

"Remember Denise Chantal, the singer at Mother Lucy's wedding?"

"The very tall woman." Tiffany had known tall women, but this singer's height was extraordinary, along with the size of her hands and feet. Tiffany had wondered about her when she'd first met her. Now, it all made sense.

"She used to be a countertenor," Reshma explained. "Before she transitioned, she sang as Dennis Chantal. She was out of work during the pandemic, and Mother Lucy hired her as the music director. Even though she wasn't clergy, she let her live in a studio in the rectory. We both liked the same music, and we'd stream concerts on the internet. Her salary was low too, so we shared meals to save on groceries. One night..." Reshma paused. She glanced at Tiffany, as if looking for permission to continue.

Tiffany stiffened her face to avoid showing how surprised she was. "Wow, that's not something I would have expected of you, Reshma."

"Me neither," Reshma muttered into her coffee. "But it happened. She said she'd broken up with Lucy's daughter, and it was over, but now, they're back together."

"You were the rebound fuck."

Reshma visibly squirmed. "I guess so. I think I took the relationship more seriously than she did."

"Of course, you did." Tiffany repositioned her backside on the stool. She'd been sitting motionless for so long that one cheek was getting numb. "Reshma John, you never cease to amaze me." She picked up the section of croissant Reshma had abandoned and began to nibble on it. "What was it like?"

"What was what like?"

"Sex with a trans woman. Did she still have a dick?"

Reshma glared at her. "I don't talk about the people I sleep with!"

"Don't get all excited, Reshma. I'm just curious. I never met anyone who'd slept with a trans woman. I read a lot of them never get bottom surgery."

"Yes, she had bottom surgery," said Reshma in an irritated tone, "not that it's anyone's business!"

"That's good, I guess. I don't know how I'd like sleeping with a woman with a penis."

"Yes, I find that hard to imagine," said Reshma, frowning.

"Have you ever slept with a man?"

"No."

"So how would you know?"

"I guess I wouldn't."

"Oh, come on, Reshma! Now, you have to tell me," said Tiffany, tugging on Reshma's arm.

"No, I don't. And don't get all weird on me. She looked like a woman...down there. That's all I'll say about it." Reshma folded her arms on her chest. It was obvious that pushing harder wouldn't make her tell.

"Okay...for now."

"Tiffany!"

"Reshma, I don't really care about that trans woman. But I do care about us, and I want us to be honest with one another."

"There's no 'us' yet," said Reshma.

"But don't you agree it's important to be honest?"

"Yes, but...not when it involves the privacy others. As a priest, I'm bound by confidentiality."

"You didn't fuck her as a priest."

"Actually, I was only a deacon, but that doesn't matter. It's still no one's business. And it was more than a fuck." Tiffany drew back and stared at Reshma in mock horror. "Close your mouth, Tiffany. I use the F-bomb too."

"Well, you're not wearing your collar."

"What I wear has nothing to do with it," said Reshma sharply. "I say it with my collar on too!"

"I bet you do." Tiffany hadn't seen this defiant, spunky side of Reshma's personality before, but she liked it. She preferred people with edges. She reached across the table to shake Reshma's hand. "Here's to telling it like it is."

"Where did you pick up that old-fashioned phrase?"

"My parents. They say it all the time. Born too late and too old money to be hippies, but they're social justice warriors, always protesting this or that. They weren't going to have kids because of climate change, but when Mom was in her forties, she suddenly decided she wanted a child and became Super-Mom. You know the type. Helicopter parent doesn't even begin to describe her. You'll get to meet her at Thanksgiving."

Reshma's face tightened. "You're inviting me for Thanksgiving? Not sure I'm ready for that."

"Why not? You want to know where I came from, don't you?"

"Well, yes, but..."

"But what? Meeting my parents doesn't mean we're getting married. You'll like them. Mom is super smart. Dad knows a lot about music. They're actually good company when they're not plotting my success."

Reshma didn't look reassured by the explanation. "Let me think about it," she said slowly. "I have a standing invitation at Bobbie's, where Teresa does an African-inspired Thanksgiving. And Mother Lucy always invites me for holidays."

"Don't think too long. It's only a couple of weeks away. Before you know it, it will be Christmas."

"Don't remind me. Mother Lucy said she has big plans for me for Advent."

"And what does that entail?"

"She expects me to come up with ideas for special services. Because of my age, I'm supposed to have special insights into what younger people want."

"Do you?"

"No, and liturgical innovation isn't exactly my specialty. I'm doing research."

Tiffany poured Reshma another cup of coffee from the French press. "You'll figure it out. I believe in you."

That seemed to make Reshma happy. "Thanks." She glanced down at her plate. "Tiffany, you ate all of my croissant!" she said with an accusing stare.

"I'll give you a bag to take back with you. Fresh ones from the case downstairs."

Reshma glanced at her watch. "I should be getting home."

Tiffany allowed her lower lip to protrude in a mock sulk.

"Stop it," Reshma ordered. "I have a job to do."

"Okay, but I'm walking you down to your car to get your clothes."

Reshma rolled her eyes, but there was no way Tiffany was letting her go outside alone with that killer on the loose. She had no idea what she'd do if they ran into him, but at least they'd be together.

***

Teresa always had a tune in her voice—whether it was the music of her native tongue that added a lilt to her marginally British accent, or the rounds sung by the native women in the tribal lands of South Sudan. This morning, as she filled her teacup with hot water in the staff break room, she softly sang an African chant.

It seemed odd to Liz that someone would be singing after a mass shooting, but Teresa was always cheerful no matter what insanity a day at the practice brought. "That song sounds so happy," said Liz, taking a coffee cup down from the cabinet.

"Yes, it does, doesn't it? But it's a prayer."

"Really?" asked Liz, filling a pod with coffee. "What do the words mean?"

"It is a call to our maternal ancestors to keep us safe through the night. I always think of my grandmother when I sing it. She taught it to me." Teresa moved away from the coffee maker to give Liz access.

"We can use all the help we can get with this crazy man on the loose," said Liz, vigorously pressing the button on the coffee maker. Repetitive use had made the controls less responsive. "Scary to think he could be anywhere, even here in Hobbs."

"Yes, only a few months ago we were burying our own children. This new shooting will be difficult for our people."

Liz discreetly squeezed her fist to hide her anger. She couldn't allow herself to get upset before seeing patients. She'd given up hope for gun reform since Congress had refused to impose stricter regulations after the Sandy Hook school shooting. If the senseless massacre of young children couldn't bend political will, nothing could. "You left Sudan to escape violence. Now, you find it here in America," Liz said in a discouraged tone.

"Violence is everywhere, Dr. Liz," Teresa reminded her gently.

"And now in your homeland. Again. Sudan is a horror show. Homes and critical infrastructure destroyed. People starving. Women and girls raped."

This litany of tragedies did nothing to change Teresa's pleasant expression. "We are so blessed to be in America, where my daughter can be a child, not fearing rape at any moment. She can learn in a real school. I am grateful to be here working for you, going to school, so that I can be a nurse again. These blessings bring so much joy!" Teresa's optimism cheered Liz. She'd been in a dark mood since last night. Lucy couldn't drag her out of it, no matter what she tried, maybe because she was disheartened herself.

"And we are happy to have you, Teresa, queen of the blood draws. No one sticks a vein better than you do, not even me." It was a white lie. Liz was proud of her ability to find even the shyest vein. Teresa beamed at the compliment. Liz reminded herself to smile back. Lucy had been encouraging her to unlearn the flat affect trained into surgeons of a certain generation.

"And today, I received the most excellent news," Teresa continued. "Miss Bobbie has told me I may continue to live in her house as long as I wish. What a relief! I dreaded seeking another place to live."

"I don't blame you. There are so few open rentals, and they are expensive. But are you sure that old office is big enough for you? Your daughter's growing up fast."

"Dr. Liz, after living in a refugee camp, it is a palace!"

Every night the news showed the terrible conditions in Gaza, stark proof that refugee camps were no place to raise a child. Although the conflict was the most visible, it was only one of many places where people were forced to live in camps. The civil war in Sudan got hardly any coverage except on public television or BBC news.

Teresa leaned closer to speak confidentially. "Dr. Liz, can you spare a moment? I have an urgent matter to discuss with you."

Liz glanced at her trusty gold watch, a gift from Yale on her retirement. "Sure. But the others will be here soon. Let's find a more private place." She thumbed over her shoulder in the direction of her office.

As Liz led the way down the hall, she tried to guess what Teresa had on her mind. She'd been promised a raise as soon as she passed her licensing exams. Perhaps she was looking for extra hours to supplement her income. Liz gestured toward the visitors' chairs, but Teresa sat down only after her boss was seated. Her old-world respect stuck out in the deliberately casual atmosphere Liz had created in the practice.

"We're all rooting for you to pass your exams next month," Liz said, tenting her fingers. "We can really use another nurse, especially with so many new people moving into Hobbs."

"You and everyone at this practice have been so supportive. I am grateful beyond words. And now that Grace and I are settled, I can think about the future."

Liz scanned Teresa's face for clues about what might come next. "I hope you're not going to tell me you're leaving."

To Liz's relief, Teresa laughed merrily. "No, Dr. Liz, not at all. I have no desire to go elsewhere. On the contrary, now that Miss Bobbie has confirmed I may remain in my little apartment, I can pursue a venture I am considering. But first, I wanted your advice."

Liz rested her ankle on the opposite knee and leaned back in her chair. "Go on."

"I am inspired by Miss Bobbie."

"Bobbie is invaluable to the practice," Liz agreed. "Now that Joyce is gone, I'm trying to get her to work full time."

"But you can't blame her for taking some time for herself. Caring for Joyce has consumed her entire life for over a decade. Bobbie enjoys working in the garden and taking hikes with my Grace." *And she's in a relationship with Susan Gedney,* thought Liz, *hopefully distracting her from obsessing about my wife.*

"That's why we're glad you're getting your license. I hope you'll stay on full-time."

"If I can. The university has a new program for family nurse practitioners. I am going to apply."

"That's great news. How can I help?"

"First, I hope you'll recommend me."

"Done," said Liz with a curt nod.

"And I hope you will accommodate my class schedule. I can do most of my practicum here. That is, if you agree to sponsor me."

"Well, I do know something about training," said Liz, attempting to sound modest.

"Hah, we all know you were chief of surgery at Yale. You must have overseen the training of so many medical students and doctors."

"I've certainly paid my dues."

"I understand. Like Miss Bobbie, you are close to retirement and want more from your life. I shall respect your time, Dr. Liz, but I suspect you miss teaching."

"And why would you think that?"

"Because you are so good at it," replied Teresa with a broad smile. What she'd said about teaching was true. Liz missed it.

"I teach gun safety classes. That helps me get the teaching bug out of my system, and of course, I'm always mentoring staff here, but not as formally as you're suggesting."

"In Sudan, I worked in a teaching hospital before the war. The one before the last war, not this one. There are so many wars, I cannot keep up." Teresa forced a smile and returned to the subject. "I have seen many teachers. You have a gift for medicine and a passion for sharing it."

"That's the quid pro quo of medicine. We learn from our elders, and we pass it on to successive generations. It's even in the Hippocratic Oath. Like anyone takes it seriously anymore." Her cynical tone seemed to disappoint Teresa, so Liz smoothed her brow and asked, "How is your exam prep going? Do you need any help?"

"Bobbie has been quizzing me, as well as the new medical student, who came to live with us. She is very knowledgeable."

The mention of Bobbie's cooperative housing arrangement made Liz nostalgic for the communal living forced on them during Covid. When Erika's refrigerator died and couldn't be replaced quickly, she and Lucy had moved into the apartment over the garage. They'd brought Stefan, Erika's elderly father, to protect him from the contagion spreading like wildfire in his senior residence. Maggie's daughter, Alina, and her girls had moved into the guest rooms. Maggie had been in her element, cooking meals for their newly enlarged household, despite the shortages. She and Lucy had planned evening entertainment that Alina had streamed on the local cable channel. All around them, the virus was claiming hundreds of thousands of victims, but in Liz's three-story home, they'd all found a safe haven.

"You're smiling, Dr. Liz. You must approve of my plan."

"Actually, I was thinking of when my extended family was living with me during Covid. It's comforting to live with other people. Too many of us are rattling around in our oversized homes, when so many people have no place to live."

Teresa nodded in solemn agreement. "You never appreciate a home more than when you are without one."

Liz thought of how much grit and stamina Teresa had needed to endure life in a refugee camp, her patience in waiting her turn to come to the US. She admired her determination to better herself for her own sake and her daughter's. "Of course, I'll help you," said Liz. "The doctor shortage isn't going away. We need smart, ambitious people like you to fill the gap."

When Teresa smiled, her teeth contrasted brilliantly against her dark skin. "Dr. Liz, thank you for your time this morning. I hear stirring in the hall, which means I must get to work!" Teresa rose to her feet. "Bless you for your kindness. I believe that the good we do comes back to us in blessings."

The religious angle made Liz squirm a little. It was enough Lucy inserted it from time to time, but she was more subtle. "Teresa, I'll help in any way I can. Good luck with your exam prep."

"Thank you, Doctor." Teresa left and Liz headed back to the break room to refill her coffee cup. Cherie, the physician's assistant, was there ahead of her. Usually, Cherie was as tuneful as Teresa, but she wasn't singing this morning.

"Hey, Liz," she said, removing her cup from the machine. The indestructible white mug with the logo of Café du Monde in New Orleans' French Quarter was a memento from her home state. Cherie guarded it jealously, and none of the staff dared to touch it. "What a night!" she exclaimed with a long sigh.

"Your poor kids can't catch a break, can they?" said Liz. "First their parents, then their schoolmates, now this. I really feel for them."

"Brenda was up all night, and I had my hands full keeping my babies calm. As much as I wanted to turn on the TV to see what was happening, I didn't. I made Brenda stick to her office with all her telephone and radio calls. The kids and I went into their playroom and sang. Singing always helps in times of trouble."

"I go into the shop and play opera really loud," said Liz. She didn't admit that she often sang along.

"Lucy doesn't sing for you?" Cherie asked with a little daring tease.

"Lucy has her hands full."

"That she does." Cherie opened the refrigerator to take out the cream. "I would like to help her. Can we ask Bobbie to come in early today? Gloria is coming up from Portsmouth to help. We are swamped with requests for therapy sessions." Cherie's blue-green eyes narrowed as she studied Liz. "You're so calm."

Liz shrugged. "Better than me hyperventilating and crawling up the walls."

"I'm surprised the shooting hasn't triggered you."

"Oh, it did. But I'm okay now."

"You sure? Not just making yourself numb? Are you taking anything?"

Cherie was unfazed by Liz's sharp look. She softened it, knowing Cherie only dared to ask her boss invasive questions because she cared. "Low-dose Alprazolam last night before bed, but nothing since."

Cherie laid a reassuring hand on Liz's arm. "If you need to talk…"

"Yup, I know, you're here for me. Lucy said the same, but I think I'm okay. If not, I'll let you know."

"None of us will be okay until they catch that guy," said Cherie with a mock shudder.

"Thanks for the reminder," Liz said, patting Cherie's shoulder. "I should tell Ginny to make sure we keep the outside doors locked today. We don't want any unwanted visitors."

***

Hands clasped under her chin, Lucy knelt in the third pew. She knelt despite her conviction that God did not require groveling as part of worship. It was a habit. As a Catholic school girl, she'd been taught that kneeling was the proper attitude for prayer, but the radical progressives in her seminary insisted it was a holdover from the time of kings and emperors, when paying obeisance was part of the culture. Lucy wasn't such a purist that she would banish it completely. Some rites required bowing and genuflection. When she felt especially stressed, assuming the supplicant's posture told her body and mind it was time for prayer.

Today, she was conflicted, praying for the grace to handle this new insult to the community and shouting at God. *Why? When will the sacrifice for the sake of the Second Amendment be enough? How many more must die?*

The little voice that sometimes popped into Lucy's mind during prayer wasn't talking today. Although Lucy often wondered where the voice came from, she wasn't crazy enough to think that the voice was God's, but maybe it was. The debate was irrelevant today. If the voice was only Lucy talking to herself, she had nothing to say either. Certainly no answers, only questions.

Lucy squeezed her hands tighter together until her knuckles turned white. She remembered the scene of the school shooting. To preserve evidence, the bodies of the dead boys had lain in their own blood on the polished gym floor. Lucy couldn't bear to visit the scene herself, but Liz had shown some photos she'd taken when Brenda had asked her to check the victims for signs of life. Poor Liz. As a surgeon in a big city hospital, she'd probably seen many horrible things, but some of those dead kids had been her patients. She knew their parents and families. A death is so much harder to bear when it's close to home.

Why did God allow this carnage? Lucy was a trained theologian and a priest. When her parishioners asked questions, she could recite all the approved answers. God never promised to make everything right, only to be with us always. Hardly a satisfying explanation.

Lucy understood why people needed certainty when events seemed so random and unpredictable. Every one of the shooting victims had been in the wrong place at the wrong time—children playing in a gym, a local bowling league enjoying a night out, friends gathered in a local pub for an after-work beer and a game Lucy had never heard of before that night. It was Lucy's job to help people make sense of the tragedy and give people God's comfort, but what could she say?

After Erika had died, Rebecca had given Lucy her own well-worn, dog-eared copy of *When Bad Things Happen to Good People.* Lucy always found it enlightening to see which passages another reader had underlined or highlighted. Knowing she'd been inspired or moved by the same thought made her experience feel part of something bigger. Other times, seeing the evidence that others had felt the same pain or sorrow brought her close to despair.

Lucy clamped her hands tighter and fought the inclination to feel sorry for herself, especially when she thought of how Liz must be experiencing this latest shooting. She seemed unnaturally calm. Like every day, Liz had gone to the office, saying people still had medical issues that needed attention. Now that Liz had her carry pistol back, she'd shrugged off the shelter-in-place order and told Lucy not to worry. Of course, she worried. The world was a dangerous place.

Liz sat on her troubles, chewing on them in silence, all alone even when they ate her up inside. She was a doctor, so she blamed too much whiskey for her indigestion and menopause for her broken sleep. The real cause was keeping everything to herself. It had broken her marriage to Maggie, which Lucy knew from both parties.

As a professional, Liz was an exceptional communicator. She used language precisely and she could summarize key information like no one else. When it came to her feelings, Liz suddenly became tongue-tied. Lucy had been trying to help Liz learn to communicate, and not only to keep their marriage vibrant and healthy. She passionately wanted to know Liz, to share her secrets, including the fears that kept her up at night. It wasn't enough to make love to Liz's body. Lucy wanted complete intimacy. She wanted to touch her soul.

The side door of the church facing the rectory opened. Lucy opened her eyes and looked up to see who'd entered. As Cherie Harrison approached, her blond hair glistened under the bright lights in the sanctuary. Being biracial, she was an unlikely blonde. Her skin was so light she had to tell people she was black.

"I hope I'm not disturbing you," Cherie apologized. "Jodie told me you were here."

"It's okay. I'm done," said Lucy, getting up from her knees. "God's not very talkative today."

Cherie made a little face. "Yeah, what can He say about another mass shooting?"

Lucy couldn't think of a response that didn't sound hypocritical, so she said nothing. She gave Cherie one of those quick therapist's evaluations, noting that she looked tired, probably kept awake by her anxious kids and the fear she shared with the rest of Maine.

"You're early, Cherie," said Lucy, stepping out of the pew.

"Liz called in Bobbie to cover for me. After Jodie called to say you're overwhelmed with requests for appointments, I thought I'd better get over here as fast as I could. I expected to find you in a session."

"I needed a break to recharge my batteries. I've been counseling people nonstop since I got here."

"I'm sorry," said Cherie, her beautiful face radiating compassion.

"I'm sorry too...for all of us. When will this violence end?" Lucy's question was rhetorical, but Cherie seemed to feel compelled to answer.

"Not anytime soon," she said, shaking her head. There are too many guns out there in the hands of people who shouldn't have them. I heard on the radio driving over that the shooter's National Guard unit had him hospitalized in New York for mental illness. Why didn't they keep him? Why didn't the army follow up with him?"

"Like always, there will be a lot of second-guessing," said Lucy, "but we know why. Too much bureaucracy, lack of communication, not enough funding for mental health. Hopefully, there will be a full investigation." She patted Cherie's arm. "But how are *you* doing?"

"I'd be better if the kids weren't so upset. First, their parents are shot, then their classmates. If Keith hadn't been in the nurse's office with one of his fake illnesses, he might be dead with the rest of his gym class." Cherie took a deep breath. "Thank God for Aunt Simone. She's got the kids. I'm lucky. A lot of parents scramble to find childcare when there's a sudden school closing."

"Fortunately, many businesses are closed because of the shelter-in-place advisory. That should help." Lucy glanced in the direction of the rectory. "We should get back. There was a line when I left."

Cherie nodded without enthusiasm. "Maybe we should do group sessions to help more people."

It was an inspired suggestion. Lucy wondered why she hadn't thought of it before. "That's a great idea, Cherie. You can use the lower hall. How long can you stay?"

"As long as you need me."

Lucy emitted a mirthless laugh. "Don't say that. You might be here all night."

"Aunt Simone said she could stay the night," replied Cherie earnestly. Lucy loved her generosity. She was such a good soul, but she would never take advantage of her.

"Just kidding, Cherie. We all need to get back to our families. They need us too."

"Mother Lucy, let me know if I'm out of bounds, but I want to talk about Liz. That's why I came looking for you."

Lucy tried to hide her anxiety, but Cherie instantly read it in her face. "Don't worry. There's nothing wrong. She seems fine, but I've worked with her type before. They're living examples of the calm before the storm. She says she's fine, but how could she be? First, she makes herself a hostage to a mass shooter, then needs to shoot him. That kind of trauma doesn't just go away."

Lucy sighed. "Thanks, Cherie. I'm aware. Liz thinks being stoic can block the traumatic responses, but we know they'll come up one way or another."

"I just wanted to give you a heads up."

"And I appreciate it," she took Cherie's arm. "Come on. Let's get back to the office. We have clients waiting."

They walked across the quadrangle. Cherie's legs were longer, so Lucy hurried to keep up with her.

"What do you say to people when they ask why there was another mass shooting?" Cherie asked.

"The only thing I can say: I don't know."

"I'm glad you're not one of those ministers who say it's God's will."

Lucy stopped short, which made Cherie stop too. "Cherie, God loves us and would never want innocents to die. This is the doing of humans, the result of our insane love of guns. It has nothing to do with God." Lucy's frustrated tone made Cherie take a step back and regard her warily.

"I know, Lucy," she said with a gentle hand on her arm, "but I'm sure people expect you to have an explanation...because you're a priest."

"Believe me. I wish I could explain why innocent people keep dying, but I can't." Lucy raised her eyes to heaven and sighed. "Let's get ourselves together for the clients. We need to put on our professional faces, no matter how much we want to scream and cry."

"It's not easy what we do," said Cherie.

"It sure as hell isn't," Lucy agreed. The mild expletive drew another concerned look from Cherie. "Sorry," muttered Lucy. "Sometimes, even priests can't pretend."

***

Liz noted that they were running low on dishwasher detergent and mentally added it to her shopping list. After she'd turned on the dishwasher, she looked at the clock. It read quarter past ten. Maggie had cooked dinner. Now, she was in her room to prepare for tomorrow's class. It had been Lucy's turn to do the dishes, but when she'd come home looking frazzled from counseling sessions, Liz had offered to clean up the kitchen.

She was equally spent. She'd barely slept since the Lewiston shooting. When her restlessness woke Lucy, she offered sex to soothe her. Feeling guilty that she was interrupting her wife's sleep, Liz would lie as still as possible, which for an active person wasn't easy.

There was too much on her mind—worry that Lucy was working too hard. Her counseling practice and the pastoral care of her congregation were taking up every waking moment. When she was supposedly winding down for bed, she was often texting a church member in an emotional crisis. Liz worried about Hobbs Family Practice, where everyone, from herself as senior partner to the medical assistants, was working overtime to address the needs of a terrified community. Requests for sleep aids and tranquilizers had skyrocketed, along with visits for stress-related illnesses like irritable bowel and other gastric distress. Small wonder. Liz's gut had been cranky too.

Although Liz knew it could make her sleep worse, she poured herself a glass of whiskey. She'd given up her beloved single-malt scotch in favor of an Irish whiskey that was smoother and considerably cheaper—not that she had to worry about money, but she'd been raised not to waste it.

She heard footsteps in the hall and Lucy appeared at the kitchen door.

"I was just going to pour you some wine and bring it up," said Liz.

"Thanks. I can use some wine," said Lucy, heading to the cabinet for a glass. "I came down to tell you they found the shooter."

"Really? Where?"

"In the back of a container at the recycling plant where he used to work. They think he shot himself."

"Jesus Christ! Why don't they fucking shoot themselves before they kill other people?"

"Liz..."

"Yeah, I know. No taking his name in vain."

"That's not it. It's the lack of compassion. That poor man is a victim too."

"I'm sorry but it's hard for me to feel sorry for a guy who shot eighteen people."

"I know, but think of how damaged he must have been to do such a terrible thing."

"That doesn't excuse it."

"No, but it explains it. And God loves him too, just like She loves poor Peter Langdon."

Mentions of Peter Langdon always gave Liz a twinge. Almost reflexively, she said, "Then why did *She* allow him to be abused by the gym teacher? Why did *She* allow him to kill all those kids?"

Lucy stood up straight, showing she was ready to rebut Liz's deliberately provocative questions. Then she suddenly relaxed and raised her eyes to heaven. "Please, Liz. I've been hearing those questions all day. Please cut me some slack."

Chastened, Liz put her arms around her. "I'm sorry. No one will do anything about the guns. It's so fucking frustrating!"

Lucy gave her a little squeeze. "It's okay, honey. I know how much it upsets you."

"We should tell Maggie," Liz said, releasing her. "She's probably plugged into her ear pods listening to music while she prepares for class."

"Tell me what?" asked a voice. Maggie came into the room, wearing a multi-colored woven shawl over a slinky yoga outfit. She always complained of the cold. While Sam had been away, she'd been keeping Sam's house much warmer than its energy-conscious owner would usually allow. Liz only knew because Maggie had asked which oil company to call to refill the tank. "I came out to get a glass of wine. What's going on?"

Liz opened the refrigerator and took out a bottle of white wine. "They found the shooter. Looks like a suicide," she explained, filling two glasses. She handed one to Maggie and one to Lucy. Liz lifted her whiskey glass. "To finding the killer."

"I'm glad he's been caught," said Lucy, "but his death isn't something to celebrate."

"Okay," Liz said slowly. "How about toasting to our life getting back to normal? The kids going back to school. Businesses reopening. Maggie being able to go home." Maggie gave her a sharp look. For obvious reasons, returning to an isolated house, where she'd be all alone again, didn't appeal to her. "There's no rush," Liz hastily added.

"If you don't mind, I'd like to stay until Sam gets back. I promise I won't be in the way. I'll contribute to the groceries."

"No need for that," said Liz, glancing at Lucy, who didn't look happy. Liz had also looked forward to regaining their privacy, but Maggie had been good company during a stressful time. With her chef's training, she could make exceptional meals with the simplest ingredients, and Liz got a break from cooking every night.

"You're always welcome," Lucy finally said. She raised her glass. "Let's drink, as Liz suggested, to life getting back to normal."

They sipped their drinks, but they all looked introspective. There was no joy in this toast.

"Tomorrow, I'll go out to Sam's and shut off the water and turn down the heat," said Liz, putting away the wine bottle.

"Are you sure it's okay for me to stay?" Maggie asked looking from Liz to Lucy and back again. They both nodded. "Maybe we can all sleep better tonight, knowing the shooter has been found." She wished them goodnight and headed to her room.

Liz poured another splash into her whiskey glass. "Are you really okay with Maggie staying here until Sam gets back?" she asked when she was sure they were alone. "She probably won't be home until Thanksgiving."

"It's fine," said Lucy with a shrug. "Maggie feels safe here with us."

Liz replaced the whiskey bottle where it belonged. When she turned around, she noticed Lucy's lips moving. "Are you praying?" she asked incredulously.

"I'm saying the prayers for the dead."

"Lucy, he was a *killer*."

"He was a human being, just like Peter Langdon."

"That's different. He was abused as a child. At least, you can understand why he snapped."

"We don't know this man's story yet. And there's no harm in asking God to have mercy on his soul."

Chapter 9

As usual, Lucy had taken off her collar and changed into her pajamas the minute she'd gotten home. Since the shooting had put non-stop demands on every counselor in Hobbs, she was even more determined to put distance between her and her job. Tonight, Lucy wanted nothing more than to hibernate in what she considered her one, safe place.

Although their unexpected, long-term guest had altered their routine, Maggie's presence had proven to be much less intrusive than Lucy had expected. Liz's ex-wife rarely rose when they did, having learned that Lucy's singing practice in the media room was a special, private time they shared as a couple. To solve the problem of morning coffee, Liz had installed a dorm refrigerator and a compact, single-serve coffee maker in the small room that Maggie had once used as an office. Now, Lucy didn't need to shower and dress before having her first cup of coffee and had the double luxury of enjoying it in bed. Liz had ceded the kitchen to Maggie, who cooked most nights. She said it was a way to pay them back for their hospitality. While she tidied the kitchen, she respectfully left them to their quiet time on the enclosed porch while they debriefed from the day.

When Rebecca Morgenstern called, Lucy reluctantly left Liz on the porch and went upstairs to their bedroom. She pulled down the covers and got into bed. She felt especially safe in the king-sized four-poster. Liz had constructed it soon after teaching herself woodworking. She disparaged it as overbuilt and claimed it was sturdy enough to support a deck. But it was the sturdiness of it that Lucy cherished and the fact that Liz had built it with her own hands. Other women had slept there, but it was Lucy's special place now. She pulled up the fluffy comforter and snuggled into the big pillows.

"Okay, Rebecca, I'm upstairs now, and you have my complete attention. I'm glad you called. I could use a long talk with my rabbi."

"What if I told you I could use a long talk with my priest?" Lucy didn't know what to say. Usually, she was the needy one, and Rebecca played the straight-talking sage with all the answers. Rebecca seemed to sense that the reversal had upset a long-standing norm. After an extended pause, she said, "I hope I didn't interrupt your dinner."

"No, no. We're done eating. I was supposed to be cleaning up the kitchen, but our house guest is doing it."

"You need to tell me your secret. I never get out of cleanup. Is it weird having Liz's ex there?"

"Yes, but so far it's been okay. She's so grateful she doesn't have to stay in that isolated house all alone. She sees Liz as her protector."

"Liz promotes that image," said Rebecca dryly. "She shouldn't be surprised when people expect her to make good on it."

"And she does. She always rises to the occasion."

"I bet she does." Rebecca giggled lewdly.

Lucy bristled. Maggie's presence had made her less tolerant of disparaging comments about Liz, even a backhanded compliment. "Okay, enough about my wife," she said. "What's going on with yours? Have you heard from her? When is she coming home?"

"Whoa, Lucy! Give me a chance to answer. One question at a time. Yes, we video chat every morning. I call her before the twins are off to school, so they can talk to their mom."

"How are they doing with her being away so long?"

"She'd planned to be away until Thanksgiving, so that part's okay. But they're old enough to follow the news on their phones. They're scared, just like I am, especially now that the IDF has invaded Gaza."

"Is she still talking about signing up for active duty?"

"Yes, but she sounds less enthusiastic now that it's turned into a real war with people shooting back."

"But she's in the reserves. Won't she have to serve?"

"No, she didn't re-up last time and let her commission expire.

She was tired of going back for training that took up half her school vacation."

"I'm sure that's a relief."

"Oh, you bet, and for Judith too. She might be a patriot, but she's not crazy. It's fine to play soldier during peacetime. Completely different when there's a war. And this won't be a quick one."

"How are they going to get the civilians out of harm's way? Gaza is so crowded."

"That's their problem," said Rebecca dismissively. Lucy noted the lack of sympathy, which was understandable as the details of the brutal Hamas attack continued to emerge. That horrible event seemed so long ago, and yet it had only been last month. So much had happened since! "Judy's parents are trying to talk sense to her, begging her to go home and get out of harm's way. The twins plead with her every time they talk. I think she's weakening."

"She's probably worried about leaving her family during a war. I can understand."

"They're free to leave Israel. Mom invited them to stay with her. And even if Judith does volunteer, what can she do to protect them? Her sabbatical from her teaching job expires in January. There's such a shortage of teachers I'm sure her district will extend it, but our kids need her. I need her." Lucy heard a long sigh of frustration. "Oh, Lucy, I'm tired of arguing with her."

"I'm sure she feels torn. It must be so difficult."

"When you see what those savages did, you can understand why she wants to fight back." Lucy shuddered as she remembered the news footage of the Kibbutz overwhelmed by masked assailants on motorcycles. Old men and women fleeing in terror. Mothers cowering in corners trying to shelter their small children. Young people at a musical festival cut down while they were dancing. Lucy shut her eyes as if it could block the terrifying images. "Netanyahu will use this war to preserve his power," said Rebecca cynically. "He's nothing but a criminal."

"How does Judith feel?"

"Oh, she's been a vocal critic. Like most liberal Israelis, she thinks he's corrupt. She was furious at his bid to take power away from the Supreme Court. The right-wing faction that's taken over the government is full of religious fanatics. My Israeli friends complain about ultra-orthodox men criticizing how women dress in public. Some Hasidic sects are as bad as the Taliban when it comes to women. They harass tourists for not dressing modestly, and that's been going on for a while. This isn't the Israel I grew up with and admired." There was silence for a moment. "But Israel was attacked. I shouldn't be so critical of my fellow Jews."

"Hey, many Evangelicals think the existence of female clergy is heresy. When we have interdenominational services, the Evangelical ministers look at me with horror and pity. They're all men, of course, and they tell me they're praying for me."

"What do you say back?"

"That I'm praying for them too."

Rebecca laughed aloud. "Good answer, Lucy. I'll have to remember that. I often get odd looks from the rabbi at the orthodox synagogue, but so far, we've been getting along. The patriarchal faiths don't have much room for women. Apart from a few prophets, all our heroes are men."

"That's one reason Liz isn't interested in joining our church. She says it's too sexist."

"Oh, I think it's just another excuse, Lucy, but she supports your ministry. That's the important thing. Where faith is concerned, Liz is skeptical, but curious."

Lucy realized that Rebecca had Liz pegged, but she didn't have the whole picture. Lucy suspected Liz's interest went beyond curiosity. She loved liturgical music. She was a traditionalist, but she saw Western religion as limited by the past. She righteously opposed Christianity's oppression of women and LGBT.

"Of course, I'm less sure of my own faith..." Lucy began to

say. There was silence on the other end of the call. Lucy listened carefully, hoping to gauge how critically Rebecca had received the message. She'd admitted to Rebecca that since her doctoral studies in theology, her own faith wasn't as secure. The old certainties couldn't satisfy her anymore. Maybe that's why she'd snapped at Cherie when she'd asked how she would respond to questions about another tragedy.

"Are you having any special services for the victims of the Lewiston shooting?" Rebecca asked.

"We've talked about it," said Lucy, sounding surprised at the sudden change of subject. "I think we'll do something with the Hobbs Religious Leaders Association like last time, but honestly, our own wounds are still so fresh."

"Of course. It's been only nine months since the shooting at Hobbs Elementary. How's Liz taking it?"

"You know Liz, stoic as always, but honestly, I worry about her. I don't want her to relapse. She was in such a dark place after the school shooting."

"Lucy, I know you want to rush in and make it all better, but you need to let her deal with it. She's a doctor. As a surgeon, she had to deal with many traumas, physical and mental."

"She's not the best communicator."

"Her type never is, but you need to trust her to let you know when she needs help. It's the respectful thing to do." It was good advice, but Lucy still worried.

"I just can't believe we have to go through this again."

"Believe it. Mass shootings happen literally every day."

❋❋❋

Watching Amber effortlessly roll out one pie crust after another, Tiffany was grateful that she'd accepted her invitation to Thanksgiving. Amber was the champion pie maker of their CIA class. Her crusts had no peer. Tiffany envied Amber's sublimely flaky pie pastry that melted in your mouth. They were so good that the filling was unnecessary, as proven by the sugar twists Amber made from the scraps. If enough survived their munching on them while they baked, Tiffany would put some in the case for sale. Maybe they should be a regular item. Customers seemed to love them.

Tiffany had repeatedly tried to recreate Amber's pastry. Somehow, it never came out like Amber's. It lacked that perfect, buttery "mouthfeel." Tiffany knew that even when two people followed the same recipe, the result was never the same. There might slight differences in technique, like how the dough was kneaded or rolled out, plus so many other variables—the quality of the water, the brand of butter or shortening, or the heat of the oven.

Another reason why Tiffany had invited Amber was her efficiency, something her friend had learned baking in a big New York City hotel. They'd already finished the blueberry pies, which were popular in Maine. The "very berry" pies, bursting with strawberries, raspberries, and blueberries, had their fans too. Later that afternoon, they'd tackle the pumpkin pies, not Tiffany's favorite, but the old-timers liked them.

Amber had lined up two dozen foil pie plates, ready for the apple and cranberry-apple filling they'd already prepared. They'd make enough pies for all the pre-orders and multiple extras for Wednesday's walk-in customers. The frozen pies had been sold out for days. When they ran out, they'd draw the blinds and put the "closed" sign on the front door.

"Stop daydreaming and get that dough kneaded," Amber ordered briskly, "or no sugar twists for you!"

"Now, there's a threat I won't ignore!" Tiffany leaned into the dough with renewed vigor, punching and twisting it into pliancy.

Amber was Tiffany's closest friend from the CIA. Her subtle humor and easy-going personality had naturally attracted Tiffany, not sexually, but in every other way. It had been Amber's idea to create their cooking club to keep their circle of school friends connected.

"What time did you say your parents are getting here?" Amber asked.

Tiffany raised her shoulders. "Sometime this afternoon, they said. But who knows? Dad works all hours. Mom too." Mary Taylor had a busy psychiatry practice, but it was her pro bono work for a women's prison in Westchester that ate up her time. Brad Taylor flew all over the world in support of the arts organizations for his foundation. His latest project was the Afghan National Institute of Music, in exile in Portugal since the Taliban seized control of the government. Music was forbidden, and the Taliban had bragged about destroying more than twenty-one thousand instruments. Brad was deeply involved in the Afghan Youth Orchestra's American tour to raise funds for the school and awareness of the plight of the arts under the repressive regime.

Her parents' causes were certainly worthy and a source of pride for their daughter, but she often wished they could spare some time for her. When it came to their attention, it was literally feast or famine. Growing up, she'd had a series of engaging and clever nannies. One had taught her French, which had come in handy when she'd apprenticed with a Parisian pastry chef.

Before Tiffany had gone off to boarding school, her mother would make extravagant breakfasts and dinners. The association of maternal love with tasty meals had inspired Tiffany to become a chef. Her father had his own version of parental extravagance. He would fly her to famous zoos to visit the pandas. Of course, he got them front row seats to Broadway shows and classical concerts.

Each parent had haphazardly dropped into Tiffany's young life based on their busy schedules. The drought of their absence was broken by a deluge of attention. Sometimes, Tiffany felt she might drown under a tsunami of riches. Then Mary and Brad were gone again, leaving her stranded in their New York apartment until next time.

An only child because her mother had run out her biological clock, Tiffany had always longed for siblings to take the edge off her solitude or share the burden of her parents' suffocating attention.

She'd gravitated toward Amber because their childhoods had been similar. Her parents were divorced now, but they were high-flyers too, both successful and wealthy New York attorneys.

"I really appreciate you coming up to help me," Tiffany said, but she meant more than the help with the pies.

"Dad is skiing in Calgary and Mom is cruising the Greek Islands with her new boyfriend. Where else would I find a traditional sit-down Thanksgiving except here with you?"

"Well, you could have taken the hotel's offer of double pay to stick around over the holiday. I bet you turned down a lot of money."

Amber shrugged. "So what? I make plenty, and I deserve time off too. My assistant is very competent. He learned everything from me. He didn't go to culinary school like we did."

"Better watch out, Amber. You might be teaching your replacement. Remember, that happened to me. Once my assistant could make decent pastries, I was out of a job. Of course, they could get her for lower pay."

"So let them fire me," said Amber, scraping dough off her rolling pin. "I get offers all the time. Maybe I'd like to go somewhere else. New York is outrageously expensive. It's not like I have time to take advantage of being in the city. You know how it is."

One nice thing about having a business in a resort town was that Tiffany would get a break after the tourists and the summer people left. The locals kept her afloat in the winter months, but being shut down for three days while the police searched for the Lewiston shooter hadn't helped her bottom line. Luckily, the Thanksgiving orders had far exceeded last year's and more than made up for the loss. After only two years, Tiffany was well on her way to paying her parents back for the seed money they'd put into her business.

Her father kept insisting they didn't expect repayment, but Tiffany wanted to prove she could make it on her own. She'd seen too many classmates, bankrolled by their parents, go from one failed restaurant to another. Covid had done in many of them, along with too much focus on "food art," as Tiffany called it, yet as a pastry chef, sculptural desserts were her specialty. Their culinary school teachers had often warned that the restaurant business meant long hours and great risk. Many of Tiffany's peers seemed unwilling to put in the hard work to succeed. She was determined to show she was the exception.

"I wish my parents agreed to have Thanksgiving here instead of renting an Airbnb," said Tiffany, mostly thinking aloud. "It's so hard to cook in a strange kitchen where you don't know where anything is."

"Yeah, but I saw photos of the place they rented. I would never turn down a kitchen like that. An Aga stove, top-of-the line cookware, every utensil and appliance to make food prep easy."

"Mom said when she read about the 'cook's kitchen' on the website, she booked the house right away. She later admitted the kitchen was a bribe to stay there with them. When I told them you were coming, they invited you too."

"That's sweet. My parents never pay attention to the things I like. When she travels, my mother buys me clothes and jewelry I wouldn't be caught dead wearing." Tiffany glanced at Amber's mismatched ear cuffs. She had eclectic tastes that no one could possibly accommodate, not even Tiffany, who knew her well. "You could do worse. That place is top-of-the line. The living spaces are right out of a HGTV, and the hosts supply everything down to the candles for the table. Must have cost your parents a fortune."

"You know Mom. She likes everything to be just so."

"When you're always being wined and dined by the rich and famous, I guess you get used to it."

Maybe you do, thought Tiffany, *but I'd rather be right here in my own kitchen.* She'd come to Hobbs because the setting was beautiful, and despite the fancy homes along the shore, it still had small-town charm. "The truth is, I would have preferred a nice down-home Thanksgiving. I don't need a meal looking like it belongs in a food magazine. I get enough of that, don't you?"

Amber thought about it for a moment. "Yeah, but I also like my food to look good. Presentation is especially important for Thanksgiving. Who wants to eat a pale turkey or scorched sides? It's bad enough the food is so monochromatic—brown turkey, beige stuffing, orange sweet potatoes and squash."

"I like the autumn color palette," countered Tiffany.

"I know. The only one in our class who actually likes pumpkin spice." Amber wrinkled up her nose.

Tiffany slapped and pounded the ball of dough she was kneading as if it had offended her. She felt disappointed that Amber didn't share her nostalgia for the kind of old-fashioned Thanksgiving that existed only in Norman Rockwell's paintings and Tiffany's imagination. Growing up, she'd often wondered how it would be to share a big table with siblings and cousins, critical maiden aunts, and a cantankerous, politically incorrect uncle. Both of her parents came from small families that were scattered across the country. Like most WASPs, they kept to themselves. Tiffany barely knew her few relations.

She was glad that Reshma was coming. She'd declined an invitation to Thanksgiving dinner at Dr. Stolz's house, which sounded like the big communal holiday meals the CIA students used to hold. Tiffany had also been invited and wished she could go, but she really wanted her parents and Reshma to meet.

So far, she'd kept information about her girlfriend on a "need-to-know" basis. She hadn't revealed that Reshma had been a refugee from Sudan, so they didn't know she was black. It would be an interesting test of whether Brad and Mary were really as color-blind as they claimed.

"I hope Reshma doesn't regret accepting the invitation to Thanksgiving with my folks," Tiffany said, sharing her thoughts aloud.

"Don't worry. They're nice people," said Amber, cutting strips for lattice-topped pies. "They won't interrogate her like my parents would, but they're lawyers. That's what they do."

Tiffany grinned. "They certainly put me on the stand when we met."

"Actually, that was mild. Dad had already looked up your parents, so he knew you had the right connections."

Tiffany made a face. "I'm sick of being judged by my so-called pedigree."

Amber sighed. "Face it, girl. It's how the game is played. That's how I got my job at the hotel. Dad called in a favor."

"In New York, maybe, but not here. So many people here had big jobs before they came to Hobbs. Dr. Stolz is an expert on breast cancer. She was chief of surgery at Yale New Haven. Lucy Bartlett sang at the Met. Olivia Enright managed a big hedge fund, and Maggie Fitzgerald starred on Broadway."

"Some people would say their time has come and gone."

Tiffany shot Amber a fierce look. "Maybe so, but none of them are wasting time playing golf. They do things to make Hobbs a better place."

"Okay. Okay. I'm sorry if I insulted your friends. I didn't mean to. Actually, I'd love to meet them. They all sound so interesting."

Tiffany scrutinized her friend to see if she was really serious. In her job at the hotel, she'd encountered many celebrities, from politicians and Wall Street executives to rock stars.

"Well if you can stick around until Sunday, you can come to the concert at the Cathedral. They'll all be there. Lucy is singing the *Verdi Requiem* to raise money for the shooting victims."

"Well, if I can get back to New York by Sunday night, I'll bite."

"Dad has a car service driving them home on Sunday after the concert. I'm sure you can hitch a ride."

"That's perfect!" Amber washed the pastry wheel in the sink. "Okay. Where are those apples?"

"Coming right up!" Tiffany headed to the fridge to fetch the bowls of sliced apples, marinating in lemon juice, sugar, and cinnamon.

❈❈❈

Liz finished bringing up the folding chairs from the basement. She'd built the long mahogany table in the dining room for twelve, but on holidays, she set up folding tables on the screen porch to accommodate additional diners. Each year, the guest list for Thanksgiving grew longer. As she set up the wooden chairs, she mentally seated the person who would occupy it. Although she hated assigned seating, she'd resorted to place cards to avoid the chaos of kitchen helpers dishing out food while dancing with diners looking for a seat.

When Liz had first suggested to Maggie that she sit on the porch with her clan, she was incensed. That was before the divorce, but things had already become unbearably tense. Up to that point, they'd cooked so well together. Then Maggie began to find little things Liz did in the kitchen exasperating. She screeched when Liz soaked her sharpening stones in the sink or forgot to leave the butter out to soften. The same was true in other shared spaces. If Liz's toothpaste wandered onto Maggie's side of the double sink, her response was completely out of proportion to the offense.

Maggie's irritability was clearly retribution after she'd forced Lucy to confess the impulsive kiss on the boat. Maggie had always been a "saver," someone who stuffed down small perceived transgressions and then released them in a blast of resentment, usually in the middle of a massive fight.

During those long, lonely nights after Maggie left, Liz had analyzed the collapse of her marriage down to the smallest detail. Their indiscretions were only partially to blame. Maggie was bored after she'd retired. She'd complained of feeling old and useless. The BRCA gene she carried meant the specter of cancer always lurked in the background. Liz had retired from the operating room. For over four decades, being a surgeon had given her life meaning. The last chapter of their life had begun, and they both feared what lay ahead.

"Still trying to figure out where everyone sits?" asked Lucy, standing in the doorway.

Startled out of her thoughts, Liz turned around quickly. "I worked out the arrangement last year, and I think I'll keep it." She carefully adjusted a chair's position to line up perfectly with the others. "People like continuity."

Lucy laughed. "You think anyone will remember where they sat last year?"

"Why not? I do."

"You, Dr. Stolz, remember everything."

In fact, Liz had a prodigious memory, but it wasn't quite as sharp as it used to be. More often now, she had to look up things online. "Not anymore," she admitted. "And I don't retain the new things I learn."

"That's why I'm not interested in learning new roles. It's hard enough to memorize an entire opera."

"I can't imagine learning all the text and the music for an opera. In college, I used to help Maggie learn her lines for plays. Even that's quite a feat."

Lucy cocked her head to one side as she studied Liz. "You're attracted to singers and actresses. I wonder what that says about you."

Liz unfolded the last chair and pushed it under the table. "Maybe I like drama?"

"No, I think you like glamor. You like the costumes and makeup. Are you disappointed when I take them off?"

"In fact," said Liz, bending to kiss her, "the costume I like best on you is none at all." Her fingers traced the curve of Lucy's breast. She tested its weight with her hand.

"Not now," Lucy said, but her laughing green eyes said otherwise. "We have company, and you have things to do." She lightly pushed Liz away. "You're such a flirt."

"I thought you liked that."

"I do."

"Maggie won't be home for hours. We have time."

"In that case..." Lucy grabbed her hand. "Let's go upstairs."

***

Lucy felt wonderfully calm after an hour of slow, sensual sex. Her preference would have been to spend the rest of the afternoon in front of the fire, drinking good wine and relaxing with her wife, but Maggie had come home looking upset. As an actress, Maggie was exceptionally adept at disguising her feelings, but her act today was paper thin. Lucy didn't need to draw on her therapist's training to perceive that something was very wrong.

Maggie came into the kitchen without saying hello and put away the groceries she'd picked up on the way. "You want a glass of wine?" she murmured with her head in the refrigerator.

"Sure," said Lucy and went to the cabinet to get glasses.

"Where's Liz?" Maggie asked, looking around.

"In the basement, looking for that hatchet she uses to split the squash."

The wine cork emerged from the bottle with a distinctive pop. "Liz never 'looks for' anything. She knows exactly where it is," Maggie said dryly. "She was always preaching to me about putting things in the same place. She follows that rule religiously. I always blamed her German grandmother, but I'm sure being a surgeon had something to do with it."

Lucy merely nodded. She was still feeling warm and intimate from the afternoon sex and disinclined to agree with any criticism of her wife, not even a backhanded compliment. "Liz has the fire going on the enclosed porch. Want to sit out there?" Maggie didn't look sure. "It's nice and toasty," Lucy added to sweeten the proposal.

"Good idea. We can keep an eye on Liz while she butchers that poor squash. It's a critical part of her Thanksgiving ritual." Under Maggie's sarcasm was perceptible nostalgia for a life she no longer shared.

They both positioned themselves for a view of the deck. Liz

came up the outside stairs with the shiny hatchet she reserved for the task. The giant Blue Hubbard sat cradled in a sawbuck like a sacrificial victim. Liz waved in their direction. With one blow, she split the enormous vegetable in half and proceeded to cut it into pieces that would fit in the oven. She neatly scraped out the seeds and placed them in a bag. The squash would yield a vat of soup for Thanksgiving dinner. The seeds would be toasted for snacks and garnish for the soup.

Lucy hadn't realized, but she'd been holding her breath while Liz wielded the hatchet. Her wife was exceptionally competent, but the primitive violence of the squash-splitting ritual put her on edge. When she glanced at Maggie, she saw that she'd been watching the process with equal attention. Instead of jealousy, Lucy felt an odd sisterly bond with her predecessor over the protective feelings they shared. She gave Maggie's thigh an affectionate pat, which provoked a curious look in her hazel eyes.

"I'm glad you're here," said Lucy warmly.

"Thanks for having me. After the shooting, it was just too creepy to stay at the house on the pond alone. I was afraid I might be over-staying my welcome, so I've tried to stay out of your way."

"You're not in the way, and we've adjusted," Lucy said. "You know how Liz loves company."

Maggie frowned. "Isn't it strange how an introvert like Liz likes to have so many people around?"

"No, entertaining guests is how Liz gets socialization in doses she can manage. She's an introvert, not a loner."

Maggie glanced out the window as she considered this informa-tion. "If only she'd talk more."

"Most of us figure things out by talking. Liz is a ruminator. She mulls things over before she decides what she thinks."

Maggie nodded. "Sounds like you've figured her out. You have more patience than I do. Maybe you'll succeed where I failed." Her voice trailed off into silence, followed by a long sigh. Lucy didn't want to get into regrets about the divorce. They'd been over this ground many times, and treading it again could disturb their delicate living arrangement.

"When's Sam's coming home?" asked Lucy to change the subject.

"Tomorrow afternoon, assuming the flights are on time. She wanted to stay in Chicago. One of her architect buddies invited her for Thanksgiving. Me too, and Sam offered to pay my airfare, not that she needs to. I can afford it. But I want to be with my family. That's not wrong, is it?"

"No, of course, it's not wrong. Thanksgiving is a time for family, those of us lucky enough to have one." Lucy thought of her parents, gone before their time. Her mother loved Thanksgiving, although it was her father who cooked the turkey. She gazed outside at Liz, who was carefully cleaning up after her task. She felt a warm surge of love toward the woman who'd brought her into this chosen family.

"This is the first time Liz invited us since the divorce," Maggie said. "I know how much Alina and the kids miss her. I didn't want to deprive them."

"Alina and the kids could have come here if you'd flown to Chicago to be with Sam."

"I know, but I want to be home for Thanksgiving." She cradled her stemless wine glass as if it were something precious. Lucy wondered if Maggie had bought it for the house.

"You miss being here, don't you?" Lucy ventured.

Maggie hesitated but then nodded. "I miss us, and I don't mean just Liz. I miss you. Our friendship. Most of all, I miss our tribe."

Without a moment's thought, Lucy put her arm around Maggie and squeezed her shoulders. "You're always welcome here, just like you and Liz welcomed me when I first came to Hobbs."

"Except I've come to regret that part," said Maggie, shrugging off Lucy's arm and moving to the far end of the settee.

"I understand, considering how things turned out. But don't regret your generosity and hospitality. No one expected it to turn out the way it did." Maggie regarded her skeptically and shrugged. Lucy sat forward so she could see Maggie's face. "Tell me what's going on with Sam. Why doesn't she want to come home?"

"You know why. She thinks the Lewiston shooting will remind everyone of how Peter Langdon got into the school. What Sam did was stupid. She should have locked the back door and walked around. I don't care how cold it was."

"You blame her, don't you?" asked Lucy, studying her. "Don't you think she deserves the benefit of the doubt?"

"Why? Because she's my partner?" Maggie made the idea sound despicable.

"No, because everyone makes mistakes," Lucy said, leaning closer.

"Not mistakes that cost children's lives. The parents of those dead kids are right to be angry."

"They're angry they lost their children, but Sam didn't kill them. Maybe she made it easier for Peter Langdon to get into the building, but he killed the boys and their teacher, not Sam."

"She did something stupid that's wrecked her life. Our life! Not just hers." Maggie said bitterly. Now, they were getting to the real issue. Maggie couldn't forgive Sam because her actions had driven her out of Hobbs, depriving her of the happy domestic arrangement she'd envisioned.

"She didn't do it deliberately or to hurt you. It was an unfortunate set of circumstances. How would Sam know Peter Langdon harbored such grievance against a teacher? Maggie, why are you being so judgmental?" Lucy asked, even though she knew Maggie held grudges, one reason it had taken so long for the feud with Liz to cool down.

"Why are you defending Sam?"

"Because we all need grace whether we deserve it or not."

"Lucy, don't minister to me," warned Maggie.

"I'm not. I'm speaking to you as a person who's made plenty of mistakes in her life. Forgiveness is a gift we give ourselves as well as others. Harboring anger and guilt doesn't change anything. It only makes us miserable."

Regarding Lucy coolly, Maggie didn't look convinced. "Maybe I'll learn to forgive Sam. She did something stupid, but I'll never forgive Peter Langdon. Sam gave that fucked-up kid a job, and he abused her trust."

"He did, and everyone finds it hard to forgive him and Robert Card, who killed all those people in Lewiston."

"How can you forgive Peter?" asked Maggie. "He could have killed Liz. She was stupid too, walking in there, thinking she could talk him into surrendering his gun. What arrogance!"

Lucy didn't see it that way. "I don't think you can simply write off what Liz did as ego. Yes, she has more confidence than most people. As a surgeon, it was trained into her, but she legitimately thought she could help. He asked for her to be his witness. He trusted her."

"Why are we always second-guessing ourselves?" asked Maggie with an enormous sigh.

"Because examining our behavior is how we learn to do better next time."

"Does Liz talk to you about the shooting?" asked Maggie.

Lucy looked into Maggie's hazel eyes, wondering if admitting her concerns would make her too vulnerable. Finally, she decided it was worth the risk. "Not as much as I'd like."

Maggie inhaled a long breath. "Sam's like that too. She's not as articulate as Liz, so it's even worse. She really didn't want to come home. I had to beg her."

"I'm sorry. But in the end, she agreed. That's a good thing, right?"

"Capitulation wasn't what I expected, especially when she said she was doing it for Alina's kids. She likes them, but I want her to come back to Hobbs because it's her home. After Liz talked to her, she was better. I wish she'd talk to her again."

"Why don't you ask her?"

Maggie shook her head. "No, I don't like to ask Liz for favors."

"What's the worst thing that could happen? She says no?"

"I don't like being in her debt," Maggie replied flatly.

Exasperated, Lucy allowed herself the luxury of a discreet sigh. Liz was right. Maggie put everything on a scale.

Maggie gazed at Lucy with a look indicating she hoped she would intervene with Liz. Lucy saw the manipulation for what it was. "If you want Liz to talk to Sam, just ask her," she said in a measured tone. "And now, if you'll excuse me, I'm going to ask Liz if she needs any help."

***

Not surprisingly, Tiffany couldn't find anything in what had been billed in the Airbnb squib as a "chef's kitchen." That's because it was an architect's idea of how chefs cooked, and no one had bothered to consult someone who actually prepared food.

Tiffany was willing to forgive her mother for not knowing better. Her parents had been trying so hard to accommodate her by not imposing on her space or demanding that she leave her business to spend Thanksgiving at their New York penthouse. Taking care of everything was the way they showed love.

She forced down her surliness and eventually located a cooking thermometer. Other than the perverse arrangement of the cookware, the large oceanfront house, so quintessentially Maine, made for a picture-perfect setting for a fall feast. Had she known, she could have invited one of her food photographer friends to immortalize it. Tiffany had never fancied herself a food writer, but her mentor at culinary school always said that articles in popular cooking magazines could put a restaurant or food shop on the map. Too late now. Thanksgiving features were planned in the spring. Maybe next year.

"Finding everything you need, dear?" her mother asked, hovering. She'd been watching her daughter rifle through the drawers with mild concern.

"I'll get there, Mom," Tiffany assured her as she continued her search for a plane grater.

"Maybe I can help."

As she bent to open a drawer, Mary Taylor's completely straight, white hair, blunt cut to the jaw, swung like a luxurious drape. Today, she wore skinny jeans that fit perfectly and a boat-neck polo with a coordinating jacket. The high-end, classic brands on the tags indicated she'd spent liberally on what she wore. Mary, like her husband, Brad, came from old money, so it didn't matter.

Brad's people had struck it rich in the petroleum boom of the early twentieth century. Mary was descended from New York blue bloods with a Dutch name that went back to Manhattan's first settlers. They both had what Tiffany's grandmother would call "good breeding," and she meant more than their manners. Yet the Taylors wore their distinguished ancestry well, never showing off, instead presenting themselves in a deliberately understated way, but that was also a sign of good breeding.

Tiffany's pedigree gave her an automatic in at Choate Rosemary Hall, a tony boarding school in Connecticut, where she'd learned not to brag like the "new money" kids. Her grandmother would call that "uncouth." Tiffany found it comforting that Reshma had also had the "boarding school experience." Although the young priest had been a charity student, at least she understood the culture of high society. She understood when Tiffany had revealed that her au pair had once been her best friend.

Tiffany finally located the grater she'd been seeking. Now if she could only find a pasta fork to fish some fusilli out of the stock pot to test the pasta for doneness. Ahead of all the poultry the next day, she was making a lighter, more refined version of lobster mac and cheese. Dinner would be ready soon, but where was Reshma?

They'd agreed it would be easier to meet Tiffany's parents before the pressure of cooking the holiday dinner. That way, Tiffany would have her wits about her if things became too uncomfortable and she had to run interference. Although he was always charming, Brad could ask probing questions. Fortunately, Mary, the psychiatrist, knew how to facilitate difficult conversations. Tiffany had decided not to shock them. She'd finally revealed that Reshma was an ordained Episcopal priest and that she'd been brought to Maine as a refugee from Sudan. What they didn't know was that Reshma was not your typical woman of color.

While Tiffany drained the pasta, she thought of Brianna's accusation that she was only dating Reshma to prove how woke she was. Had she missed the fact that Reshma was drop-dead gorgeous? Or her gentle way of deflecting challenges with a smile? Brianna loved ethnic dishes. Why couldn't she even acknowledge that Reshma's Yassa had been delicious?

The simple answer was she was jealous. That was to be expected. Brianna was jealous of everyone who paid attention to Tiffany, even Amber. Tiffany worried that bitterness over the breakup had made Brianna downright vindictive. If she'd hit her once, she was probably capable of doing it again. Tiffany would have preferred not to see her, but she'd been part of the cooking group since the beginning, and there was no way to cut her out gracefully.

Tiffany half listened to Amber and her father, trading stories about the many celebrities they'd met in the course of their work. Laughter bubbled up spontaneously, a positive sign. Mary finally left the kitchen and went out to join her husband. That freed Amber to come into the kitchen, not that Tiffany needed the help. Her confidence in her cooking was unfailing, but she worried about what Reshma would think of Brad and Mary. Would she dismiss them as vapid, knee-jerk liberals who adopted every leftist position? She knew that no matter what, Reshma would be kind. Even if she thought her parents were complete assholes, she'd never show it.

"Looks amazing," said Amber, watching Tiffany fold in chunks of fresh-picked lobster meat. "Is this from a recipe?"

"Sort of. I adapted a lightened version of mac and cheese from *Eating Well.*"

"I love those, especially since I'm always dieting." Amber patted her ample thighs. She leaned on the counter. Tiffany felt her eyes scrutinizing her. Under her breath, Amber ordered, "Quit stressing. You know they'll love her."

"I hope so. I just wish she'd show up! We're ready to eat." The doorbell rang. "Thank God!" Tiffany muttered. Since Reshma had come into her life, she'd reined in her spontaneous appeals to the deity, but this was an unusual situation.

"I'll open the door for her," Amber volunteered.

A moment later, Reshma came into the kitchen with her antique stock pot. "A Sudanese vegetable stew. I hope it goes with the meal you're cooking. I made it this morning. It just needs a quick reheat."

Tiffany stretched for a quick kiss on the cheek and accepted the battered pot, which she handed off to Amber. "Glad you brought something healthy. We're having mac and cheese."

She stepped back to take in Reshma, who was wearing one of the colorful cardigans over her clerical blouse. She'd removed the white tab from the collar and opened a button. "Sorry I didn't have time to change. My bereavement group ran long." She wrapped her long arms around Tiffany and pulled her into a delicious, full-body hug. Over Reshma's shoulder, she could see Amber watching with a sappy smile on her face.

"How's it going?" Reshma whispered into Tiffany's ear.

"They're on good behavior so far. Amber's been keeping them entertained." Tiffany resisted letting go of Reshma. "Are you nervous?" she asked in a whisper.

"You want the truth?" asked Reshma. "Terrified."

Tiffany watched Brad and Mary get up and head toward the door. "Don't worry. You'll charm them to death."

"If you don't mind," said Reshma, eyeing the approach of Tiffany's parents, "let's not talk about death. There's too much of it going around."

***

Smiling, the Taylors approached Reshma with outstretched hands. She didn't know whose hand to shake first, but finally, she chose Mary's. She'd perceived that Brad with his affable smile would be easier to win over. Mary's eyes keenly scrutinized her in the way only another woman could. Plus, she was a psychiatrist and could decipher every word and body movement.

Their smiles had the overly earnest warmth that successful professionals use at public events. Reshma could see the genetic mix in Tiffany. Her parents both had blue eyes that had blended to create Tiffany's unique celestial shade. Mary's hair was white now, but here and there were yellow wisps. Brad's hair, what remained after male pattern baldness, had been shaved, so it was hard to tell if he'd been blond too. But maybe Tiffany's hair color came from neither parent. The perfect golden shade could have been chosen off a hair-dye chart. Until this moment, the possibility that Tiffany colored her hair hadn't even occurred to Reshma.

Out of the corner of her eye, Reshma could see Tiffany nervously watching the introductions. She had an endearing habit of biting her lower lip when she was anxious. Of course, Tiffany wanted her parents to like her new girlfriend. Reshma gave them a high-wattage smile. Brad instantly melted, but Mary's eyes remained subtly critical. Being black and female, Reshma was used to being judged. Every time she climbed the pulpit she felt the weight of expectation. Can the black woman really preach or was she another DEI hire?

Mary held Reshma's hand longer than she would have expected. "Tiffany said you were pretty, but that's an understatement. You're absolutely stunning!" Reshma was never more grateful that her dark complexion hid the blush. "Come sit down and have a glass of wine." Mary led Reshma by the hand into the sitting area, where a charcuterie platter lay abandoned.

"No, Mom. We're going to eat now," said Tiffany, putting down trivets on the table for the hot dishes.

With a gentle hand at Reshma's elbow, Mary diverted her to the dining area and seated her to her right.

"What a lovely place this is," Reshma said, remembering her boarding school manners. "How lucky that you could get it for the holiday weekend."

"It was pricey," Brad admitted, apparently listening from the kitchen, where he was opening wine for dinner, "but the ocean view makes it totally worth it."

"Did you have a chance to take a walk on the beach?"

"Unfortunately, we were delayed in New York and just arrived this afternoon," Brad said. He grunted as he pulled the cork. "By the time we got here, it was dark."

"An emergency at the prison," Mary explained. "A thwarted suicide attempt in the minimum-security section. A poor mother whose children were prevented by relatives from visiting her for the holiday."

"That's sad," Reshma said.

"Oh, but so common. The stories you hear in urban prisons are heartbreaking. You have no idea."

"I served as a chaplain to a battered women's shelter while in seminary in New Haven, so I do," said Reshma, instantly regretting the competition she'd unwittingly set up. All she needed was a pissing contest with Tiffany's mother. "The holidays can be so hard on marginalized people," she added quickly, trying to find common ground. She wanted Mary on her side for Tiffany's sake. She was still trying to figure out Brad, but he seemed easy-going compared to his wife, whose smile seemed a little too perfect.

Amber brought the salad to the table. With all the tension of the introductions, Reshma had barely had a chance to say hello to her. Reshma grabbed Amber's arm as she passed on her way to her seat.

Amber bent near Reshma's ear and whispered. "I'm here to make sure her parents don't eat you alive."

Tiffany shot her a warning look.

"Much appreciated," Reshma whispered back. She glanced around to see if anyone had heard.

Brad raised his glass. "Happy Thanksgiving to family and friends, old and new." They all raised their glasses. After he sat down, Brad asked, "Reshma, do you still have family in Sudan?"

The question put her completely off balance. "None that I am aware of. Only my mother and I survived the war."

"And now there's another one," said Brad. Tiffany gestured for her father's plate, and he handed it over. "Geez, why is that country so unstable?"

Although Reshma understood why Brad's job would make him interested in geopolitical hotspots, it hardly seemed a topic for a family dinner. Maybe he was testing her knowledge of world events. "It's complicated, as is most political unrest in Africa. Some of it is religious, Muslims versus Christians. There is government corruption, fighting over control of territory and resources. There are tribal rivalries that predate colonialism."

Brad's eyes indicated satisfaction with her succinct answer. He dug into his lobster mac and cheese with gusto. A rapturous smile came over his face as he chewed. "Oh, honey, this is delicious!"

"Thanks, Dad," Tiffany said, looking pleased. "I know how much you like it, but we probably should have had something healthier before tomorrow's food orgy."

"No, Tiff, this is just right," Brad assured her. "Everything is great. And I'm glad we postponed our return to New York, so we can go to that concert on Sunday." Reshma had patiently listened to Tiffany complain about her parents extending their stay. "I live streamed the *Verdi Requiem* from the Met," Brad continued. "Wow! Lucille Bartlett is fantastic. I'm really looking forward to hearing her sing live."

Reshma puffed up with pride at hearing Mother Lucy praised by such a musically literate person. "You won't be disappointed," Reshma said loyally.

"I could kick myself for missing her early career. Quite a story about the Met apologizing for not dealing with her sexual assault."

"It was very brave of her to be an example to others," said Mary. "I admire her."

"You'll be at the concert, won't you, Reshma?" Brad asked.

"Of course. I'm one of Mother Lucy's biggest fans."

"You work for her, don't you?" Mary asked. The real interrogation was beginning.

"She's the rector, which means she oversees the spiritual life of the church and the clergy," Reshma explained. "So, yes, she's my boss."

"When Tiffany told me she was dating a minister," said Mary, "I found it hard to believe."

"Priest, Mom," Tiffany muttered. "In the Episcopal Church, they're called priests."

Her mother glared at her daughter for correcting her. "Tiffany has never shown any interest in religion. I suppose she told you that we're atheists."

"It's Reshma's job, Mom," said Tiffany in an annoyed tone. "It has nothing to do with why I like her."

"Maybe not, but it was your job that made me like you," said Reshma. "It was those chocolate croissants."

"Shh!" hushed Tiffany. "They don't need to know that."

Fortunately, Brad began laughing, and it was contagious. Mary and Amber joined in.

"They say that chocolate is an aphrodisiac," said Mary after the mirth sputtered out.

Across the table, Tiffany locked eyes with Reshma. "Is it?" she asked.

✳✳✳

The Cathedral was packed. Lucy's concerts had become popular beyond the Portland area. This production of the *Verdi Requiem* had been written up in newspapers as far away as Boston and New York. There was even a longish piece in the *New York Times*.

"Thanks for saving me a seat," said Sam, sliding into the pew.

"You're welcome," Liz replied. "You can help me keep an eye on the kids."

Sam waved to Maggie's granddaughters. Then she crossed her arms on her chest and from under a furrowed brow watched the other concertgoers.

Liz gave her a jab with her elbow. "Smile, Sam. It won't kill you."

"I didn't want to come," she replied in a sullen whisper.

"Yes, I know, but it's good for you to be seen," said Liz curtly. "It's *your* foundation."

"It was your idea. It's *your* foundation."

"So? It was my idea, but you provided the seed money."

"You did too. Oh, Liz I HATE these things!" said Sam, scowling.

"I know you do. I hate them too, but if you smile, they're less painful. Trust me, Sam. When I was in New Haven, I attended more fundraisers than you can ever imagine."

"They're all staring at me," Sam complained, glowering at the person sitting in front of her.

Liz glanced around, but no one was looking at Sam. "So what if they are?" said Liz. "You keep hiding like this, Sam, and people will think you're guilty."

"The judge dismissed the last case. Said it had no merit."

"Doesn't matter. If you act guilty, people think you're guilty. That's how it works."

"Like you after that actress sued you for malpractice. You quit your job. Did that make you look guilty?"

Sam knew Liz during the very public malpractice suit that had finally convinced her to quit her Yale New Haven job and come to Maine. She also knew how furious Liz had been over being dragged through the tabloids. "It's not the same," Liz replied in a measured tone. "I quit because I couldn't deal with bean counters making medical decisions. I was tired of a bureaucracy that worried about the bottom line, not the patients."

"Right," said Sam dismissively. "You didn't feel you belonged there anymore. That's how I feel."

"Sam," Liz said softly but with obvious affection. "Please don't run away. You've faced your critics before and proven them wrong. When everyone was saying your architecture was passé, you proved them wrong."

"We should all live so long that we become retro," Sam said glumly.

Liz never liked to pull the emotional card with Sam because she considered it a dirty trick, but she was out of reasonable arguments. "I'd miss you."

"You'll do fine. Liz, I need to get out of here. And being an architect again feels good. It means I need to go where the work is. Maggie knows that. If she doesn't like it, well, that's too fucking bad."

Liz sighed deeply and stared straight ahead. "Are you leaving her?"

"More like she's leaving me."

"Shit," muttered Liz under her breath.

"Yeah. Shit," Sam repeated.

Further discussion was precluded by the chorus filing in to take their seats, which drew polite applause. The soloists followed. Lucy appeared last, drawing shouts and cheers. The clapping for the conductor, who led the Portland Symphony, was tepid by comparison.

Liz patted Sam's hand. "We'll talk later," she promised.

"No, we won't," Sam said tersely. "I'm done talking about this."

After the concert, Liz found a quiet corner of the hall and withdrew to sip her bland chardonnay. The bottle label from a large winery, known to blend its wine for a consistent taste, explained why it was as predictable as a McDonald's hamburger. Liz wasn't a wine snob, but she liked what she drank to have a point of view.

When she'd traveled Europe with Maggie, early in their marriage, they'd visited the wine regions of France, Germany, and Portugal. Liz's insatiable curiosity caused her to seek out every book and website she could find on wine production and the history of winemaking practices. Soon words like "*terroir*" and "*ullage*" were falling off her tongue. Staring at the pale liquid in her plastic glass, she wondered if the makers of this tasteless product ever spoke in such terms. Although their ads and websites showed picturesque fields and antique barrels piled high, this wine had been produced in an industrial-sized vat.

She glanced around the room. The overflow concert audience had packed into the cathedral hall to await the principals. By any standards, it had been an impressive concert, with musicians from the BSO supplementing the Portland Symphony Orchestra. Lucy and Denise had been joined by a tenor and bass from the Met roster. A competent chorus drawn from local churches and singing groups had accompanied them. No one expected the performance to compare to Lucy's Met version of the *Verdi Requiem*, but everyone involved in the production could be justifiably proud. No doubt, the wealthy donors had gotten more than their money's worth.

It was easier for Liz to think about the indifferent wine or the contributions to the shooting victims' fund than what Sam had said before the concert. A split between Sam and Maggie would change the ecology of Hobbs. In their small, tight-knit LGBT community, a single breakup could be as damaging as a winter Nor'easter. After another mass shooting, a shocking war in Gaza, and unsettling political currents setting up another pivotal election, everyone was longing for some stability. Liz was no exception. Change was inevitable, but so much, all at once, could be overwhelming. The key, Liz reminded herself, was not to overreact.

She was giving herself this little lecture when Lucy appeared at her side. She took Liz's glass out of her hand and took a gulp.

"I can get you one," Liz offered. There hadn't been much left in her glass, and Lucy had left barely a sip.

"No, let's stay here for a moment. I'm hiding too." Lucy took Liz's elbow and pulled her closer to the wall.

"It's not like you to avoid your fans," Liz said, moving to block the view of Lucy from the crowd.

"It's not my fans. It's Tiffany's father."

Liz searched her mind to understand why Lucy would perceive Brad Taylor as such a threat. They'd enjoyed the Taylors' company when Reshma had brought them over after Thanksgiving dinner, along with pies to feed the extra guests. They were still eating the pies, thanks to the abundance Maggie had created. Liz guessed that Reshma had felt the need to pay obeisance to her rector after declining her invitation. Other than an excessive liking for Liz's expensive whiskey, Brad seemed harmless. As he approached, minus his entourage, the reason Lucy was fleeing him finally connected in Liz's brain. Brad ran a performing arts foundation.

Liz's eyes scanned the hall for an available exit, but she'd backed herself and Lucy into a corner. As Brad came closer, Lucy quickly drained Liz's glass.

Brad gave Liz a broad politician's smile, revealing beautifully veneered teeth. "I'm glad you're here, Dr. Stolz. Your wife tells me that you founded the Gun Victim's Fund, and I need to talk to you." Surreptitiously, Lucy reached for Liz's hand.

"I'm one of the founders, but now it has a board, and the fund is administered by an attorney, Melissa Morgenstern."

"But I'm guessing you know how to convey a proposal to the principals," Brad answered smoothly. Liz resented being forced into her executive persona, but she resolved to remain cordial.

"Well, of course, but it would be easier for me to give you her contact information."

"That's great, but I'd like to preview the idea for you...get your feedback, if you don't mind."

Liz stared at him coldly, hoping he'd back off.

"It concerns your wife," Brad said, glancing at Lucy, who

tightened her grip on Liz's hand, not enough to hurt but with enough pressure to transmit her anxiety.

"If it's something professional, you might want to talk to her agent," said Liz. She stood straight and looked him in the eye. In heels, she was taller than he was. She was glad for the height advantage, which forced him to look up to her.

Brad was undaunted, probably used to being pushy to get what he wanted. "Oh, does he also schedule her charity events like this one?"

"No," Lucy admitted. "I set this up with the diocese, but otherwise he needs to be in on all my bookings."

Brad whipped out his phone, obviously prepared to take notes. "What's his name?"

Lucy hesitated.

"Roger Weinstein," Liz supplied. "You can find him online. Also, the contact information for the victims' fund," Liz said, hoping that would satisfy him, but by now, her curiosity was getting the better of her. "Okay, Brad. I'll bite. What's this idea you want to pitch?"

Now that Brad knew he had a willing audience, he slipped his phone back into his pocket. "I knew you'd be interested, Dr. Stolz. I saw your interview on *Sixty Minutes*. Obviously, you know first-hand the damage guns can do. My idea is simple. Concerts in cities near towns that have experienced mass shootings. Find the biggest classical music venues to host them with proceeds split between a local support agency and our foundations. I'll arrange for one of my youth orchestras to accompany the singers. Madame Bartlett, I hear you do Broadway tunes as well as classical singing. Maybe we can find some pop singers to participate to mix it up for a wider audience."

Liz looked at Lucy, trying to read her reaction. She could see a glimmer of interest in her green eyes but also hesitation.

Liz had been giving Brad her most skeptical look so he couldn't read her enthusiasm for the idea. "You do know that Lucy has a full-time job as the rector of a church?"

"Yes, but we can work around her schedule, so it's not a burden. I'm sure your agent can figure it out."

"It's a worthy cause," Lucy finally said. "But as Liz said, I have a job. I only sing part time, and my agent is always pushing me to do more."

Brad laughed heartily. "Hah, agents always push you to do more. That's how they make their living. But I'm not telling you anything new, Madame Bartlett. You've been doing this for a while."

She doesn't need to be reminded of her age, you asshole, thought Liz.

"Please call me Lucy. No need to be so formal."

Especially not after parking yourself at my house and draining my bottle of single-malt scotch, thought Liz, but she followed Lucy's gracious example and asked him to call her Liz.

"I'm sure the foundation will give your proposal the consideration it deserves," Liz said noncommittally. "The main issue is Lucy's time. Only she can decide how much she can handle." She glanced at Lucy urging her to speak up.

"I've got a lot on my plate, but I'll think about it," Lucy finally said.

"Do you know other artists who might want to collaborate on this project?" asked Brad. "I hear you know the contralto, Denise Chantal, who sang today. I'm sure there are others."

"I know some people," Lucy said noncommittally. "But you'll have to contact them directly."

"Great. Send me some names, and I'll take care of the rest." Brad shook Lucy's hand and reached out his hand to Liz. "Thanks for listening to my idea. I think this program can raise a lot of money." While Brad had been talking, Liz had been mentally calculating the kind of money Brad's project could raise. Lucy's contacts would guarantee the best venues for the performances. It could turn into something big.

Brad withdrew a business card from his jacket pocket. "Here's how to find me." Liz fingered the card as she watched him disappear into the crowd.

When she turned to Lucy, she sensed her conflict. The poor woman had finally gotten Roger off her back, and now someone else was pursuing her. "You're interested, aren't you?" Liz ventured. "I can tell."

"It's a brilliant idea, and it could raise a lot of money for the foundation."

"A shitload of money. For his foundation too…and raise their media profile. It promotes classical music. A win-win."

"But will it be too much for us?" Lucy asked, anxiously searching Liz's face.

"I don't know," Liz replied honestly.

Chapter 10

Lucy finished singing her exercises and drained her water bottle. Her throat was always parched after a vigorous round of arpeggios and scales. She gazed at the last row of home theater seats, where Liz usually sat, missing her presence as much as her criticism of whatever Lucy was rehearsing for her next performance. Liz's absence had allowed Lucy to lean more heavily into the technical exercises, which could be auditory torture to anyone who wasn't a singer or a vocal coach, never mind boring.

Liz had only skipped morning practice because she was preparing her statement to the Maine House of Representatives. The Maine Gun Safety Coalition had invited her to speak in support of stricter gun laws proposed after the Lewiston shooting. With her usual thoroughness, Liz had prepared for the five-minute speech like she was writing a medical paper. She'd reviewed the police and coroner's reports from both shootings, compiled talking points from her interview on *Sixty Minutes*, and made a detailed timeline, including links to news stories. By the time Liz addressed the state representatives, she would dazzle them with her command of the facts.

Melissa Morgenstern, a trust attorney and administrator of the Gun Victims Fund, liked to say that if Liz hadn't gone into medicine, she would have made a brilliant attorney. When Lucy asked Melissa to elaborate, she said, "Liz can weave the driest details into an engaging story. That's a real gift."

After that, Lucy started paying more attention when Liz gave a public talk. She'd even learned a few tricks to use in her sermons. Unlike Erika, who always used the shortest route to win an argument, Liz built up her case gradually. Then, bam! She clinched it. Liz had a comedian's sense of timing, waiting for exactly the right moment to deliver the punchline.

It was Liz who'd taught Lucy how to organize her thoughts when she was writing her doctoral dissertation. Erika had tried, but she was too indulgent, letting Lucy get away with what she now recognized as sloppy thinking.

Looking back, Lucy realized she'd fallen in love with both women because they were so smart. She'd always doubted her intelligence and saw in them something she thought she lacked. She was a pretty face with a beautiful voice, not an intellectual. She saw herself as the beating heart of the relationship, the one with the high EQ, who could interpret the social world for them, while they were the brains. But each of them had seen her potential. Erika had encouraged Lucy to pursue her doctorate. Now, she had a PhD from a prestigious institution after her name, and she could style herself *The Reverend Doctor Lucille Bartlett.*

Usually, Lucy didn't compare her two wives. She loved them each uniquely, although they used to joke about being twins, two sides of the same coin. Liz's intellect was sharp and wide-ranging. The sheer diversity of Liz's interests was staggering. She could cogently discuss anything from the most abstract aspect of epistemology to hydraulic engineering and the microbiome of the human gut. She could probably teach the history of nineteenth century music at Juilliard.

Equally brilliant, Erika preferred to play on her own turf, namely political philosophy, which she'd taught for over thirty-five years at Colby College. Although she was highly literate in music, she'd always deferred to Lucy because she was a professional. She was humble, whereas the buccaneer confidence that had enabled Liz to become a surgeon also tempted her into believing there was no subject she couldn't master. Liz gorged on information until she had her fill. As a result, the knowledge she accumulated was as deep as it was wide.

Lucy turned off the sound system and the lights in the media room and went to look for Liz. She found her wife in her office, hunched over her laptop. The blue light of the screen reflected on her face. Whatever she was reading was so engaging that Lucy had to rap sharply on the open door to get her attention.

"Hey, babe," said Liz, looking up. "Done with singing?"

"Yes, I could sing the boring stuff because I didn't have an audience."

"Sorry, but I need to get this done."

"I know," said Lucy, rubbing her shoulder affectionately. She kissed the top of her head. "Don't apologize."

"Want some breakfast?" asked Liz. "I'll make you something."

"No, don't stop what you're doing. I can have some yogurt and fruit. After all that pie at Thanksgiving, I can skip a few calories. They wouldn't miss me."

"Maybe not, but you would miss them," said Liz, massaging Lucy's bottom in the most seductive way.

"Stop that," said Lucy gently pulling away. "We can't this morning."

"Why not? It's Saturday and we have nowhere to go. Now that Maggie's gone home, no one will care if we disappear to the bedroom."

"You have things to do today, and so do I."

The phone buzzed in the pocket of Lucy's fleece, and she pulled it out. "Hmm. It's Emily. She hates to talk on the phone, so this must be important." Lucy tapped the call open. "Good morning, sweetie. How are you?"

"I woke up thinking of blueberry pancakes," replied the young voice. "Do you suppose I can get Aunt Liz to make me some?"

Meanwhile, Liz was once again deeply engrossed in whatever she was reading. "I don't know," Lucy said. "Why don't you ask her?" She handed Liz the phone. "Emily," she mouthed to clue her in and listened while her daughter negotiated with her wife. Finally, Liz closed her laptop again and got up.

"I guess we're having blueberry pancakes this morning," she said, handing back Lucy's phone. "Emily needs to talk to us."

"About what?" asked Lucy, hurrying to catch up with Liz as she headed to the kitchen.

"She didn't say, but I guess we'll find out soon."

Liz was in the basement looking for a bag of frozen blueberries when Emily arrived, looking sleepy but dressed for the day. Often when Denise was away on a singing engagement, she came over for breakfast in what she'd worn to bed. Lucy liked the informality, which reminded her of when they'd all lived together as a family.

Now that she'd reached her full adult height, Emily was a hair taller than Liz. She towered over her petite mother as she gave Lucy a light half hug. Since Emily had turned twenty, her face had settled into its adult proportions. She resembled her mother even more closely. She helped herself to a cup of coffee like she lived there all the time. Lucy was glad to see her make herself at home.

"Liz says you need to talk to us," Lucy said casually while Emily waited for her coffee to brew. "Want to give me a quick preview?"

"Let's wait till Liz comes up so I don't have to repeat it. What I have to say isn't easy."

Well, that was a clue, but it sounded ominous. Fortunately, Liz returned from the basement with a bag of blueberries, which would end the wait. "Feeling hungry this morning?" she asked Emily. "I can make some bacon."

The idea brought a genuine smile to Emily's face. She loved bacon. "Absolutely! Thanks, Aunt Liz."

Accustomed to feeding a hungry crowd at breakfast, Liz had preparation down to a science. She carefully laid out strips of bacon in a cold skillet, then oiled the griddle. "Can I help?" Lucy offered, too late to be useful.

"Nope, sit and talk to your daughter. We don't often have the pleasure of her company at breakfast."

"Maggie was here," said Emily with a big yawn. "I didn't want to bother you while you had company."

"Maggie's not exactly company," Liz reminded her. "And you know you're always welcome."

Lucy was sad that her daughter hadn't felt welcome but pleased at the advance in her daughter's social perceptions. The religious people who'd adopted Emily had laid a good foundation in how to behave with others, but their social network had been limited to their traditional small-town community. At Yale, Emily needed to navigate the academic hierarchy to survive the politics of graduate school. Denise had been a positive influence, coaching her on appropriate responses as if she were teaching a budding actress to express an emotion. It was still hard to know how much of Emily's behavior corresponded with her feelings, but she could pass as "normal."

"If you want more coffee, now's the time to get it," Liz warned from the stove. "Pancakes and bacon will be ready soon." Lucy and Emily lined up to refill their cups. "I forgot to ask if anyone wanted eggs too."

"No, sit down," said Lucy, "This is wonderful." Then she saw the hopeful look on her daughter's face. To Emily's credit, she didn't protest that she would like some eggs. Lucy refused to feel guilty about depriving her daughter. Denise was a good cook. Emily certainly didn't look like she was starving.

Liz demolished her pancakes while Lucy and Emily were just warming up and jumped up to start another batch.

"Okay, Em," Lucy said. "You've kept us in suspense long enough."

Emily compressed her lips into a flat line and looked from Liz's back at the stove to her mother. "I'm moving out."

"Oh," said Lucy, trying not to sound as surprised and hurt as she felt. "Where are you going?"

"To the faculty residence at Yale. They found me a studio." Emily played with her phone. "I'm sending you photos."

"Thanks. I'll look at them later," said Lucy, taking her daughter's hand. "When will you be moving?"

"Next week, if Aunt Liz can help take my stuff down in her truck."

Liz came to the table with another stack of pancakes and distributed them. "Sure. I'm off on Monday."

"How did you get into faculty housing?" Lucy asked.

"They hired me as an assistant professor."

"Before you pass your thesis defense?" asked Liz in between bites of pancakes. "Isn't that a little unusual? I bet Stefan had something to do with it." Erika's father, who'd once held a named math professorship at Yale, was the co-author of the theorem that had won Emily a scholarship to Yale and admission to the PhD program.

"I don't know." Emily focused on her plate. "He didn't say anything."

"What about music school?" Lucy asked, trying to hide her disappointment.

"I can do that later, Mom," said Emily confidently.

How lucky to have such a luxury, Lucy thought, but with Emily's many talents, it must be hard to choose.

"Congratulations." Liz, mindful of Emily's aversion to touch, gently patted her on the back. "When did all this happen?"

"A couple of days ago," Emily admitted, drawing designs with her fork in the leftover syrup on her plate. "Denise and I needed to talk before I told you."

"I assume she'll be leaving too," said Liz. Lucy shot her an annoyed look for getting down to business so quickly. Sometimes, she wondered if Liz was on the spectrum too.

"Denise is moving in with a friend she met in Milan," Emily explained.

"Oh?" said Liz, raising a brow. "A friend-friend or a romantic friend?"

Lucy had wanted to ask the same question. She was glad that Liz had no qualms about being blunt. Emily's face darkened.

"They're involved, if that's what you're asking. He's a baritone."

"He? A man?" Liz's eyebrows rose, but Lucy wasn't surprised. She'd always suspected that Denise was bisexual. When she'd first interviewed Denise for the position of music director, she'd mentioned she'd suddenly been forced to vacate an apartment she'd shared with a male friend.

"Yes, a guy."

"You don't seem all that broken up about it," Liz observed tactlessly.

"I've known something was going on for a while."

"I'm sorry," said Liz with genuine sympathy. "That sucks."

"It's okay. It was time for her to move on. Me too."

Lucy couldn't tell whether Emily was upset or not. Her face registered no distinct emotion.

"We're here to support you, sweetie," Lucy assured her.

Emily turned her blue eyes on her mother and looked puzzled. "I'm okay. I just need help with the move."

"When will Denise be here to get her things?" Liz asked, refilling her coffee cup. "She has stuff in the barn over my workshop. I need to be home to let her in."

"She said she'd call you." Emily picked up a piece of bacon and began to nibble on it. "Please be happy for me. It's a good thing."

Lucy forced herself to sound pleased and optimistic. "It is a good thing. I'm very proud to call you Professor Bartlett and happy they found you a nice place to live. I'll look at the photos after breakfast."

"And you'll come to my thesis defense?"

"You bet we will. Right, Liz?"

"Only if you get us front row seats." Liz's crooked grin was endearing. "Just yanking your chain. Wouldn't miss it for anything. Congrats, kid. Well done."

***

"You didn't have to come with me," said Liz, turning to glance at Lucy in the passenger seat. "I'm sure you have other things to do this morning."

Lucy was tapping away on her phone and appeared not to hear her, but then she said, "Sorry, sweetie. I need to answer this text."

Liz rolled her eyes. "For fuck's sake! Another crisis?"

"What's a church without a crisis?" murmured Lucy in a tone dripping with acid. She added the last decisive stroke to her message with a finger poke that could take out an eye and dropped her phone in her lap. "Of course, I have to come with you, Liz. Number one, you're my ticket into the House chamber, and also number one, I want to support you and gun safety."

"What's the crisis?" Liz insisted.

Lucy shook her head. "You don't want to know, and besides, you should be thinking about what you're going to say to the lawmakers in Augusta, not the craziness at St. Margaret's."

"Come on, Lucy. You're going to tell me anyway."

"An elderly man in hospice is nearing death. His family called for pastoral care. Reshma asked for the day off to come up for the rally. Tiffany even closed her shop to come along. Tom is in Connecticut visiting friends. Susan is teaching..."

"So, who will respond to the request? Not you, I hope," said Liz, watching for an opening in traffic so she could change lanes. She cut in quickly. She glanced at Lucy for signs of disapproval but saw none, such a difference from Maggie. Lucy's lack of reaction almost made daredevil mischief not worth doing. It finally dawned on Liz that Lucy might be ignoring her stunts as a strategy. *Damn! Why did I have to marry a shrink?*

"I texted the chaplain at the hospice," explained Lucy. "She'll stay with the family until someone from St. Margaret's can get there. And she's a Lutheran minister, so she can administer the last rights if we can't get there in time."

"Saved by Lucy's contact list."

"And our full communion with other denominations. I'm grateful for interdenominational services where I can get to know local clergy, who can help in an emergency."

"Except the Evangelicals. They hate you."

"They keep saying they'll pray for me, and I say, 'thank you. I can always use prayers.'"

"Bet that makes them mad as hell," said Liz. "And people think you're so sweet and kind."

Lucy affected an innocent smile. "I am, and after all, it's true. I'm a mess like everyone else, and I can use all the grace and prayers I can get."

Liz saw the green sign indicating the exit to Augusta was coming up in two miles. They were in plenty of time for the hearing, but when Liz pulled into the entrance to the parking area, she found it packed with vehicles.

"Wow, they weren't kidding about this hearing drawing a big crowd," said Lucy, sitting up to look around.

Liz followed the directions of the waving traffic officer. "Both sides were counting on their supporters to show up."

"Look, there's Reshma and Tiffany!" Lucy pointed to the walkway running parallel to the drive.

The young priest's black coat was open, showing her rainbow stole. Tiffany was bundled up against the January chill in a dusty rose down coat. A huge, white scarf wound around her neck like an albino boa constrictor. Liz stopped the car and rolled down the passenger window. "You ladies look a little cold. Want a ride?"

Reshma's eyes raised to the sky. Liz guessed she was thanking God for a warm ride. They whipped open the doors and jumped into the backseat and not a moment too soon. The traffic had backed up behind Liz's car. Behind her, someone leaned on the horn. Liz glanced in the rear-view mirror. "And fuck you too!" she muttered irritably.

Lucy glanced at their passengers, pleading for understanding. Tiffany giggled softly. Liz engaged her eyes in the rear-view mirror. "Yes, the old lady swears, but I'm sure you've heard that word before." The vehicle behind them honked again. Liz gave him the middle finger, figuring Lucy would find a silent epithet less offensive. A truck, flying the yellow 'Don't Tread on Me' flag with its coiled rattlesnake, roared past them. The driver shouted unintelligible, angry words from his open window. "You fucking nut!" Liz snarled back.

"Liz," Lucy said in a quiet but firm voice, now looking very disapproving. "Honey, you need to calm down. You don't want to sound angry when you're giving testimony."

"Maybe I should sound angry. It's outrageous that eighteen people are dead!"

"Yes, it is, and your righteous anger is appropriate, but you know a calm voice persuades better than an angry one." Lucy reached over and rested her hand on her thigh. "Breathe, sweetie. Come on. Deep breath...and another..."

After a few breaths, Liz felt calmer. She patted Lucy's hand on her thigh. "Thank you. Good advice."

I love you, Lucy mouthed and smiled. "It will be okay," she added aloud.

The legislators' lot, where they had reserved parking, was crowded, so they had to walk quite a distance in a cold wind that cut like knives of ice. Liz clutched her coat closed at the throat. Her hair, which she'd fussed with a little more than usual, would be a complete mess. Maybe she could duck into a ladies' room to comb it before the hearing.

She had only had two passes for the gallery in the chamber, but the guard saw Reshma's collar and waved her through the door. They needed to part at the balcony entrance. Lucy traced a cross on Liz's forehead with her thumb. "I'm blessing you, so you can do God's work," Lucy said. When she reached up to give Liz a kiss on the cheek, she whispered into her ear, "You'll be great. I love you so much." Reshma offered a hug, and Tiffany gave Liz an encouraging pat on the arm and wished her luck.

The guard directed Liz to a page. The young man led her to the section of the chamber reserved for those who were testifying. Before she took her seat, Liz looked down the row and spotted a portly, older man with a flat-top crew cut. The style was still popular with Maine's retired military men. He was also an NRA-certified gun instructor, and Liz knew him from regional training meetings. She smiled and waved to him. He responded with a filthy look. Obviously, he would be speaking for the other side today.

Liz sighed. Before the gun rights advocates had become so entrenched in the idea that all regulation was bad, they could have reasonable conversations. Not anymore. Now, they claimed that everyone had an absolute right to have a gun. They'd succeeded in getting rid of the requirement to have a permit or even safety training before carrying a concealed weapon. They fought any attempt to regulate assault rifles or high-capacity magazines. Meanwhile, mentally ill shooters rained death on innocent Mainers.

Liz had decided to focus her talk on Maine's weak yellow-flag law. Clearly, it had failed in the case of Robert Card. His family had reported their concerns about his odd behavior to local law enforcement, hoping they would take away his guns. The police had gone out to talk to him, but he wouldn't come to the door. Failing to confront him in person, they legally couldn't do anything and left.

A handsome, elderly gentleman approached where Liz sat. He was the House rep from the Hobbs district, who'd invited her to speak. Liz got up to shake his hand.

"Thanks for coming, Dr. Stolz. You're a real celebrity, but you certainly speak from experience. Your words will have a real impact."

"I hope so, Dan. You know I'm not on board with all the proposals, but I'll keep that to myself."

"Good idea. Which legislation don't you support?"

"I'm not sure the seventy-two-hour waiting period will save any lives. It will just hurt local gun dealers and drive business to New Hampshire."

"Even if it saves one life," said the rep.

Liz nodded but she still wasn't convinced the law would be effective. "Maybe it could prevent some suicides."

"Half of gun deaths are suicides, so that's something."

"Yes, something, but it's an area where we need national reform. Same with the carry laws. They're too loose in some states. Too strict in others. I can't even stay overnight in New York with my unloaded gun locked in a safe in my trunk. That's crazy."

"Let's take what we can get," the rep said, patting her arm. "Thanks for offering to speak out. You're our star witness."

"You're welcome, but I don't need any more pressure." She thumbed over her shoulder toward the gallery above. "I've got a bunch of people in collars with high expectations up there."

The House rep was also gay and smiled knowingly. "I'm glad Dr. Bartlett is here to support you. I never turn away support from a higher power." He raised his eyes.

Liz laughed. "Don't tell my wife, but neither do I."

He was called away and Liz sat down. Before she opened her tablet to review her notes, she glanced down the row of seats. She caught the eye of the gun instructor she knew. Again, she smiled. He responded with a scowl.

***

Reshma leaned over the gallery railing, trying to find Liz. They'd been early enough to get front-row seats. She finally spotted Liz almost directly below, hunched over her tablet. Reshma called softly, but Liz didn't stir.

"Do you see her?" Lucy asked, interrupting her conversation with Tiffany.

Reshma pointed down and Lucy's eyes followed the direction of her finger. "I tried to get her attention," said Reshma, "but I guess she didn't hear me."

Lucy rolled her eyes. "If Liz is involved in something, the building could fall down around her, and she wouldn't know it."

Watching Liz ignore what was going on around her, Reshma envied Lucy the deep knowledge of her partner that allowed her to predict her behavior so accurately. She wondered if she could achieve such a close connection with Tiffany. Her girlfriend had attracted the attention of the two young men sitting behind her. She laughed at something one of them had said. They were obviously flirting with her. *What was she thinking?* Reshma wondered. Of course, she could lean across Lucy and ask. How different from Liz and Lucy, who often seemed to communicate without speaking. Their deep well of shared understanding went beyond familiarity or a physical relationship. They always seemed almost preternaturally aware of each other, as if connected by an invisible golden cord.

Reshma knew that having sex alone didn't mean the partners were intimate. Her brief relationship with Denise had included sex, but the act of touching a person's naked body isn't the same as truly knowing someone. Often, words got in the way. Reshma knew, because no amount of explaining on Denise's part had enabled her to comprehend the trans woman's deep need to change her gender. "You don't need to understand," Denise had finally explained in a frustrated voice. "Just love me as I am."

Although Reshma always tried to meet each person where they were, she simply couldn't wrap her brain around Denise's need to transition. Listening to the recordings she'd made as a countertenor confused the issue even more. She loved hearing the strong, incredibly pure tones Denise had sung before Lucy's coaching had helped her add the complexity and warmth of a natural female alto.

"It's going to be so cold for the people outside," Lucy said, interrupting Reshma's thoughts. "We're lucky Liz could get us into the chamber. I hope the protestors outside dressed for the weather. Otherwise, they're going to freeze!" Thinking of the windy walk from the parking lot made Reshma involuntarily shiver.

"This is exciting," she confided. "I've never been to a public hearing before...or a political demonstration."

"Really?" Lucy's green eyes searched hers. "What brought you to this one?"

Reshma discreetly looked in Tiffany's direction.

Lucy leaned closer to whisper, "Whatever your reason, we're glad you're here. I'm sure Liz appreciates the support. Gun safety is a worthy cause."

Usually, Reshma avoided politics. Their denomination supported the separation of church and state, but keeping her opinions to herself also helped her to stay out of trouble. People often made assumptions based on the color of her skin. Her seminary friends expected her to be all in for "Black Lives Matter." Historically, the lives of people of color mattered less, but that didn't mean they should matter more. She perceived the implied racism that went both ways. She wouldn't say it out loud, but she had more sympathy for the idea that *all* lives matter.

In her Episcopal school, they taught that every human being was one of God's beloved children and equal in his eyes. Whatever happened to the goal of equality? Why should people in the present compensate for wrongs committed before they were even born? The idea of "defunding the police" was even more ridiculous. After working with marginalized people in rough urban settings, Reshma knew how much they depended on the police to protect them. The reality of social justice was far more complex than the slogans invented by rich kids at Ivy League schools.

She glanced at Tiffany, relieved to see the young man beside her was now busy talking to his friend. She was more worried about what Tiffany would think if she knew she harbored beliefs that didn't coincide with her own. Tiffany shared her views freely, assuming Reshma agreed. Reshma simply listened.

When Tiffany had invited her to this gun safety rally, she didn't need to ask twice. Gun safety was a cause Reshma could get behind. As Lucy had said in the car, keeping innocent people safe from madmen with guns should be everyone's priority.

Below, the roar, amplified by the vaulted ceiling, had softened into a low hum, and Reshma could see why. Rachel Talbot Ross had stepped up to the podium. Reshma could only identify her by name because Ross was the first black woman to be elected to the Maine House, and the first person of color to become its speaker. She banged her gavel on the table of the lectern.

"The House will come to order!" she demanded in a booming voice. Except for a few stragglers, the sound in the hall stilled. "Welcome, members and guests. This special joint session of the Maine Legislature to hear public comment on proposed gun legislation is now open. First we will hear from those who oppose the proposed legislation. Our first speaker will be Bob Garrison of the Maine Sportsman Alliance."

A tall, bearded man headed to the lectern set up in the front. He sounded perfectly reasonable recounting Maine's long history of hunting and outdoor sports. That's what made sorting the arguments so tricky. Some positions made sense. It was taking them to an extreme that made them dangerous. The man's main point seemed to be that more stringent laws would penalize gun owners who followed the rules. At the end of his speech, the Speaker asked if there were any questions. A member near the back raised her hand, and everyone turned around to look at her.

"With all the hunting rifles and shotguns available, does any hunter need an assault rifle? I mean, you can kill a deer or a moose, or even a bear without one, isn't that right?"

"Yes, that is correct," said the man from the Maine Sportsman Alliance. "But you never know what you might encounter in the woods. You might disturb a bear den, or you could run into a lynx or a fisher. They are nasty little critters with a mean bite. You want to be able to neutralize them quickly."

"But wouldn't a pistol do that just as well?" the rep asked in a persistent tone.

"Yes," he said after a moment of hesitation. "It could."

"Thank you," said the woman and sat down.

The next five speakers offered the usual reasons why gun regulations would impede the rights of law-abiding gun owners and wouldn't reduce deaths or injuries as promised. A spokesman from a major outdoor and sporting goods retailer railed against the seventy-two-hour waiting period, saying it would only drive business to neighboring states. The final speaker flatly said that Second Amendment rights were absolute, and the legislature had no business writing any legislation.

As she listened, Reshma could see the plausibility of some of the arguments. But like all government regulations, how much gun laws protected or inconvenienced citizens was a matter of degree. "And there are already too many gun laws on the books," said the last speaker. "Why not just enforce them?"

"And now we will hear from the speakers in favor of the proposed gun laws," said Speaker Ross.

The anti-gun speakers cited facts and figures, hoping to prove why their pet legislation would benefit the citizens of Maine. Reshma wondered if the lawmakers in the chamber were as bored as she was.

Finally, it was Liz's turn to speak. When she rose, there was a ripple of applause. Liz's *Sixty Minutes* interview had made her the best-known of anyone on the roster, and many considered her a hero for ending the standoff in the Hobbs School shooting. As she took her place at the lectern, Liz frowned and patted the air to silence the applause.

"Thank you," she said, adjusting the microphone for her greater height. "I'm here today as a certified gun safety instructor and a physician who has seen the harm to the body that guns can do. But I'm also here as someone who must decide whether a gun owner is mentally fit to have a gun. Understand that you don't have to be criminally insane or ready to be committed to an asylum to be unfit. All gun owners go through periods when their emotional stability is questionable. It even happened to me after the Hobbs Elementary shooting. Fortunately, my family realized that I needed a break from my guns. I voluntarily surrendered them to the Hobbs police chief, who locked them up.

"But not all of us are able to see the problem, or if we do, we might deny it. Maine's Yellow Flag Law was designed to protect the rights of gun owners while taking guns out of the hands of dangerous individuals. As I said, we can all find ourselves in an emotional state that can make us a danger to ourselves or others. Clearly, in the case of Robert Card, the law failed to protect Maine citizens. Mr. Card's family reported his odd behavior to local authorities. They followed the law and tried to interview him, but he wouldn't cooperate, so their hands were tied.

"From the point of view of law enforcement, they'd done their duty. If they had been more persistent, eighteen people might be alive today. But hindsight is twenty-twenty. Predicting whether an emotional disturbance will result in violence is tricky. It's not a precise science. But to protect the public, we need the opportunity to evaluate the situation. That means bringing in the subject to be examined by mental health professionals. Right now, the barriers are too high, and often it's too late to make a difference. The Lewiston shooting was the result.

"Full disclosure, I would rather have a red flag law like they have in other states. Erring on the side of inconveniencing a gun owner is better than allowing him to kill innocent people or himself. I say 'him' only because the subject is usually male, but as my own story proves, the problem could be a female. I support the governor's tightening of the current yellow flag law that makes it easier for police to approach and bring in gun owners for evaluation. I hope you will support it too. Thank you."

Liz closed her tablet. The Speaker asked if there were any questions. A dozen hands shot up. Speaker Ross smiled. "Now you know why we saved Dr. Stolz for last." There was a murmur of laughter in the auditorium. "Questioners, come up to the front and form a line, please."

"Was Liz expecting a lot of questions?" Reshma asked Lucy.

Lucy leaned closer to speak in her ear. "When she agreed to do this, she knew she would be putting herself on the line."

The first questioner was a representative from Aroostook County. "Dr. Stolz, you are in favor of stricter gun laws, but aren't you proof that a good guy with a gun can be a deterrent?"

Liz looked directly at the questioner when she spoke. "I often get this question, and the simple answer is no. While I hope I'm a 'good guy,'" she paused for the laughter, "I am not a good example of that idea. I am an NRA-certified safety instructor, who practices regularly, not your average citizen who gets to the range a couple of times a year. Second, I was at the scene at the request of local law enforcement. In an active shooting situation, the biggest danger to a Good Samaritan is being mistaken for the assailant or a conspirator. In that case, the so-called good guy gets shot instead of the perpetrator. I think you'd agree that's not a good outcome."

Liz answered each of the remaining questions, which ranged from technical details of how being shot with an assault rifle impacted the body to the mental health criteria for taking away a person's guns. Each information-packed answer was brief yet completely addressed the question. Finally, the last questioner, a tiny older woman, took the microphone.

"Dr. Stolz, in your TV interview, you were asked which one thing you would like to tell the audience. You said, 'It's the guns.' Can you please elaborate?"

From the gallery, Reshma could see Liz compressing her lips into a flat line. She was weighing her answer carefully. Finally, she said, "I'm a gun owner. Like most gun enthusiasts, I enjoy the pleasure of accurately hitting a target, even the sound of the gun firing. Like watching fireworks, the noise and smoke are part of the fun. Mechanically, guns are marvels of engineering, and they fascinate me. But guns were invented for one purpose: to kill. They must be handled and operated with great care. Not everyone is careful.

Many gun owners never learn how to use them safely, which makes them a danger to themselves and others. I teach gun safety in the hope of preventing unnecessary injury and death, but there's only so much I and other instructors can do.

"Yes, I believe what I said in my interview. There are too many guns in private hands. Because we don't require registration or keep a reliable database of ownership, no one really knows how many guns are in circulation, who owns them, or where they are. Many are owned by criminals, but even legal owners may be too impaired to have a gun. You might be perfectly sane when you buy a gun but later have mental issues. Some guns are owned by dementia patients, which, as the population ages, will be a bigger problem. No matter how many gun laws we pass, if a gun is in the possession of the wrong person, it can kill someone."

There was absolute silence in the room. Reshma looked around, seeing the effect of Liz's answer on the audience. Even the gun rights advocates appeared reflective. There were no more questions. Without another word, Liz returned to her seat.

Chapter 11

Liz glanced in the rear-view mirror as she passed the old TV re-pair shop. The Hobbs police liked to hide next to the building, waiting to catch speeders on their way out of town. The shop was closed now. No one had their electronics repaired any more. They became obsolete too fast and when they broke down, they ended up in a collection box at the dump. Rumor had it that the building would be torn down soon. Liz wondered where the police would hide afterwards.

They seldom went after a driver with M.D. plates, but Brenda had warned Liz not to expect special treatment. Liz knew most of the Hobbs cops by name and didn't need to trade on her friendship with the chief. Mostly, the patrol officers just ignored her speeding.

She was almost fifteen minutes late, but she'd left on the heat in the garage apartment, knowing Denise would be coming to clear out her things. Liz reminded herself to ask for Denise's keys, not that she didn't trust her, but she liked to keep track of who had access to her property. Now that Denise's singing career had been successfully launched, it was unlikely that she would ever live in Hobbs again. But who knew? Denise had left before and returned.

When Liz pulled up to the house, her headlights caught Denise carrying long dresses out to her car, probably her concert gowns. She hung them carefully in the back seat which already looked crammed full of bags and boxes.

"Good timing," Denise called as Liz got out of her car. "I just finished getting my stuff out of the apartment." She handed Liz the keys.

"Sorry I couldn't get here before dark. A staff member needed to talk to me."

Denise shrugged. "Always dicey when you make a date with a doctor."

Liz led Denise through the house to the back door. "I left a hand truck down by the barn. Hopefully, we can be quick. Pretty cold tonight." Inside, she flipped on the lights along the path to the barn.

"Do you have a place to store this stuff?" she asked on a cloud of vapor as she unlocked the door. It had been less than a year since Denise and her young trans friend had brought her things up to the loft over Liz's shop.

"I rented storage space near Logan. I figure if I leave my stuff near an airport, I can always get to it."

"I have the space. I'm not in a hurry to get it out of here."

"Thanks, Liz, but you've already been so kind."

Liz threw the main workshop switch. The brilliant lights flashed on, illuminating the gleaming machinery. Everything looked ready to go, but Liz hadn't had time to do woodworking since Lucy had gone back on the singing circuit.

She led Denise to a pile of boxes at the foot of the stairs. "I think I brought everything down, but you should go up and check to see if I missed anything." She switched on the stairwell light.

"Everything was clearly marked. I trust you, Liz."

"If I find anything that belongs to you, I'll set it aside."

"Thanks." Denise looked grateful that she hadn't been permanently banished. She began piling the boxes on the hand truck.

While Denise brought the first load up to the car, Liz found a flashlight and went upstairs to double check for any stray boxes. She heard Denise come in and stack the second load. One box remained. Liz carried it up to the car.

Denise brought down the hatch door. "Well, I guess that does it."

After a year of the young woman living right next door, sharing meals, and traveling together, it felt wrong to let her just drive away into the night. "How about staying for dinner?" Liz asked. "I can use the company. Lucy's at a basketball game in South Portland. Rebecca's twins are playing."

"I don't want to impose."

"Denise, you know me. If you were imposing, I wouldn't invite you. Come in."

Liz left Denise with a glass of wine and a plate of cheese and crackers while she figured out what to make for dinner. With Lucy out for the evening, she'd planned to eat leftovers, but there wasn't enough for two.

"I'll get the fire started," she said when she returned from the kitchen. She built a little tower of kindling over some crumpled newspaper. Above it, she constructed a counter-levered stack of logs and touched a match to the paper. In less than a minute, she had a blazing fire.

"You do that so efficiently," said Denise in an admiring tone.

Liz tossed the spent match into the flames. "Lots of practice."

"Your home is so cozy. I've always enjoyed being here."

As Liz looked around the room, she noted the items that made it feel like home. A colorful Afghan that Liz's grandmother had cro-cheted lay on the leather sofa. Beside the cast-iron wood stove stood a tidy stack of firewood. The old-battered copper pot held carefully proportioned sticks of kindling. Liz was glad that she'd never let Maggie change the rustic, Maine cabin look although she'd talked about it many times. "When I lived in Connecticut, I had a fancy, formal place. I had a big job, and I wanted to impress people to show I was someone important. When I came up, I just wanted to enjoy life."

"And do you?"

"Most of the time, yes. Being with Lucy makes me happier than I've ever been."

"I can see that." Denise slipped off her shoes and sat with her feet under her. Liz tossed her the Afghan.

"Here, if your feet are cold, put that over you." Liz went into the kitchen to get a drink for herself.

After Liz settled down with her beer, Denise asked, "How's

Emily doing?" Liz forced her brows to remain level. As far as she knew, Emily and Denise had parted on good terms, so she was surprised to hear they hadn't spoken. But Emily had enough trouble communicating in person, never mind at a distance.

"She's fine," said Liz. "We moved her into the new apartment last week. It's as tiny and cramped as you'd expect for junior faculty. She has friends in the building, so she won't be lonely. The grad students and faculty Stefan recruited to look after her while she was studying seem to genuinely care for her."

"She's very likeable when you get to know her," said Denise, loyally defending Emily. "And she's so smart and interested in absolutely everything. You can learn a lot just by spending time with her."

"You've done so much to help her adjust to campus life. I'm sure she's grateful, even if she can't express it well. Are you going to her dissertation defense?"

Denise sighed. "I can't. I'm singing in Buenos Aires that week. I'm sure she doesn't need me there as a distraction." Liz knew that Emily's unbreakable focus made it unlikely she would even notice, but that was not something to say aloud. "I'm glad she's doing well," Denise added, her eyes shining with affection.

Liz nodded and sat back, waiting for her to say more. Faced with silence, people inevitably felt the need to fill it. "You're probably wondering why we broke up," Denise finally said.

Liz shrugged. "Not really my business." Her seeming lack of interest ensured that Denise would tell her why.

"It's not easy being with Emily."

"People with Asperger's probably say that about us." Liz took a big slug of beer, a pleasantly bitter double IPA. She smacked her lips in satisfaction. "But I'm sure being with Emily can be challenging."

"May I speak frankly?"

"I hope you will." Liz settled back to show that she was ready to listen.

"And don't tell her mother."

"I'm a doctor, Denise. Whatever you tell me stays between us."

Denise stared at her wine glass, apparently searching for a place to begin. "Emily isn't very sexual."

"But you knew that before you got involved."

"I did, but I thought I could teach her about sex and draw her out. Arrogant of me, wasn't it?"

"Was it?" Liz asked honestly.

"No, I really loved her. I thought I could make her love me too. There was one problem. She isn't really interested in sex and…" The lengthening pause made Liz want to lean forward to urge Denise to finish her thought, but she held her position without even blinking. "Neither was I, as it turned out. I've always been attracted to both men and women. Maybe I transitioned so I can be with a man. That's what women want, isn't it? To be desired by a man."

"Not all women," said Liz, arching a brow.

"No, of course not. Lesbians want to be with other women. But maybe I'm not a lesbian. Maybe I'm straight."

"Which is why you're with the baritone now."

Denise visibly blushed. "Emily told you."

"Don't worry. That's all she said. Emily doesn't talk much, as you know."

"I'm hoping it will be easier with a man. But honestly, the sensitivity is not what I expected."

Liz studied Denise to judge how honest she could be. "When you operate in a highly innervated area like the genitals or breasts, you risk severing the connections. I worked on the problem of preserving nipple sensitivity for a long time. I finally discovered it's not merely a matter of technique or skill. It depends on the body's own abilities to heal. That's unpredictable."

"I know. They keep telling me it might get better, but it's been two years. Don't you think by now…?"

Liz shrugged. "Can't say, but don't give up. Nerves can take a long time to knit back together."

"But the hormones I'm taking depress my sex drive."

"They're reversing the effects of the male hormones your body still makes. Even women have testosterone."

"My therapist keeps telling me that attraction is in the mind."

"It is in the mind. How do you think a postmenopausal woman like me can lust after my wife?" Denise's blue eyes grew large. Maybe she didn't want to imagine her doctor and her former boss getting it on. "But it helps to have a willing partner. If you were doing all the work and getting no help from Emily, I can see why sex wasn't satisfying."

"And there's another thing…"

There's always another thing, thought Liz. Patients seemed to reserve the embarrassing details until the last minutes of an appointment.

"I find the maintenance difficult. Sometimes, I'm so busy, rehearsing or traveling, and I can't do it. When I finally do…" She picked at the Afghan over her legs.

Liz completed her thought, "The dilation is painful."

"Yes," said Denise, blushing crimson. "They explained it to me, but I never thought it would be so hard."

Liz modulated the intake of breath so it wouldn't seem like a big sigh, but that's how she felt. "Do you regret transitioning?"

"No," said Denise without a moment's hesitation, "but it's not what I expected."

"In what way?"

"I thought it would solve my problems, but instead it created new ones."

"It's like the geographical cure. Moving to another place doesn't get rid of the problems you brought along with you." Liz waited for Denise to say more, but she didn't. "How can I help you?"

"Just do what you're doing. I need someone to listen. No one in the trans community wants to hear about my issues."

"But aren't there support groups?" asked Liz. There were support groups for every medical condition. Why not transitioning?

"There are, but any doubts or complaints are written off as negative self-talk. The doctors are all in. The surgeons only show you photos of the best possible outcomes, not the failures."

"I've seen their work on you," said Liz after taking a long pull on her beer. "It's certainly not a failure. A very good cosmetic result."

"Yes, but it's not a success if it only looks good."

"No," said Liz. "I'm sorry you're disappointed."

Denise batted her lashes, thick with heavy mascara, and Liz realized she was trying to blink away tears. "You're the only doctor who's ever been completely honest with me. Now that I'm moving away, I won't have you anymore." Now the tears finally came. Liz got up to offer the box of tissues near the sofa.

"Would it help to talk to me from time to time?"

"Of course, it would, but I don't want to take up your time. You and Lucy have already been so kind to me."

"Denise, if you need to call me, just pick up the phone. If it gets to be a problem, I'll let you know."

Denise yanked a handful of tissues out of the box and wiped her face. The dissolving mascara left ghoulish black circles under her eyes.

"If you want to tend to your makeup, you can use the bathroom. You know where it is," Liz said quietly.

"Why are you being so kind to me?" asked Denise, her voice still thick with tears. "I know you have strong opinions about transitioning."

Liz finally allowed herself the luxury of a long sigh. "Knowing you has helped me see things differently. I've softened my positions, and after all, who am I to judge? It's your body."

"Yes, but you're a doctor, and people come to you for advice. Not all doctors give good advice because they're too wrapped up in the ideology. You can be tough, but at least I can trust you to tell me the truth."

Liz leaned on her knees. "People often say that to me as a backhanded compliment."

"It is a compliment," Denise said with unexpected adamance. "Not everyone has the guts to tell people what they don't want to hear."

"My wife does. If you think I'm brutal, you should hear what she says to me."

Denise's bright red lips curved into a smile. "That would be interesting to hear, I'm sure."

Liz glanced at the clock. "I should get dinner going if you're driving down to Boston tonight. With Lucy at the game, I was going to eat leftover stew, but there's not enough for two. Would a pantry meal of pasta with greens and chicken sausage be okay?"

"I don't often get a home-cooked meal these days, so I'd be grateful for anything you put in front of me, but I do have a request."

"Okay.... What did you have in mind?"

"You once made me the most delicious grilled cheese sandwich. I hate to say it, but it was better than my grandmother's."

"With tomato soup? I have some in the freezer. I'll bring it up to defrost. You can keep me company while I cook," said Liz, getting up. "I'll even give you another glass of wine."

"How can I turn down an offer like that? Let me just clean myself up first," said Denise, pointing to her ruined mascara. "And I will call you when I need to."

"I hope you do," said Liz and went down to the basement to get the soup out of the freezer.

❋❋❋

Lucy had already had a headache before the sound of a dozen basketballs pounding the polished gym floor made it worse. As she awaited Rebecca's arrival, she wondered about the wisdom of meeting her after such an overscheduled day. It had begun with a lengthy meeting with the vestry wardens and the treasurer. They'd failed to include an ongoing renovation project in the budget. The diocese wouldn't look kindly on them adding a twenty-thousand-dollar line item after the fact.

She sighed and tried to push church business out of her mind. If only she could banish the sound of bouncing basketballs. She tried a technique she'd learned as a singer to tune out voices other than her own. Unfortunately, it was only partially successful. Plugging her ears with her fingers would work better, but she couldn't do it surrounded by all those people.

One of Rebecca's daughters noticed Lucy sitting in the bleachers. She stopped dribbling her ball to smile and wave. Because they weren't actually twins, the girls were easy to tell apart. Lucy could always tell Rebecca's biological daughter, Sarah, because she had dark curls like her mother. Judith's daughter, Naomi, had straight hair that was as dark and smooth as a crow's wing.

Rebecca often praised their athletic ability. "Being good at sports isn't usually encouraged in Jewish families, but Judith is all in for teamwork after growing up in a Kibbutz." The girls were both tall enough to be an asset to their team. Fortunately, they'd both landed on the starting line-up, avoiding the potential for sibling rivalry. Even if they hadn't shared the same womb, they seemed to have twins' uncanny ability to communicate without words, which made them even more formidable on the court.

Lucy spotted Rebecca entering the gym on the other side. She sat up and waved so she would see her. Her friend waved back and headed in Lucy's direction. As Rebecca wound her way around the gym, stepping over small children in her path, her eyes were focused on the floor. Rebecca excelled at putting on a good face. For her to scowl in public was an ominous sign. Obviously, her day hadn't been any better than Lucy's. Rebecca managed a smile for her friend and caught her in a half hug. "Thanks for coming," she murmured into Lucy's shoulder. "Sorry it's the girls' game night."

"Hey, if this is the only time you can see me, I'll take it."

It felt like Rebecca released her with reluctance. With Judith gone all this time, she was probably starved for affection. Lucy knew what that was like. She was affectionate by nature, and when she was away from Liz, even for a couple days of rehearsals, she hugged everyone in sight.

"I hope this is a good game," said Rebecca, squinting critically as she evaluated the girls on the court. "If they win this one, they have a good shot at the state championship."

"We could pray for them," Lucy suggested.

Rebecca laughed. "A priest and a rabbi walk into a gym," she quipped in a twist on the old joke. "Yes, we could pray for them." She reached for Lucy's hand and closed her eyes for a moment of silent invocation.

After Rebecca finally let go of her hand, Lucy said, "I've always thought asking God to choose sides makes no sense. God is supposed to be on everyone's side."

"Not if you were a Jew in ancient Israel. That God definitely took sides. And you can't ignore the primitive impulse to sway God in your favor. I'm sure Judith and her family are desperately praying for the defeat of Hamas."

"We all are. It's the only way Israel will have any peace."

"Peace," Rebecca repeated cynically. "There will never be peace in the Middle East. Not in our lifetime, anyway."

Lucy heard the unspoken anger in her friend's voice and decided to steer away from the war in Gaza. "Has Judith set a date to come home?"

"No, and I just found out today that she's asked her school district to extend her leave."

"Oh, no! Doesn't she realize how much you and the girls miss her?"

"I'm sure she does, and she misses us too, but she doesn't want to leave her parents with this war going on. There are warning sirens every night. The sky is lit up with rocket fire. One fell only a few miles from her parents' house. I want her home. It's too dangerous there."

"That's what we should be praying for—a ceasefire," said Lucy passionately.

"A ceasefire? Israel won't stop fighting until Hamas is destroyed."

"But the loss of civilian lives in Gaza is horrifying. People are starving. The IDF keeps telling the Gazans to move, then they bomb them, doesn't matter if it's a school or hospital. They're even bombing refugee camps."

"Serves them right for harboring terrorists in buildings meant to help people."

Lucy turned and stared at her old friend. "Becca, you can't mean that."

Rebecca refused to engage Lucy's eyes. "I do. You've heard about the rapes during the October attack? The sheer savagery of it is unthinkable. My in-laws lived in a Kibbutz like that when Judith was growing up. It could have been them. It wasn't enough to kill those people. They had to humiliate and torture them."

"It was horrible," Lucy agreed. "But that doesn't justify killing women and children. Women have no political sway in Gaza, and children are innocent."

Rebecca's piercing eyes engaged Lucy's. "Israel has a right to defend itself."

"Becca, be honest. This is more than self-defense. It's genocide."

Rebecca's face hardened. "I never knew you were an anti-Semite."

"What?" Lucy asked, too shocked to put her feelings into words. Did her long-time friend even know her? Lucy took a moment to collect her thoughts before saying, "Just because I don't agree with Israel's aggressive attacks on Palestinians doesn't mean I'm anti-Semitic. Rebecca, you know I'm not."

Rebecca turned away and focused on the gym floor, where the coach was calling the forwards to the center to jump for the ball. Lucy tried to focus on the game, but she realized she was shaking. Rebecca's accusation had unnerved her. She'd wanted to say that it was possible to feel compassion for the people of Gaza *and* the Israelis who'd been unjustly attacked, but she sensed this was no time for rational arguments. Rebecca was afraid for her wife. When danger was so close to home, the most liberal views took second place to loyalty.

Fortunately, the home team sunk a ball in the basket and the roar from the home crowd was a distraction. Lucy jumped up to cheer in solidarity. She glanced at Rebecca's face but saw it was stony. The hot dog Lucy had wolfed down in lieu of dinner before the game sat heavily in her stomach. It was going to be a long, tense game.

Chapter 12

Tiffany had been trained to prepare the trendiest, most artful meals from exotic and expensive ingredients. But when she was cooking for someone she loved, she preferred to cook comfort food, especially braises with rich meat that melted into silken, shimmering sauces. She wanted to fill the belly of her loved ones with tasty, high-calorie meals that would stick with them. She gave them the gift of her time in the hours of preparation and the many layers of flavor each step imbued.

She'd been looking forward to cooking this dinner for Reshma since she saw lamb shanks in the butcher's case. Last years' lambs were finally ready for slaughter. Whenever possible, Tiffany preferred to source her ingredients from nearby growers. Eating local supported small farmers and lessened the environmental impact of long-distance transportation. In other parts of the country, spring peas and baby vegetables would be available this early, but not in Maine, where the snow from the plowing hadn't yet melted. Instead, Tiffany would rely on fresh greens from one of the many hydroponic gardens that had sprung up in New England.

She'd been mentally cooking this meal for over a week. She hoped Reshma would savor this meal for the offering it was. Maybe this would be the night they finally made love. Reshma hadn't stayed overnight since the Lewiston shooting. Tiffany knew it would look bad for her to spend the night in Reshma's rectory studio. Plus, it was microscopic. Tiffany had only gotten a quick peek inside when they were going out and Reshma had forgotten her scarf. She'd asked how Reshma could live in such cramped quarters.

"After living in a refugee camp for years, I am grateful to have a home," Reshma explained quietly. "Except for some books in the basement, this room contains everything I own." The admission made Tiffany want to protect Reshma and make up for what she'd suffered. Ironically, on the night of the shooting, she'd looked to

Reshma as her protector. Maybe that's what people in love were supposed to do—protect one another from life's hardships while trying to make up for past hurts.

Tiffany's bright red Le Creuset pot had been in the oven for an hour, and the whole house already smelled delicious. The knock at the door made Tiffany's heart rate speed up. Maybe Reshma had finished her pastoral care visits early. Tiffany unlocked the door with trembling fingers. She flung it open, expecting to fall into Reshma's arms. Slouching, Brianna stood there with a menacing smirk. Tiffany's hand involuntarily flew to her chest, protecting her heart.

"Brianna! What are you doing here?"

"I was up at a professional cookware show in Portland. Since you haven't been taking my calls or answering my texts, I decided to see if you were still alive." Brianna grinned, which slightly eased the threat Tiffany felt in her presence. "I came all this way to see you. Aren't you going to ask me to come in?"

Tiffany's mind was racing as she tried to find an answer. One thing she was sure of was she didn't trust Brianna, but she knew that if she outright refused, her anger would be explosive.

"I'm expecting company," Tiffany said. It sounded convincing because it was true.

Brianna sniffed the air appreciatively. "I can tell. What are you cooking? Beef stew?"

"Braised lamb shanks."

Brianna grinned. "My favorite. How did you know I'd stop by?" She took a step forward, but Tiffany blocked the door.

"I didn't know, and I didn't invite you, so you should leave."

Brianna assumed that little-boy, pleading look that could always melt Tiffany into a puddle of compliance. "Please, Tiff. I've missed you so much."

"No, I have plans for the evening. Now, please go." Tiffany tried to close the door, but Brianna held it open with her foot. Brianna took another menacing step closer, her movements at odds with the pleading look on her face. Tiffany felt conflicted, but she continued to block the entrance.

"Come on, Tiffany," Brianna said, unflinchingly holding her gaze. "I promise I won't stay long."

"No, Brianna, and I don't have time for this. I'm cooking for my guest. Just go. Now."

"You heard the lady," said a strong voice from the stairwell. Reshma came up the remaining steps. "I think she wants you to leave." Reshma was wearing clerical garb because she was coming from visiting the shut-ins. For the first time, Tiffany was glad to see her collar, which confirmed her authority. Reshma was taller than Brianna, who took in her height. When Reshma stood behind Brianna, she spoke more gently. "Brianna, you need to go. It's what Tiffany wants. Now, if you care for her, you'll do as she asks." Reshma's tone was firm but reasonable. Anyone normal person would be convinced by it. Tiffany tightly clutched the doorknob and waited to see what would happen.

At first, Brianna seemed to go along with the suggestion. Then Tiffany saw her face darken and cringed. "Who are you to tell me what to do, *priest?*" Brianna turned to Tiffany. "You still dating this black girl? Does it prove how woke you are? Not to me."

"That's not why," Tiffany protested helplessly, as easily drawn into an argument with Brianna as ever. What was it about Brianna that always hooked her?

"Yeah, right," said Brianna. "You want to prove you're as liberal as your parents, no matter how much you complain about them."

"Leave my parents out of it," Tiffany protested, jutting out her chin defiantly.

"Why? They own you and everything you have, including this shop." Brianna pounded on the door that barred her way. "Even this fucking building."

"Go away!" Tiffany snarled back.

Brianna looked startled by the vehemence of the order and took a step back. Meanwhile, Reshma, who'd maneuvered around her, interposed herself between Tiffany and her unwanted guest. Tiffany finally let go of Brianna's gaze, which she'd held to avoid giving away Reshma's strategy. For the first time, she noticed the gold pin that fastened Reshma's collar to her shirt. She murmured a silent prayer of thanks to a deity she didn't really believe existed.

"Brianna, it's time to go," Reshma said in a steady voice full of authority.

Brianna's eyes flashed anger. Her jaw muscles tightened until her temples twitched. "Fuck you, priest," she said as if she were spitting in Reshma's face, but she turned around and headed down the stairs.

Once they heard the downstairs door close, Reshma turned around and took Tiffany in her arms. They gratefully clung to one another. "I'm so sorry you had to deal with her alone," Reshma whispered into Tiffany's ear. "Are you all right?" Her warm breath tickled. The excitement it caused confused Tiffany. This was the second time her desire for Reshma had gotten mixed up with terror. "Should we call the police?" Reshma asked.

"No, the last thing she needs is a police record." Tiffany released Reshma. "I'll go down and lock the door."

"No, you go inside. I'll do it." Reshma's bravery made Tiffany fling her arms around her. When she finally let her go, Reshma descended the stairs. Tiffany stood in the open doorway until she returned.

"Thank God you came!" she said, pulling Reshma inside.

"Something told me to hurry. I was done with my pastoral visits, and I wanted to surprise you by showing up early."

Although the downstairs lock would keep out any intruders, Tiffany carefully locked the door behind them. "I never expected her to show up here."

"Tomorrow, you should probably text her to stay away from you."

"But I don't want to provoke her into doing the opposite. She's good at that."

"Do it anyway, so you'll have a record for the police that you'd warned her not to come back."

The thought chilled Tiffany. "I never would have thought of that."

"I was a chaplain in a battered women's shelter while I was in seminary. The police don't always believe women's complaints. You might need evidence to prove your story."

"That's terrible."

"I know, but the police chief here is a woman. I know her. She'll listen to you. If you need to go to court, it's important to have proof."

Tiffany was horrified at the thought that Brittany's possessiveness could ever go that far. She threw herself into Reshma's arms and clung to her with all her might.

***

Tiffany began to cry, and she was still trembling. Reshma held her close. "She's gone now. She can't hurt you anymore," she whispered into Tiffany's blond curls. Her hair smelled of flowers and fresh grass. Even after the crying stopped, Reshma was reluctant to let her go, but she led her to the sofa and nudged her to sit down.

"Can you tell me what happened?" she asked, engaging Tiffany's tear filled eyes.

Tiffany instantly responded with a fearful look. Clearly, she didn't want to answer the question, but she glanced at Reshma's collar, and her expression softened. "I never expected her to resort to stalking. I thought she'd eventually realize the relationship was over and let it go." Tiffany brushed the tears away from her cheeks with her fingertips. "That's why we broke up. She was jealous of everyone, even Amber, who's as straight as they come! We had so many fights about it. Brianna always wanted to know where I was going, who I was seeing, and why. I'm an adult woman. I can come and go and see anyone I want, but Brianna thought she owned me."

Reshma had heard this story before, but she listened silently, holding Tiffany's hand while she described how Brianna had tried to manage her life. "Did she ever hurt you?" Reshma asked gently. Two flaming patches on Tiffany's cheeks confirmed her suspicion. "Can you tell me about it?"

"I came home late from an appointment. I was seeing my gynecologist for God's sake. Brianna kept texting to ask me where I was, but I was so annoyed at being tracked all the time, I refused to answer. When I got home, she demanded to know where I'd been. When I refused to tell her, she shook me and told me she'd get it out of me one way or another. That made me even more determined not to tell, so she slammed me against the wall, really hurting my shoulder. I went into the bedroom and locked the door. Fortunately, we were in a rental, or I think she would have broken the door down. She'd already put a few holes in the drywall slamming doors, but she always fixed them right away so no one would know."

Reshma finally allowed herself the luxury of a long sigh. "Tiffany, I'm so sorry."

"Why? It's not your fault. I was the one who stayed with her. The last straw was the tracking app she put on my phone when I wasn't looking."

"You're not joking," said Reshma, unable to restrain her shock. "That's such a violation of your privacy!"

Now that Tiffany had begun her confession, all the salacious details spilled out. "She regularly read my text messages to make sure I wasn't seeing anyone else. Like I said, she was suspicious of everyone. At first, I let it go, figuring that was common in lesbian relationships. But when I found out about the tracking app, I called my Dad. While Brianna was at work, he came and helped me move out. I stayed with them for a while. That's when I got the idea to open my own shop. I wanted to get as far away from Brianna as possible, which is why when this place was up for sale, Mom and Dad helped me buy it. Then, Brianna took a job in Boston. That's too close for comfort."

"Why do you keep including her in your chef's nights if you feel so threatened?" asked Reshma.

"She keeps saying she's changed. Tonight, she proved she hasn't." Tiffany chewed nervously on her lower lip, a sign she didn't want to admit something. "I never told our friends about the abuse because I was afraid they'd cut her off."

"I'm sorry Tiffany, but Brianna won't change until someone calls her on her behavior."

"They'd throw her out of the group."

"That's too bad. I know it's harsh, but there must be consequences, or she'll continue to be abusive. For your own safety, I think you should talk to Brenda Harrison. Tell her the whole story so she can ask the police to keep an eye on the shop. You don't know what Brianna will do if she gets desperate enough."

"But I don't want to get her in trouble. I just want her to stop." The tears came again, making shining trails down Tiffany's cheeks. "And now she ruined our evening. I've been planning this dinner all week. You're being a priest and counseling me instead of being my girlfriend!"

"I'm being your friend and supporting you," Reshma said, putting her arms around her. "That's different."

Tiffany sat back and eyed Reshma's collar with a frown. "I wish you could change out of your work clothes so we could relax."

Reshma reached back and unfastened the collar pin. She removed the starched linen band. "There. Is that better?"

"Yes, a little. I have a huge sweatshirt that might fit you."

Reshma couldn't resist a little guilty smile. "I have a bag in the car…just in case."

Tiffany's face went from stormy to beaming a sunny smile. "Really? You're going to stay?"

"Let's see how things go," Reshma said. "The night has gotten off to a rocky start."

"I could bring out the quilts and pillows, and we could cuddle like that night the shooter was on the loose."

"Wouldn't your bed do just as well?"

Tiffany's blue eyes grew enormous. "Now?"

Reshma lowered her lids and gave her a sultry look. "We've waited this long, and you want to wait longer?"

"But I was going to seduce you with a fantastic meal!" protested Tiffany like a disappointed child.

Reshma laughed softly. "You can do that later. Seduction doesn't have to be a one-time thing. How long until dinner?"

Tiffany glanced at her phone. "At least another hour and a half. But it's a braise, so it will be fine if it's longer."

"Okay. Let me go down to my car and get my bag. I think if I get out of my work clothes, we'll both feel more comfortable."

"No!" said Tiffany, grabbing Reshma's hands. "She might still be out there."

"Unless she wants to freeze her ass off, I doubt it. I'm parked in a place where you can watch me from the window. If you see anything, call the police right away." Reshma took out her phone. "I'm texting you the chief's direct number. She's very responsive and understands sensitive situations."

"Her wife is a regular. She comes in to buy a bag of croissants every couple of days. Says her aunt likes them too."

"That wouldn't surprise me. Cherie and Simone grew up in the French-speaking part of Louisiana," said Reshma, getting up. "Now, don't worry. I promise to be right back."

As Reshma descended the stairs, she remembered Tiffany's worry that Brianna might be lurking outside. She looked both ways before hurrying out to her car. She'd deliberately parked under a light, a trick she'd learned in her self-defense class. The cold was shocking after being in Tiffany's warm apartment. The temperature convinced Reshma that Brianna probably wasn't hanging around. Even so, she unlocked the car on the way, so she could rip open the door and grab her bag quickly. On her way back, she raised her eyes to the third-floor window and saw Tiffany watching.

Reshma double checked after she locked the outer door. Tiffany was waiting for her on the second-floor landing. "Did you see anyone?" she asked in a whisper, as if a potential intruder might overhear.

"No, there's no traffic on Route One. You know how it is in February. The whole town shuts down."

"Get in here," ordered Tiffany, grabbing her hand. "I turned down the heat in the oven so we can have more time."

"You didn't need to do that," Reshma said with a grin. "We've been waiting so long, I'm sure we'll both be quick."

"Not if I have my way." Tiffany's seductive threat heartened Reshma because it meant the worst of her fear was behind her. Reshma dropped her bag inside the door. She slipped off her black pumps as she hung her coat on the hook by the door. "Should I change clothes?"

"Don't bother," said Tiffany, grinning rakishly. "I'm just going to take them off." She drew Reshma down into a long, deep kiss that made Reshma's toes tingle. Tiffany smiled into her eyes when she finally released her mouth. "Come on. I can't wait another minute!"

With trembling hands, Tiffany unbuttoned Reshma's cardigan and slipped it off her shoulders, but she was baffled by how to proceed with her clerical shirt. Reshma peeled back the placket to reveal the concealed buttons. Tiffany grinned with delight, and her fingers went to work. Soon, Reshma was standing there in the new front-open, lacy, black bra she'd bought just for this occasion. Tiffany ran her arms appreciatively over Reshma's bare arms. "Your skin is like silk," she said, her eyes admiring each newly revealed place. She leaned closer and sniffed Reshma's cleavage. "That's a unique scent. Hmm, let's see. Rosemary, citrus, lemon probably, and something else." She looked puzzled.

"A little lavender," Reshma supplied. "My own deodorant. You add those herbs to a little oil and baking soda. My mother showed me how to make it. In the camp, personal care items were hard to come by, as was water for washing."

"All edible and yummy. Perfect!" Tiffany released the bra fasteners and planted a line of delicate kisses between Reshma's breasts while gently pinching the nipple. Reshma's knees became weak.

"I need to sit down," she said, "but first, let's see you." She reached under Tiffany's sweater and opened her bra. Then she pulled everything off together. She feasted her eyes on Tiffany's soft breasts. The nipples were so pale she couldn't find their edges.

The image of a pink fairy-tale princess on a child's birthday cake suddenly popped into Reshma's mind. She bent to kiss Tiffany's creamy flesh and sighed in pleasure.

"I need to sit down too," Tiffany said and plopped onto the bed. She shed her yoga pants and panties at the same time, then lay down with her legs slightly parted, making Reshma weak with desire. But she carefully took off her black pants and neatly folded them because she'd have to wear them again tomorrow. She retrieved her clerical shirt from the floor and hung it on the back of a chair.

Tiffany's head popped up. "Come on, Reshma. You're driving me crazy! Get over here!"

"I thought you'd enjoy a slow approach."

Tiffany groaned. "You've already made me wait too long!"

To quiet her, Reshma kissed the place where her thighs met her body and worked her way up to her breasts, giving each pink nipple equal attention before arriving at her mouth. "You liked the suspense, didn't you?" she asked with a grin.

"Stop talking and touch me," Tiffany ordered, placing Reshma's hand between her legs. Tentatively, Reshma explored the warm place and found it wet and completely open to her touch.

✳✳✳

Parked at the board members' table in the front of the room, Liz tried to look interested in the treasurer's report. Winter meetings of the Hobbs Fish and Game Club were often poorly attended. The members who were seasonal residents headed south, and the outdoor ranges were closed. Not much happened during the cold months. There would be little business to discuss.

The old barn, retrofitted for their clubhouse, was poorly insulated. In the upstairs room where they met, the timber-framed walls had been preserved. The original wide floorboards had gaps as wide as a pinky and bled cold air. At winter meetings, Liz always wore heavy socks and thick soled boots. Downstairs was the indoor range, where they trained and held regular events like "ladies' night," a popular get together for women shooters. Liz used to lead the group, but now she'd turned managing it over to a younger woman.

Liz had been a member of the Hobbs Fish and Game since she'd bought her first pistol and needed a place to practice. She had enough property in the back of the house to shoot, but she'd already pissed off her neighbors by cutting down trees for the view. The sound of gunfire made her even less popular.

She came to winter meetings of the club because she enjoyed seeing the other members, many of whom had become friends. It took a while for the members to accept her, but she'd figured out the key long ago.

When she'd started her residency back in the eighties, surgery was still a boys' club. Same with woodworking. The guys in the hardwood lumber yard ignored her when she showed up to buy some rough-sawn cherry. She'd needed to prove, just like in the OR, that she could talk the talk. If you knew the right words, you were one of them. When Liz taught women's firearm classes, she always made sure everyone used correct terms. Bullets were held in a "magazine," not a "clip." She kept telling gun safety advocates they needed to learn firearms vocabulary, but no one seemed to listen.

She put on her "I'm not bored look," which was different from her "I'm engaged look." It was hard not to be distracted by what had been a busy day. She'd had too many catch-up appointments after returning from Emily's thesis defense in New Haven. The examiners went easy on her, almost deferential to the young woman, and they should be. A mathematical mind like Emily's came along once in a generation.

Stefan Bultmann, Emily's honorary grandfather through Lucy's marriage to his daughter, Erika, was the co-author of the famous theorem that had propelled Emily to fame. They'd offered to include him in a Zoom presentation of the defense, but he'd insisted on attending in person. In front of the faculty, many of whom Stefan had taught and mentored, he wanted to present himself as robust. At ninety-seven, he needed no excuse for his frailty. He insisted on walking into the meeting room on Liz's arm, using a cane instead of his wheelchair. Exhausted by the effort, he'd been forced to retreat to the wheelchair for the reception. Liz, standing nearby in case he needed her, enjoyed listening to his laughter while he held court near the bar.

Jenny and her wife were gracious hostesses, giving him the first-floor bedroom that had been refitted with handicapped appliances. The aging in place trend hadn't passed them by, and after paying Liz a huge amount of money to buy out her interest in the house, they intended to stay for good. Liz was grateful for their hospitality and their kindness as she helped Stefan get ready for bed. He'd become so thin that she could easily lift him out of his wheelchair to help him into the shower. It was the least she could do for her old friend Erika, who'd been like a sister to her.

The treasurer finished his report. A motion was made to approve it. They voted on it but then backtracked because no one had seconded the motion. The obsession that volunteer organizations had with *Robert's Rules of Order* amazed Liz. She'd seen fierce arguments break out when all they were trying to do was end a meeting.

While they reviewed the thin program planned for March, Liz found herself thinking about the Netflix series that she and Lucy had been watching. Finally, the chair called for new business. Usually, people were anxious to get home, so there were only a few hurried announcements, but someone in the back raised his hand. When the chair acknowledged him, the member stood. "I make a motion to remove Liz Stolz from the board of this club."

Startled, Liz sat up and studied the middle-aged, paunchy man. He wore an NRA cap and spoke with the long A's and dropped R's of a lifelong Mainer. The chair glanced at her for an explanation, then turned his attention to the man standing in the back.

"Can you explain your rationale for this motion?"

"She doesn't support Second Amendment rights."

"How do you know?"

"I was at the hearing up at the legislature."

"Did she say she doesn't support the Second Amendment?" the chair asked, seemingly playing for time. He'd been surprised too.

"No, but it's obvious."

Another man rose. "I second the motion," he declared. "And I'd third it, if I could."

Stunned, Liz sat back in her chair. She'd been teaching safety classes with this member for years. They'd gone out for beers many times.

"That's crazy," said Liz. "Without question, I support the Second Amendment."

The head of the board raised a hand in her direction. "You'll have your chance to respond, Liz. Hold your thought."

Liz stifled the impulse to make a face at being officially silenced. Instead, she assumed a stony expression while another member described how she'd betrayed the club and its members in her state house testimony. "And while we're at it, maybe we should throw her out of the club. Who needs a traitor like her here?" a man shouted from the back.

The chairman banged his gavel on the table. "Out of order! Raise your hands, and I will call on you." He surveyed the room with narrowed eyes. An angry murmur rose, but to Liz's relief, no one raised a hand. "Okay, Liz, now it's your turn."

Usually, Liz didn't stand when she spoke. The posture seemed too formal for this group of usually affable, older men, but this time she got to her feet.

"I don't know where this is coming from. You've all known me for years. I carry concealed every day, everywhere I go. I joined the NRA back in high school. My dad taught me to shoot, and he believed in safety first and foremost. I thought you all did too. I spoke out for commonsense gun laws because if we don't engage in the process, people who know jack shit about guns will decide for us. We need to show that we can regulate ourselves."

"But a seventy-two-hour waiting period to buy a gun? What bullshit is that?" a man in the back called out.

The chairman smacked his gavel on the table with a loud bang. "I said, raise your hands, if you want to speak."

"I agree that idea is stupid and hopefully, it won't pass," said Liz. "But there are some good ideas in the proposed legislation. Has anyone read it?"

She scanned the mostly blank faces in the crowd. Some people shook their heads. Others scowled. One man spat on the floor.

"Who has time to read that crap?" a member shouted. "Never mind understand it if I did. Bunch of bullshit, if you ask me."

The chairman slammed his gavel on the table. "Raise your hand! Anyone who can't follow that rule can leave right now." He turned to Liz. "Anything else to say?"

Liz thought for a long moment. Sure, she had plenty to say, but not to this sullen bunch. There was so much that could be done to make people safer, like requiring owners to store guns with trigger locks. If you needed a registration and insurance to own a car, why not the same for guns? How about standardizing gun restrictions nationally, like traffic laws? Liz could fire off a long list of reasonable suggestions, but she was not about to share them with these angry men.

"No," Liz said, unwilling to provoke a full-scale war within the club. Maybe she could talk sense to them when tempers weren't as hot or lobby them individually, but not tonight. She sat down and crossed her arms on her chest.

The chairman shot her a sympathetic look. He allowed the grumbling in the group to settle down before speaking. "Okay. Does the motion to remove Dr. Stolz from the board still stand?"

"What about the motion to throw her out of the club?" someone asked.

The chairman glowered at the speaker. "Mike, what don't you understand about raising your hand?" he challenged. "Watch it, or I'll throw you out personally." The color in his cheeks faded by degrees. "Is there a second for the motion to cancel Liz's membership?"

The member who'd made the original motion sat forward and looked around for allies. No one would even meet his gaze, so he sat back with a huff and crossed his arms on his chest.

"Is there a second for the motion to remove Liz from the board of directors?" asked the chairman.

For a moment it seemed this question might get the same response as the first. Then someone in the back tentatively raised his hand. "I second the motion to remove Liz Stolz from the board of directors until she comes to her senses."

Liz shot him a chilling warning like she'd used on junior staff in her surgery days. The man crumbled back into his seat, but he glared at her.

"All in favor, raise your hands and say 'Aye,'" the chairman instructed.

The vote was far from unanimous, but the show of hands indicated a clear majority. The chairman's sigh of disappointment was audible. "Well, it looks like Liz Stolz is removed from the board. At our next meeting, we'll have a vote to fill her seat."

Liz got up from the front table and went to sit in the back of the room. The man sitting next to her leaned over and whispered. "I'm sorry, Liz. You didn't deserve that. You've done so much for this club."

"Thanks, Jake," she whispered.

After the meeting was adjourned, Liz grabbed her coat from the rack and made a beeline for the door. On the ride home, the anger buzzed in her ears like a swarming hive. Jake was right. She'd done so much for Hobbs Fish and Game. Whenever there was seasonal cleanup, she was out there raking up spent shells. She'd given the money to install new bathrooms because the ladies' group was tired of waiting in line outside the single toilet. She'd taught classes even when she was swamped at the practice.

Fuck them, she thought, *I should resign.* Then she reminded herself that someone needed to talk reason to gun owners or things would only get worse. It was easier to work from the inside than try to influence the outcome from the perimeter. "Fuck!" she screamed aloud in her truck and thumped on the steering wheel. "Why are people so damned stupid!"

✳✳✳

As much as Lucy loved Liz's company, she coveted the nights when she was home alone. The silence was different when the house was completely empty. She could savor a passage in a book and stare into space to consider its message without Liz looking up from her iPad to give her curious looks. She could use the time to meditate or catch up on her prayers. She could touch up her Sunday sermon. The best part was not having to answer to anyone. She loved Liz with all her heart, but even the most devoted couple needed a break from one another. Lucy regularly suggested the practice in her marriage counseling sessions.

She sighed when she heard Liz's truck come up the driveway and the lights flash through the front windows. Her precious interlude of privacy was about to come to an end. She listened to Liz come into the hall and hang up her coat. Liz wasn't the quietest person, but she was neat. The sound of her flinging her boots into the closet got Lucy's immediate attention. Liz came into the room in stocking feet. Her scowl confirmed Lucy's suspicions.

"Tough meeting?" she conjectured lightly.

"I need a drink. Want anything from the kitchen?"

"You could bring me a glass of wine, if you don't mind."

Liz heaved up a grunt, which Lucy took as agreement to bring the wine. Liz returned after a few minutes later. After setting the glasses on the coffee table, she flung herself on the sofa. Her blue eyes stared straight ahead. Her jaw was clenched, but her temples were pulsing. Lucy recognized the struggle to control seething anger.

"Okay, Liz. What happened?"

"They kicked me off the board."

"What?" said Lucy, putting aside her book. "Why? You've done so much for them."

"Doesn't matter. Because I spoke at that hearing, I'm one of those *libruls* who want to take their guns away. Meanwhile, kids can't go to school without being killed. Or they find their parents' guns and shoot themselves. Or bring them to school and kill other kids. Any nut can get a gun, and there are guns everywhere! I fucking give up. Maybe I should just resign from the Fish and Game. That's what some of them want."

Lucy listened sympathetically to Liz's litany of grievances. She wanted to put her arms around her, but when Liz was like this, she hated to be touched. "Honey, please, don't resign. Teaching safety is important to you. It's the election year rhetoric. It winds people up so they can't see reason."

"I know, but it even turns gun owners against their allies, like me. I've been in that fucking gun club for years. I'm going to lose friends over this."

"We are so divided." Lucy sighed. "I never told you about the argument I had with Rebecca Morgenstern."

Liz's eyes sharply refocused on Lucy. "You had a fight at the basketball game? Let me guess. It was about the war in Gaza."

Lucy nodded sadly. "A few weeks ago, she told me Israel's war policy was criminal. But when I said the civilian casualties made it look like genocide, she accused me of being anti-Semitic."

Liz's lips parted in surprise. "Rebecca said that? I don't believe it."

"Neither did I. I was so shocked I didn't know what to say. Fortunately, the game got started and interrupted the conversation."

"Have you talked to her since?"

Lucy shook her head. "No, and she won't take my calls. She texts saying she's too busy with the kids."

"Well, I'm sure it's not easy suddenly becoming a single parent. Why hasn't Judith come home? She's not still talking about enlisting again, is she?"

"No, I think the idea of being shot at by real bullets doesn't appeal to her, but she did ask for extended leave from her teaching job. She's worried about her parents."

"So, bring them to Maine. Jack Dreyfus told me Rebecca's mother invited them to stay with her. God knows they have plenty of room in that big house."

"But Judith has a large, extended family in Israel. Not as easy as it sounds."

"So, what will you do? Can't you talk to Rebecca? Jeez. You two have been friends since forever."

"I know, and she's my rabbi. I feel lost without her. She's helped me figure out some of the most difficult things I've ever had to face, like deciding to marry you." At least, that brought a smile to Liz's face.

"It must have been a tough decision, considering how long we stayed in bed the first time we made love."

"All afternoon, if I recall," said Lucy, returning Liz's lewd grin.

Liz sighed, serious again. "Give her time. Maybe she'll come around."

"I don't know about that. Gaza is in the news all the time. The students at Ivy League colleges are still demonstrating. Poor Claudine Gay, forced to resign over a charge of plagiarism."

"What bullshit! I've been writing and reviewing medical papers for decades. It's so easy to make a trivial mistake in a citation. That was a witch hunt. The Republicans just want to discredit academics, especially female academics. It was no accident all the college presidents they called were women. I'm so sick of those fucking hypocrites complaining about free speech and then forcing people to resign when they support it!" The number of f-bombs Liz had been throwing around proved how agitated she was. Her face looked like a storm cloud.

"Well, I for one, refuse to give up," said Lucy in the most hopeful tone she could muster.

"Yeah?" said Liz doubtfully. "What are you going to do?"

"Things that can bring people together. Like giving Brad Taylor's idea a try. He's been leaning on Roger to talk me into doing his fundraising tour."

"Great. Now you have the two of them up your ass, as if the pressure from your agent wasn't enough."

"But maybe Roger is right. I need to perform while I can. I'm going to be sixty this year and not getting any younger." It was the first time Lucy had said aloud how much she dreaded her milestone birthday. "Now that I'm singing opera again, I realize how much I've missed it."

Liz sat up, looking worried. "You're not going to quit being a priest?"

"No, but I might have to step back from some of my duties so I can perform more often. That means more practice...and travel."

Liz's brows bent toward her nose. "Lucy, are you sure?"

"No, but I've been thinking about it. Maybe I could work something out with Tom. He really misses being in Florida with Jeff in the winter. He only came back to help because of the school shooting." Lucy studied Liz's face to judge how this idea was being received, but she'd already reverted to her inscrutable doctor look. "More performances would mean a lot more travel. I can understand if you don't want to come with me and leave your practice."

"You're really serious," Liz said, sounding mildly surprised.

"Yes."

The ice cubes in Liz's whiskey glass settled with a soft tinkling sound. She drained the remaining contents. "When you said you wanted to go back to singing, I said I'd support you. Amy Hsu is ready to step into the role of managing partner. Teresa was accepted into her nurse practitioners' course and wants to stay in Hobbs, maybe it's time for me to cut back my involvement in the practice."

Lucy held her breath. She knew what a big step this would be for Liz. For years, Maggie had begged her to retire so they could travel. Liz's identity was so wrapped up in being a doctor. Erika used to joke that Liz would die strangled by her stethoscope. "But you'll still practice medicine?" Lucy asked tentatively.

"Oh, sure, I'll just reduce my hours. There's such a shortage of doctors in Maine I can't quit. But I promised to be with you if you went back to singing, and I will be." Liz picked up her empty whiskey glass and stared at it, meaning she wanted another drink. "That is, if you want me along. Maybe you just want to hang out with your singing buddies and leave your old wife at home."

Lucy raised a brow. If this was a game, two could play. "Well, you do make an excellent manager and personal assistant when I'm on the road."

Liz stood up and made a deep, courtly bow. "I am honored to serve you, my gracious lady." She looked up from her bent position and grinned. Lucy smiled too, relieved to see that Liz's sense of humor had returned.

Lucy extended her hand. "Then take me upstairs, my loyal knight, and show me the extent of your devotion."

Liz chuckled and lowered herself into another bow. "My lady, it will be my pleasure..." She approached and kissed Lucy's hand. "...after I rinse out the glasses." She snatched them from the coffee table. "See you up there."

"I'll be ready for you," replied Lucy with a sultry shrug of her hip. "Don't be long."

Chapter 13

Reshma was the first to arrive in the meeting room. Since she'd been seeing Tiffany, she was late for everything. Fortunately, her girlfriend respected her need to be at religious services on time and actually shooed her out the door. Less fortunately, Tiffany hadn't attended another church event since Joyce's funeral.

"Good morning," said Tom, striding into the meeting room. He put his tablet down on the worn mahogany table and looked around. "I guess we're the first." He glanced at his watch. "We're not *that* early. Where is everyone?"

"Lucy was on the phone when I passed her office," said Reshma. "I haven't seen Susan yet today."

Tom raised his brows. "Reshma, are you your sister's keeper?"

"No, Tom," Reshma said pleasantly. "I respect the privacy of my sister priests."

"Only your sisters? How about me?" He grinned to let her know he was teasing.

"You're happily married, so privacy is unnecessary."

"Hmm. You never know what scandal can pop up...out of no-where." He mimed the sudden appearance of an imaginary threat by tossing up his hands and bending them back at the wrists. The gesture was unmistakably gay. Reshma was pleased to see him so fully embrace his identity. "Remember, Reshma. None of us is exempt from unintended embarrassment. It goes with the collar. We're supposed to live such an exemplary life that each tiny misstep gets magnified out of proportion."

Lucy breezed into the room. "Good morning, people. Thanks for coming on short notice."

"It's not often that you summon the clergy outside of our regular weekly meeting," said Tom. "This must be important." He and Lucy exchanged little smiles suggesting he already knew the reason for the impromptu meeting.

Lucy turned to look at the door. "Where's Susan? She sent a reply saying she'd be here."

Susan appeared, looking out of breath. "Sorry. I hope I'm not late."

Lucy had been stern with Susan lately, but she smiled and casually waved her to a seat. The reason for calling them together must be positive. So often, unscheduled meetings meant bad news. "Come in, and sit down. This meeting shouldn't take long."

Eyes downcast, Susan slid into the seat next to Tom. Although the church had provided her with a new iPad, she rummaged in her bag and took out a ruled copy book with an old-fashioned ball point pen. She clicked it open and wrote the date on the top of a fresh page.

Lucy looked at each of them in turn. "Thank you all for coming. I hate to take up time on your weekend, but we have some important announcements. Tom, will you be chaplain and pray us into the meeting?" They all bowed their heads, and Tom offered a thanksgiving for their work together and a short entreaty to the Spirit to inspire them. Lucy beamed a radiant smile, and Reshma instantly melted. Lucy may have fallen off her pedestal, but Reshma still adored her.

"To allay any anxiety you may be feeling," Lucy began, "I want to assure you that what I have to say is good news. As soon as the vestry approves the change, and I was assured when I met with the wardens that it will pass, Tom Simmons will be co-rector of St. Margaret's."

The announcement was followed by murmurs of congratulations. Tom brought his hands together in the supplicant's position and bowed his head. "And it will be an honor."

"Susan and Reshma, here's a quick version of why we're making the change. My administrative duties in the parish constrain me from taking more singing engagements. My agent warns me that, because of my age, I don't have much time left to perform, and

I must make the most of it. A foundation headed by Brad Taylor has created a program of recitals near cities impacted by school shootings. One of the beneficiaries will be the Gun Victims Fund. I've agreed to sing in some of those recitals. I've also committed to a busy schedule of operatic performances and concerts. I thank God for my many blessings, including a voice that brings pleasure and inspiration to many. Unfortunately, I'm not a saint gifted with bilocation, so ordinary human scheduling needs to prevail. Tom only wanted to come to Maine to retire and live as his true self. He never wanted full responsibility for a church, but he has graciously volunteered to share St. Margaret's with me. While I am traveling, Tom will assume full duties as the rector in charge."

Reshma patted Tom's shoulder. Susan kept her hands modestly out of sight, but she nodded an acknowledgement of Tom's changed role.

"Tom has asked for a blackout period during the winter. He intends to spend the colder months in Florida with his husband. Both were kind enough to come out of retirement to support us after the Hobbs Elementary shooting. Now, they've generously agreed to work around my schedule, and I will give them the same courtesy. I won't take any engagements while they enjoy their time away. While Tom and I are both here in Maine, we will share duties, but for the sake of clarity, Tom has agreed to give me the last word in cases where we disagree. Of course, those instances are almost nil, but it has been known to happen."

Reshma wondered if Lucy's decision to share her authority with a man had been difficult. Lucy had confided how hard she'd found being a first-time rector who needed to prove herself worthy of a large, affluent parish like St. Margaret's. Despite a clergy shortage, women found it difficult to convince churches to hire them, and female rectors were still paid less than men.

"I am honored to share the leadership of this church with Lucy, whom I admire more than she knows. As she said, after the burden of leading a church in Connecticut under the pretense that I was straight, I was happy to disappear into anonymity here in Maine. While I explored my identity as a gay man, she supported me every step of the way. Now, I am grateful that I can support her in her singing career. God has given her the gift of a superb voice, and it would be a crime not to share it with the world."

"Hear! Hear!" said Susan and began to clap. Everyone stared at her. Usually, Susan looked to others to initiate the response to an announcement and followed their lead.

After they'd settled down, Lucy asked, "Are there any questions?"

"Before we end, I could use some advice," Reshma said, surprising herself. She hadn't planned to bring up her dilemma about Tiffany and Brianna with this group, but now she realized it was a perfect opportunity.

Lucy gestured toward Reshma. "Go on. I hope we can help."

Reshma engaged the eyes of each person at the table. "I feel privileged to serve with clergy who can look beyond heteronormative conventions and see that things aren't the same for us...and yet they are. One of those things is domestic violence."

Tom's eyes narrowed in a mixture of anger and sadness. Lucy tensed. Susan leaned forward in what Reshma interpreted as a gesture of encouragement. "I have a friend who suffered abuse in a previous relationship. Unfortunately, some of the abuse was physical. A few nights ago, her ex showed up at her residence unannounced and made threats. Fortunately, she left without the need to call the police, but what should we do now? My friend is reluctant to talk to law enforcement. She doesn't want her friend to have a police record."

"She should tell the police," Susan said without a moment's hesitation.

Tom trained his blue eyes on her. "If she hasn't hurt anyone and has no past record, there's little they can do."

"No matter," said Susan. "They should be aware that someone is stalking the young woman."

Lucy sighed. "No one ever thinks of domestic abuse between female partners, but it does exist."

"Chief Harrison would certainly give her a fair hearing," Susan said.

"Of course, she would," Lucy agreed. "But as Tom says, there's nothing she can do unless there's a documented threat."

"They could keep an eye out for the stalker once they have a description," said Susan. "The chief could make sure a patrol car drives by the shop regularly. If the perpetrator is trespassing on private property, that's illegal." Susan looked across the table and gazed directly into Reshma's eyes. "I know you're bound by confidentiality, but so are we. Can you share the identity of the victim?"

Reshma tensed. She hadn't expected that. "I'm sure you can guess. She's Tiffany Taylor, the owner of the pâtisserie."

"The police should know that she's been threatened," Lucy said. "They'll be more attentive because there's a business involved. Hobbs prides itself on being a safe place for commerce. Reshma, I hate to ask, but are your perceptions of the danger to Tiffany colored by your personal relationship? I don't doubt you. As a victim of sexual abuse, I would never minimize another woman's concerns, but we should be sure the threat is real before running to the police."

Reshma considered the question before answering. "I was a witness to the threats. We're dealing with a very angry woman. According to Tiffany, there were previous episodes of violence. I'm no expert, but from the description, I'd say it was an assault."

"Then you have an obligation to report it," Tom said unequivocally. "I am happy to invite Brenda Harrison to listen to Tiffany's story as part of an off-the-record meeting. That way, you are only involved as a friend, not in any official capacity."

"The hardest part will be convincing Tiffany to speak to the chief," Reshma said, looking defeated. "She still cares for this woman, and she's part of her social network."

"She needs to decide what's more important," said Susan, "her safety or keeping her friends happy. We all make mistakes in our lives, Reshma. But unless we're called to account for our bad behavior, we seldom change it."

Reshma felt torn. She'd hoped her fellow clergy could suggest another alternative, not confirm what she knew but didn't want to hear. She turned to Tom. "Thank you for offering to moderate a meeting," she said. "No offense, but I think it would be better if it were a woman."

"No offense taken," Tom said, reaching across the table and patting Reshma's hand.

"I'll do it," said Lucy. "I know what it is to be assaulted by someone you trusted."

"If it came to that, Lucy could break Tiffany's friend like a stick," Susan added, reminding everyone of Lucy's martial arts skills.

Tom grinned. "Tiffany's stalker would be no match for Lucy, but she has better things to do than play bouncer at Wicked Pleasures. I say, let the police handle it."

"Check my calendar and give me some dates," Lucy said. "I'll talk to Brenda. Tiffany shouldn't have to live in fear."

***

When Liz told Amy she had something important to discuss she could hear Olivia in the background. "Tell her to come for lunch," she said in a loud, officious voice. "And tell her I won't take no for an answer!"

Liz held the phone at a distance so she could see the time. It was getting on to noon, so it was logical that Olivia would invite her to lunch. Usually, Liz didn't mind accepting her invitations because Olivia's culinary prowess was rivaled only by Maggie's. Both had gone through chef's training.

Liz weighed the option of spending hours at Olivia's against setting a time for a short visit later. Being in her shop to help Denise collect her belongings had inspired her to start a woodworking project. She'd picked out some cherry boards from her wood stash and planned to mill them that afternoon.

Olivia got on the call. "Don't be stubborn, Liz Stolz," she scolded. "Amy sees you all the time. I haven't seen you in ages. Now get yourself over here. I'm making seafood crêpes, your favorite."

How could Liz refuse? No one made crêpes like Olivia. The light, delicate pancakes were like air in solid form, and Liz never turned down lobster. "Okay. You don't have to twist my arm. I'll be there as soon as I change."

"Oh, Liz. Come as you are," Olivia said. "We're not exactly dressed for a ball here. I'm sure whatever you're wearing is just fine."

Liz looked down at the worn hoodie she reserved for working in the shop. It had been washed so many times the fabric had no nap and resisted sawdust, but the frayed cuffs were coming away from the sleeves. Being a surgeon, Liz was excellent with a needle, but she'd been too lazy to sew the old shirt. Olivia might say she didn't care, but when it came to appearances, she had high standards. Liz decided to change into a fleece without holes.

Heading to Gull Island, Liz formulated her pitch to Amy. They'd already discussed the long-term plan for Amy to assume the role of managing partner. What Liz had to say shouldn't come as a surprise, although the timing might. The subject had come up during Amy's interviews, but lately, they hadn't formally discussed it. Maybe it was the perfect moment to make the change, now that Amy seemed to have settled in Hobbs. Although she hadn't given up her apartment in town, she was basically living with Olivia.

Liz wondered what it would be like to live with Olivia. Although the former hedge-fund manager came from humble circumstances, she was one of the richest people in Hobbs. Her Neo-Victorian home was the biggest house on Gull Island. She drove the most expensive cars, but she was always scrupulously tasteful in how she presented herself. To climb to the highest echelons of Wall Street, she'd made a study of how to avoid the social faux pas of the new rich. Mostly, she'd succeeded, but occasionally a few cracks in the façade showed the simple woman beneath the perfectly turned-out image. In the beginning that seemed to bother her, but now that she'd been accepted by Liz and her Hobbs friends, she was much more personable.

As expected, Olivia looked Liz over from head to toe when she opened the door. "You're looking well for someone who's been in hiding for weeks," she announced after her inspection. "Come in, Liz. You're bringing in the cold air." She pulled Liz down with a firm hand to plant a kiss on the cheek. "Amy's in the kitchen minding the sauce so it doesn't break. Lunch will be ready shortly." She led Liz into the dining room, where the furniture and table settings looked like they came out of a home design magazine. Liz could see why Sam, as an architect and designer, had been drawn to Olivia's impeccable taste, but like all of Sam's relationships, it had ended quickly.

"Take a seat, Liz. Of course, you'll have wine with lunch." It was an order, not a suggestion.

"No, thanks. I'm going to work in the shop later. I don't want to cut off a finger."

"No, we can't have that," Olivia agreed. "Isn't there a saw that stops when it senses danger? I thought I read something about that."

Liz knew that Olivia regularly scanned the business pages for investment opportunities, an old habit from her Wall Street days. "It's called a 'Saw Stop'," Liz confirmed. "It's been around for a while. A sensor detects when human flesh comes too close and sets off a small explosive that instantly stops the blade. Supposedly, it works great, but I'll keep my old cabinet saw."

"You're so old fashioned, Liz. Even an old-fashioned doctor. You still touch patients when you examine them. No one does that anymore."

"I know," said Liz, frowning. "But they should. Physical diagnosis is becoming a lost art."

"Soon you doctors will be replaced by AI. You should buy stock. I can make a few recommendations."

"Thanks, but I try to invest ethically." Liz wondered if Olivia would perceive the little dig. Not much got past her.

"I understand, Liz, but the point of investment is to *make money*." Amy came out of the kitchen, apparently to see what was taking so long. "Excuse me, Liz, but I need to make the crêpes," said Olivia. Liz would have made them beforehand and kept them warm in the oven. Of course, Olivia, with her insistence on perfection would make them to order. "Sit down, Amy, and let Liz discuss her business with you before we eat." Olivia disappeared through the door to the kitchen.

Amy gestured to a chair, which was Liz's usual place at the table. Olivia believed in designated seating with herself at the head. "What's going on, Liz, that it couldn't wait until Monday?" asked Amy, taking her assigned seat.

"It's not something I want to discuss in the office. Sorry to interrupt your weekend."

"You're not. We weren't doing anything special. Just catching up on reading." Amy eyed her curiously. "You've made some kind of decision...an important one."

Liz chuckled. "How can you tell?"

"You have that look of determination which means something has fallen into place."

"You read me too well," said Liz, but one reason she'd chosen Amy to succeed her was she understood how her mind worked. Liz wasted no time on a preamble. "I think the time has come to implement the succession plan."

Not a muscle in Amy's handsome face moved. "You're not retiring, are you?" she asked cautiously.

"No, not completely. But I need to cut back. I'll be traveling more. Lucy has decided to be more active in her singing career. A singer's sixties are considered the last hurrah. With her big birthday coming up, Lucy's has been mentioning her age more often."

"She still looks terrific."

"She takes good care of herself. The break in her career probably bought her some time. By her age, most opera singers have dragged themselves all over the world and strained their voices. They're exhausted and ready to quit the stage. Lucy's voice has changed, but it's still pure and strong."

"I'm glad for her, and brava that she's willing to seize the day. But what will that mean for her church?"

"She's worked out some kind of time-share deal with Tom Simmons. Like me, she's not ready to quit her day job completely." Liz studied Amy's face, but she was the consummate professional and effectively hid her thoughts. "I want to travel with Lucy," Liz continued. "I want to get more involved in gun legislation. I've talked the foundation into creating a division for political action. Don't tell Olivia, but I'm going to ask her for another large donation."

"I'm sure she'll give it to you. She hates guns, especially since her son used one to kill himself. She insisted on viewing the body. Apparently, it was a horror."

"I bet. A 9mm round through the mouth can be ugly."

Amy visibly shuddered. "She considers herself tough as nails, but it really affected her," Amy said under her breath. "She still talks about it."

Liz was glad to hear that Olivia had confided in someone. She'd been seeing Lucy for therapy but had quit some time ago. Liz suddenly thought of Cherie, who helped in Lucy's practice, and now would likely take it over. "That reminds me. I agreed to mentor Teresa Gai in her nurse practitioner's training…"

Amy shook her head. "Don't worry, Liz. Yes, of course, I'll help. And if the practice keeps growing, we may need even more help. Maybe we should hire another doctor. I've been impressed by the D.O. who's living at Bobbie's. She's very smart."

"I'll look forward to hearing your plan," said Liz, reaching for Amy's hand to shake it. "Congratulations, Dr. Hsu. I'm pleased and proud to leave Hobbs Family Practice in your competent hands."

Olivia burst through the kitchen doors with two beautifully composed plates. "Lunch is served. I just need to get my plate, and we can eat." She put the plates in front of Liz and Amy, scrutinizing them as she did. "What's this? You both look so serious. Did Liz bring bad news?"

"No, she came to promote me to managing partner."

"Well, then congratulations are in order! No arguments, Liz. I have champagne in the fridge. Let me get it, and my plate."

Amy rose to get the flutes. "She'll want the right glasses, of course."

"Of course," agreed Liz, partial to using the proper glasses herself. She knew she'd soon be pressed into duty. Olivia hated to open champagne bottles after she'd broken the glass door of her antique China cabinet.

They toasted Amy's promotion, but then the conversation turned to politics. The March primaries had confirmed that a rematch of the 2020 candidates was inevitable. Olivia, a former Republican, spoke with the vehemence of the newly converted. She despised the former president and made no secret of it, even though she was preaching to the choir.

They were eating an excellent panna cotta for dessert, when Liz's phone vibrated in her pocket. She glanced at the screen and saw it was Sam. She usually texted because she hated to talk on the phone, so it must be important. "Excuse me," said Liz, getting up from the table. "I need to take this."

"An emergency?" Olivia asked.

Amy shook her head. "She's not on call today. Cathy is." Heading into the living room, Liz smiled because Amy knew the duty roster by heart. She'd been exactly the right choice to succeed her.

"Yes, Sam?" said Liz, trying not to sound impatient.

"I'm not bothering you, am I?"

"Nope, I'm just finishing up lunch with Amy and Olivia."

"Oh," said Sam, sounding strange. She'd once dated both women. Usually, Sam moved from one relationship to another without regrets, so jealousy probably wasn't the reason.

"What's up?" Liz asked, glancing into the dining room where Amy was clearing the table.

"I was hoping we could get together. I could use a friend." Her voice had dropped a few notes on the last sentence. With a sigh, Liz pictured the gorgeous wood she'd left on her workbench. The project would have to wait for another day.

"Sure. I can meet you. Where would you like to go?"

"We can meet at the diner. I feel like having some blueberry pie."

"Maggie makes the best blueberry pie. She's not baking anymore?"

Sam didn't answer the question. "I'll meet you at the diner," she said and hung up. Liz didn't take offense that she didn't say goodbye because she was often guilty of doing it herself.

Approaching the diner, Liz saw that the parking lot was empty except for Sam's truck. A banner over the sign read "closed for winter vacation."

"I forgot they were closed," Sam said after Liz rolled down her window. "Awakened Brews will be closed by now, and none of the cafes are open this late. Where can we go?"

"You can come home with me," said Liz.

Sam shook her head. "I need to talk to you *alone*."

Liz thought for a moment. "I left some beer in Lucy's beach apartment. The place will be freezing, but that mini split you installed heats it up fast."

"Meet you there." Sam rolled down the window and started her engine.

Sam arrived before Liz. She was standing outside the garage next to Lucy's beach house, hands in pocket, a plume of lazy vapor rising from her head. It was wicked cold for this time of year. Usually, by March the weather warmed up a little. Today, the cold wind at the shore was like an icy slap in the face.

Liz found her keys and opened the door as quickly as she could. They went upstairs and Liz turned on the heat pump full blast. She rubbed her hands and blew on them. "God, it's cold. Sure you want beer? There's probably some coffee in the cabinet. Only powdered creamer, I'm afraid."

"Beer's good," said Sam, plopping down on the sofa.

When Liz looked in the cabinet, she found only one bottle of beer. She'd forgotten that she'd consumed the others when they were shutting down the place for the winter. She brought out the lone bottle.

"Sorry, Sam. Only one. You can have it. I had alcohol at lunch."

Sam waved her hand dismissively. "Put it away. I have something better." She took a plastic tube out of her pocket.

"Weed?" The one word was half question, half surprise. "Sam, I didn't think you smoked. I find it hard to believe, especially after you had such a problem with Peter Langdon being high at work."

Sam stretched out on the couch. "One of my architecture students got me started." The way she smiled made Liz wonder if Sam was involved with this student. "Got matches?"

"Yeah, I think so. Let me look." Lucy liked candles for atmosphere and usually kept a box of stick matches on top of the refrigerator.

"I haven't smoked in forty years," said Liz, handing Sam the box. "Back then, doctors could lose their licenses for pot possession. Erika enjoyed a joint now and then, but I just watched."

"Erika," repeated Sam, puffing on the joint to get it going. "Bet you miss her."

"Hell yeah. Can't tell you how much."

"It used to piss me off that you talked to her, not me. Now, I don't envy her one bit. Dead at sixty-two. What a shame." She handed

Liz the glowing joint. Liz took a long drag. She began to cough and couldn't stop. Her windpipe burned like it was on fire. Her lungs were out of practice. She'd quit cigarettes years ago, except for an occasional guilty smoke on social occasions, but never inhaled. She took a more measured toke this time and held her breath while she talked.

"Sam, don't take it personally. Erika understood me in a way no one else could." Liz finally released her breath along with the irritating smoke.

"Yeah, you could talk about Hegel with her."

Liz laughed. "What do you know about Hegel?"

"Nothing," Sam admitted with a grin that showed the pot was working. She took a long drag before handing the joint back to Liz.

Before taking a drag, Liz said, "Okay, Sam. What's going on?"

"We broke up."

Liz couldn't stop herself from shaking her head. "Sam, I told you not to get involved with Maggie."

"Yeah, I know, but I thought you were jealous."

"I was...a little, but it was to protect you...and her, of course." Liz studied her friend and wondered why Sam was so restless. Her relationships never lasted.

"She told me she was leaving me," Sam said, taking the joint out of Liz's outstretched hand.

"That's Maggie's MO. She leaves people before they can leave her. Is she involved with someone? Usually, she has an affair before she breaks up a relationship. She likes to have someone lined up ahead of time...as a buffer."

"Wow, you have her pegged," said Sam, puffing a few perfect smoke rings.

Liz shrugged. "I've only known her for fifty years."

"I don't know if she has someone on the side," said Sam, looking thoughtful. "I don't think so, or she wouldn't be so scared to stay out at the pond alone. I offered to sell her the house for practically nothing, but she's not interested."

"I'm not surprised. She doesn't want to live there without you."

"Which is crazy," said Sam. "She knows it's safe."

"Doesn't matter what she knows. It's how she feels."

"Lucy teach you to say that?" Sam grinned.

"No, I figured that out on my own," said Liz. "So, are you going to sell the house?"

"Not right away. I put a shitload of work into that place. I'll close it down for now. I might come back for a while in the summer. Now that I'm not working in town, I don't have to see anyone. I can shop for groceries in Sanford. It's closer anyway."

"You really don't have to stay away, Sam. People don't hate you."

"Oh, yes, they do. Someone walked right up to me in the hardware store and told me so."

"I'm sorry," said Liz and meant it.

"Don't be sorry. You didn't do anything wrong. You're the hero now."

"I'm not a hero," Liz muttered. "I hate it when people say that."

"I know you do, but once people get an idea in their minds, it's hard to change. That's why I need to leave."

Her mind wandering from the pot, Liz suddenly remembered an article she'd read about how hard it was to change people's beliefs with facts and reason. "Is Maggie going to move back in with her daughter?"

"I don't know," Sam said, exhaling smoke. "She says she doesn't want to disturb Alina's love nest. The kids are getting older, and they're involved in activities, so they're not around much. And that basement apartment is so dark!"

"It is. I wouldn't want to live there. Like living in a dungeon," said Liz, reaching for the joint. She was determined this would be her last toke. The furniture was moving like she was on the boat.

"Maggie talks about moving back to the city, but I doubt she will. She loves those grand kids too much."

"Where is she now?"

"Home, packing her stuff."

Liz gazed out the picture window overlooking the ocean. "I guess she could stay here for a while. It's big enough for one person. Courtney and Melissa are quiet neighbors. It has a nice view." Against her better judgement, Liz took another drag. "But don't say anything to Maggie. I'd have to talk to Lucy first."

"That's generous, Liz, but you don't have to take care of Maggie."

"Of course, I do. It's what she expects. That's why she keeps me around."

Sam made a face. "It's more than that. She loves you."

"Yeah, I guess she does. I love her too. I've slept with lots of women. I can't remember most of their names, but some meant something to me, like Jenny and Maggie. I still love them."

"And Lucy. But it's different with her. She gets you in a way the others never did." Sam's perceptive observations were infrequent but always made Liz think.

"Yes, she does," she agreed, drifting into the pleasant high.

Sam lay back and gazed admiringly at the ceiling. "Remember when Erika commissioned me to turn this place into a practice studio for Lucy? I'm glad we could keep the ship-lapped boards. You did a nice job, Liz."

"Thanks," replied Liz in a lazy tone. "That seems so long ago." She closed her eyes and tried to imagine Erika's face, now blurred by time. Then those pale eyes, brilliant with intelligence, came into focus. Erika's thin lips smiled ironically, and Liz smiled back.

Chapter 14

Tiffany came to a sharp halt in front of the door and refused to budge. "I can't do it," she whispered.

Reshma sympathetically took her hand. "Yes, you can!" she insisted, trying to sound encouraging rather than frustrated. "This is important, and it will give you some peace of mind. I promise."

"But what if she finds out?"

Reshma fought the temptation to roll her eyes. "Unless she does something incredibly stupid and gets caught, she won't." Reshma gently but firmly pulled Tiffany in the direction of the door. They'd been having this argument for days. Just when Reshma was sure she had convinced Tiffany to talk to the police, her resolve wavered and they were back to square one.

Tiffany's face was pinched with anxiety, but she allowed Reshma to lead her like a small child. The rectory door of wooden planks tied together with iron fittings was so heavy that Reshma had to lean against it with all her weight to open it. She often wondered how tiny Lucy was able to open it. But as Reshma had admiringly observed, nothing ever stopped Lucy.

Tiffany's grip on Reshma's hand suddenly tightened. Reshma turned around to see a police car pulling into the parking lot. With casual precision, the white SUV swung into a space, and a tall woman got out. She reached into the rear seat and came out with a campaign hat. She perched it jauntily on her head, carefully adjusting the brim. Brenda Harrison cut a dashing figure as she strode toward the door.

"Ignore the swagger," Reshma whispered near Tiffany's ear. "It's part of her cop act."

Tiffany narrowed her blue eyes, scrutinizing the policewoman as she approached. Brenda touched her hat brim with her fingertips. "Good morning, ladies," she said cordially with a special nod to Reshma. "Rev. John, please introduce me to your friend."

Reshma took her cue from the chief's formality. "Chief Harrison, you must know Tiffany Taylor. She owns the new pastry shop in town."

"Not really new," Tiffany protested. "It's been open for two years."

"So you're the one responsible for my expanding waistline," said Brenda, amiably patting her belly over her service belt. "My wife loves your croissants. She has French blood, so she knows a good croissant when she tastes one." Brenda winked rakishly.

Tiffany seemed charmed by Brenda and soaked up her compliments like a sponge.

Out of the corner of her eye, Reshma noticed Lucy come out of her office and head across the hall to the meeting room. "I think we're expected," Reshma said, tugging Tiffany's arm gently.

Brenda showed the way with an extended hand. "After you, ladies."

Lucy and Cherie Harrison were already seated at the long table when they entered the conference room. Cherie beamed a sweet smile at her wife. Lucy rose and extended her hand to Tiffany. "Hello, Tiffany. Nice to see you again. Sorry, it's under these circumstances."

The chief took off her hat and seated herself next to Lucy. Reshma led Tiffany to the empty chairs on the other side of the table. Once they were all seated, Lucy opened the meeting. "Tiffany, Mother Reshma shared that you had an uncomfortable encounter with your former partner. We understand that you don't want to file a formal police report, but Chief Harrison would like to hear what happened so her people can be prepared if it happens again."

"Would you mind if I took some notes?" asked Brenda, taking an old-fashioned black leather-bound notebook out of a compartment in her belt.

"But this won't go on her record?" Tiffany asked anxiously.

"No, this information is for me. I'll verbally share it with the patrol officers and ask them to be on the lookout for any strangers lurking near your shop. They keep an eye on all the businesses in town, but they'll drive past yours more often." Brenda asked some basic questions—names, dates, addresses, phone numbers, but she didn't ask for any details of the relationship other than the number of episodes of violence and a description of what had happened. "I'm only asking so I can assess how dangerous the subject could be. To your knowledge, does she own a firearm?"

Tiffany shook her head. "No, and she's usually not the angry type. Most people really like her."

"Unfortunately, intimate relationships can bring out the worst in some people. That's why they call domestic murders 'crimes of passion.'" Brenda scribbled some strange symbols in her notebook. Reshma realized she was writing in shorthand. "Are you still in communication with her?"

"On Reshma's advice, I sent her a text telling her never to show up at my house unannounced."

"That's good," said Brenda. "Would you mind taking a screenshot of the text and air dropping it to my phone?"

"Is that really necessary?" asked Tiffany.

"No, not if it makes you uncomfortable."

"I just don't want to violate her privacy."

"Understood, and we'll keep this informal unless there's another incident. But having this information in advance will help us keep you safe."

"Okay. Here," said Tiffany, taking out her phone. There was a distinctive click as she took the screen shot.

Brenda flipped closed her notebook. "I think that does it. Thanks for giving us a heads up about this situation. As the old saying goes, 'to be forewarned is to be forearmed.'" Brenda put on her hat and touched the brim. "Thank you, ladies." She turned toward Tiffany. "Miss Taylor, call us right away if this woman bothers you again. Meanwhile, we'll keep an eye on your place."

"Thank you, Chief Harrison," said Tiffany. "You've been very kind."

Brenda nodded to acknowledge the compliment and left.

"Are we done now?" Tiffany asked, her eyes watching Brenda's retreating figure.

"There's one more thing," Lucy said. "We thought you might like to have someone to talk to about this situation. Any domestic violence, no matter the gender of the partners, is traumatic. I was a victim of rape, and it took years of counseling to recover. It's not something you 'get over.' I know your situation is not the same, but we'd like to offer you the opportunity to talk about it."

"But I've been talking to Reshma," Tiffany said, turning to her and smiling warmly.

"And that's a good thing, but if I'm not mistaken, you're in a relationship now. While Reshma can support you, it might help to talk to someone who can be more objective. I'm happy to give you pastoral counseling, which means there's no charge. And if you're uncomfortable talking to a priest, Mrs. Harrison has offered to make herself available. She's also a PA and can prescribe medication, if you need it."

Tears suddenly clouded Tiffany's blue eyes. "I don't know what to say." Reshma passed her a tissue from the box on the table. "Do I really need counseling?"

"That's up to you," said Cherie. "But we wanted you to know that we're here to help."

"Wow," said Tiffany, blotting her eyes. "I've never met such kind people. Thank you so much!"

Reshma sighed in relief. Her effort to support Tiffany, which could have gone so wrong, had been a success.

***

Lucy anxiously scanned her phone for a reply to her text. She'd read online that the South Portland girls' basketball team had qualified for the state championship. Without a second thought, she'd shot off a message of congratulations to Rebecca. That was three days ago. Lucy knew that being a single Mom kept Rebecca busy. In addition, Rebecca was the rabbi to the largest Reform congregation in Maine. But couldn't she spare a quick word for an old friend? How long would it take to key the word "thanks"? Being cut off from the woman with whom she'd shared some of her deepest secrets wasn't only painful, it was scary. Who would be her 'rabbi' now?

With a long, cleansing sigh, Lucy put down her phone. She remembered when they'd met at a conference on gender roles in religion. Rebecca was living in New York, and Lucy was still a deacon in Boston. They instantly decided they were kindred spirits, who found the patriarchal dominance of their faith stifling. Next, they found themselves volunteering to work on a project to protect vulnerable LGBT youth. Despite their fifteen-year age gap, Lucy looked up to her younger friend because she had more experience in ministry.

In the beginning of their friendship, they'd spent many hours on the phone together. Lucy often wondered why Rebecca's wife was never jealous. But she had nothing to worry about. Lucy loved Rebecca Morgenstern like the sister she never had.

She scanned her text to see if she'd written anything that could offend Rebecca, but the message couldn't be simpler. "Hey, I saw the girls' team made the state championship. Congrats and hugs to them and you." Nothing wrong with that, but maybe the purple heart that followed was presumptuous. They hadn't talked since the argument at the basketball game, and that was almost a month ago.

The screen on Lucy's phone went dark as it went into sleep mode. The black screen was a metaphor for how this rejection felt to Lucy. The space between her and Rebecca had become a void.

Lucy briefly panicked at the idea of living without Rebecca there to talk her through a crisis. She'd been there for Lucy when Susan left. When Lucy met Erika at that first lessons and carols service at St. Margaret's, Rebecca was the first person she'd told. Rebecca had been there for every one of Lucy's moral dilemmas, including how long she should wait before telling Liz she was interested in a relationship. When Lucy's graduate school theology classes challenged her faith, it was Rebecca who talked Lucy through her dark night of the soul. Lucy couldn't imagine anyone else being such a perfect combination of spiritual counselor, advisor to the lovelorn, and BFF. Now there was only a Rebecca-shaped hole in Lucy's heart.

In the beginning, Lucy had hoped Maggie could be that kind of friend. She'd listened patiently to Lucy's anxieties about Erika's silence. Forays into the local thrift shops helped them forget their worries. Lucy bought so many clothes that year. Her tiny rectory closet couldn't hold them all. She ended up donating many of the items to Goodwill.

Lucy stared at the dark screen. Now she'd lost Maggie AND Rebecca. She could understand why Maggie found it hard to forgive her, but this argument with Rebecca was ridiculous. How could disagreement about Israel's policies come between two educated, adult women? Women, who also happened to be faith leaders.

But it wasn't that simple. Being Jewish was such a big part of Rebecca's life that she'd become a rabbi. Anti-Semitism was on the rise all over the world. It was easy to conflate the two, especially when Rebecca's wife was debating whether to re-enlist in the Israeli army. Lucy wondered if she had decided. With Rebecca's silence, she might never find out.

With her fingertips, Lucy tried to ease the headache forming at her temples. She wished she could talk to Liz, but she was at Sam's helping her pack up the house. On impulse, Lucy picked up the phone and found Maggie's number. The call rang and rang on the other line. Then Maggie's voice said, "Hi, Lucy. Nice to hear from you."

"I hope I'm not interrupting anything."

"Nope, I'm in the faculty room, grading papers. Not like I have any place to go."

"Have you moved out of Sam's? Where are you staying now?"

"I've been up in Scarborough, but I think Alina and I have already had our fill of one another. I'll need to find a rental soon."

"It's a tough market," said Maggie with a sigh.

"Tell me about it."

"Come for dinner." There was silence on the other end of the line. "You're cooking?" asked Maggie dryly. It was a mild barb. Maggie knew Lucy's cooking skills were limited. Lucy decided Maggie hadn't meant any harm. She was merely asking for information.

"I can order takeout," Lucy said quickly.

"Don't be silly. I can pick up something on the way down to Hobbs. Liz will be tired after working at Sam's and appreciate coming home to a hot meal."

"You don't have to do that," Lucy said.

"I know I don't. I want to."

Lucy hesitated for a moment before saying, "Tell me how much it costs. I'll give you the money."

Maggie's quick laughter unnerved her. "Oh, Lucy, don't be ridiculous. It's just a few groceries. I'll see you in half an hour."

Lucy glanced at the clock over the sink. She still had plenty of time to change clothes and set the table for dinner.

***

"Maggie," said Liz when she came into the kitchen. She was too tired to have much more of a reaction. After packing up the stuff Sam intended to move, they'd had to fix a leaking shut off valve in the crawl space. Liz was achy and exhausted from the adventure.

She sniffed the air appreciatively and determined that someone had a savory braise cooking. She could bet it wasn't Lucy. "You spared us Thai takeout, Maggie. I don't have the energy to cook after moving all those boxes. And people ask why I don't join a gym!"

"I'm sure Sam worked you hard," said Maggie. "She doesn't have much time before she leaves. She booked a flight for Thursday." Liz already knew Sam's travel schedule, but she was surprised Maggie was so well informed.

"Hi, Lucy," said Liz, bending to kiss her wife, just a quick peck that wouldn't stir up trouble. "You'll forgive me if I don't kiss you, Maggie. I'm filthy and probably stink."

"I've smelled you much worse," Maggie said in a blasé tone. "But you have half an hour until dinner, if you want to take a shower."

"I think I will, but first, I'll have a beer." Liz looked from Lucy to Maggie and back again. They were smiling at her in a way that said they were up to no good. "Catching up?" she asked, smiling back.

"I was just telling Maggie about my fight with Rebecca," Lucy explained.

"She still hasn't answered your text?" asked Liz, surprised. She took a beer off the refrigerator door and rummaged in the drawer for the opener. "She's an idiot if she thinks you're anti-Semitic. She herself admitted Israel is wrong."

"It's complicated," Maggie said, rolling her wine in her glass. "One of my friends is Jewish, non-practicing, but I wouldn't dare say anything against Israel to her."

"What a fucking mess," muttered Liz and took a long pull on her beer. "You never know when you're going to say the wrong thing that will make someone hate you forever. It's like a rip tide. You can't even see it from the surface. Then you step into it, and the next thing you know, you're drowning."

"Lucy told me your gun club threw you off the board."

"They did. Someone even made a motion to throw me out of the club. Fuck it. I don't care anymore."

"Sure you do," Maggie said. "You love teaching classes and talking about guns. Those guys are your friends."

"They were my friends," Liz said in a gloomy voice and wiped some beer foam off her lip. She inspected the label. Good beer. She'd buy it again.

"It's hard to tell who your friends are these days," said Maggie.

"You think you know someone, and then they come out with something you can't believe they said. If you don't toe the party line, people will cancel you in a heartbeat. I'm talking about both sides."

"That's because people can't talk to one another anymore," said Liz. "We've lost the art of civil conversation. I can get hot and bothered about politics as you both know, but I know when to end an argument and move on. Nowadays, most people don't know when to shut up."

Maggie glanced at the clock. "Liz, if you're going to take a shower, you'd better get moving,"

Liz made a face. "I thought you said I didn't smell that bad."

"I said, I'd smelled worse. Now, get going. You have twenty minutes."

Liz glanced at Lucy, who'd been watching the exchange intently. They hadn't been married long enough to start bickering. Liz hoped the preview wouldn't scare Lucy.

The hot water was like a balm on Liz's shoulders and back. She was too old to be crawling under houses like a crab. The entire time she was thinking of the filth and the critters creeping around her. Her knees ached. Her elbows too. But she wouldn't admit to Sam, who was younger, that she couldn't do it. It was a butch thing. Men would do crazy things before they'd admit weakness to one another, but why would two women be so stupid? Next time, she'd tell Sam to call a plumber. *Next time*, Liz thought sadly. *When will that be?*

After Liz blew her hair dry, she pulled on a Yale sweatshirt, skipping the bra because she wanted to be comfortable. She arrived at the table just as Maggie was dishing out their dinner. Liz looked it over. "Let's see. Chicken thighs. Preserved lemons. Olives. Smells good."

"Hope so. It's a new recipe. *New York Times*. If it's any good, I'll send it to you."

"Thanks. I hate it that they make you pay extra for sections we used to get for free." Liz poured wine into their glasses. "Cheers."

She glanced at Lucy, who'd been quiet since she came home. "How was your day?"

"Interesting. We met with a young woman who's being stalked by her ex. A woman."

Liz grunted. "Unfortunately, the straights don't have a corner on the market when it comes to domestic violence. I saw some weird cases in the ED at Yale, mostly males, though." She'd been enjoying her meal so much she'd forgotten to tell Maggie how good it was. "I really like this recipe. Don't forget to send it."

"I like it too. I'll put it on rotation."

"You going to stay up there with Alina?" Liz asked, demolishing her serving of Maggie's good stew and looking into the pot for more. Wordlessly, Maggie reached for her plate.

"No, I don't think so. That little apartment is so small after living in a house again."

Liz made a face. "You kidding? That place you were living in when we met was a tomb."

"But when I was in New York, I was always somewhere else—at school, at the theater, with my friends. My apartment was only a place to sleep."

"That's how New Yorkers live," said Liz with a shrug.

"I know what you mean, Maggie," Lucy said. "My Manhattan apartment was a place to store my stuff and get my mail. Sometimes, I even slept there."

Liz put her cutlery down and studied her wife. "I've been so busy helping Sam, I haven't had a chance to ask, Lucy. What do you think about letting Maggie stay at the beach house until she finds a place?"

Maggie sat back in surprise. "Don't let Liz put you on the spot like that, Lucy. She's good at that."

"I know," Lucy agreed. "But it's not a bad idea. We're not using it now. It has a beautiful view, and you can walk to the beach." She sounded like a real estate agent extolling the virtues of a questionable property.

"I'd rather find something more permanent. I don't want to move twice. Plus, it's so deserted down at the beach this time of year."

"Courtney and Melissa are next door. They're good company," said Lucy and took a sip of wine.

"They're so young. It would be like living with Alina and Steve."

"It's good to have multiple generations living together," Lucy said. "Keeps you young." Liz studied her wife to see if she dared float the idea that had just popped into her mind. Lucy's green eyes looked straight into hers when she said, "Now that Emily's moved out, the garage apartment is free."

"Reading my mind again?" Liz quipped.

Lucy smiled slyly. "Sorry, dear, but it's so easy."

Maggie had apparently ignored their little sidebar. "Huh. I hadn't thought of that. That garage apartment is a cozy place."

"When Courtney and Melissa were living there, I turned the sleeping nook into a real room. It would make a nice guest room or office. I spared no expense when I built that place for my mother. Too bad she hated Maine so much she never lived there."

Maggie put down her wine glass and gave Liz a penetrating look. "I might be older than you, Liz, but I'm not your mother."

"No, thank God!" said Liz, laughing.

"But could you stand me living right next door?" Maggie asked, looking directly at Lucy.

"You were here for almost a month after the Lewiston shooting," Lucy said with a shrug. "We managed. And it's not like you'd be living with us. I've been watching Bobbie's experiment with her boarders, tenants, whatever you want to call them. It seems to work for everyone. There's a housing shortage. People have too much space after their kids leave. I think there should be more experiments with space sharing."

"You're serious," said Maggie.

Liz crossed her knife and fork and sat back. As usual, she was finished before everyone else. "I was reading an article the other day…"

"Ah, we're about to hear about the latest medical advance," said Maggie, rolling her eyes.

Liz shot her an annoyed look, but she went on with what she was about to say. "A study found a surprising risk factor for Alzheimer's. Guess what it is."

"Why don't you just tell us?" asked Maggie impatiently.

"What fun is that? Guess."

"Bad diet," said Maggie.

"That's one factor."

"Sedentary lifestyle," volunteered Lucy. "Not enough exercise."

"Yup, those are big ones. But guess what the biggest hidden risk factor is."

They looked at one another and shook their heads.

"Lack of social interaction. The biggest risk factor for Alzheimer's is *loneliness*."

Lucy nodded as if she'd already guessed what Liz was going to say. "Human beings need one another to survive. We need conversations and connections."

"We need to eat together…like this," said Liz, gesturing toward her plate. "Nutrition is more than eating food. If you lived here, Maggie, you could cook for us more often. I get tired of cooking all the time."

Lucy shot her a furious look. "I can cook. You never let me!"

"You make too much mess in the kitchen," said Liz, leaning her elbows on the table. "If I cook, there's not as much cleanup."

Lucy huffed, but she didn't argue.

"Why would I want to live next door to you, Liz?" Maggie asked. "You just insulted your wife in front of company. You haven't changed a bit."

"You're not company, Maggie, and you haven't changed either. And at our age, it's unlikely we will."

"Probably not," Maggie agreed.

"You should live here," Liz said, continuing her argument. "You'd have the apartment all to yourself. It's a nice size. You wouldn't even have to see us unless you wanted to. I'll put up the hoop house for the truck, so you'd have space in the garage for your car."

"You must be special, Maggie," said Lucy. "She never offered to do that for anyone else."

"Well, our previous tenants had two cars. I wasn't about to give up *two* bays."

Maggie was frowning, but Liz could see she was considering the idea. "I don't know... If I move in, I insist on paying you fair rent."

Liz waved her hand dismissively. "It's not a legal apartment. I never charged Courtney rent or Emily. Pay the utility bills. That's all I ask. Buy groceries when we eat together, if it makes you feel better."

"That's quite a deal," said Maggie. She drained her glass and looked at Lucy as if expecting her to offer an opinion.

"You could try it for a month or two and see how it goes," said Liz, refilling Maggie's glass. "If you find a better place, you can move out. No harm. No foul."

"Liz, don't pressure her," said Lucy.

"I'm not."

"Yes, you are, Liz. When you get an idea, you just won't let it go." The stubborn look in Maggie's hazel eyes showed she was digging in. "I said I'll think about it, and I will."

"But..." Liz began to say.

"Liz..." Lucy warned quietly. "Let it go."

Liz realized that when those two formed an alliance she had no hope of winning. She'd been in this position before and knew when to cut her losses. "Okay," she said and got up to clear the table.

Chapter 15

Liz slammed the tailgate closed to make sure it locked. "Thanks for helping me put on the cap."

Sam, standing with her hands in her pockets and puffing white vapor in the cold, nodded. "Feels like snow. Don't want my stuff getting wet on the way down to Logan."

They hoisted themselves into the cab. "You sure they're going to let you take all this shit on the plane?" asked Liz, starting the engine.

"That's what they said. I gave them the sizes and weights of all the bags and boxes, and they said okay, bring it."

"Bet it's going to cost you a mint," said Liz.

"Not as much as you'd think." Sam ran her hand along the dashboard tenderly, like a caress. "I'm going to miss my truck, but I don't need two vehicles sitting in the garage, inviting the mice to nest. I had to blow all the cracked acorns and nutshells out with compressed air before I showed it to the buyer. Hope I didn't miss any. But I sold it as is."

"You can use my truck when you need it," said Liz to ease the pain of the loss. She knew how Sam felt because she loved her truck too. Heading toward the main road, she glanced at Sam's house in the rear-view mirror. "I'm glad you didn't sell the place."

"Me too. It's paid for. I don't need the money. And I like the idea of having a place where I can relax and fish. I trust you to keep an eye on it. Brenda makes sure her patrol comes out here."

Liz noticed Sam watching the image of the house get smaller in the side mirror. Because she'd worked alongside her, Liz knew how much effort Sam had put into the renovation. They'd turned the old, run-down cabin into an architect's showpiece. The sweat equity was the main reason Sam couldn't let the place go. "I probably never should have moved up here," she said in a rueful tone.

"Don't say that. It was a good idea. People need contractors with design skills. Another year, and your business would have taken off."

"The shooting killed more than those kids," replied Sam grimly. There was an extended silence in the cab. She pointed with her cocked thumb over her shoulder. "Who's going to help you take off the cap? Lucy doesn't have the strength."

"Oh, I'll probably leave it on until spring," Liz replied casually, but she hadn't thought that far ahead. "I guess I'll ask Brenda."

"Yeah, she can be your buddy now." There was no jealousy in her voice, only matter-of-fact honesty. Liz could always count on Sam for the unvarnished truth.

"Brenda's too busy with those kids and her new wife. She doesn't have time to hang around with me. And now my friends in the gun club don't want me around either. What strange times we live in." She thought of Lucy's argument with Rebecca.

"I guess you'll have to make some new friends, Liz," said Sam. "I've done it in Chicago. It's not hard. Maybe it wasn't a good idea to bring all your friends to Hobbs. Maggie, Erika, me..."

"Brenda was here before me. So was Tony. He's the one who convinced me to buy the practice."

"How is Tony? I haven't seen him for a while."

"He's fine, now that the Playhouse has recovered from Covid. Lucy volunteered him and a bunch of other Playhouse people to get involved in Brad Taylor's concert series. She's working on Maggie too, but she's in such a dither over your breakup, she can't focus long enough to give her an answer."

"She left me," said Sam. "Let's just be clear about that."

"I know. Like I told you, that's her way. She leaves people before they leave her."

"I know she's worried about finding a place to live. I offered her the house for pennies. When I went to Melissa to see about the paperwork, she told me I was nuts to sell it for that price."

"Is that the real reason you didn't sell it?" Liz asked.

"Yes...No. I told you. It's not the money. I love the place." Sam added in a soft voice, "Maybe when things settle down..."

Liz smiled to herself and nodded.

***

The sheet of chocolate croissants was both clumsy and heavy. Carrying the trays from the kitchen counted as Tiffany's morning workout. She arranged the pastries in the glass case. When she stood up, she saw Reshma grinning at her. "First in line today?" asked Tiffany.

Although they were alone in the shop, Reshma leaned over to whisper, "Hungry to see you." She added a suggestive wink.

Tiffany looked Reshma over and noticed an absence. "No collar today?"

"I was out late on a sick call, so Mother Lucy gave me the day off."

Tiffany was disappointed that Reshma was free, but she had to work. She looked outside, where the bright spring sun was melting the last of the snow. "I wish I'd known. I could have called in someone to help. It's such a nice day. We could have gone for a hike."

"Kind of muddy for a hike," Reshma said. "But I can hang around here with you." Her eyes focused on the apron embroidered with the shop logo, hanging by the door to the kitchen. "Maybe I can help you."

"No way. Too many people know you work for the church." Tiffany tried to imagine what the people would think when they saw their priest standing behind the counter.

"So? Other priests have second jobs. Lucy is a therapist. Susan teaches. Why can't I help in your shop?"

"I can pay you." Tiffany didn't want Reshma to think she was taking advantage of her.

Reshma rolled her eyes. "You think you need to *pay me* to spend time with you?" She looked over her shoulder. "Doesn't look like you have much business today."

"It's early. Just wait a few minutes. They'll come." On cue, the little bell over the door began to tinkle, and a group of five came into the shop. Reshma handed out cups while Tiffany put their pastries on plates. She turned to see Reshma looking baffled by the register. "You okay over there?"

"I've never used one of these before."

Tiffany handed the customer his order, then went to Reshma's side. "It's easy. I've entered every item and its unit cost. You just put in the quantity, like this. If it's a chip card, they slide it in there or tap here. Then you just follow the screen prompts. They can add a tip if they want, but most people just throw cash in the jar. Easy peasy."

"Everything's easy when you know how," replied Reshma skeptically. Tiffany remained for a moment to watch, but Reshma got it right on the first try. She was so smart.

A steady stream of customers came in, keeping them both busy, especially when a line began to form all the way to the door. Tiffany was dishing out pastries as fast as she could. Reshma was efficiently keeping up with the coffee requests.

In a brief lull in customer traffic, Tiffany turned to admire her new helper. Reshma looked as professional in her "Wicked Pleasures" apron as she did in her clerical shirt. She had a lithe figure, but with curves in all the right places. "You look good in that apron," Tiffany said. "Want a job?"

Reshma laughed. "I told you that you don't need to pay me."

"You did, but I know you don't get paid much in your job."

"But I manage, and now that Susan's moving out, Lucy says I can have the big apartment. I can't wait! Finally, I can use the oven without taking all the pots and pans out first!" Reshma moved closer and reached down to give Tiffany's hand a quick squeeze. "I don't want your money, Tiff. I know how hard you're working to pay back your folks."

"They're not pushing me."

"I know, but it's a matter of pride for you to show them you're worthy of their trust."

Tiffany smiled, mostly to herself. One good thing about having a priest for a girlfriend was her insight into complex situations. "What did I ever do to deserve you?"

"Nothing. God thought we might be good together, so here we are."

Tiffany was about to make a face at the religious overtones, but she knew Reshma was sincere. She believed God meant them to be together, and that was okay.

Tiffany turned and saw Cherie Harrison on the other side of the counter, waiting patiently. "Good morning, ladies," she said in her warm Louisiana accent. "How are you on this bright, sunny morning? Looks nice but not too warm out there. Hard to believe Easter is only a few weeks away." She bent over to peer into the case. "I see *les pains au chocolat* are fresh this morning. I'll take half a dozen. My aunt Simone likes them. My kids too."

Tiffany got a bag and whipped out some sheets of wax paper. It felt odd to be bagging pasty for her therapist, but that's how it was in a small town. She finished counting the croissants and slipped in an extra. "Six croissants," she said, passing the bag to Reshma to ring up the sale.

"See you later," said Cherie with a warm look in her striking blue-green eyes.

After she left, Reshma asked. "You have a session today?" she asked, surprised.

"No, she always says that. I asked her why and she said it's an old superstition in her family. It's a hope there will always be a next time, in case there isn't."

"Interesting practice," said Reshma, nodding thoughtfully. Tiffany could practically hear the gears in Reshma's amazing mind turning as she processed the new information.

When Tiffany turned, she saw the campaign hat first, then the bright blue eyes shining in Chief Harrison's attractive face. The chief leaned over the counter. "I'm dying for a cup of coffee," she whispered with a grin.

Tiffany laughed. "Your wife was just in here."

"Yes, I saw her in the parking lot. She slipped me a croissant. I hope you don't mind me bringing food back into your store."

"Not as long as it's *my* food," said Tiffany, handing the chief a large paper cup. "The coffee carafes are over there." Tiffany pointed the way.

The chief looked over her shoulder, but there was no one behind her. "I don't want to alarm you, Miss Taylor, but one of my patrol officers saw a car parked outside your place." Tiffany's heart started to thunder in her chest.

"When was this?"

"Last night. The officer pulled right up beside the car before it could get away. He warned the driver that it was private property, and she needed to leave. He didn't ask for ID, but he got the license plate number. It belongs to your friend."

"Shit," said Tiffany under her breath.

"The officer made a formal report, so it's on record now. I'm sorry, but there's nothing I can do."

"Then it's on her. I told her to stay away. What happens if she comes back?"

"I doubt she will. Officer Bolanger is a big guy." Chief Harrison measured with her hand to a distance way above her head. "Believe me. When he warns someone about trespassing, they know he means business. But I'll make sure the patrol cars keep your place on their routes."

Tiffany nodded her appreciation.

"Call right away if you see anything. Okay?" The chief glanced at Reshma. "You gave her my direct number, right?" Reshma nodded. "Trespassing is against the law. Promise you'll call me. Remember, we're here for you." She patted the counter top to emphasize her message before walking away.

Reshma gripped Tiffany's hand. "I'm so sorry. But at least, the police know you were telling the truth."

"Oh, I think they believed me."

"We're really lucky to have a woman as our police chief," said Reshma. "It makes a difference."

***

A green text message popped onto the screen of Lucy's laptop. *Is the garage apartment still available?* The question startled her, but she instantly understood who'd sent the message. Lucy had been so deeply involved in writing her Maundy Thursday sermon that she had to think for a moment to come up with an answer. They hadn't discussed the apartment since the night they'd offered it to Maggie. Lucy knew she couldn't hesitate too long, or Maggie would assume they'd rescinded the invitation.

As far as I know, she typed. *Liz isn't home right now.* She wondered if Maggie knew that Liz had driven Sam to Logan.

Mind if I invite myself to dinner? I can pick up something to cook.

Liz would like that. She'd be coming home from the airport during rush hour, when traffic would be heavy.

Sounds great. When will you be here?

The gray bubble started to move on the screen, indicating a response was on the way. Then the motion paused for some time. Finally, there was a response. *As soon as I pick up dinner makings. I'm in town. I can come later if now's not a good time.* There was another long pause before the next message. *I really need to talk to you.*

What now? wondered Lucy, scrolling through the text of the half-finished sermon. She glanced at the time on her computer and estimated she might have a half hour to work on it before Maggie arrived. Good thing the service wasn't until next week.

Lucy decided to get dressed first. She was still wearing yoga pants and one of Liz's old sweatshirts, even though she swam in it.

It wasn't fresh from the laundry. Liz had worn it before, but Lucy liked wearing clothes that held her wife's familiar scent. Before the breakup, it wouldn't have mattered what she wore when Maggie arrived, but their friendship still wasn't back to its old casual ease. By getting dressed, she'd be showing respect, and it would establish some important boundaries. If Maggie moved in next door, they'd need them.

By the time Maggie arrived, Lucy had dressed, brushed her hair up into a loose ponytail, and put on some makeup. She'd put away her books and papers and tidied the living room. She'd been working there to be near the comforting heat of the wood stove. As she added a few logs to the fire, she remembered Liz saying she'd started cutting the wood shorter to make it easier for Maggie to handle. Lucy realized she was also benefiting from the length adjustment. After Maggie had left, Liz had tried to erase every indication that Maggie had once lived there, but some signs had persisted.

Maggie arrived looking as carefully made-up and coiffed as she always did, but it was obvious she was completely exhausted, and not only physically. Her eyes were bloodshot, either from drinking too much or crying. Under them were dark circles. Her cheeks were pinched, showing the delicate web of fine wrinkles under the concealing foundation she always wore. Lucy stiffened her face, trying not to show her surprise at the condition of her visitor. Maggie, the theater director, saw right through it. "Yes, Lucy, I know I look like hell. You don't have to pretend."

"Come in," said Lucy, gently pulling her inside. "What's wrong?"

"I left my daughter's house in the middle of the night. Maybe I should tell the truth. She threw me out."

"What! Why?"

"She had a temper tantrum like I've never seen."

Lucy took Maggie's coat and hung it on the hook by the door. "Come in. You look cold. The fire's going in the living room." She led her to the sofa nearest the fire and sat down beside her.

"Thanks for letting me come on such short notice."

"Of course, I would. Can I get you something to drink? A cup of tea? Something stronger?"

"No, just sit and talk to me." Maggie stared into the fire and nervously chewed on her knuckle. Clearly, she was in a bad way.

"Tell me what happened." Lucy reached for Maggie's hand.

"Alina threw my clothes and shoes into my suitcases and carried them out to the driveway. She told me to leave and never come back."

"My word!" exclaimed Lucy. "Where did you go?"

"I checked into a motel. Good thing it was a high-end place. They gave me a courtesy toothbrush and some toothpaste and deodorant. Alina threw in my makeup bag, but she forgot my toiletries."

"Oh, Maggie, I'm so sorry," said Lucy. "Why didn't you call us?"

"It was two in the morning. No time to be showing up on somebody's doorstep."

"Did you and Alina have a fight?"

"A fight?" Maggie gasped. "This was World War III! It began as an argument between Alina and her boyfriend. The house is well insulated, but they were so loud I could hear every word. The girls were scared, so they knocked on my door. I let them get into bed with me. Lucy, they were shaking!"

"It's good you were there for them."

"When the screaming stopped, I tiptoed upstairs to make sure everyone was still alive. Alina was in the kitchen guzzling a glass of bourbon. It's a new thing since she started dating Steve. She's not supposed to drink because of all that anti-anxiety medication she takes. She's so tiny, even a little bit of alcohol can throw it off. When she saw me standing in the kitchen, she glared at me. 'What are you doing here?' she asked. I told her I'd come up to see if she was all right, and the girls were with me. Then she started to shriek and accused me of interfering in her relationship. I mean, you should have seen her. She was in a full-blown psychotic meltdown, throwing dishes, kicking the cabinet doors, knocked one right off the hinges. That's when Steve came out of the bedroom and told me to go back downstairs. 'For your own good!' he shouted. 'Can't you see she's lost her mind?'"

"That must have been terrifying for the children."

"I can't even imagine. Katrina told me there's been a lot of fighting while I was living at Sam's. I was worried because Alina left an abusive marriage. I was afraid Steve was too."

Lucy had heard the story of how Alina secretly left her husband right before Christmas. She'd arrived in Boston with only the few belongings she could stuff into her kids' backpacks. She'd paid cash for the plane tickets so her husband wouldn't know where she'd gone. Liz had driven down to Logan in a snowstorm to pick up her stepdaughter. When she'd arrived, she found Alina lacked even the money to buy her hungry children something to eat.

"When I listened to the argument last night," Maggie continued, "I realized Steve wasn't the problem. Alina said things to him I wouldn't say to my worst enemy, never mind my fiancé."

"So did you leave when he told you to go?"

"No, I stayed and tried to reason with her. Alina threw her drink in my face and demanded I leave the house. When I refused to go, she stormed downstairs and began throwing my things into my bags. She dragged them outside and left them in the driveway. I don't even know how she got them out there. She's so tiny. It was like she suddenly had Herculean strength. The kids were crying and terrified." Lucy could see in Maggie's face how upsetting it was to revisit the scene. "I kissed the girls and told them to go to their rooms. I managed to grab my shoes and coat and left. I was in my nightgown when I checked into the hotel."

"I'm sure you're not the first person to do that," Lucy assured her. "Hotel night clerks must see all kinds of things."

"You're probably right, but it was embarrassing."

"What do you think caused Alina to behave like this?"

"Her doctor put her on a new medication. And she's not supposed to drink. I've seen her flip out after being triggered or when her meds were off, but nothing like last night."

"Oh, dear," was all Lucy, who was seldom at a loss, could say. This nightmare made all the comforting clichés sound ridiculous. Maggie was staring vacantly into space, obviously reliving every moment of the horror she'd just described. Lucy squeezed Maggie's hand to get her attention. "Can I get you a glass of wine? It might help you calm down."

Maggie sighed and shook her head. "I need to get the groceries out of the car first."

"I'll help you."

The activity seemed to calm Maggie, but it looked like she'd bought enough food to feed all of them for a week. Lucy helped her unpack to avoid complaints about Liz's rearrangement of the kitchen.

"I had nothing to do this afternoon and nowhere to go, so I bought some new towels and sheets for the bed in the apartment," said Maggie. "It's still queen-sized, isn't it?"

Lucy hadn't thought of that. "We have sheets and towels, but I'm not sure the place is ready to be occupied. Liz turned off the heat and water. Ellie cleaned the apartment after Emily moved out, but I'm sure it needs to be dusted."

"I don't care. I don't want to be more trouble than I already am."

Lucy gripped her arm and shook it for emphasis. "Maggie, I don't want to hear that kind of talk. You're not trouble. What you went through last night is just awful. We're glad to help. Now, let's get this stuff put away, and we'll have some wine. I'll put out some cheese and crackers. Did you eat today?"

Maggie shook her head.

"Okay, you go get warm by the fire. I'll get us something to drink and some snacks."

Once Maggie had a glass in her hand, all her worries spilled out.

She was terrified that Alina was regressing after Maggie and her husband had tried so hard to mitigate the terrors of her early life in a Romanian orphanage. Lucy knew there had been long periods when Alina could keep it together, but other times when she totally broke down and couldn't even come out of her room. Maggie's main worry was for her granddaughters. Fortunately, Katrina, the older one, was resourceful. When Maggie had called her that morning, they were at a friend's house. The mother had taken in the girls without question. Apparently, the neighbors were aware of the problems in the family.

Maggie finally paused her description of the situation and took a breath. "I haven't been gone from there that long, Lucy. How could things get out of control so fast?"

"It happens," said Lucy with a sigh. "Families are complicated. And psychotropic medications can stop working. New ones can cause unexpected reactions."

Maggie perked up at the idea that the medication could be to blame. At least, that meant there might be a remedy. "She just started the new medication this week. At first, I thought she was doing better, and then this insane behavior. Lucy, I've never seen her like this."

"What about her fiancé? Could he be the problem?"

"I don't think so. Steve is a decent guy. Their relationship has been good for her. He helped her get ahead at the news station. But every so often, Alina just flips out like this. You know. You've seen it happen."

"She had a lot of trauma in that orphanage. Maybe she'll never get over it."

"Her sister did. She's a practicing oncologist now."

Lucy shook her head. "Kids are different, even with genes from the same parents." She glanced at her watch. "I should call Liz and let her know that you're here and she doesn't need to worry about dinner. Unless you're not up to cooking. She can cook whatever you brought."

"No, I can do it. I just hope she's not mad at me showing up on her doorstep again. After all, I am the ex."

"Don't even think about that," said Lucy. "You know she's not like that. She takes in strays all the time."

Maggie assumed an expression of profound indignation. "Lucy, I've been called many things, but never a stray!" Then she burst into laughter that almost sounded deranged. It had been a performance, and a convincing one.

"Glad to hear you laugh," Lucy said uncertainly.

"If I don't, I'll cry," said Maggie, her shoulders sinking like a deflating balloon.

"So cry. It's okay. I'll give you privacy if you need it."

Maggie's hand clenched Lucy's wrist fiercely. "No, don't leave me."

Maggie sobbed for a good five minutes. Lucy recognized the deluge as a response to cumulative grief. Maggie had lost her relationship with Sam, her home, and the security she'd thought she have in her daughter's house. While Maggie cried, Lucy strategically fed her tissues to mop up the mess and made soothing circles on her back. Finally, Maggie sat up, sighed deeply, and announced. "I feel better now."

"Nothing like a good cry to vent your feelings." Lucy took her hand. "Now, will you be okay for a few minutes while I call Liz?"

"Of course," said Maggie, nodding as if to assure herself as well as Lucy. "Go ahead. I'll be okay."

Lucy held the phone with her shoulder while she emptied the bag of crackers into a bowl and opened another bottle of wine. Liz finally answered the call while Lucy was rummaging through the cheese drawer.

"Hey, babe, where are you?" asked Lucy.

"Coming through Portsmouth. I'm thirty minutes out."

The way Liz drove, it was thirty minutes. For everyone else it was forty-five.

Lucy quickly explained the situation and told as many details as necessary for Liz to get the picture. "I think she intends to move in tonight, but I told her we weren't ready."

"I can turn on the water and the heat, but the place needs a good once over before someone moves in. She can stay in the downstairs guest room tonight. Let's get off the phone, so I can call Alina. Let me find out what this new medication is. She should probably stop taking it right away."

"Liz, I think you should wait until you talk to Maggie."

"I'll handle it, but thanks for the advice, Lucy." Lucy knew she had just wasted her breath. She put the cheese and crackers on a tray and returned to the living room to sit with Maggie.

A short time later, she heard Liz's truck drive in. Lucy glanced at her watch and saw that thirty minutes had passed, just as Liz had predicted. After hanging up her coat, Liz came straight into the living room.

"I'm so sorry," she said, reaching out her hands to Maggie, who catapulted herself into Liz's arms. Over her shoulder, Liz exchanged a look with Lucy, sympathetic, but not overly so. Lucy knew that Liz still doubted the validity of Maggie's emotions. She often said she could never tell when Maggie was acting. In this instance, Lucy could see that Maggie's distress was genuine.

Liz eased Maggie back down on the sofa and spoke in that calm, deliberate voice she used with patients. She looked directly into Maggie's eyes and carefully enunciated each word. "I called Alina from the road. The drug she's taking is known to have adverse reactions like those you described. I told her to stop taking it and go back on her old medication until she can talk to her psychiatrist. And absolutely to stop drinking alcohol. She's very sorry about last night. She said she'll call you later. The girls are fine." Lucy always admired Liz's ability to describe a situation so succinctly. For a busy doctor, it was an essential skill.

Liz glanced at the tray on the coffee table. "I'll get another glass and join you." She was gone less than a minute and sat down to pour herself a glass of wine. "I hear you're making dinner, so I can relax and put my feet up." She grinned in Maggie's direction. "But if you're not up to it, I can cook."

"No, it will give me something to do. I need a distraction. Plus, I want to make up for showing up unannounced."

"Well, we did invite you," Liz said dryly. "We just didn't expect you so soon."

"Neither did I. I wanted to give living with Alina again a chance before deciding. Obviously, the experiment failed." Maggie's careful elocution had returned. She was approaching her old self, or at least, a convincing facsimile.

In the end, Maggie deferred to Liz's need to be the caregiver and let her cook dinner. "Not as fancy as you would have made," Liz said, levering portions of haddock cooked in browned butter and capers onto warmed plates, "but it's food." She plopped creamy mashed potatoes beside the fish. "Eat up, Maggie. You look like you've lost some weight. You can use a few extra calories." Maggie looked up in fear. Liz quickly added, "I'm sure it's just the stress. Don't worry."

While they ate, Liz described the confusion at the airport when they'd arrived with so many boxes. They'd had to bring them to the freight drop off, which was hard to find, and Sam had nearly missed her flight. Lucy wished Liz would stop talking about Sam. Maggie's face showed how much the conversation distressed her.

❊❊❊

Liz enjoyed watching Maggie savor the meal. From a trained chef, it was like an unspoken compliment. She'd finally gotten Lucy's message and ended the conversation about the fiasco at the airport. After the meal, Maggie jumped up to clear the table, obviously a gesture to mean she was grateful for the invitation to stay. The subtext announced that she lived there now and wasn't just a guest.

"Maggie, we should work out a way to eat together more often," Liz said casually.

Maggie didn't look up. "Sounds like fun, but I don't want to invade your privacy."

"You're not. I'm sure Lucy wouldn't mind a break from my cooking. She's probably bored with it by now." Lucy shot her a look that clearly said, "Don't blame it on me!" Liz grinned back. "We could set up a schedule."

"You and your schedules." Maggie rolled her eyes.

"Well, they work. You and I used to make a weekly calendar of who was cooking when."

"We did, didn't we?" Maggie said, reflecting. It sounded like she was warming up to the idea.

While Maggie and Lucy cleared the table and put away the leftover food, Liz sat back, admiring their efficiency. "This is so cool. Like having two wives."

At the sink, Maggie spun around and glared at her. "You only have one wife, Liz, and *that's Lucy.*" She'd pronounced it with the ominous ring of a Shakespearean curse. "And you're damned lucky, because I bet she enjoys sex a hell of a lot more than I do."

The bright pink spots on Lucy's face made the statement impossible to deny. Maggie flung the dishcloth into the sink and huffed off to her room.

"Liz, what the hell were you thinking?" Lucy said, shaking her head. "Sometimes, you're such an idiot."

Lucy never called her names. Obviously, she'd defeated even her patience. Lucy picked up the dishcloth and wiped the dishes with a vigor that underscored how angry she was. Liz got up to help her, but Lucy forcibly nudged her away with her hip. "Go. You're annoying me now. I don't need your help!"

"I was just fooling around."

"It wasn't funny, and you can see how upset she is. Don't you have *any* sensitivity?"

"You're right," Liz conceded. "I guess I should apologize."

"If I were you, I'd just leave it alone."

Liz realized it was good advice. Instead, she cleared away the remaining dishes and wrapped up the leftover food. When she finished, she headed upstairs to turn on the evening news. The first scene was the devastation in Gaza, so she clicked it off. She had enough on her hands dealing with the war in her own house.

She sat up when Lucy, her green eyes smoldering with anger, came into the room. She sat down in her usual spot without even looking at her. Liz moved to the far side of the sofa. Finally, she said. "I was just kidding. I was trying to be funny."

Lucy got up and stood right in front of her, so close that Liz could see the golden specks in her eyes. "What did you mean by saying it was like having two wives?" Lucy asked with an unflinching stare.

"Nothing." Liz squirmed under the scrutiny and tried to sit further back, but Lucy only leaned closer. "Okay," said Liz. "I was uncomfortable being with my present wife and my ex, so I made a joke. Is that a sin?"

"No, not a sin. But we're in uncharted territory, Liz, so we all need to be careful what we say. Are you still attracted to Maggie?"

Liz couldn't get away from Lucy's eyes, just inches from her own. "Yes, she's an attractive woman," she admitted.

"Do you want to have sex with her?" asked Lucy, reminding Liz of a prosecutor cross-examining a witness.

Liz grinned rakishly. "I want to have sex with every attractive woman."

Lucy's auburn brows dipped toward the bridge of her nose. Then she sighed and finally stood straight. "Up to your old tricks, I see. Well, if you must know, I find her attractive too."

Involuntarily, Liz's lips parted. "What?"

Lucy looked down at her with a little smirk. "Why do you look so surprised? You said yourself she's attractive."

"Yes, but..." Eventually, Liz remembered to close her mouth. "Do *you* want to have sex with her?"

"I don't know..." said Lucy, tilting her head to one side while she considered the question.

Liz's words came out in a torrent. "But...but that would go against all your preaching, your book on sex, Christian dogma. True love is between two people, etc."

"Biblical sex is much more than one man and one woman. I'm a theologian who writes about sex. Maybe I should be open to different experiences."

"You're serious."

Suddenly, Lucy broke into peals of laughter. "No, Liz, I'm not. You're so gullible sometimes. Yes, I find Maggie attractive, but I also know that sexual intimacy can be a minefield that needs to be navigated *very* carefully. You're mine, and I'm not sharing you with anyone. Got that?" She poked Liz's shoulder for emphasis.

"Got it," Liz assured her smartly. "So maybe we should go upstairs so you can lay claim to territory."

"Exactly, what I had in mind," said Lucy, tugging on Liz's hand. "Come on, wife. Time to show me who you belong to, and it's not the woman downstairs."

Their sex was by turns fierce, passionate, sensuous, and finally reverential. Liz made love to Lucy as if it were a sacrament. They'd confirmed their bond and found it was secure and solid.

Afterward, Lucy lay in her arms while Liz lazily teased her nipple. "Feel better?" Liz asked.

"Much."

"I'm hungry," said Liz.

Lucy raised a brow. "You're always hungry after sex." She gave Liz a kiss followed by a little shove. "Go on. Get something to eat. If you're so inclined, bring me a glass of wine."

"We should keep a few bottles up here in that little fridge we bought to keep milk cold for our coffee."

"No, then we'd have to have glasses. And knowing you, they would have to be the *right* kind, so forget it." Lucy gave her another nudge. "Go on and be quick. You wore me out. I had a wild day, and I need to sleep."

Liz crept down the two flights of stairs quietly. She grabbed a bag of chips and poured a glass of wine. When she came out of the kitchen she noticed the orange reflection of the fire on the hallway wall. She'd banked the fire to burn to coals, so the flames shouldn't be that high. She walked down the hall and peeked into the living room. Maggie was sitting in the dark, staring into the fire.

"Are you okay?" Liz asked quietly, not to startle her.

"No," said Maggie. "I'm not okay." Liz came in and sat down beside her. She put Lucy's wine and the bag of chips on the table. "Ah, an attack of the munchies," observed Maggie. "The sex must have been good."

"Maggie..." Liz warned.

Maggie covered her face with her hands and rubbed her forehead. "I'm sorry. That was uncalled for." She sat up straight.

"I know you're upset," said Liz. "Alina's attacks always upset you."

"They do, and that's a big worry. But now I'm homeless again. I never should have given up my New York apartment."

"Maggie, that was years ago. And you admitted it was just a place to sleep."

"It was, but at least it was *mine*. You don't know how it killed me to sell the Connecticut house. But that's what Barry and I agreed to in the divorce settlement, that I'd sell it after the girls moved out."

Liz noticed Lucy standing in the doorway and motioned to her to come in. She sat down on the club chair, the one farthest from where Liz and Maggie sat. She was signaling that she was there as an observer, not a participant.

"Maggie, why are you rehashing this old shit?" Liz asked. "You can't change any of it."

"But why does the same shit keep happening to me?" Maggie asked, shaking her fists. "I'm seventy years old. You'd think I would have learned by now."

Lucy's voice pierced the darkness like a prophecy. "We repeat the lessons until we learn them."

"The Eternal Return," Liz added solemnly.

"Oh, Liz! Stuff your philosophy!" said Maggie impatiently. "I'm old. My daughter is a mess. And I'm homeless."

"Maggie, you're not homeless," Liz said. "You'll always have a place here with us."

"That's what Alina told me," Maggie replied bitterly.

"But we mean it," Lucy said.

Liz got up and went into the hall. She opened the closet where she kept all the property keys in a little box screwed to the wall. Even in the dark, her fingers could locate the key to the garage apartment. When she returned to the living room, she placed it into Maggie's hand and rolled her fingers over it. "Here. It's yours...*to keep.*"

Maggie's fingers tightened around the key. She raised her closed fist, pressing it close to her heart. "Thank you," she whispered softly. "Thank you."

Also by Elena Graf

Hobbs Series

HIGH OCTOBER

Liz Stolz and Maggie Fitzgerald were college roommates until Maggie confessed their affair to her parents. When Maggie breaks her leg in a summer stock stage accident, she lands in Dr. Stolz's office. Is forty years too long to wait for the one you love?

THE MORE THE MERRIER

Maggie and Liz's plans of sitting by the fire, drinking mulled wine, and watching old Christmas movies get scuttled by surprise visits from friends and family.

THIS IS MY BODY

Professor Erika Bultmann, a confirmed agnostic, is fascinated by Mother Lucy, the new rector of the Episcopal Church, especially when she discovers Lucille Bartlett was a rising opera star before mysteriously disappearing from the stage.

LOVE IN THE TIME OF CORONA

Police Chief Brenda Harrison shows an interest in Liz's biracial PA, but first Cherie needs to get past her loathing for all law enforcement since a state trooper shot and killed her sister.

THIRSTY THURSDAYS

Liz Stolz initiates Thirsty Thursdays, a weekly cocktail party on her deck, so her friends can socialize safely during the pandemic. Pretentious, overbearing Olivia Enright pursues Liz's friend, architect Sam McKinnon, and tries to push her way into the tight-knit group.

THE DARK WINTER

Erika hires Sam to build a soundproof practice room for Lucy. Fortunately, the early Christmas gift is ready before tragedy strikes. As the women of Hobbs pull together to help a beloved friend deal with her loss, the dark winter brings tension and realignment in their small community.

SUMMER PEOPLE

Melissa Morgenstern, a high-profile lawyer from Boston, is spending the summer with her widowed mother. She's doing some trust work for Liz who introduces her to the attractive Courtney Barnes, Hobbs Elementary's new assistant principal. The arrival of Susan, Lucy's ex, complicates her deepening relationship with Liz.

STRANDS

Cherie hears her biological clock ticking and would like to start a family. When a shocking tragedy creates an opportunity for her and Brenda to become parents, their friends need to step up to make it happen.

THE RECTOR'S WEDDING

The sudden opportunity for Lucy to return to her singing career throws everything in her life into doubt—her vocation as a priest, her settled life in Hobbs, even her upcoming marriage to the woman she loves.

THE VANISHING BRIDGE

Rev. Susan Gedney tries to rebuild trust after her humiliating exit from Hobbs. Bobbie Lantry always needs to rush away to take care of a mysterious elderly woman. They need to share their secrets, but do they dare?

EXTENDED CAPACITY

A school shooting was a nightmare that only happened in other towns until it came to Hobbs. Liz finds herself in the middle when the shooter's identity is revealed. The town is shocked to learn how the shooter got into the school.

PASSING RITES SERIES

THE IMPERATIVE OF DESIRE

A coming-of-age story that takes a brilliant aristocratic woman from La Belle époque through a world war, a revolution that outlawed the German nobility, and the roaring twenties to the decadent demi-monde of Weimar Berlin.

OCCASIONS OF SIN

For seven centuries, the German convent of Obberoth has been hiding the nuns' secrets—forbidden passions, scandalous manuscripts locked away, a ruined medical career, and perhaps even a murder.

LIES OF OMISSION

In 1938, the Nazis are imposing their doctrine of "racial hygiene" on hospitals and universities. Margarethe von Stahle has always avoided politics, but now she must decide whether to remain on the sidelines or act on her convictions.

ACTS OF CONTRITION

After the fall of Berlin, Margarethe is brutally assaulted by occupying Russian soldiers. Her former protégée, Sarah Weber, returns to Berlin with the American Army and tries to heal her mentor's physical and psychological wounds.

About the Author

In addition to the Hobbs series of contemporary novels set in a small town in Maine, Elena Graf has published four historical novels set in twentieth-century Europe. Two of the titles in the Passing Rites series have won Golden Crown Literary Society and Rainbow awards for best historical fiction. She pursued a Ph.D. in philosophy but ended up in the "accidental profession" of publishing, where she worked for almost four decades. She lives in coastal Maine.

Find out about events and new books at her website, www.elenagraf.com. You can write to Elena at elena.m.graf@gmail.com. Find her on Facebook and BlueSky: @elenagrafauthor.bsky.social.